The
Scandal Clause
Can $700,000 Buy a Life?

Sydney Stern

Bridgeland Books

The Scandal Clause by Sydney Stern

©2020 by Sydney Stern.
All rights reserved.
Printed in the USA.

ISBN:

978-1-7336435-9-7 - Amazon KDP Paper Back

978-1-7336435-5-9 - Ingram Spark Case Laminate

978-1-7336435-6-6 - eBook via D2D

978-1-7336435-7-3 - PDF

978-1-7336435-8-0 - Kindle

Bridgeland Books
PO Box 4277
Winter Park, FL 32793
www.SydneySternBooks.com

Disclaimer:

Permissions:
Photo 94328901 © Anna Ivanova - Dreamstime.com
stock photo ID: 629979566 © wavebreakmedia / Shutterstock
stock photo ID: 383752165 © G-Stock Studio / Shutterstock
stock photo ID: 101675857 © kropic1 / Shutterstock

Cover Design: Asli Cemiloglu, Asli@RavenSigns.com

Editing and Marketing: www.Rick.Feeney.com

Dedication

To all the women, men, girls and boys who have the courage to create a conscious and healthy relationship with their sexuality in the world, at work and at home.

The Scandal Clause

Contents

Dedication..3

Contents 5

Chapter 1..9

Chapter 2..14

Chapter 3..21

Chapter 4..27

Chapter 5..33

Chapter 6..37

Chapter 7..40

Chapter 8..47

Chapter 9..53

Chapter 10..60

Chapter 11..67

Chapter 12..70

Chapter 13..77

Chapter 14..86

Chapter 15..92

Chapter 16..95

Chapter 17..101

Chapter 18..108

Chapter 19 111

Chapter 20 118

Chapter 21 123

Chapter 22 133

Chapter 23 139

Chapter 24 144

Chapter 26 156

Chapter 27 164

Chapter 28 176

Chapter 29 186

Chapter 30 192

Chapter 31 202

Chapter 32 205

Chapter 33 214

Chapter 34 222

Chapter 35 231

Chapter 36 234

Chapter 37 244

Chapter 38 251

Chapter 39 268

Chapter 40 273

Chapter 41 279

Chapter 42 284

Chapter 43 292

Chapter 44 298

Chapter 45 302

Chapter 46 314

Chapter 47 323

Chapter 48 329

Chapter 49 336

Chapter 50 343

Chapter 51 351

Chapter 52 356

Chapter 53 364

Chapter 54 376

Chapter 55 386

About the Author 399

Ordering Information 401

The Scandal Clause

Chapter 1

The computer screen lit.

Damn. That ad again.

$700,000.

Black bordered numbers bold and real.

A typo. She was positive.

Except they would have fixed that mistake.

Not one comma had been shifted, not one number removed.

Shit.

She read it again.

> *$700,000/year.*
>
> *Nurse with Administration Master's Degree. Surgical skills. Prominent neurosurgeon practice.*
>
> *Passport. Ability to travel at a moment's notice and work under pressure. Psychological testing required at interview.*
>
> *Two-year commitment. $50,000 bonus at completion.*
>
> *Cover letter, resume, recommendations. Apply to address below*

The "below" was a New York City P.O. Box. The $700,000 too enormous to ignore.

Laura stretched out on the couch. These past three years, work at the hospital had exploded into spirals of too many pills, too few nurses, too much documentation, and too many days filled with grief.

Then there was yesterday's blowout with Morris Havershaw, the hospital's lawyer-guy. He was the high paid legal shield for streams of complaints that could threaten doctors, nurses or hospitals, no matter how good—from malpractice and following federal regulations to sexual misconduct and tripping on icy sidewalks.

She'd met him on his first day of work two years ago.

"I'm the legal beagle around here," he'd said walking unannounced into her office and extending a hand. "The powers that be commanded me to go on hospital walkabout my first day here." He waited for her response.

He'd interrupted her focus on finishing last night's drug disappearance report—a major problem at the hospital.

"Crap!" she spat at the mistyping. She looked up. "Who are you?"

He was six-feet tall, dressed in grey suit, white shirt and blue tie. *My age,* she thought. *Decent build. I bet he works out. Wonder if he's...* Then she grabbed her jabbering mind and squeezed it to silence. *Oh, for God's sake,* she chided herself. *Just ask the man what he wants.*

He's wearing a wedding ring—definitely off limits. "What did you say?"

The man smiled. "I've interrupted important work."

"Yup. Unless you want to write my report, come back later." She looked back at the computer screen.

He went on unperturbed. "Maybe I can help. I'm the new hospital lawyer."

Laura sat back to assess her visitor. "After my bad manners?"

"I've heard worse." He nodded at the chair in the corner. "Let's give it a try."

That was their first meeting. Many hours of working together since then had not changed her opinions—good at his job, too glib and still married.

But yesterday, Morris got stupid.

On Friday afternoon he'd barged into her office. "Tight schedule," he announced. "You got time tomorrow?"

"It's Saturday, Morris. I don't work."

"Accreditation problem just came up. We need a response—and fast."

So, she agreed to meet at South Station in Boston's financial district the next afternoon—a lifeless, January day. Morris led her on a cold walk ending at a small alley and down a flight of steps. At the bottom, a wooden door opened to a dining room with dangling lights and basement windows.

"Mr. Havershaw," said the maître-d walking over, "your business is overflowing if you come Saturday, yes?"

"Up to our necks."

"We have our most intimate room reserved for you," continued the maître-d, and bid them follow to the end of the hall. "This chamber has the only private restroom. No need to disturb for any reason." The maître-d winked, then inquired, "May I bring you wine, sir, before the dinner menu?"

Laura choked.

Dinner, wine, bathrooms, intimate? He was married with children. And they had to face each other every day at work. What the hell was he thinking?

Stupid question. She could guess. A familiar sick feeling came creeping over her again. She couldn't stay here—not in the room, not in the restaurant. "I don't drink when I'm working," was her most face-saving response.

The awkwardness was palpable.

"Listen, Laura," Morris explained, "We're working on the weekend—I thought a private, comfortable place..."

"Yeah, right," she'd interrupted. "Why not the office?"

Morris flushed; she offered fake apologies; he waved away the cost; she refused to order; he said yes; she said no. The maître-d kept eyes downcast and canceled their reservation. They trudged to a diner near the Tremont Street Subway Station with uncomfortable

11

chairs and fishbowl windows. Three bruising, document-revising hours later, she fled home in the darkening afternoon.

I can't do one more minute of this, she thought. The job was bad enough. Morris had just made it a fucking mess. *Why does it have to be such a mess*, she wondered, *this men, work and sex thing?*

The computer screen still flickered on $700,000. The numbers pulled her out of her irritating daydream.

$700,000. She looked at the number again and said out loud, "Double crap" *I hate writing cover letters.*

You gonna ignore $700,000? an inner voice retorted. *After Morris's out-of-line behavior? Get a grip, Greenwald.*

She typed.

To Whom It May Concern,

With an advertised salary of $700,000, I'm sure you will receive hundreds of resumes for this job.

Enclosed is mine. Attached are references.

If my credentials pass initial inspection, I would be pleased to accept an interview.

Thank you.

Sincerely,

Laura Greenwald MBA, MSN, NP

Done. Quick, simple, and didn't matter how good. *Job's probably a hoax, anyway.*

Too irritable to relax, she shrugged off her bathrobe, pulled on a crumpled coat, top and pants and double-timed downstairs into the frigid cold. A narrow alley stretched between the houses. Seven miles lay ahead of her—seven miles to unkink tangled thoughts and bring her back home.

***

An hour later, Laura checked the computer screen again. The ridiculous salary still existed. "Just do it," she said talking to herself in the mirror. "The application, the update, copies of licenses, diplomas, the whole thing. If the job is yours, you'll get it. That's what everyone says."

Yeah, right, she thought, *I don't have a chance in hell.*

Chapter 2

Monday morning. Laura's alarm kept ringing. The Hospital Accreditation Committee and Morris loomed in front of her. She hated the 6:30 am times for these meetings. Way too early to talk about life threatening crises and deal with staff rudeness. Too much to do, too little money, too few people, too much at risk. 'Time to get serious about another job,' was no longer a distant thought.

The speed with which Laura wrote her cover letter the day before hadn't translated to anything else. The rest of the application consumed the entire Sunday. As reward, this morning she sported a stiff neck, big headache, circles under both eyes and a manila envelope to be mailed to a nameless post box in Manhattan.

She finished dressing, grabbed a snack, and ran out the door towards the subway. On impulse she tossed the envelope into the first mailbox she encountered.

Forget the post office. Now it was done.

Mailed with no retreat.

Next stop—work.

***

"Are you with us or what?" Dr. Saunders annoyance jolted Laura back to the meeting. She'd drifted into daydreams on the droning flow of his too-early-in-the-morning speech. Ten disgruntled faces glared at her, including Morris.

I gotta get out of this place." The job had eaten away her energy and skill and replaced it with irritable impatience.

"Thank you for your time, everyone," said Laura, taking charge of the meeting again. "Attorney Havershaw and I will review your suggestions for improving post-surgical care. As you know, the upcoming hospital accreditation will be crucial. We are adjourned." The semi-command quashed further discussion.

She stood, gaze directed to Morris. "We've got work. Let's go." Unpleasant memories of Saturday afternoon with him might just get washed away in the avalanche of problems facing them this week.

***

Laura struggled to reach the end of the day. Morris had remained blank throughout, refusing to acknowledge anything about the weekend. With no time to eat and stacks of paperwork to sort through, she found herself exhausted by the biting January coldness of the evening commute.

Long ago, out of desperation, she'd developed a 'night routine' to shatter the black moods which too often overtook her after-work thoughts. Tonight was different only in its intensity. She kicked off boots at the door, hung her coat, chose a Merlot from the wine cupboard, and sank onto the sofa to rub frozen feet. A glass or two each day dispersed the bone-deep stranglehold of winter darkness. She poured a large glass and sipped for ten quieting minutes. Then she headed to the bedroom, shed work clothes, and pulled on a leotard.

Finding a proper stance, Laura began slow, lazy neck rotations. Tension leaked away in the movements. This time was hers alone. Stretching, exercising, and meditating followed by a long, hot shower, a second glass of wine and dinner removed most of the stress absorbed during the day. Afterwards, she wasn't bothered if emails or phone messages lingered for days as she curled into a cocoon of quiet safety.

There had been a time when she hadn't been so smart, when she'd been vulnerable to… well, dangerous things. It was a long time ago— but not nearly long enough for her. Saturday afternoon with Morris ripped open a festering wound. She shook her head, trying to scatter her thoughts about it, but they would not go, even as she pressed fingers against her temples and squeezed her eyes shut.

Seven years ago.

The other hospital.

Her first job.

Her first 'love'—or so she thought.

She had been the new girl on the block. Just graduated from nursing school, ready to break out, to play, to throw the rigidity of study habits out the window. She'd sat in too many front row seats taking notes, studied too late at night for too long. She was ready for whatever came next.

They met on a late afternoon. Laura, tall and slender, was reaching over a patient's head as she readjusted oxygen tubing.

"What are you doing?" asked a no-nonsense voice from behind her.

Startled and still stretched over the bed, she whipped her head around, dislodging one of the two barrettes holding up her hair. The back-length auburn mass, loosened by a day's worth of nursing activities, cascaded onto the patient's face and tangled into the oxygen tubing. The patient, beginning to cough, raised his arms to disentangle hair from his face.

"Oh! I'm so sor…" Her blue eyes locked onto the doctor advancing toward the bed. *What a mess,* she thought.

The doctor shrugged, then began untangling the whole mess. His only comment was, "You've got some beautiful hair—just don't throw it in everybody's face." They laughed about it in the end. And that was their first meeting.

He was the top earning, head doc in surgery—attractive, sexy, self-assured, knowledgeable, attentive, powerful. She was the background—assistant nurse, new to hospital life, at his beck and call, learning the job, submissive in an environment full of technology and skill. He'd say, "bring me the scalpel, take these clamps, sponge the wound," and she'd do it, instantly, as required. The head nurse was a guy and didn't figure in the equation.

One time, after an exhausting eight-hour surgery, he invited her for a drink. She'd accepted. Over a scotch and soda, they'd talked. The afternoon drink turned into supper. Afterwards, he gave her a ride to her nearby apartment in his Porsche. That day was followed by other afternoon drinks and rides home. Until the day he had come up to her apartment and hadn't gone home.

16

The routine went on for a while. Tiring surgeries, drinks, dinner and back to her apartment. Until one afternoon, after a particularly difficult operation, he simply said, "Laura, my wife and kids are coming home tomorrow."

Her mouth dropped. She stared, without moving, unbelieving. She'd fallen in love with him, this magnificent man. He'd never spoken of a wife or children and she'd never guessed—or never wanted to. She'd been a jerk to imagine he'd be interested in her. A convenience, that's all she'd been. A supplier of necessities, a provider of comforts, someone who didn't know his story, who could be taken and used.

His next words jolted even more. "You can't stay here," he said.

"What the hell do you mean by that?" she flung at him.

"It's too awkward. It won't work."

"Awkward? You want me out of your life because it's awkward? You should've thought of that before this, you bastard!" She didn't know what else to say, how else to feel except consumed by hot, unreasoning rage. He looked down at her but did not retreat.

"Look. I'm sorry. Really. Melinda had the opportunity to lecture in Europe. We thought it would be good for the kids to live overseas, you know, get educated, that kind of thing. I was so busy it didn't seem to matter. What happened between you and me, well, it just happened. It shouldn't have gotten this far."

"Well, it did. You think I'm going to disappear?"

"It would help if you transferred out." Said without hesitation. Without a blink, as if their four months together had no connection to him, no impact to her.

"Well, think again!"

Those had been her last words before she exploded out of his office.

She did not request a transfer. *No fucking way I'm doing that.*

He filed a sexual harassment charge, backing it up with colleagues.

She filed a counter charge, but it had been too late and too little. He was the "big doc" who brought in the money. She was just the 'new girl.'

When Laura approached the senior administrator, he took her complaint. He asked for her signature, then dated and stamped the whole packet with the time. He seemed pleasant enough.

"Ms. Greenwald, I'm sorry the necessity for this has occurred. Situations such as these are always difficult and affect everyone. We try, in many ways, to reduce contention in the hospital. I hope we can be effective in your case." He'd paused, then said, "It's late. I see from your address here you don't live far from the hospital. May I offer you a ride home?"

It was late and rainy so she accepted. Her apartment building nestled on a quiet neighborhood street close to the hospital. This was what had made it so easy to slip into an affair. Her handsome doctor explained how his home was over an hour away—that he stayed overnight in the hospital rooms if surgery went late. So, she'd invited him into hers instead. She never saw his home, family pictures, family rooms, family history, family anything.

She remembered how the administrator stopped the car. She opened the door to get out. "Thank you for the lift. It's a bad night for walking."

"A pleasure," he'd replied. She turned. As her foot went on the pavement, bending to get out, he asked, "Ms. Greenwald, It's a little embarrassing, but, well, I...would you mind if I used your bathroom?"

She smiled weakly, tired, wanting the day to be over. "Sure," she said.

He followed her two flights upstairs. She opened the door; he walked in and shut it quietly. He never made it to the toilet room. He shit on her life right there.

"You know, Ms. Greenwald, this is going to look very poorly for you." She swung around to face him.

"What are you talking about?" Alarmed, uncomprehending, she began to back away.

"You asking me upstairs. Surely you haven't forgotten inviting me? Especially since Dr. Holder already filed sexual harassment charges against you."

"What about the bathroom?"

"Who said anything about a bathroom?" he responded with a small, tight smile. Then he moved. She stood paralyzed. The rest happened as if to someone else. But, like a horror movie, it etched deep and profoundly into memory.

He grabbed her arm, ripped off her blouse, pulled her head back, whispered how if she screamed, she'd involve the neighbors; how the whole story of her messing around with just about everyone at the hospital would really get out; how she went for married men; how she violated professional ethics.

With her arm bent behind, he pushed into the bedroom, pelvis thrusting into hers. The erection was hot, throbbing, disgusting, terrifying. Her hair fell from the knot at her neck and cascaded down her back. His hands tangled into it, arching her body. She shrieked in pain. He reached behind to turn on the television. As the noise blared, he muttered in her ear, "This assignment is going to be a real pleasure."

It only lasted ten minutes and he kept the most humiliating part for last.

"Sweetheart," he'd said as he zipped up his fly, never having stripped out of his pants. "You come in tomorrow, and we'll give you recommendations and a job opening in Boston. Someone I know real good up there is looking. Owes me a favor. Like Doc Holder said, you can't stick around here anymore. Tonight was a little motivator, just so you could think it over. You want to think any more let me know. If not, I'll see you in my office at 9:00 am sharp."

And he'd left. She'd vomited, then again, and once more, took five showers, scrubbed, cried, and dry heaved. She'd gone in the next day, left with a recommendation and a job interview in hand. She never returned to those New York hospital streets. Her move to Boston came a month later.

Laura catapulted back to the present, her workout had left her panting, sweating, hands clutching hair. "Oh, God," she whispered as the memories surged forward, "get out of my head—just leave me alone."

With a vengeance she began the movement routine—kick front, kick back, side, side, side. Kick front, kick back, side, side, side.

Chapter 3

Laura's week lurched forward with appointments, disagreements, occasional successes. She and Morris worked side by side, stiffly efficient, the coldness between them a new standard. A picture of wife and children appeared on his bookcase where none had been before. She worked hard, didn't bother with breaks and arrived home so exhausted she couldn't think. Several people remarked on it but went no further.

The 'Thing' happened Friday afternoon. Stephanie, her assistant, interrupted Laura in a meeting. With raised eyebrows questioning the failure to take a message, Laura left the group.

"They wouldn't give me any information. It had to be you," said Stephanie with an apologetic shrug. "It sounded official."

Laura punched a button on the blinking phone. "Greenwald here," she said.

"Ms. Greenwald?" said the disembodied voice, "We apologize for interrupting your meeting."

"What does this concern?"

"It is about your employment application."

The pounding in her chest began so suddenly she couldn't think. The phone became slippery in her shaking hand from sweat that had come out of nowhere.

"Further documents will arrive by overnight mail via US Postal Service. They should arrive Saturday. Please return them by Monday. The forms take time to complete. You may need to clear your weekend schedule. Is this acceptable?"

"Yes. Uh…yes, of course."

"You will need to be at home to sign for the package. If not, it will be returned immediately. Unfortunately, we cannot determine exactly what time delivery occurs. Are you able to comply?"

Laura nodded her head, heart still thudding its beat.

Silence on the other end of the line. "Ms. Greenwald, are you still there?"

"Oh, sorry. Yes, I'll be home. Of course, yes."

"Then that is all. Thank you for your time." The clicking sound disconnected them.

Laura looked at the phone. She held her hand to her chest, breath coming in erratic gasps, thoughts flying in bee circles around her head. Concentration shattered, heart pounding she forced herself back to the meeting, leaving behind a silent and confused secretary.

The struggle through Friday afternoon was worse than usual. Irritations of the day floated in spicy mixtures of wild imagination all the way until 6:00 pm when she pushed stiff muscles into the windy-cold night.

Reluctant to go home, she ended up at Hondie's, a mostly bar and sometimes grill restaurant, close to home. Good for wine, good for beer, lots of sports, no CNN and no pressure-talk.

"Hey, Laura!" a voice called. "Grab a glass and come on over!" She rose on tiptoe, looked for the face that went with the voice and saw Sam, a many-Friday-evenings friend. She waved and swam over through the chaos of the crowd. It was time to shut out the rest of the world.

***

That noise again.

Insistent. Intrusive. Unpleasant.

Over a too-many-drinks-and-not-enough-food aching head she peered at the clock. An impossible 11:30 am. Last night had gone on way too long.

That noise—again. She turned to pull the covers over...then jack-in-the-boxed out of bed.

"Oh, m'God! The post office! Oh, my God! Wait!" She struggled with her robe, clasped it, forgot slippers, jiggled knobs, pulled at latches, hurdled down the hall.

"Wait! Wait!" The hallway echoed. She burst barefoot through the front door onto cold concrete steps. A postal van was just edging into traffic.

"Stop! Stop!" she yelled, voice frantic, panicked. "Please, stop!" Lurching forward, she pounded the fender. The driver, glancing in the rear-view mirror, saw a woman waving frantically, standing in January weather with white satin gown clutched by one hand around slender waist, long auburn hair swirling wildly in the wind. He would have stopped for the sight even if she hadn't pounded on his van.

Seconds passed as he maneuvered back to the curb. By now, Laura was hopping first on one foot, then the other, arms clutched, teeth chattering, limbs shivering, feet frozen.

God, it's cold outside.

"Yes, miss? How may I be of assistance?"

"Thheee package, the package you were supposed to deliver…I wa-wass sleeping. I di-didn't hear the buzzer." The words cold-froze in her mouth.

"Oh, sleeping, were you?" An Irish brogue flavored his voice. "Well you get yourself back into that hallway lickety split and I'll pull out this package you're talking about. Go on; go on, you'll catch your death out here."

She retreated to the hallway but kept the door open fearing he might disappear. He pulled out a canvas satchel. She'd expected a brown envelope. Instead, he pulled out a box—confirmation of a weekend to be lost.

"Here you go. Lucky you caught me. Instructions say 'Immediate Return.' Can you sign just here?" She scrawled illegibly with shaking hands. It didn't matter. She had the box—a wooden one with the top nailed tightly and precisely to the bottom.

***

The box sat like a grenade where she'd left it on the table. One-inch slabs of pinewood for sides, an address label with her name glued direct center. Numbers making no sense were printed where a return stamp should be.

She found a hammer and screwdriver, then wedged the screwdriver tip between the layers and tapped with surgical skill. She pried off the top and began to sweat. What did she expect? Shrapnel? Poison darts? Thousand-dollar bills? What?

She looked.

Inside lay a smaller box. It had an unsealed lid with eight screws taped to its top. Tiny holes were drilled indicating where the screws should go later. An address label, glued to the center of the lid held the numbers she'd seen on the return label. Inside were documents. And a letter on top.

Laura picked up the letter and began reading.

The first two pages requested basic information—education, employment, references along with a request for supporting documentation. She'd already sent all that. Okay, no sweat, but she felt a creeping annoyance at having to send everything again.

Then came the third page.

The three short paragraphs changed her life.

Dear Ms. Greenwald,

> *This application will intrude on your weekend. We may pay you for your time, regardless of whether we invite you to an interview.*

> *Present each of the following cases as if you were in a medical conference—facts first, opinions and diagnostic impressions following. Attach information from national research sites to support responses. Case studies are actual patients—details and identities shifted sufficiently to maintain privacy.*

> *Place completed application in the small box. Deliver directly to Daniel Demers at Special Packages window in the Somerville Post Office Monday morning. If you wish to with-*

draw from this process, place all materials in small box. Drop into any US mail receptacle.

Sincerely,

Dr. Manhattan's Office

"Give me a break! 'Dr. Manhattan?' What kind of lame name is that?" She grabbed her computer and ten-minutes later was no closer to knowing anything about Dr. Manhattan. There were too many doctors of that name who practiced all over the world. She didn't even know if Manhattan was a name, a location or some "sufficiently shifted identity."

$700,000 floated in the air. It wouldn't go away. "Oh, Lord, here goes my whole weekend again."

Laura spent it on line; she spent it missing Sunday brunch with Leanne and Lily; she spent it with Tylenol when her headache raged; she spent it ordering Chinese; she spent it exhausted and ready for Monday to escape back to work.

Twelve cases! Hard, gut-wrenching cases. When she nailed the box shut with the completed case studies inside, she thought she should include a bill for hand, neck, and brain damage.

***

On Monday morning, when Laura looked at the mirror on the back of the door, it reflected a woman with droopy, baggy eyes—a funeral reject who needed bed rather than work.

She called a cab and headed to the post office. A few strides inside took her to a door with typing paper pasted on but sagging. 'Special Packages,' it proclaimed. Daniel Demers' name was nowhere present. Her finger rang the call button.

"And how are you this fine mornin'?" inquired an Irish brogue from behind her. Laura recognized the Saturday postal driver.

"I was told to give this package to a Mr. Demers." Laura pulled the box from under her arm.

"Well, that'll be me," he said and took the box.

"The address label doesn't make sense to me..." she began.

"Oh, don't go an' worry your head about that. These here are special codes—customers pay a pretty penny for them. Computers scan the code, then direct the delivery—keeps things private, you see."

"Oh," she responded. "You're in charge of Special Packages Division?"

"No, Miss, just sometimes I fill in. So here I be. I'll post this straightaway. Top a' the mornin' to you, Miss."

He smiled, opened the door with a key and disappeared inside. As it shut, the sagging paper loosened from the tape and slipped to the floor. Laura stared at it. Special Packages Division? She'd never heard of it.

***

Laura never made it to the end of the day. By noon, she took sick leave, called for a cab and wondered what kind of job started with an application in a tight-nailed box and a sagging paper falling to the floor.

Chapter 4

The special delivery arrived at her office almost to the hour two weeks later.

Once again Stephanie interrupted Laura as she led a meeting. "It has to be you," reported Stephanie with another apologetic shrug. "It's very official."

The delivery came with special instructions.

"I have to do *what?*" she said, incredulous.

"It says here," the delivery man flipped through several pages on his clipboard. "The recipient shall read instructions out loud, sign the statement, and only then receive the package." He shrugged.

Laura gave up, reached for the paper and read out loud "I must keep this parcel with me and in sight at all times the day it is delivered. When I arrive home, I will store it in a secure location." She signed her name and received the item. Dr. Manhattan's name and code occupied the return address space.

She brought the packet into the meeting, held it tightly under one arm and once again found her concentration shattered for the rest of the day. A headache blossomed, muscle cramps clutched at her neck and her mouth turned dry. She couldn't wait for the day to end.

At rush hour she took a taxi, afraid of losing the package on the subway. Forty-five minutes and $39.00 later the cab arrived at her apartment. Add a tip and she could have paid cell phone charges for the month. Laura ran the steps, and, once inside, poured herself a large glass of red wine. She sat to open the envelope, cramps and headache still plaguing her.

"Tomorrow," the instructions said, "at 2:00 in the afternoon, be prepared to conduct a telephone interview. The letter followed with a list.

"Personal prereview questions are provided below.

Be prepared to answer whatever is asked.

If you do not wish to respond, do not answer the phone.

Non-response will terminate the application process.

If that occurs, kindly return the packet using the enclosed envelope.

We thank you for your time."

"We," she thought, "who the heck are 'we'?" That was all she'd had the energy to read. The rest could wait until morning. Laura tucked the envelope in the closet, as if clothes and closet doors might keep the boundaries of her old life intact. It would have to do because she wasn't going to sleep with the wretched thing.

***

Saturday morning sunlight streamed in the window. Phone interview at 2:00. Last night she'd hung out with Sam at Hondie's but ordered food along with wine. That had been the mistake two weeks ago—no food, too much drink. The next day she'd overslept and almost missed the package delivery.

This time she wanted exquisite clarity. She had to prepare her answers for the personal questions. What did they mean by "personal," anyhow? For a $700,000 salary, she couldn't imagine anything too offensive to answer.

That was what she thought before she opened the packet. The raspberry colored, sticky note said simply, "These are sample questions only."

The first questions were a little "not-so-normal."

Why are you not married?

What do you think of medical practice in other countries?

Are there any countries you would not travel to?

How do you feel about operating on a political leader charged with genocide?

What do you think about marriage?

Do you plan to have children? If so, how many?

And on and on.

That was the first page.

But the second page made her eyes pop and blood pressure rise. These questions weren't "personal." For a job application, she thought they came closer to being illegal.

How do you feel about current Congressional and White House morals?

What sexual practices do you think are illegal?

How many sexual partners have you had? For how long?

What is your stance on abortion?

Have you had any abortions?

The list went on to the bottom of the second page and the top of the third. It read like a Peeping Tom's grocery list. The last paragraph stated, *"If you wish to continue with the application, answer the 2:00 pm phone call."*

Laura dropped the papers on the table. Where could such extraordinary questions lead except to headaches and complications—and a $700,000 salary?

She paced irritably looking at the clock. It was 12:00. She had two hours to take a run, grab a latte at Pete's Coffee to clear her brain and be back with time to spare. The package would be fine babysitting itself in her closet.

She looked around for her cell. It lay on the counter where she'd dropped it last night. Snatching her coat from the door hook and grabbing the phone, she bolted out of the apartment.

Less than two minutes later she stopped and felt in her pockets. *Damn. I need some money.* She ran back upstairs, fumbled for keys in her pocket but first dragged her phone out to get at them.

"SHIT," she screamed. The battery on her phone was dead—completely gone, below the redline dead. Okay, it was an old phone; she needed a new one, yes, but forgetting to charge it the night before the interview? *Totally stupid.*

"Oh, SHUT UP." she boomed in the hallway. She shouldered her way inside the door, slammed it, went straight to her charging cords and plugged in her cell.

You'd better stay here and wait while it charges, said a part of her.

"I'm not sitting here watching my phone charge," she said out loud in response. "Gotta get outside or I'll go crazier than I already feel." She looked. There was way more than an hour left.

One thirty-minute run and two blocks from home later, friendly chatter and bustling counter lines at Pete's Coffee dissipated Laura's tensions. She purchased a mocha java, found a high stool by the window and cupped cold hands around the warm paper mug. Then she sat. And watched. And let her mind run blank.

***

The phone was ringing by the time she reached her apartment. She could hear it in the hall. This wasn't right. It was just 1:45. She was sure of it. She'd checked her watch.

Where were the keys? She dumped her pack upside down and four keys on a chain tumbled to the floor. Inserting key in lock, she opened the door and ran inside. The ringing had stopped—gone totally, deadly silent. Caller ID showed "Unknown number."

Laura stood and stared at the silent cell phone.

"SHIT," she screamed. She hit her head with her hand. "SHIT." She'd missed the call. Her heartbeat thudded, and she paced.

"Just breathe; calm down; you missed the call and that's that." Talking to herself helped. She paced some more, breathed more deeply. "Good riddance," she said, "Not a big deal. You've got a job. The last two weeks you've been way too caught up with this business, anyway."

Her apartment felt claustrophobic. "Distraction. That's what I need. I'll stop at Diane's and see if she's home."

Laura went to the bathroom, snatched a brush, yanked hard strokes through tangled hair. She punished herself for having left the phone, lost the opportunity, been too smug. She changed jogging sweats for jeans and sweater, then on went hat and gloves again. She could feel her mind marching back to practical borders and knowable landmarks.

Then the phone rang.

Once.

Laura lunged. It slid off the counter.

Twice.

She grabbed it from the floor.

Three times. On the fourth ring call answering would pick up.

"Hello!" she choked into the receiver

"Ms. Greenwald?" came the response.

"Yes?"

"Are you ready for the interview?"

The clock said 2:01 pm. "Yes, yes, I am, thank you."

***

Provoking, demanding, intrusive, intimate, professional. When it was over, the questions left her feeling alternately naked and suited up.

They ended with a simple, "Thank you, Ms. Greenwald. We will be in touch."

Click.

That was it.

Done.

Over.

She looked at the caller ID. "Unknown number." Of course.

This time when the phone went silent, she danced around the apartment in twirls, full of dreams, laughing. How she could go from such despair to such excitement in so short a time?

"Go run!" said her brain. "Now!"

And she did.

The rest of the weekend couldn't compare. Sam called wanting to hang out; Diane joined them. They walked, ate pizza, and went home separately. She didn't mention the interview. The weekend slid into Monday.

Chapter 5

The next special delivery came Monday afternoon. Her secretary paged Laura who was, at that moment, in the middle of defusing a "difference of opinion" between a surgical doc and his nurses.

They've been going at it for months, thought Laura trying to keep her exasperation under wraps. "Hi, Stephanie. What's up?"

"Special delivery. I thought it might be important."

Her heart thudded. *Already?* she thought.

"I'll be right up," she said out loud. When she turned to her arguing colleagues, they had disappeared—as had the argument. "I'll have to try interruptions more often."

Two flights of stairs, four corridors and one office door later, she held the special delivery in her hands and watched everything tremble. Her anxiety made Laura want to rip away parts of the envelope as she opened it. When her right hand steadied, she grasped a sheet of thin, watermarked paper from inside.

Dear Ms. Greenwald,

Thank you for the case review data you submitted two weeks ago. Your clinical analysis and writing style show an excellent grasp of the medical field

Enclosed is a check reimbursing you for your time and expertise.

Attached to the page was a check for $3,000. The signature line was unreadable, and the bank routing numbers were composed of dots and lines rather than numbers.

Perhaps she would take that unaffordable ski and spa trip after all.

***

Friday night at Hondie's. Background noises from the bar formed a bubble of privacy around the corner table where Sam liked to sit.

"They haven't called," she said to Sam. It had taken months for Sam to morph from acquaintance to after-work friend. They'd shared laughs and drinks, thoughts and annoyances, and finally, friendship. "It's been two weeks," she complained. "They've always contacted me within two weeks."

"Laura," he said. "let it go. You've had a hard few days." His voice was low—intimate in a way she'd not noticed before.

Monday night, Laura had broken her wall of silence. The $3,000 had been too exciting to hide. She called Sam, swearing him to secrecy. She hadn't told him everything—just about a great job possibility and a hefty consulting fee. He'd laughed and imagined fantastic futures along with her, lush consultation fees and brilliant beaches upon which to spend her disposable income.

He'd called back, said they should celebrate the next day at his favorite deli restaurant where you eat gourmet sandwiches on stools slung around a ridiculously high and tiny table. So, Sam's intimate tone wasn't surprising—or unwelcome—but it was new.

"How about we order some takeout and watch a movie at my place?" she suggested. Tonight Laura wanted the comfort of home.

Sam raised his eyebrows in mock disbelief. "You have etchings for me to see?" he joked.

"Don't get any brilliant ideas," she retorted, "Just a movie."

It had turned into more than a movie, but less than sex. Laura, always wary and suspicious since her "big-doc-on-the-block" disaster, took time when getting into new relationships. They watched the movie, ate the food, snuggled, and fell asleep on the couch. When it got too late to go home, she invited him into her bed, both more or less clothed—her in rag-tag pajamas, him in shirt and briefs. He held her close and muttered sweet nothings; she muttered "not-tonight's." Eventually they fell into sleep, arms forming a cocoon against the outside world.

***

The phone jangled them awake at 7:30 Saturday morning. Sam, groaned and pulled pillows over his head. Laura grappled with the charging cord, and the cell fell out of her hands into the quilt. She poked around, mussing up the covers. Early calls meant emergencies. Sam turned over, taking the pillow off his face.

"Hello?" she responded, attempting to wipe sleep from her voice.

"Ms. Greenwald?" came the reply.

Instantly awake. She knew that voice. "Yes?"

"Dr. Manhattan's office calling. We'd like you to come for a full process interview. Would you be willing to do that?"

"Yes. Yes, of course." She paused. "I'd like to...but, what do you mean 'full process interview'?" It was hard for her to hear over the pounding of her heart.

"It means, Ms. Greenwald, you are a finalist for the job."

Laura stopped breathing so quickly she choked. Her iron grip on the phone threatened to break it. Finalist? Finalist for *The Job*? She'd never dreamed she'd have a chance—not really—not for a $700,000-a-year-job-Job.

"Ms. Greenwald?"

"Uhhh...yes. It's just...it's just this is a surprise..."

"We apologize for the early morning hour."

"Oh, no, it's no bother, just that, well, I'm thrilled you called. I thought..." She hesitated. "Well, to tell you the truth, I thought there would be thousands of applications and what could be so special about mine?"

"Apparently. Ms. Greenwald, it was special enough or I wouldn't be making this call. Would you care to take time to consider?"

"No, that won't be necessary," stammered Laura. "I'll be glad to come for an interview. But..." She took a deep breath.

No further explanation followed from the phone.

"What do I do now?" she finally asked into the silence.

"All conversations are recorded from this point onward. Your verbal acceptance, once digitalized, will be considered official." Silence. Then, "Will you do so now, please?"

Laura's brain sparred with The Voices of Caution clamoring in her head.

It's crazy.

Who cares?

Your whole life might change.

That's what I want.

Who are these people?

We'll find out soon enough.

The arguments could have gone on. But Laura's throat made the decision. It uttered the necessary, "I understand all conversations will be recorded."

Oh, my God. I did it.

Chapter 6

Silence.

"Ms. Greenwald, are you still there?"

I just did it. I can't believe I...

"I will explain the interview schedule if you are still there." A pause.

"I'm here, yes." Laura found it hard to control her breathing.

"You will be at our home office location for three nights."

"Oh."

"We arrange all air and ground transportation, lodging, and meals." A pause. "There will be psychological testing."

"I see."

"Some clinical work is required."

"I understand."

"Several social engagements are involved."

"That's nice." *Did I really say that?*

"There will be face-to-face interviews."

"It sounds thorough."

"The process is demanding." No further comment came from the phone.

Laura waited. Then, "Is there time for a question?"

"Certainly."

"Where will I be going?"

"I'm sorry. Until you sign a confidentiality agreement, I can only tell you the location is in the continental United States. I can tell you our office is a fully licensed, legitimate practice with the highest medical and ethical standards. The people with whom you will be dealing are trained professionals in their fields."

"Okay," she said, the tension in her neck beginning to ache.

"Thank you for your time, Ms. Greenwald. We will contact you with the interview schedule." The line disconnected. Laura hung there, looking at the receiver in her hand.

"They called," said Sam.

"They did."

Silence followed. He kissed her then, gently, softly, without pressure or demand, and she responded without resistance or fear. Wrapped in each other's arms they breathed quietly until her body relaxed.

***

The suitcase wasn't shutting. She slapped it in frustration, sat on the unclosed side and yanked the zipper until it slipped around the corner. Yesterday had been consumed raking through her wardrobe. Clothes packed in the suitcase were tossed out, tried on and taken off, steamed and then ironed. Hours passed until she slammed the bedroom door and went for a run. Not one word passed her lips to anyone besides Sam except to ask for days off. Mostly, she kept to herself. No one inquired why; they knew she'd been working too hard and chalked it up to stress.

Laura, in tailored grey pants suit, white blouse and diamond necklace, rolled the suitcase into the hall and down the stairs. A special taxi had been ordered to take her to a special airport where a special plane would fly her to the special interview.

The journey had begun. She had no idea where it would end.

***

The taxi picked her up. The driver knew her name, stored her suitcase, and drove her to the Belmont airfield. He escorted her through the hanger to the plane and refused when she offered him a tip.

"I've been well paid, Miss Greenwald. Enjoy your flight," he said and waved good-bye.

38

A black-suited airline steward welcomed her into the plane. "Once the seatbelt light is off, we'll serve refreshments," he explained, giving her a cream-colored menu board with gold printing. The flight would last one hour, and would she please strap in?

Laura knew she was flying to Washington, DC. The location of the home office and the name of the doctor, however, were still privileged information.

She ordered a glass of wine. The steward sat with her and chatted about interesting places to visit in the city. Before her wine was finished, the seatbelt light signaled descent. From the Virginia executive airport, she was escorted to lodging at the Lincoln Inn where staff greeted her with smiles and trays of sweets. It was 7 pm.

The room, which was to be her home for three nights, overlooked southern style gardens, held one four poster bed and two antique dressers along with a brocaded corner loveseat.

"Would you like a bath, then dinner at 8:00?" the bellhop asked.

"That would be lovely." She closed the door and sat on the bed, turning her head one way and then another as tension eased from tight muscles. An envelope with her name rested against the night stand lamp. She opened it. The elegant script flowed across an embossed ivory card.

> *Dear Ms. Greenwald:*
>
> *Welcome to Washington, DC. Enjoy your dinner.*
>
> *Be ready in the lobby of the Inn at 8:00 am tomorrow.*
>
> *Your wakeup call is at 6:30. We look forward to meeting you.*
>
> *Sincerely,*
>
> *Office of Dr. Manhattan*

Chapter 7

Laura barely stirred when she heard the knock.

"Ms. Greenwald?" The knock continued. Her eyes flew open. The interview.

Today.

Soon.

"Yes?"

"This is your 6:30 wakeup call. Breakfast is served in the dining nooks downstairs or in your room, as you wish."

"I'll come downstairs." Sound of receding footsteps, then silence.

Sunlight illuminated the walls. She stood, slipped on a white plush bathrobe left for her convenience, and ran fingers through her long auburn hair. In the tossing and turning of night dreams, it had tangled. That meant a fifteen-minute brush-out, at least.

Her plan was to look professional with discrete sexuality painting the edges—a hard combination to pull off. She'd spent hours combing and pinning hairstyles that reflected her intelligent, no-nonsense style. Determining how much sexiness to let peek through was part of the "dress for success" art.

Today she chose semi-tailored, with a flowing skirt that swirled mid-calf around her legs. Open-toed two-inch heels revealed a red-polish pedicure. Her plunging V-neck blouse stopped the prying eye with contrasting neck scarf. She worked her hair into a French knot and decorated it with a single pearl hair clip. Makeup, minimal with a slight touch of perfume.

The whole procedure, including shower, took just under an hour. When she was done, she locked her door and went to face the day.

***

The black Lincoln Town Car with liveried driver picked her up at exactly 8:00. He welcomed Laura by name, opened the back door of the sedan and offered her refreshment which she declined.

The ride took twenty minutes in mild morning traffic before the car slowed and the chauffeur eased onto a private lane. Leafless dogwood trees and flower patches awaiting March blooming lined the walkway to the doorway steps. The driver opened her door, offered his hand and accompanied her to the building.

Behind the door a wide spacious foyer opened to a large salon. Sunlight poured through French windows overlooking landscaped gardens.

"Welcome, Ms. Greenwald." An impeccably dressed woman with warm smile and perfect pronunciation stood in front of her. "Welcome to Long House. We are pleased to have you with us. Our staff is waiting for you in the conference room."

The woman guided her down a hallway and into a room of high ceilings and tall paned windows. Around an oval conference table sat five men and women of varying ages and body types.

"Please sit down, Ms. Greenwald," said one gentleman.

Clasping her purse with both hands, she willed her blood pressure to stabilize. *It's just a fancy interview, that's all,* she thought. *No big deal.*

"I'd like to introduce myself and my companions. I'm the company coordinator, and everyone else is a lawyer." The gentleman's name was Phillip Williams and conversation moved too quickly for her to remember anyone else's.

"Ms. Greenwald, we start right away at a crucial agreement. You must sign a confidentiality document before we can proceed."

Laura smiled, confused, tentative, reluctant and willing all at once. She counted to five before she answered.

"I don't understand what's going on."

41

Everyone nodded.

"We wouldn't expect you to sign anything without proper review of the details," answered Phillip Williams. He pulled a sheaf of papers from a briefcase and spread them on the table. "These documents attest that you will not talk about these proceedings to anyone at any time, ever."

He smiled as if what he had said was a typical, ordinary, everyday statement.

She blinked. "Excuse me?"

"Ms. Greenwald, what you are about to get involved with touches on matters of national security.

Laura blinked again. "National security?"

"Yes, national security."

She shouldn't have been surprised, right? Not much could be worth a forever secret and $700,000.

Laura cleared her very dry throat. "Well," she said, "this is a little unusual for me."

"This job *is* 'a little unusual'," replied Phillip Williams.

It helped to hear him say it out loud. Her stomach knot eased; she uttered the word, "Okay," then looked at her watch. Only 8:45 am. It felt like hours.

Williams stacked the papers and placed them in two piles.

"These documents," he said, placing his hand on the smaller of two piles, "state you will not describe this interview or details of employment, ever. Authorized staff is the exception." He looked up, waited for a response.

She took a breath. Then nodded.

He continued. "For your convenience, we provide a synopsis of information you may tell family and friends."

"That will be helpful." *What the hell am I getting into?*

"You will never be required to do anything illegal. We want to be clear on that last point."

"That's even more helpful," she said. *I can't believe I just said that* but he appeared unperturbed.

"This second set of documents," he continued, hand on the larger stack, "outlines all job requirements except one. That requires a separate signature process depending on the outcome of this interview." He paused. "Any questions?"

Questions erupted in her mind. She didn't know which to ask or how many mattered.

Phillip Williams waited. She finally spoke.

"How would you know if I were to break confidentiality? Forever is a long time. I could be anywhere."

"That's very true, Ms. Greenwald. We have access to federal and state record systems. Any leakage of confidential information traced to you would result in negative recommendations to state and national licensing boards. This would include requests to permanently revoke your professional licenses as well as presenting a civil law suit against all your assets. And we would win. That is a guarantee."

She visibly stiffened.

"Ms. Greenwald." They locked eyes. "Our focus is health care. We must be assured each candidate appreciates the responsibility demanded by this position. We have all signed similar contracts. We engage in nothing illegal. We are not criminals, nor do we deal in drugs or violence. You have the option to step down from your position whenever you choose. But you do need to agree to absolute confidentiality. I hope this assurance allays your concerns."

Laura reluctantly let go of her fears under Phillip's direct, professional manner. She tried on a smile.

"Well, yes, thank you. That does help." She reset her posture. "May I review the contract?"

"Yes, of course," he responded and reached over to hand her three sheets of paper. Tension around the table eased—water and coffee refilled, clothing rustled, china clinked. Laura began to read.

***

The documents were written in legalese, a never, ever straightforward language. With years of hospital administration behind her, she translated her way through. Mostly a repetition of what Williams stated, once more going over consequences of contract breach. In a sudden movement of decision, she took a pen, signed her name to the contract and handed back the papers.

Done.

First point of no return.

She didn't know if she'd make the second.

***

"Yes, I'd like that very much," she said.

What would I like very much? Only 9:15 a.m. and she felt she'd been sitting all day. *When did I lose track of the conversation?*

Phillip Williams' right arm was extending in a semicircle over the table. "This building is a southern style mansion called Long House. Dr. Russell purchased it for administrative and clinical purposes."

"Dr. Russell?" she blurted out. *They dropped his name just like that?* She'd been asking for weeks.

"Yes. Dr. John Russell. We can mention names now."

"Then who's Dr. Manhattan?" *Would she never stop interrupting?*

"Ah, yes. Dr. Manhattan."

Laura waited. She'd been doing that for weeks.

"Dr. Manhattan is John Russell's financial foundation. The financial end of the business is separate from the clinical side. It's a typical business arrangement. The medical work is conducted under his, shall we say, 'regular' name."

"Oh."

"He's a board-certified neurosurgeon, well-published, and in demand nationally and internationally. But DC is his home base."

"I see," said Laura forcing her overloaded brain to focus.

"He bought Long House because this location provided an unusual amount of privacy for his high-profile clients as well as for himself."

Williams paused his explanation, took a sip of cappuccino. "Wonderful taste, this. Our chef brews the coffee with spring water. Exceptionally good. Would you like a cup?"

"Thanks, but no." Laura's anxiety wouldn't tolerate more caffeine and her bladder didn't need excuses to make her miserable.

"Dr. Russell lives on the second floor of this building. He's got a private drive to his residence on a different street than the clinic entrance and parking." Phillip Williams smiled pensively. "He does go on and on about separating homelife and work."

"He's upstairs right now? I mean, doesn't he ever come down through one of the doors or something?" exclaimed Laura. *Would she never stop interrupting?*

"There is a door linking the two floors," responded Phillip Williams. "Required by fire codes. But he was adamant. The door was specially reinforced with a coded lock. He is the only one who knows the combination. Special fire routes had to be designed for anyone else on the second floor."

"So, is he upstairs?" persisted Laura.

"No, I don't believe he is. Hmmm, let me see..." Williams punched a few keys on his laptop and scrolled down the screen. "He always leaves us his schedule. So...at the moment...no, he's in surgery. That means he'll be at Washington Memorial Hospital in DC most of the day." He looked up. "Any other questions before we take a break?"

***

With fifteen minutes to herself, Laura sought the safety of the 'powder room.' An antechamber with mirror, inlaid marble sink, and ivory-colored loveseat overlooking winter gardens welcomed her. She stared out the window, body locked away from the flood of information on the other side of the door.

She'd heard stories of people stepping beyond their comfort zone into places for which they were not prepared. Lives exploded, like thermostats on extra high heat. One Los Angeles waitress won the million-dollar lottery. Before the week was over her life had turned into a living hell, people at her door, asking, wanting, needing, demanding.

"I've bumped into the 'big time," Laura whispered into the silence of the empty room. She wasn't sure if she was ready, or if life would explode in her face.

Chapter 8

She returned to the conference room. At the head of the table sat the woman who had greeted Laura in the foyer. She had not paid much attention then. Now she did. This woman radiated power.

"Good morning, Ms. Greenwald. I'm Eva Jormand. It's a pleasure to meet you in person." She re-introduced everyone around the table. A grateful Laura realized she couldn't remember topics of conversation, much less names of people here to judge her.

"They won't say much for the moment," said Eva. "That's my job—I created your position." She paused. "I'm also the person who decides if you pass or fail the interview process."

No one spoke and Laura couldn't have, even if she'd tried.

"When we advertise this position," she continued, "everyone gets distracted by the $700,000-dollar figure."

Laura felt the tug of a smile.

"A lot of people make more than $700,000—millions more—but not in nursing."

Laura's nod started at the top of her head. It didn't make it to her chin before Eva spoke again.

"Things other than salary make this job unusual. The first is that you'll work with the President of the United States."

The President?" Her startled interruption made Laura wish she could slide under the table.

"Yes. Not every day, sometimes not even in a year," continued Eva, "but he is the most important client. We work with many high-level dignitaries, national and international—which is very confidential information."

Eva paused. In the silence Laura heard the winter wind rustling against the trees.

"Of course, daily activities are different. If chosen, you'd work as Dr. Russell's executive nurse in Washington and wherever he travels."

Eva took a deep breath.

"John was the first to diagnose President Reagan with Alzheimer's when he was only a neurosurgery resident. He was watching Reagan on TV and saw verbal and facial changes—really little ones. Not very noticeable. What he saw worried him. He'd been studying early Alzheimer's treatment as a sideline—his maternal grandmother..." Eva did not finish her sentence.

"I see."

"He made calls and wrote letters—to Health and Human Services, the Surgeon General, even to Nancy Reagan. Of course, that didn't get very far."

Laura nodded. She could imagine it wouldn't.

"People brushed him off as a crank. So, he dropped it. A couple of years later, two men show up with FBI badges and tell him he's needed in DC. He thought it was a practical joke, except they ended up in Washington. The Surgeon General and some mucky-mucks from Walter Reed wanted to ask how he knew about President Reagan's condition."

Eva looked at her. "Still with me?"

Laura nodded.

"Anyway, they called 24-hours later and offered him the position of Presidential Neurosurgeon. It wouldn't be just for Reagan, but for every President in office. The President's ability to think can never come into question. Routine checkups to be conducted every three months unless a 'situation' occurred. Then he'd have to stay until the issue resolved. They quoted a retainer and expenses that would have made him rich even if he never saw anyone else. Except that's not Dr. Russell's personality."

Eva took a sip of coffee before continuing.

"He moved to Washington, and began his practice here. It expanded exponentially. To maintain his case load, he needs a discreet, highly skilled executive and clinical nurse working with him." She paused. "It's a very demanding relationship."

Eva studied Laura's face. "That person has to be okay with unconventional schedules. Sometimes…" Eva kept her posture very composed. "…sometimes the work interferes with personal life."

Laura had the uncomfortable feeling Eva had just left out something important—except Laura had no idea what it could be.

"That's how all this got started. Although Dr. Russell sees other patients, they all know he might get called on emergency." Eva glanced at the clock. "We'll take a break. You still have a long day ahead, Ms. Greenwald. Any questions about what I've said?"

Laura's million-and-one questions evaporated as soon as Eva asked the question. No, I don't think so," she said. Chairs creaked; papers shuffled.

"Well, then, we are finished with this part of the interview. If I'm needed, my office is just down the hall." Eva stood and exited the room.

***

Fifteen minutes later, Laura returned to the now unoccupied conference room—unoccupied except for one woman of medium height, dressed in tweed suit, tan blouse, with hair arranged in a too tightly bound French twist.

"Let's get started, shall we?" she remarked a somewhat prim yet gentle voice. "My name is Dr. Vona DeCambrio." She sat in Eva's chair at the table.

"I'll work privately with you before lunch, Ms. Greenwald, on some evaluations." Vona paused, then said, "I'm a psychologist. All candidates undergo two psychological tests that require about an hour and a half. We'll move to one of the private offices for that.

Laura waited for further information. Seconds passed.

"If this is not acceptable, we thank you and the interview process will terminate," said Dr. DeCambrio.

"I'm sorry. I was waiting for, well, anything else you might have to say." Laura figured she could always walk out if she didn't like the testing.

"Good," said the psychologist. "A written report will be written and ready for Dr. Russell in the morning." She gathered her files and walked to the door. "Please follow me."

***

The testing office was windowless. A mission style table with water pitcher and two chairs occupied the room's center. Tall plants, extra chairs, and a fountain pouring water over a six-foot-tall etched glass pane occupied the wall and corners.

"Please, sit, Ms. Greenwald," Dr. DeCambrio gestured to one of the chairs at the table. "I'll explain our task." She pulled several files from a briefcase and began speaking.

"We already know you are an organized thinker, intelligent, and successful with people and administrative responsibilities."

"Thank you," replied Laura.

"This is not flattery, Ms. Greenwald. What is true is true. However, what we do not know—and have to evaluate as best we can—is your character. Not just values, but how you might act under duress, split second decision-making, flexibility of thought, and so forth. We are looking for areas of concern even you are not aware of."

"These tests will tell you that?" asked Laura.

Dr. DeCambrio smiled, "A lot of people think psychologists gaze into crystal balls and pronounce the future. It's not so fantastic. But research, training, and experience can be predictive about potential behavior—what someone is likely to do given their profile."

The psychologist sat back in her chair. Laura shifted forward.

"We're not 100% accurate. *That* would be magic and I'd be worth millions. Sometimes we're not even close. But most often a good psychologist with the right diagnostics can suggest behaviors that are 'in the ball park' for a particular client. I'm pretty good at what I do."

She stopped to fill a water glass. "Would you care for some?"

Laura shook her head.

"Are the questions going to be like the ones I answered over the phone?"

Dr. DeCambrio gave a small laugh. "No, they'll be quite different." She pulled a folder from her briefcase and laid it on the table. "You've heard of the ink blot test?"

Laura nodded,

"Yes, I have."

"That's layman's terms for the Rorschach. People nicknamed them inkblots because they look like someone folded a paper in half with a blob of ink on it. The test has been around for a long time. It's developed into a very sophisticated tool." She paused. "Shall we begin?"

Laura nodded. Curiosity had overcome her anxiety.

"Please sit next to me on this side of the table," requested the doctor. She retrieved a chair from against the wall and Laura changed seats.

"I'm going to show you 10 cards, one at a time," explained Dr. DeCambrio. We'll go through them a second time once you're done."

She showed Laura the first card. "Each card has a different design. Tell me what you see in this design. Tell me as many things as you can think of."

And that is what Laura did. The doctor took notes throughout. When they were done, Vona questioned Laura again about some of the items. It had taken less than 40 minutes.

"That's it. Well done, she said. "How are you feeling?"

"I'm good," answered Laura. "It was fun." She paused. "How does finding shapes in inkblots tell you anything about me?"

"Lots of people wonder that." Dr. DeCambrio talked as she pulled a pamphlet from her briefcase. "We compare your responses and behaviors to what many other people have done. Algorithms and normative tables developed over years, guide our interpretations. The same is true for all psychological tests, including this next one."

Vona placed pamphlet and pencil in front of Laura. "Inside are a little over 300 true and false questions. Please answer everyone. When you can't decide, think in terms of 'mostly true' or 'mostly false.' Take as long as you wish."

When I get home, thought Laura before she began, *I'm going to brush up on psychiatric nursing. None of this makes much sense at all.*

***

An hour later, Laura put down her pencil. "Done." She rubbed her eyes. "I'm exhausted."

"Testing gives the brain a thorough workout." Dr. DeCambrio smiled. "Lunch in 20-minutes."

Laura rose, legs stiff and protesting. She slipped into the restroom, slapped water on cheeks, massaged her neck and rolled her shoulders. *At least at lunch I can relax with my food and hide in a corner.*

Laura walked to line up at the dining foyer without oomph enough to think. She watched as Vona DeCambrio approached.

"Laura, I forgot to tell you—there's a special event today. Dr. Russell usually can't get away from surgery, but he had a cancelation. He's joining us for lunch. Afterwards, he'll take you back to the hospital himself. You get extra time with him." Vona's smile showed how pleased she was about the "exception."

Thought you'd get a quiet lunch? Laura thought. *Good luck.*

Chapter 9

The dining room doors opened. Laura saw sunlight streaming through the windows, bouncing off crystal water glasses and polished silverware. A woman in white and black uniform stood beside a soup tureen waiting for everyone to be seated. Laura almost forgot her exhaustion as the elegance of the setting overtook her senses.

Then she noticed the man standing beside the chair at the center of the table. Tall, dressed in tailored suit and grey tie, diamond cufflinks, and expensive haircut. This was Dr. John Russell. She was sure of it.

She studied him. Attractive in that lean, runner's way. Focused, intense, alive, radiating energy. Powerful men had that energy—used it like electric power. When the energy wasn't focused on work, sports or project, it vibrated into the social scene. It could be shaped and trimmed, disciplined and curtailed, but it could not be contained.

Laura sensed an unwelcome quickening in her gut. Adrenaline flooded her system. She stared at him, and dropped her eyes, for an instant, to recover composure. He wasn't her type. She preferred men heftier, muscled, thin-waisted, strong-armed, like Sam, sweet Sam. Only Sam was not magnetic. Sam was comfortable, sometimes sexy, sometimes not. But never magnetic.

She smiled.

He smiled back.

"Welcome, Ms. Greenwald," she heard him say, "It's a pleasure to have you with us. I've been fortunate to have time to meet you a day early."

A day early? she thought. *What's he talking about?*

"Thank you," responded her alter ego, currently managing the situation while Laura was still assessing his hair cut. "My visit so far has been an experience I won't forget."

He laughed. "Always direct. From the documents I've reviewed, you don't slice your opinions or dice your words, but it all comes out so pleasantly. Please, have a seat. You must be hungry after this morning's activities."

He motioned to a chair next to him. She sat.

"Ms. Greenwald," he said, "at meals I do not discuss work. A habit I learned to appreciate in Europe. In the United States, we insist on ruining our digestive systems with business."

And then, the food was served.

Salmon tartare, mozzarella roasted asparagus, spicy pumpkin soup, Chesapeake Bay crabs and oysters in a reduction of butter, croissants, baguettes, stone fruit salad, Key Lime pie.

Sumptuous dining. Flowing conversation. Attentive wait staff. The intensity that was John Russell softened. She enjoyed his wry sense of humor, awareness of current events, ability to relax while still in control.

Lunch hasn't been a mindless eating retreat, she thought.

"….to the hospital this afternoon," Dr. Russell continued as he rose from his chair, folding his napkin and laying it on the table.

"Oh…yes, that sounds lovely," she said, without any idea what she'd agreed to.

"We'll have Daniel drive us over. If you wish to stay longer, you're welcome to watch."

Go? Watch? Watch what?

"I'm sorry, Dr. Russell, I…well, I think I've…I'm not sure what I just agreed to do."

She felt the blush run from her neck. He burst into laughter. The others in the room turned to watch. John Russell was rarely this relaxed.

She thought she saw his eyes twinkle.

"Well, you've just agreed to spend the rest of the afternoon at the hospital on a tour of neurosurgery—and, possibly to observe my last operation—or return early to the amenities of your hotel. I promise your honor shall remain intact, whatever you decide."

Laura relaxed. She liked this man. "Agreed."

"At your service, madam. Your skills in being straightforward precede you."

He called to Phillip Williams who waited in the doorway. "Phil, would you have Daniel pick us up at the front door in ten minutes?"

With that, Laura began the second half of her very long day. This part included Dr. John Russell, alias Dr. Manhattan, in flesh and blood. It didn't feel real. But even less real, although just a bit closer, was $700,000 a year.

***

The Town Car waited at the mansion's clinic entrance. Dr. Russell opened the rear door and held Laura's elbow as she stepped in. When they pulled out of the driveway, he turned to her. "Thank you for lunching with me. I hope you'll enjoy this afternoon."

He pulled a folder from the seat pocket. "Time for work. You'll find it's a frequent infringement on personal time." He bent to look for his briefcase.

"When we get to the hospital, I'll leave you with Jeanne Sharmont. She'll help arrange the special permission for you to participate tomorrow."

Laura paused before she spoke. "Special permission for what?"

"No one told you?"

"Told me what?"

"You're working with me tomorrow."

"Oh."

He opened his briefcase and removed another file. "I need a final review for one of my surgeries. You're on your own for the rest of the drive." His tone was so business-like it took a moment for Laura to understand what he's said. He'd closed a door and they now existed in two separate rooms. She stared out the window without speaking until Daniel dropped them at the hospital.

Jeanne Sharmont guided her through pages of legalese that would allow Laura, who did not have a DC nursing license, to assist in the operating room the next day under strict supervision. Once that was complete, Jeanne guided her through corridors, patient rooms, operating rooms, conference rooms, the pharmacy, and administrative offices, introducing people from doctors to executives. By the end of the tour, everyone had become a blur with a smile. Her exhaustion left no desire to observe Dr. Russell in surgery. She wanted only to retreat to her hotel.

"So, we'll see you tomorrow morning at 8:00." stated Jeanne.

"I don't know what the schedule is," said Laura, over-tired and on edge.

"John asked me to tell you arrival time. They'll let you know if it changes. She looked for a long moment at Laura. "I imagine you've had a long day."

"That's an understatement."

"Being around Dr. Russell is an intense experience," smiled Jeanne. "All the time and for everybody."

***

Daniel drove Laura back to the Lincoln Inn during rush hour traffic. The ride took time, but the car felt safe and restful amidst the swirling unknowns engulfing her. When they arrived, she headed to her room, shut the door, and leaned against it, closing her eyes. When she opened them. she noticed the bouquet of cut flowers on the glass table by the windows. A small note card with italic script was clipped to one of the roses.

"Thank you for participating with us today and tomorrow. Enjoy your dinner. John Russell and Staff."

An envelope with her schedule for the next day lay under the vase.

Arrival at hospital by 8:00; Participation in two surgeries with Dr. Russell; observe one more. Afternoon is free. At 5:00, your driver will take you to a dinner engagement with Dr. Russell at his home—

Long House Mansion. Arrival back at the hotel may be as late as 11:00.

Laura replaced the schedule on the table, lay down and fell asleep as soon as her head hit the pillow.

***

The next morning Jeanne Sharmont waited for her by the front door of the hospital. They took elevators, walked down corridors, past locked doors, and into to the locker room. She gave Laura a wrapped bundle and pointed to a locker.

"These are your scrubs; there's your locker. I'll take you to the operating room when you're ready." Jeanne smiled at her. "Dr. Russell's already there. He said not to worry. He's a great doctor. You'll be fine."

Laura put on the scrubs and took a deep breath. The day had begun.

The operating room was like all such rooms—high tech, clean, metallic. A quiet hum of equipment filled it with purpose. John Russell stood at the center. He turned as she entered.

"Ms. Greenwald, welcome to my second home." He paused, then continued. "You have official permission to practice at this hospital today under my supervision. You'll be doing basic back up today. It will give me an idea about your work style. If you're hired, we'll train you for complex procedures."

"The morning's busy. Today's operations are short but can be life-threatening. You can handle that without a problem?" He was both telling and asking. He already knew of her yearlong surgical specialty.

"Not a problem, Dr. Russell."

"Good." He walked to the instrument tray. "Ellen Bronston is the head nurse. Just do what she says as soon as she says it. If this is too much, you can leave and return home today."

He turned to check his instruments, the time, the medical record. She had disappeared completely from his radar screen. His abrupt rudeness made Laura feel as if he'd slapped her in the face. *Was he really so oblivious to his gut wrenching lurches between charm-*

57

ing gentleman and horrific autocrat? She'd seen it yesterday and here it was again.

"Glove up!" called Ellen Bronston. "Patient on the way. Here in three-minutes." She was tall, efficient, and curt with eyes that scanned the room and noted everything. They stopped on Laura.

"Get the patient chart from Dr. Russell and glove him up," said Ellen.

Laura was getting used to the abruptness. *It's contagious.* Laura did as she was told. The room quieted. Ellen spoke.

"Listen up folks. This is a cauterization of a ballooning neural artery in the posterior portion of the left hemisphere. We're attempting to prevent future hemorrhage. Patient headaches were the alerting symptoms. We'll open the skull in the back, move to the artery and cauterize. Dr. Russell will be attending neurosurgeon for the cauterization with the opening and closure of the skull attended by Dr. Antrum. Everyone clear?" Heads nodded. Operating room doors were flung open and the patient wheeled in.

Laura retained vivid impressions of that morning's surgeries—the intensity of focus, curtness of orders, open skulls, precision responses, machine noises, heightened energy, and adrenaline surges as the operations proceeded. John Russell's journey into a patient's brain tissue was a choreographed dance. Not once did he flex a muscle without a purpose; not once did he draw his eyes from the target; not once did he falter in his instructions to staff, or in his level of intense focus.

Laura handed instruments to Ellen but otherwise remained uninvolved. Staff knew why she was there and gave her viewing points close to the operating table. Even so, by 11:00 she was exhausted and shaky. The three of them had moved to a second operating room as another doctor completed closure of the patient's skull and scalp. There was one more surgery to go this morning, but she would be protected from exhaustion by watching from the observation room.

He turned to her as they walked out, his eyes crinkling behind his mask. "Tired?" he inquired with gentleness. She looked up, surprised he had noticed anything but his patients this morning.

"Yes, I am," she replied. He chuckled, his voice, for the moment, laced with professional camaraderie.

"You build up to it. We run an intense schedule. Not every day though, thank God. Between four of us neurosurgeons, we share the load and cover each other. Makes life a bit more manageable."

He paused, then continued, "I'm doing back up for this next operation. Get yourself a coffee and relax while you watch." Then he and Ellen moved through the doors, and she found herself alone in the hallway. She shook her head. What a bundle of contradictions the man was.

It was 1:00 p.m. by the time Laura called Daniel to bring the car. Watching Dr. Russell's final morning surgery had been engaging, but the coffee was no match for the tiredness that engulfed her. Dr. Russell had said nothing to her when he finished the morning's work.

Fine, excellent, great, she thought. *I don't care. It doesn't matter. It's fine. $700,000 is fine. It's all fine.*

And with that, she realized it was. Tired, over-stimulated, away from home, unsure of what would happen next, it had still been unforgettable.

Chapter 10

When Laura arrived at the Lincoln Inn, the desk clerk handed her a letter, no stamp attached, and clearly not delivered by the post office. John Russell's name showed prominently in the return address. Once upstairs, she tore it open in tired irritation. *Can't they just leave me alone for a minute?*

> "Dear Ms. Greenwald.
>
> *I look forward to enjoying cocktails with you at my Long House Mansion home, dinner to follow. Daniel will come for you at 5:00. The evening will afford us time to discuss details of the job and answer any questions you have.*
>
> *Thank you for your excellent efforts this morning.*
>
> *John Russell."*

Her irritation vanished in an instant. *Now that's annoying too*, she thought. Russell was a high- handed, dismissive, arrogant man yet she kept finding herself intrigued and interested. *Roll out your backbone,* Laura chided herself, but without noticeable effect. She stomped around, felt her blood pressure rising and finally decided on the Jacuzzi.

I need my wits about me before I get near that man again. Her mind was a haze of tumbling thoughts just before she slipped into the frothing water.

***

Her cell phone alarm rang. The only way to turn it off was to get out of the tub, dripping and disoriented. She caught a glimpse of herself in the mirror. A strange moment—watching her image react to being caught by its owner.

Laura studied herself. Long legs, auburn hair pinned out of the way, defined arms, graceful fingers, taut stomach, rounded breasts. And then it crept up, that old, familiar fear whose name was Rape. She stood frozen, trying to push it into the background, back behind the thick, mental fortress she'd built over years.

"Focus, focus, focus, now, now, now." This was the mantra she repeated over and over until heart slowed and breathing stabilized.

She dressed quickly but the moves felt tedious and uninspired. Her hands automatically went to the eveningwear in the closet. She shook it out, laid it on the bed and went to the bathroom. She applied makeup and combed her hair. She used a pearl clasp to pin back the sides but the rest spilled down her back. She slipped into her clothes, put on earrings, necklace, and shoes—she was ready. The clock showed 4:45. Fifteen minutes left to kill.

Was that the right word to use? she wondered.

Laura left her room and went to wait in the lobby trying all the while to shake away the strange mood overtaking her.

***

The drive to Long Mansion took a different route. This time she was going to Dr. Russell's home—around the back—or was it the front? Anyway, she was going to the private home of this doctor-man of many abilities. Every time one part of her wanted to tell Daniel to turn the car around, the other part countered with $700,000.

"Chill out. No one's going to hurt you." *Didn't I just tell myself that an hour ago?*

The mansion appeared at the end of the driveway, a gauntlet lined by leafless tree trunks.

"Here we are ma'am," said Daniel, pulling the car to a stop, getting out, and opening her door.

"Thank you, Daniel," she said and took his hand. Her heels were high and she had to balance carefully.

He escorted her to the entrance, rang the bell, and waited. A moment passed before the door swung open. Dr. Russell appeared in the entrance. He was clothed in 'gentleman's casual elegance,' looking alert and fresh, as if this morning's work happened weeks ago.

"Come in, come in! Daniel, thank you for bringing our guest. Your service continues to be much appreciated here." Daniel nodded, performed a shadow of a bow and left them alone.

Dr. Russell ushered Laura through the oakwood entry door, up a wide stairway with hand-carved banister and to the second floor. He turned to her on the ascent. "There is an elevator, if you prefer." He smiled, his warm manner blending professional and personal interest. "But somehow I thought you'd like to walk."

Laura relaxed. "You're right," she said, "I prefer to walk."

"Welcome to 'The Loft," he said opening the upstairs door. "That's staff lingo for the boss being over your head at work—literally."

Laura could imagine the feeling. Then she stopped dead. The room in front of her was a masterpiece. Cascading light, floor to ceiling windows, garden views, muted colors of cushioned sofas on hand-loomed rugs, and sprays of flowers contrasting the stark winter landscape beyond the window panes. She remained silent, staring, breathing it all in.

"Thank you," he said, although Laura had not spoken a word. "That's how I feel every time I come home." He stood behind her. "When I bought the house, I worked with James DeWillis to design the inside. He's the best in the field—interior designer turned architect. DeWillis designs his building 'while painting the interior environment,' as he calls it. One comprehensive plan. I never get used to it."

"I can see why," she said.

He steered her toward a window expanse where two wing chairs stood kitty corner to each other overlooking the garden. A small writing table held papers, pens, and wine glasses.

"Have a seat, Ms. Greenwald. May I offer you a drink?"

"Yes. Thank you."

He selected a deep red wine from a wall cabinet. With a deft wrist movement, he uncorked and poured a small amount into her glass and handed it to her. She swirled the liquid against the crystal sides to release the aroma, and then tasted.

"This is excellent." She placed her glass on the table. He filled it and his own, then sank into a chair. For moments, they gazed at the garden, sipping wine and letting the atmosphere settle. Laura could feel her pulse, hear the creaking of the chairs, appreciated the warmth of wine as it settled into her stomach.

He turned to face her. She was struck again with his physical angularity, strength of features, and taut movements. She wondered about his background, about who he was, and about his girlfriends. So much was distracting her it was hard to focus attention on the conversation.

"...of immersion therapy, what do you think of our little operation?" He smiled and finished with, "No pun intended."

Immersion therapy? What's he talking about? Laura attempted to formulate a response.

He laughed. "Lost in thought again?"

She blushed.

He repeated.

"So...after 36-hours of immersion therapy, what do you think of our 'Operation', so to speak?" He was not annoyed, but waited, unhurried, calm. She swirled her wine, taking time to answer this complex man.

"I'll be as direct as I can," she started.

"You usually are," he said, almost interrupting her. "I'm planning to do the same."

Oh, jeez, what else is he going to tell me? She shifted position.

"I, well...I..." she said, tongue tripping, heart pounding. She should have known wine was the prelude to 'The Interview.'

Laura cleared her throat and collected scattered thoughts. "Let me start over." Deep breath. "I never thought I'd be here. I applied because I was fed up with my job, my life."

He nodded.

"I thought the $700,000 was a typo. The application filled up a very discontented Sunday. I threw it in the mail and forgot about it."

She looked at him. He was watching, observing, evaluating.

"The rest of your—what should I call them—tasks? Anyway, the rest of the 'tasks' took me by surprise. I'd get annoyed. They'd be inconvenient, and they kept showing up. I kept being surprised I'd made it to the 'next level.' Who wouldn't with that kind of salary?"

She took a sip, then continued, "The 'Operation,' as you call it, is complex. It gets taken care of without a hitch. Your people are competent, efficient, friendly and pretty much everybody seems professionally happy. That's a huge achievement. So, yes, I'm impressed. Very."

She gritted her teeth. *Talking to him isn't so bad—only here comes the hard part.* "Dr. Russell," she began, but he interrupted.

"Would it upset you to use my first name? And may I call you Laura?"

Laura blushed.

"No, of course not. I mean yes, that's fine."

"Good. So, Laura, please continue."

Here goes, she thought.

"Questions allowed?" asked Laura, just to be sure.

He nodded. "But I remind you this conversation is covered under your confidentiality contract."

Laura readjusted herself in the chair. "It's hard to remember every word I utter is under contract—sort of like being a spy—or a politician."

He laughed. "There's truth in that."

With the wine softening her increasing tension, she made the plunge.

"The job is a career changer. But you could get a zillion people to do it for half the price and still be ecstatically happy."

He nodded.

"It's too good to be true" She paused. "So, what's the catch?"

He took a deep breath and settled more comfortably into his chair.

"I demand a lot from my staff. I'm concerned about their welfare and I also pay exceptionally well. In return, they give me their time, loyalty, and willing cooperation. The work is often annoying and difficult. I have an unpredictable schedule. In an instant, it can take days out of your life. I call and they come. My presidential responsibilities are top priority over everything in life, even someone's funeral. Disruption to family and personal life can be particularly aggravating."

He stopped, leaned over for the wine bottle and refilled both glasses.

"That doesn't sound so terrible. Not for the benefits you're offering," Laura countered.

"Perhaps. But the job requires two years of that behavior. It's the only position in my organization that requires consistent travel. That can be a real drag. If I call, you drop everything. Right then. Right there. You might be on vacation, or in a friend's wedding, at an event, or I don't know what. It takes a while to get used to, and another while before you can't stand it anymore. Two years is usually the limit. The people before you left their exit interview saying, 'I'm glad I was paid well.'"

A rueful smile appeared. "And I've heard I'm not the easiest person to work with."

Laura almost laughed out loud. She'd already been pissed off with him and they'd only been together a few hours. She shrugged. "I've worked with some pretty impossible people. I suppose a $700,000 salary would make me forget most of it. Not all, but quite a lot I think."

He nodded, "Well, it's an issue."

She waited, chewed over her thoughts, still not satisfied.

"More questions?"

"I still can't wrap my head around the $700,000," she finally said.

"In what way?" he inquired.

"Okay—do the math. At the end of two years at $700,000 a year I'd have one million four hundred thousand dollars plus a fifty thousand bonus. Then I get to quit and ride off into my own sunset as long as I don't say much. That seems like a top of the line trade to me—except it's still too generous." She stopped.

"And so…?" he encouraged.

"My brain is saying something like, this must be illegal, or, there's some other angle I'm not getting, or *something*." She held her breath, then asked, "What part of that is true?"

John's hand swirled the wine in his glass. Red liquid crept up the sides and slid back in a graceful arc, mesmerizing to look at.

"Laura, we do nothing illegal here. I want you to understand that clearly and completely. This job is more likely to thrust you into the big time than put you in jail."

"So, what is it am I not getting?"

Her crossed leg began to swing slightly. She waited. He put his glass on the table, placed his hands on his thighs and readied for a speech. Her heart began to pound. Wildly she thought, *Maybe I'll just leave now*. But it was too late. He had started to respond.

Chapter 11

"The salary is generous, but I don't agree it's too generous," he said, taking a sip of wine. "There is one part of the job we still have to discuss."

Laura waited, no longer breathing. *Get out while the goin's good, Greenwald!* But she couldn't make herself move.

"Being the President's neurosurgeon doesn't take a lot of time. But when I'm needed, I have to be perfect. The Institute I created here at Long House and my researchers keep me busy and ready for any kind of emergency. It takes practice: it takes focus; it takes time. A lot of time."

Please get to the point! she thought. Her throat was parched dry but she couldn't pick up her cup or swallow.

"There is no such thing as personal time when I am that busy," he said, his eyes locked on to hers.

She nodded in response.

"So, I asked the question."

What question? Had he asked a question she hadn't heard?

She waited.

"I asked my lawyers what to do about sex."

This time she gaped at him. *What the fuck is he talking about?*

***

Ten years ago, five lawyers sat around a table with their briefcases and their papers—not a smile on anyone's face.

"Sex, sir," said Jennine Punati. "Don't have it if you're not married. If you get married, everyone's got to know you go to church and sleep in pajamas."

"You're joking," he said, irritated and out of patience.

"You're in DC, sir. Everybody's got an eye on who's around the President," replied the lawyer.

"I'm a doctor—not a politician." He didn't bother hiding the edge in his voice.

Jennine shot right back. "Everyone in Washington is a politician, sir. Particularly in the President's circle. You're living in fantasyland if you don't understand that."

John Russell glared at her.

Jennine Punati didn't notice. "Read this," she commanded handing over a document.

He reached for the paper. Names were typed in two columns down page.

Bill Clinton, Harvey Weinstein, Bill Cosby, Eliot Spitzer, Anthony Weiner, David Petraeus, Charlie Rose, Tiger Woods, Arnold Schwarzenegger, Mark Sanford, John Edwards, Michael Jackson, David Letterman, Brett Kavanaugh, Clarence Thomas, Newt Gingrich, Barney Frank, Woody Allen, Joe Paterno, Jerry Sandusky.

The list went on and on.

"You get the picture?" she asked.

"I don't like quizzes," he replied.

"Then I'll spell it out. That is a list of men who had stupid sex in stupid places. And then they got caught. In Washington sex scandals demolish people faster than a Katrina size hurricane. It can drown you and wipe out a life's work in days."

John Russell leaned forward "Since my divorce I've been titled DC's 'Most Eligible Bachelor' by every gossip columnist. And the advice you give me is—*no sex if I want to keep my job?*" He shook his head. "Not even the Catholic priests do that."

Jim Johnson's next sentence derailed the impending argument. "We have another suggestion."

Dead silence.

"What?" asked John, controlling his irritation.

They arranged papers in front of him. They explained the idea and debated the fine points. When it was over, John Russell nodded and said, "I can work with that."

One key point required extraordinary confidentiality.

When John signed his name at the bottom of the documents, *The Scandal Clause* was officially born.

***

Laura still waited for John's response. *He's gotten lost somewhere,* she thought.

Outside, the sun's rays slid further towards night. John swirled his wine and gazed at the patterns. He cleared his throat and got ready to speak.

"Would you consider being my only sexual partner for the next two years?" he asked.

Chapter 12

Laura's clenched her fingers. Her throat locked down and her pulse rate doubled. She tried wrestling it to obedience. *This isn't a rape. Not a rape.* Words tumbled against themselves, over and over in her head. *He's just asking you to consider a question; that's it. No big deal. Get a grip!* "Stop this," she murmured, but chaos careened ahead, refusing to slow down. Rigid and still, she stared at her lap.

"Laura?"

Wood crackled in the fireplace behind them.

It's such a comfortable room, so beautiful here, she thought.

"Laura?" he asked again.

She lifted her gaze, met his eyes.

"I didn't mean to upset you."

She coughed, tried on a smile, felt her nose start to tingle, tears not far behind.

Talk to the man! she thought through panic. *He hasn't come near you.* Her lips and jaw began pre-speech movements. Another cough and she tried words.

"I was... I mean... it was just... well, it was unexpected."

"I know," said Dr. Russell. "This isn't an easy interview—for me—or for you."

She couldn't look up. "How many of these interviews have you done?' she asked. *Am I just one of a string of women—or what?* she bit at her lip.

Moments passed before John Russell interrupted the silence.

"I have no problem answering your question."

"But...?"

"But I'm not willing to do so until we have an agreement. Can you understand that?" He shifted his legs.

"Can I take some time to think about it?" she asked.

"How much time would you like?" he asked.

"I, well, I'm not—I don't know. I've never quite—I've never made a decision like this."

Dr. Russell picked up his wine glass, took a sip and put it down "May I make a suggestion?"

"Yes, please."

"Take a walk with me in the garden. Lucille will serve us dinner when we come in. See how you feel. If you need more time, we'll talk about it then." Laura cleared her throat, unclasped her hands, shifted them from lap to thighs and looked up.

"Thank you. Yes, that sounds like a good idea."

"Good."

He retrieved their coats and helped Laura into hers. Outside, the crisp air, intricate walkways, and skeletal forms of winter shrubs steadied her mind. Dr. Russell strolled the winter pathways pointing out plants. He talked about their history, their selection, his passion for having the garden in constant bloom once spring arrived.

She felt his body moving next to hers, watched his movements, listened to his speech patterns. Her thoughts ran rampant. *Who is this man? How is he in bed? Does he jam it in? Do his fingers linger where they need to? Or, is he just after the orgas...?*

"...and because of that we left the willow over there by the brick wall. The trouble is it's likely to damage the structure and then we'll have to..."

How often does he like sex? What would I have to do? Does he shower before he gets into bed? Is he a sex-in-the-office type guy?

"See over there?" John Russell was pointing to a gnarled tree trunk and bench in the center of the garden. "Legend has it that the first owner's daughter died of a broken heart waiting for..."

The garden was in darkness by the time their walk ended and Laura still had no idea what she wanted to do.

Dr. Russell opened the mansion door, helped her out of her coat and hung it with his own. The warmth of the room carried dinner smells from the kitchen—soup, roasted root vegetables, spices she couldn't identify. A growling stomach left no doubt of her hunger. Logs crackled in the fireplace. Next to it was a round table with service for two.

"Would you care to freshen up before we begin?" he asked, pointing down the hall.

"Yes. Great idea." She headed towards the privacy of the bathroom, her thoughts still flapping every which where.

From the beveled mirror above the sink, Laura stared back at a reflection startlingly different from how she felt. Out of the glass gazed a well-dressed, well-coifed professional woman with eyes softened by concern. The ravaged girl-woman who had been raped years earlier was nowhere to be seen. *Am I still naïve Laura who got used and raped?* she wondered. *Or, have I learned how to take care of myself?* She shook her head trying to make sense of it all. She wet the corner of a white hand towel, and patted cheeks and forehead, *I guess I'm gonna find out if I've gotten any smarter or not.*

Time to return. Laura felt calmer, even though she wasn't sure she'd settled anything inside herself.

"Refreshed?" asked John. He was pouring wine as she re-entered the room. He moved to pull out her chair and she sat.

"Thank you, yes."

"Ah, Lucille!" he exclaimed, "What luscious flavors have you brought this evening?" John turned to Laura. "She's a treasure to have working here," he said.

Lucille flushed with pleasure as she served the first course of smoked salmon garnished with caviar on grilled garlic toast. Then came citrus salad with avocado slices.

As she ate Laura watched John Russell's broad, lean frame moved without effort when he spoke. His intelligent face edged toward handsome when he laughed, but lost the designation when he spoke more seriously.

"Do you cook for yourself?" His casual, interested question led them back and forth between discussions of restaurants, work demands, marriage, gender roles, health, nutrition, and taste buds.

Is this the same guy from the hospital? wondered Laura. *He's actually listening.*

Lucille interrupted their conversation with more dishes—cold eggplant-chicken-pastrami rolls and hot baby back ribs on asparagus spears. Laura put up her hands. "I can't believe this dinner," she cried.

John winked. "I told you she was good."

Lucille flushed. "Thank you, sir."

"Don't ever leave me, Lucille," he said, "or I'll die of starvation."

Laura watched the interaction—how much he appreciated her work and how much he let her know it.

"No, sir," she said, pleased, blushing furiously, backing out of the room as fast as she could.

That was sweet, thought Laura as she ate, smiled, chatted, imbibed, and watched Dr. Russell charm his way through dinner.

"More wine?" he finally asked.

"Perhaps." She smiled. *Jeez, when did I forget to be nervous?*

"Perhaps an after-dinner liqueur by the fire would be better?"

"Much better," she said. *He can be so entertaining. And thoughtful. I think I'm starting to like this Mister Doctor John Russell.*

And that was a surprise she hadn't expected.

***

They were sitting by the fire when John Russell asked, "How are you doing?"

Laura flushed and took a sip of the ebony liquid in her liquor glass.

"Pretty well," said a voice.

Laura startled. *Did I just say that?*

You did, she said to herself. *And you meant it.*

"I guess I did."

"Did what?" asked John, a quizzical look on his face.

Shit, I said that out loud. She ploughed ahead, ignoring his remark. "The question about being your sex partner shook me up," she said bluntly. The words floated between them. "But you have a gift for putting me at ease."

"I'm sorry to have caused you distress." An apologetic smile appeared.

She shrugged. "Goes with the territory, I guess."

"Laura, I would be honored to have you on our team." He sat back in his chair.

To have you on our team, she repeated to herself. *But also, in my bed. To sleep with you, touch you, have sex with you.* She twisted in her seat and crossed her legs. *Who gets job offers like this?*

He needs an answer, nagged her brain.

I know that. I just don't know what I'm going to say when I open my mouth.

She rose from her chair, hands clasped behind, pacing forward and back as if she were a lawyer and John Russell the jury. She opened her mouth. An avalanche of words tumbled out.

"So, one Sunday morning I wake up and say I want to change my life; my job is driving me nuts and life is dull. I apply for a crazy job; it makes me feel better and I forget about it. Now I'm here, far away from home, after an exotic dinner with a guy who offers me a job even crazier than what the advertisement described and says I'm perfect for it. So—what to do?"

She twirled around and addressed John directly.

"The Prince wishes the young damsel to join his team but the offer hides nefarious underpinnings. She is intrigued but perturbed and time is a-wasting. A decision must be made. Will she choose to remain home where safety abides while dying of boredom or compromise her honor for swashbuckling excitement?"

Abruptly, Laura dropped the melodrama and asked, "What happens if I don't join your team?"

"Fair question." He raised his glass. "Care for another?"

She shook her head, stood and waited for a response.

"We keep a list of active candidates. It's not long, but several other people passed initial screening, which, as you know, can be arduous. Eva, my executive director, will contact our next candidate and begin the interview process. I only get involved at the end. You were first-choice candidate this time."

"I see..." Laura bit her lip, pondering the new information. She was not the first nor the last in this job. Judging from the success of his business, this arrangement would be repeated for some time to come.

Walk out now and chalk it up to a weird experience, screamed one part of her brain.

The very loud other part kept yelling, *Do it! Do it!*

Laura breathed in. She breathed out, not at all sure which side would win.

You wanna go back to that icky, old hospital job? asked a quiet little voice in her head she'd not heard before. *You wanna hang out with that boss of yours who's never gonna give you a raise while he still ogles your boobs? You won't get another chance like this and you know it. Don't you at least want a try at the big time?*

John waited, swirling liquor in his glass.

Her mouth opened. "I—I think," she said, "I'd like to give it a try." Her surprised lips didn't know what shape to take. Laura stood stock still. She brushed hair out of her eyes. "This is awkward," she said.

"Always is at this point," he replied. "But I guarantee it will never be dull."

"I've noticed," Laura said.

Dr. Russell took a slow, sip of his drink, glanced at the clock, then placed the glass back on the table. "You're taking a big step.

I'm sure you've got questions. But I also think you might be pretty tired."

Laura laughed out loud and sat down. "Near collapse is closer to the truth."

He smiled. "Then I propose we meet in the morning to hash out details."

"That's a great idea," she said.

"Agreed. I think it's high time for bed," he said standing up. Then he shouted, "Laura—what happened? Are you sick?"

Her face drained pale, respiration doubled, and knuckles clenched white. With one hand held over her mouth, he barely heard her raspy, "I'm not ready—I can't..."

"Oh, my God!" In two strides he closed the distance between them. "I'm so sorry! I didn't mean—I just thought, you know, it's time to go to sleep."

Her trembling slowed.

"Time for a deep breath," he said.

"Yes, Doctor. Thank you for the treatment plan."

He burst into laughter. She joined him until tears dripped down her cheeks. "I really am ready to go to bed," she said.

He swept into a low bow. "May I get mademoiselle her coat?"

"You may" she grinned.

He walked her to the chauffeured car and opened the door. She slid in the back seat, closed her eyes and kept thinking, *What the hell have I just done?*

Chapter 13

The next morning Laura found herself in the same car, going back to the same mansion, for a meeting with the same man to discuss—what?

To discuss the rest of your life, kiddo, said the voice in her head.

It's just a job with a super great salary.

Good luck believing that little fantasy, sweetheart.

By this time, Laura was in John's sitting room. Several sheets of paper lay on his lap, a cup of coffee rested on the side table and a small fire cast its heat into the room.

"You slept well?" he inquired while his hand gestured to a Chippendale table with a silver decanter and cups. "Coffee?"

"Yes, to coffee. No, to sleeping well," she said.

"I'm sorry to hear that," he said. "Try the coffee. It's a brand I found in Brazil." He leaned over and stirred his cup. "Except I think it's the spring water we use that makes it so good. Daniel collects it on trips to my Shenandoah cabin."

Laura shrugged off her coat, hung it up and then and poured a cup of steaming liquid. *A Shenandoah cabin, too?* she thought just before sitting down.

He arranged the papers on his lap.

She cleared her throat.

He uncrossed his legs.

Her anxiety turned to impatience. She crossed her feet at the ankles, clasped her hands in her lap and started, "My brains went all over the place last night. I stared out the window a lot. The street lights are nice."

He chuckled. "Planned them myself—just for you." He began to sort the papers on the coffee table in front of him.

"I have surgery at noon. So, we'll need to go over your contract now. You can review the materials while I'm gone. Dinner's at 8:00. I may not be back. Regardless, we'll take our leave tomorrow morning at 7:00." His business crisp tone made the room cold. "Questions?"

Back to work mode, she thought. *Sharp and short. When did I think he was charming?* It took a moment to realize he'd asked her for a response. *I don't have time to think and he's talking about questions?* She shook her head. "No questions right now."

"Good." He bent over an open briefcase and retrieved more documents.

"So, complete, total, confidentiality. First—last—and always. All the time and about everything to do with the job." He paused. "How you explain your life to others is your business. We can help develop a cover story if you wish. What you can't discuss are the details of your contract, where you go or what you do. It's a bitch to live this way. I guarantee that."

This is real.

Her back muscles tightened.

Blood drained from her neck.

Coldness crept up her legs.

"Do you want me to go on," he asked watching her, "or have you changed your mind?"

"No, I'm all right."

You are? nagged the voice in her head.

Women do this all the time. Secretaries marry their bosses. Tons of people have sex with people at work. No big deal about having it written down instead of winging it—everybody knows what to expect—right? she thought in a wild attempt to calm down.

John was talking again.

"Two-year contract, $700,000 yearly salary, $50,000 bonus at completion. You may be given the choice to re-up at the end—depends on how things go."

"I see," she said.

No, you don't see.

Yeah, I do, she snapped back silently, *it's better than being raped and dropped like the piece of crap I was turned into in New York. It'll be fine.*

The voice in her head had no comment.

"I must show that no coercion to sign the contract has occurred at any point. This must be clearly stated," he said, "by you to me and to the legal experts reviewing my contracts." He searched her face. "If you are thinking of backing out, now is the time—except for what you already signed."

"I'm fine," she lied.

"We can't turn back from here," said John. He stopped speaking.

Let's get on with this, pleeeese, before I run out screaming, she thought. "I agree no coercion has taken place," is what she said out loud.

"If you leak, drop, lose, or move from where it belongs, *any* information pertaining to this organization or its work, your professional licensing boards wherever you go will be notified of your breach of professional privacy, with recommendation to suspend. Future wages you might earn will be garnered until you've paid a half-million-dollar privacy penalty. When that is done the license complaints will be removed. My organization is able to follow through on this. We do not employ leniency concerning these penalties."

John Russell cleared his throat. He had been reading from a legal document. "Is that clear?"

Laura sat in rigid attention, hands still clasped in her lap. Her hoarse utterance of each word scraped the air. "Yes, quite clear." *God help me*, she thought.

"Point of no return," he stated and handed her a pen and one of the sheets on his knee. "Please read and sign this preliminary statement. It indicates I have verbally reviewed confidentiality requirements, duties, salary, and benefits. When I leave, my lawyers will finalize things."

She bent over to sign but he interrupted.

"This job has strong incentives—good and bad. The balance can be a strain."

He pointed to the bottom of the paper. "After you sign, if you could just initial the space where it says you agree to being recorded."

Recorded? What the ...She held his gaze. Life was not going to be the same—and he was making sure she knew it.

Laura's hand signed the document. She returned it to John Russell and stole a glance at the mantel clock. *Oh, my God! Only fifteen minutes since I got here? That's all?* A small throb of a headache was beginning at her right temple. *It's gonna be a long day.*

John took the paper, checked her signature and slipped the sheet into his briefcase.

"Okay, let's go over your duties."

"May I take notes, sir?"

"Notes? No. You don't need to take notes. And drop the 'sir' business. You can call me John when we're in private."

And fuck you, too! she thought.

He ploughed ahead, not seeming to notice her irritation.

"You will assist my hospital surgeries for two, maybe three days a week. The rest of your time is at the clinic seeing patients. You'll shadow me for the first couple of weeks, watch what I do, see how I do it. Your physical stamina and diagnostic skills have to be top notch. Working alongside me should get you on up to speed." He stopped, then added, "Oh, yes... carry your passport at all times" Another pause. "Thought of any questions yet?"

Who has time to think at this pace? she wondered and shook her head.

"Your employment date is one month from now," he continued. "That should give you time to close out your job and relocate. You'll get four weeks of training. When you're done, we revert to 'normal' mode, if there is such a thing around here." He stood and walked to the decanter. "Coffee?"

That's it? she wanted to yell. *What about the rest of the fucking contract—the 'will you be my sexual partner for two years' part? Not a chance in hell that's gonna disappear.* She took a breath and unclenched her fists. *Time to be blunt.*

"What happened to your explanation of the sex part?" *Let's see him avoid that question.*

"Ah, yes," he said. "The sex part." He poured fresh coffee.

He's acting like this discussion happens every day. Am I crazy, or is he? Laura crossed her arms. She'd let him talk first.

"I'm interested in work and research—not dating games, one-night stands, social niceties, babies, wives," he paused, "or scandals—of any kind."

"I see," said Laura. *You do?*

"Hobnobbing with powerful people in DC, which I have to do, is its own ballgame. Power attracts money. It attracts women. Sex gets thrown around a lot. You never know if someone wants something or how far they'll go to get it. Sex is the hook. It's a serious issue. People lose careers when they get stupid about sex—especially powerful people. I don't want that happening to me."

"How can you stop it? You can't control what people say or do."

"No. But we insure against damages."

"How?" *Just get on with it.*

"By working with a scandal clause contract."

"*Scandal clause*? What are you talking about?" Laura's grabbed her coffee and drank, hoping the caffeine would steady her brain.

"It's the part of your contract that describes how and why our sexual partnership works."

"What do you mean? Like the contract in *Fifty Shades of Grey*?" Laura stood up, pulse doubled, breathing shaky.

I'm not doing that shit, she yelled in her head, *I'm not stupid. I don't even know this guy.* "Dr. Russell, I don't think this will wor…"

"Laura!" John's voice rang out.

"What?"

"Sit down." It was a firm command.

She sat.

"That is nowhere near what I mean."

"Oh."

"The scandal clause is a paragraph in the larger contract of your duties. It provides for a non-coercive, exclusive, on my end—not yours—sexual partnership with my executive nurse. You are free to have other partners; I will not. I will always, so to speak, go home with you."

"Is that even legal? To write a contract about sex like that?" Laura felt her headache expanding.

"Well, it's not illegal." He stood up and started to walk. "There are a number of on-line sex contract forms available. Of course, my lawyers devised this section. The operative terms are *consenting adults* and *non-coercive.*"

"Oh."

"It's the one part of the contract that might raise eyebrows—besides the salary."

Oh, right. The salary, she thought. *I forgot to remember that.*

"That paragraph is going to keep me from being manipulated into a sex scandal. And that makes my business and everyone who works for me safer." He stood up; looked directly at her and asked, "Don't you agree?"

Laura blinked. The question surprised her. *Do I agree?* She hoped some opinions might surface, but none floated up.

"Well, let's sit on the sofa while you figure out what to think."

He picked up the papers from the table. "You'll review these papers after I leave, then finalize details and signatures with them."

"I see."

"First—any sex between us will be non-coercive."

Besides not giving him a license to kill me, what does non-coercive mean? "What does that mean?" she asked out loud.

His eyes locked with hers. "It means I won't rape you."

She recoiled, the words slapping her in the face. "I didn't imagine you'd say that, much less do it." The shock of his words clutched at her throat.

"I did it for effect. I want you to realize the sexual part of our relationship is going to be real."

"Like rape?"

"No. But there will be times I may try to be a bit more persuasive…" He let the meaning run forward on its own.

"So, if I scream, you'll stop?"

"I'm not a monster, Laura. I'm good in bed, I like women, and I like sex. I'm told I can be quite seductive. I'll leave it at that."

Greenwald, you can always quit. Just say 'yes' and get on with things.

"Yes," she said. "Okay." She'd argue with herself later.

John Russell plowed on.

"Second—If employment difficulties occur, either party may bring these to mediation with my firm's lawyers. You will pre-select a lawyer on the team and develop a relationship with that person. This legal advocate will represent you for all company matters as well as in the other spheres of the contract, such as medical, life insurance, and so on—things the company pays for that you might have concerns about."

He waited.

She looked at him.

He continued to wait.

So, she said, "Okay."

"Third—the contract states no children may be produced by either party separately or between the two parties while still employed in this position. Such biological and familial responsibilities would render job requirements unmanageable. If pregnancy occurs and is maintained, the job position and all benefits end immediately."

He stopped speaking.

Silence.

Seconds passed.

Laura felt a deep, profound irritation which made her breath short and raspy.

"How is that fair? A pregnancy is made by both parties. Regardless of all measures taken, a pregnancy can occur."

"I am sterilized," he replied, and watched her react to the crude terminology. "Vasectomized might be a more polite way of saying it. But we're not here for niceties. If you have a child with someone else, then you have a decision to make."

"Oh," she said, and blanked out on how she felt about that provision.

"The issue here is *if* you get pregnant, *you* have a decision. Prevention is the best decision in my opinion."

"I see." Laura let it go for the moment and asked her next question.

"How do you see me managing other male relationships that might occur?" she asked.

"You are required to be available for any emergency or travel on a moment's notice. How you manage outside relationships within that context is up to you."

"That sounds intrusive."

"Compensation is substantial because of the intrusion. It seems you find that difficult to comprehend. Do you wish to withdraw?"

Silence hovered between them. Laura's posture relaxed slowly limb by limb. She shifted position and shook her head.

"No, no. I don't want to withdraw. It's just a lot to absorb all at once."

"We couldn't give you details of the contract until we had your signature. If concerns arise, you may consult with your lawyer, who you will select later today." He paused and watched her face.

"Okay," she responded. Not a facial muscle twitched in betrayal of her thoughts. Actually, she had no thoughts. *I'll find the perfect response as soon as he leaves.*

"The learning curve here is steep—I admit that," he said, voice neutral, neither guiding nor cajoling. "I'm certain you'll do fine."

Laura noticed the clock over John's shoulder. *Oh, my God—it's only 9:45. I'm ready for bed.*

He shuffled papers, laying aside several pages. "Read through these first, then those." He pointed to the ones he'd separated. "Make notes; write down any questions you have. If you have questions use the phone over there." He gestured to a desk phone near the coffee pot. "My team of lawyers is on the other end."

"Okay." Two more minutes had struggled by.

"When you're done, call them and they'll meet with you. Final outcome—you sign everything. Then it all comes back to me for approval and I sign—or not. This goes on till we reach an agreement."

John Russell stood up, shook her hand and left. Laura blinked, her mouth still open. She shut it.

"What have I gotten myself into?" she said for the umpteenth time to no one in particular.

Chapter 14

The language was formal and detailed. She plowed her way through the contract and thanked her time as a hospital administrator for teaching her how to do it.

Laura phoned the lawyers several times to clarify contract details. When she called for the last time they came and led her to a room perfumed with essence of fresh coffee. Three people sat at the mahogany table. Each had a single file folder and pen laid in front.

The lawyer's den, she thought.

"A pleasure to see you again, Ms. Greenwald," said the one whose hair was longest and tumbled to her shoulders over an open-necked blouse. "I'm Attorney Punati—Jennine Punati. You remember my colleagues?"

She waited, so Laura nodded in agreement.

"Attorneys George Penunos, and Marina Brown."

George Penunos rose and gestured for Laura to sit. "We're here to witness your signatures on the documents," he said.

They sat, she signed, and the documents were notarized.

"Well, then, that's that," smiled Marina Brown. "Now is a good time to pick the lawyer you will work with." she said.

Laura's face drooped. *They want me to make another decision?*

"Or would you like a lunch break first?" suggested Jennine Punati. "We can reconvene in an hour if you wouldn't mind reviewing these during your break." The lawyer bent down and pulled an envelope from her satchel.

Laura slumped. "That sounds lovely," she said, tired lines playing around the corners of her mouth.

"Lunch break," said George Penunos.

Laura looked at the clock. Twelve noon. Her very long morning had finally ended.

***

She sat on a large, fluffy couch in a quiet room with a private bath.

"This is our 'retreat' room," George had said leading her down the hall and around the corner from the conference area. "Designed to be the go-to place for a rest. Lunch delivered in…" he looked at his watch, "ten minutes. Wash up; enjoy your break."

He'd left her alone with the documents, now torn open and scattered over the cushions and between plates of her room service lunch. She wished she'd finished everything before the break. But there it lay—in writing, on the couch. Orientation details, medical insurance, life insurance, passport requirements, health exams, moving allowances, identification cards, and on and on.

She'd rifled through the papers. The details, like gnats against a screen window, buzzed in her brain. When it was time, she shuffled everything back into the folder, brushed down her skirt and ran a hand through tousled hair. The lawyers were waiting

***

"Rested?" inquired George Penunos.

"I needed the break." *Rested? I wish.*

"I can imagine," responded the lawyer. "Dr. Russell makes us all feel the need for a break."

Laura laughed. *Good to know it's not just me.*

"Let's start," said Jennine Punati. "The sooner we start, the sooner we're done. Introductions first—meet our secretary, Jim Johnson."

In walked a man with a silver computer and a name card which he placed on the table in front of him.

"Jim is one of us," said Jennine. "We rotate secretarial duties. He's the one attorney you can't select to represent you in anything. Jim is your 'employee case scribe.' Interaction between you and him," she paused, shaking her head, "is discouraged. He has to remain neutral for recording all contract issues."

Laura nodded. *Better than John's secret tape recorder,* she thought.

"Well, let's get to it. My goal is outta here in an hour." And the afternoon began.

Laura got the details—all of them.

30 days to end her career in Boston. $20,000 cash to reconfigure life in DC. Check handed over.

A standard wardrobe required with sufficient options to ensure individual flair while presenting unity of form. Catalog to be mailed.

Passport to be tendered for administrative review.

Social and family information given for emergency contact and background checks.

And so on and so on.

Whoo-ee! Big changes a-comin.' How to dress, when to move, what to say, where to go. She could feel her headache coming back.

At 3:00 pm sharp, Jennine said, "Ok, that's it."

Jim Johnson raised his fingers from the keyboard, rubbed his hands together and said, "Not bad." His question bulldozed into her mental haze. "Ok, which one?"

"Which one what?" *What do they want now?*

"Which lawyer do you choose?"

"Choose for what?" She felt like a sinking ship. *Will this morning never end?*

"To represent you. Remember? Choose which lawyer you want—just not me."

"Oh, right. A lawyer." She sighed. "I guess, well, I thought I'd have more time to think about it."

"Best choices are made right after you meet us the first time." Jim Johnson had taken over. The other three attorneys receded into a background line-up across the table.

What the hell. What's one more decision?

She liked Jim Johnson's easy style, but he was out. Jennine was pushy; Marina too much of a listener. Then there was George Penunos. Not an attention grabber either in looks or manner, but, well… he'd attracted her confidence step by step through the afternoon. Combed back hair, white shirt, loosened tie by 2 pm, charcoal trousers with Ecco slip-ons. No glasses—contacts, maybe? He didn't look like a muscle guy but something had to keep his arms thick in the sleeve and stomach concave to his pants. George sat with quiet presence, a pleasant smile, and easy grace. She could work with George.

So, she said, "I pick George."

Jennine's judge-like gavel hand slapped the table. "Done! Ladies and gentlemen, our business is complete. Laura, we'll have this written up today so you can sign and take your copy with you tomorrow. We'll see you at dinner. Unfortunately, Dr. Russell told me he's unlikely to make the meal." In one motion, the entire group stood, collected papers and filed out of the room. The door was left open.

Laura sat unmoving in the executive chair at conference table, alone except for the ghosts of the lawyers whose writings had just changed her life. Her heartbeat pounded into the silence of the room.

A scrape of shoe on carpet made Laura focus.

"All quiet on the Western Front?" said a voice. Daniel, the chauffeur, slipped around the door jamb of the conference room.

Laura nodded, adrenaline drained and droopy.

"Then, come along." He lifted her arm and slipped it through his. Their retreat passed through the hallway and spacious clinic foyer into the car. Somewhere in-between, he'd slipped a winter coat over her shoulders.

"Dinner is served at eight o'clock. I've been told to inform you a masseuse is at your service—that is, if you like massage."

What kind of a question is that? she thought, her body already tingling with something besides stress. *Want, desire, need. That is my massage response,* she thought and actually began to smile.

***

Mee Sue composed Laura's massage of buttery relaxation sandwiched between hair raising pops. "Oh, goodness, you are jump frog!" She'd laughed the first time it happened. Laura's right foot had almost boxed Mee Sue on the chin.

"Not to worry, miss. It is only unhappy pressure point. I work. I keep tight hold. You must relax. And it is feet first," she told Laura. "You must ground the body, Miss Lori. Oh, yes, I can tell, you are spending much time in the head today—yes?"

Laura nodded. Nods were all she could manage—way too relaxed to do more.

"The feet, you must pay attention," continued Mee Sue in a fluty voice. "People say, oh, my neck, oh, my back. But I say, 'It is feet.' You must honor feet. The feet—they are the ground."

A tinkling laugh burst out of the slender woman as she attacked a resisting trapezius muscle making Laura's torso jump.

"We get you very ready for nice dinner tonight with Mr. Russell." continued Mee Sue in cheerful chat.

Laura turned and said, "He isn't coming."

The masseuse's head shook with disapproval. She pushed Laura back to the table. "Must relax everything. No head up. You lose all my work." A pause. Then, "This is too bad. Mr. Russell does not miss End Dinner. Business must pressure him very much."

This time Laura spoke without moving a muscle. "What is 'end dinner'?"

Mee Sue's hands stopped prodding. Her head tilted. "Ah, yes. End Dinner—this is your number one?"

"My number one what?"

"Number one End Dinner."

"What is 'End Dinner?'"

Another tinkling laugh. "End Dinner? It is dinner at the end of contract. We all have special contract. It is big deal."

"Oh," mused Laura, relaxing further as Mee Sue hammered the side of Laura's neck. "Who's leaving?"

"Ani. It is Ani who is leaving."

"Who's Ani?"

"Ani? Ani is very nice person. She have your job now. One month only left, she tell to me. Busy month, so have to have End Dinner now. Mr. Russell, he like that everyone know about job they take. So, invite old person and new person to meet. If many people come, then we all smile more. We all come very tired after work day."

Laura blinked. An adrenaline burst jump-frogged Laura to sitting position.

"What? No one said..."

She never finished. Mee Sue placed both palms on Laura's shoulders to ease her back to table. "Miss, you throw away my work. Lie down—yes... just like so. You do not wish to meet Miss Ani? Very nice, very nice—I know."

"But I don't—I mean, no one said..." A whiney exhaustion crept around the corners of Laura's words. Even she could hear it. She'd expected—well, dinner with known elements—or at least a little bit known. Now Russell's current lover was in the mix.

"Oh, jeez," she said. Laura was too pumped now to relax. She lifted her legs over the table side and stood up.

"Sorry, Mee Sue. I'm overloaded. You've been great. Thanks."

"No worry, Miss Lori." She patted Laura's shoulder. "I sit near you tonight and remind—'feet on floor.' Respect feet; they keep brain in right place." Mee Sue's smile followed Laura through the swinging door and into the steam room.

Chapter 15

The evening moon back lit Laura as Daniel opened the limousine door, caught her elbow and held on. "Be careful, Miss. It's slippery outside." He guided her up the steps.

Two hours earlier she'd bolted from the massage room. They'd offered manicures, pedicures, hair do's, work out rooms, swimming pool, movies, even the game room and fully stocked bar. It was the Tibetan salt room that finally worked. A chamber of minimal lighting, quiet arrhythmic chanting and the floor spread six-inches deep with Himalayan salt. She lay flat on the crystals and fell asleep. A gentle knock roused her in time to dress.

And now she was here. At first End Dinner.

Low hung chandeliers, inlaid wall mirrors and crown molding. Italian style paintings of clouds and cherubs covered fourteen-foot ceilings, softening the formal dining furniture. Buffet tables were sprinkled throughout the room. Waiters carried trays of alcoholic drinks. Music played in the background.

She recognized faces. Those who caught her eye smiled. Nowhere could she find anyone who might resemble Ani, the woman who currently held Laura's job-to-be.

Time for 'feet on ground,' Greenwald," she thought. So, she straightened her walk, broadened her smile, relaxed her eyes. Litheness came to her step and color to her cheek. She saw George Penunos take a second look as she passed. Laura recognized the feeling—she was on the prowl, but she had no idea for what.

And then Ani was there.

Choruses of "Ani!" "Hello!" "Longtime no see!" "Give a hug!" Well-wishers crowded toward a tall woman standing in the frame of the entryway. The grey silk Armani suit emphasized a severe-cut hairstyle—one that drew a harsh line of obsidian black from one cheekbone to the other. Brooding Cleopatra eyes and full shine red lips completed her visage.

"Ooooo-lah-lah's," "Honey, you look great!" Wolf whistles and applause followed the runway style entry into the room.

This was Ansonia—the soon-to-be-ex-predecessor. In that instant, Laura decided never to imitate such a Hollywood style. She was about to turn away in disgust when a hand touched her right elbow. Mee Sue struggled between clapping, laughing, and trying to stop Laura from leaving.

"No, no! This is End Dinner for Ani!" she said to Laura, then laughed and clapped again. "You not see what happen! Look!"

More clapping and laughing. Ansonia had reached the center of the room and now held a champagne flute high in her left hand. She executed a graceful twirl, bowed deeply to the crowd and showed a goodly amount of cleavage. The crowd clapped and hooted its approval.

"Who will be my first dahnce?" The English accent was more than Laura could take.

"No, no," repeated Mee Sue grabbing Laura by the waist and planting her. "Wait, see! Feet on ground!" Then Mee Sue laughed, and stomped her feet. The crowd picked up the beat. A young man in black suit and red tie swirled Ansonia into a small circle of open space. The raised champagne glass threw drops outward onto the clapping crowd.

Suddenly, Ansonia doubled over. Just as suddenly, everything stopped. Silence dropped into the crowd like a tombstone. Gurgling noises like sobs emanated from the circle center.

"No, I can't!" Cough, more gasps. Emergency room training flooded Laura's muscles. She shoved through the circle to its center and bent over Ansonia's bent form.

"Are you okay? Can you breathe?" Laura grabbed her wrist to check her pulse.

It began as a ripple, became a quiet thunder as it reached the back of the group. "She's laughing!" "Oh!" and, "I thought she'd had a heart attack," and "Very funny!"

Ansonia, holding her stomach was doubled in laughter. Her worried dance partner was still crouched next to them. His eyes widened with relief and a grin followed.

"Too much," she yelled, laughing, standing, tossing more champagne onto the crowd. More "oooo's and ahh's" and suddenly Laura found herself face to face with Ani. Flushed skin, sparkling eyes, grey silk spattered with champagne. Ansonia winked. Laura blinked—then smiled back—and found herself laughing.

On tiptoe behind, Mee Sue peeked over Laura's shoulder. "End Dinner very funny. Everyone get chance for extreme makeover. You see TV show like that? Ani do well. Not look like Ani. Look like Hollywood star! Very good, Ani!" called Mee Sue, clapping and stomping with the rest of the crowd.

Well, thought Laura, *joke's on me,* and began to clap.

The rest of the evening fled by, balancing manageable moments and rushing jolts. Skits, standup comics, and gourmet dinner. Presentation of gifts, good-bye's, and a final dance by Ansonia ended the event. Laura's exhaustion had snuck off somewhere and she found herself hugging new friends and meaning it.

And then, somehow, it was time to leave. Laura watched Ansonia break away and come toward her, extending a hand.

"Laura, such a pleasure! I'm glad we could meet tonight. Here," she held out a card. "Take my contact number. John wants us to have some time to talk before you come on board." Ansonia folded Laura in a warm hug, kissed her on the cheek, and returned to the dining salon.

Dr. Russell did not show up. Conversations suggested a new top-level client or emergency. No one knew for sure. The announcement of his absence dampened team spirits enough to leave an impression on everyone, including Laura.

Chapter 16

Diminutive and unsophisticated in comparison, she could never mistake her Porter Square subway stop with the DC Metro underground. The 100-foot escalator to street level was Boston's attempt at large-ness. But after DC—well—not much could be considered big here.

Laura used commercial airlines for the flight home—Dr. Russell's emergency pre-empted an executive plane ride home. But a first-class seat to Boston's Logan airport was not a bad exchange. Mid-morning crowds were minimal so she decided to take the subway home. She needed to unclutter her head and make the transition back to everyday life.

Her suitcase clattered over uneven sidewalks where snow had been cleared by homeowners. When it wasn't, she picked up the case and lugged it as best she could. Perspiration collected and fingers stiffened. The mile walk was a 'slap up the side of her head,' as mom used to say. It cleared brain fog.

The key struggled into her door lock. It opened it with raspy sounds. Her suitcase fell over the threshold. The warmth of home hit her in the chest. Still in the hallway, tears welled in her eyes. They expanded to sobs. Minutes passed before she bent down, pushed her suitcase into the room and shut the door.

Laura went straight to bed.

I'll just lie down for a minute she thought. Half a day later, street clothes still on she woke, turned over and went back to sleep.

***

What woke her the next morning she wasn't sure—an empty stomach or her alarm she'd never turned off? Habits too hard to break found her dressed and on the 6:30 am Friday train into work, a half-eaten egg croissant-wich in hand.

She checked her phone, something she'd not done for three days.

Sam's text popped up—Sam, her Friday night recently turned friend with benefits.

Shit! I haven't thought about him since I left. The five text messages after his first one became increasingly concerned.

Not good, said that same annoying voice in her head.

Oh, for heaven's sake. Way too early to start an argument in my own brain. She scrolled to work messages. They were even worse. Several nurse complaints, one operation needing review, two security breaches involving drugs, and a meeting request by her supervisor. What was that about? Didn't matter much. *Good,* she thought. *I'm gonna tell him I'm quitting. I can't wait.*

***

"What do you mean, you're leaving?"

Elevated voice, a bit red in the face—quintessential icky boss. Laura, patience worn thin, still smiled with feigned politeness. Johnson had no idea how uncharming he could be. Bulldoggish to the end.

"The hospital has a new proposal—just about to suggest it to you. Job expansion with increased benefits and 3% raise—that's pretty good these days. I'd have told you earlier, but, well, you know how things get."

He looked at Laura. Her smile remained solidly unchanged. *I bet if I hold out, he'll offer more.* She waited.

"Well, maybe we could get you 4%..."

She shook her head. "I appreciate your esteem. It's that..." she paused. "I have an offer I'm not prepared to refuse."

Johnson stood up, came around the large cherry wood desk, draped one leg over its corner, and leaned closer, a confidential smile on his face. "I can speak to the board," he whispered. "I'm sure I could get you five, maybe 6% and a week's extra vacation. What do you say?"

What she wanted to say was, "Fuck you," and slap him. She'd been slavishly proving herself for five years. The last three she'd asked for acknowledgement of her time and skills. He'd met each approach with his 'poor Richard' face, quoting hospital budgets, health care cuts, reduced patient stays, and all the rest of the bottom-line side step administrators told their clinical staff.

She stood up, realizing how much this man reminded her of the rapist monster from New York. "It's way too late."

She took a deep breath, added a bright smile and decided to lie. "I can give you a week before I leave for my next position. If you need less, I would gladly leave today."

Observe, turn, leave.

The expression on Johnson's face was almost worth her years five years at the hospital—open mouth, slack jaw and no pre-determined *no can do* forming on his lips—just plain old shocked surprise.

***

Laura spent the rest of her Friday morning dealing with mis-placed drugs, operation reports and salary complaints. At lunch time, she locked her 'one more week to go' office door from the in-side and called Sam.

"What do you mean, you're leaving?" protested Sam after she'd apologized at least ten times.

"Welcome back to you, too," she quipped.

"Oh, right, sorry, just, well… I'm surprised is all." Pause. "I missed you."

"After two days?"

"Yup—and it was three if you count right."

"Sounds serious," she responded.

Silence.

"Sam?"

"Yeah?

"You still there?"

"I am." He hesitated. "How about dinner tonight? You can fill me in over escargot and sauvignon blanc." Sam dangled Laura's foodie passions in front of her.

"I know what you're doing," she said.

"I don't care as long as it works. You coming?"

"Of course, I'll come. You give me no choice."

"Great! Six o'clock then at the Brasserie du Coin."

"Wait! You had this all planned out?"

"Never hurts to be prepared," he said hanging up.

A knock at the door signaled her telephone-lunchtime was over. She hadn't eaten anything since breakfast and the possibility didn't look any better for the afternoon.

***

Laura exited the hospital on Brookline Avenue and took a cab to the restaurant. Sam waited at a small table with wine bottle and glasses already set. When he rose, his sandy hair flopped around.

That's cute, she thought. She smiled at him. Then she burst into sobs.

He enfolded her. "Sit," he whispered.

She sat. He poured wine.

"Drink," he said. She drank.

"Now talk." She talked. At least she said what she was allowed to say—which was not much.

He listened.

They ate.

She invited him home.

***

Somewhere in the middle of the night, Laura wiggled out of Sam's arms her mind already running an irritating dialogue.

98

Secret sex with the boss and boyfriends don't go together, Greenwald. Unless you enjoy being stupid.

He's not my boyfriend, she shot back at the ever-present inner voice. *And just shut up for once. What's the big deal if I invited him home?*

And home he stayed for the next two days while she fled from thoughts of her future secrets. They woke late, made coffee and went back to bed. He would lean over, kiss her neck, blow away the hair and cool her skin where his lips touched. She would laugh, kiss him down to his waist, lick her tongue back to his nipple and push into him with her sex over and over again.

Halfway through Sunday afternoon Sam quit.

He leaned against the headboard, brows knit together. "We're started something that's already got an end in sight. A couple more weeks then—poof! You're gone, like nothing happened. The idea makes me crazy." He pulled an arm away. Rough and sudden.

"I can't do this, Laura."

She touched his shoulder. *I don't want Sam to disappear, too,* she thought. *Not when everything else is disappearing.* "We've had a great weekend, Sam, and three more before I leave. Let's just see what happens."

He looked doubtful.

"I'm not working," she coaxed.

He raised his eyebrows. "I thought you said…"

"I gave a week's notice." She crossed her arms in self-satisfaction. "But I've decided to use sick leave instead of going in to work. My boss is such a jerk I don't even feel bad."

Laura paused and cocked her head. "So…you want to try?"

Sam's grin spread from his lips to his cheeks as the question dangled between them for a while. Then he said, "I just might do that."

So, Laura kissed him and let her tongue meander to his ear—and then elsewhere.

***

99

Laura called her family, told them her news, informed friends, suffered congratulations and good-bye parties, and continued to take severe and utter pleasure in her boss's discomfiture. She also became heart-wrenchingly close to Sam.

Her $20,000 relocation money took them twice to DC. Together they searched for a neighborhood that could human-size DC's enormous government buildings with their miles of hallways, the oversized shopping malls and four-wheeled congestion clogging the capitol city from distances over fifty miles away.

They searched for an apartment she liked and something to put in it. Nothing from Somerville, Massachusetts was worth transporting.

The realtor listened patiently.

They drove around a lot.

She said no a lot.

They got back in the car a lot.

Late on the third day, Laura cried, "Stop! This place feels right. Where are we?"

"Mt. Pleasant," said the realtor. "Not so upscale, but it's 'neighborly.' Second floor apartment's for rent around the corner. Thought you'd like to see it."

The converted row house had three stories and four apartments. When they walked in the second-floor rental, three six-foot-tall windows dominated the living room. They overlooked a wooded hill sloping to Rock Creek Park. A brick wall at the end of the room formed the kitchen with its row of appliances. The island counter had a place for stools and divided living and kitchen space. Shower and washroom accompanied bedroom and tiny balcony. Small was too big a word for the elf-sized living space.

"I'll take it," she said.

With that statement, Laura felt her new job in Washington become real. This apartment would be home, hold her in joy and sorrow, keep her safe, keep her grounded. *I wonder how often Sam will come here,* she thought, then shook her head. She banished the question from her mind. *Too much happening to think about that now.*

Chapter 17

Time was up.

One DC lease signed at $2,300 a month, utilities included and she counted herself lucky.

One Somerville lease legitimately broken four months early.

Conversations with Sam—unresolved—to be continued.

Pack everything she could use and give away what wouldn't fit in her car—which had already been shipped.

Final visits with doctors—updated shots, birth control researched, and best IUD inserted (ouch!)

No complications to show up on my end, she'd thought. *Doesn't matter what kind of vasectomy Dr. Russell or anybody else has. No babies, no scandal, no complications. Not from me.*

That was where clarity ended.

One afternoon, in the middle of packing, she clutched her stomach and vomited on the floor. Heart pounding, Laura wobbled around the icky wet pile and headed toward the one chair still left in the living room. She sat immobilized, her now acidic esophagus burning—and cried. The scribbled to-do list lay on the counter, still a mile long. That day she'd been unable to shove her fears out of the way and vomited from tense anxiety. It helped to have an empty stomach, but now she had the floor to clean up.

And so it went until the last day.

Papers signed; documents rendered to appropriate lawyers.

Flight tickets purchased.

Hugs given.

Last night in Somerville with Sam.

Cab called.

Goodbye to life as she knew it.

***

Eva Jormand's precise telephone voice from three days earlier still rang in Laura's ears.

"A same day flight would be personal suicide."

"I'm sorry?" Laura asked.

"Your flight to DC."

"What about it?"

"Orientation starts at 9 am. It can run up to fourteen hours. We don't suggest adding air travel to an already exhausting day."

So here she was on the day-before, at Washington's Melrose Hotel with its polished-to-high-shine marble, large windows, and trendy interior. Her two bags followed in the hands of a doorman more elegantly dressed than her father at his wedding. The receptionist behind the desk called out, "Ms. Greenwald, I hope you had a pleasant flight. We've been waiting for you."

How did she know my name, thought Laura, *I just walked in.*

Laura never quite found out. Check-in consisted only of having her keycard handed over. In seconds the doorman was escorting Laura to an executive suite on the third floor. When they arrived, she took a $10 bill from her purse. The doorman raised a white gloved hand and shook his head. "Thank you, Miss, but I've been well compensated by your employer." He bowed, backed out of the room and shut the door.

She stood in a large central room with ten-foot windows, curtain-covered side walls, an overstuffed designer fabric couch and mahogany coffee table. An uncorked bottle of cabernet sauvignon and large fruit basket welcomed her.

I could get used to this, she thought sliding her hands along the richly padded back of the sofa and polished wooden table

She sighed. Tensions from the trip eased muscle by muscle. A smile tugged at her. *"You're here; you made it; Hip, hoorah.* She raised her arms, arched her back and twirled, hair and skirt swirling high in the air. *This room is gorgeous. I love it. And,* she thought looking around, *I'm ready for that glass of wine.*

Which is when the corner of an envelope stuck between two bananas in the fruit basket caught her eye.

What now? She bent to pull it out with no inkling of how many times those same words would haunt her days and nights.

The unsealed envelope of parchment paper held an embossed logo for Dr. Manhattan Enterprises in the upper left corner. In the center, her name was written in calligraphy style script. She opened it. Inside lay one folded sheet of paper.

Dear Ms. Greenwald,

The schedule for your first day of orientation has been changed.

Please arrive at the Washington Memorial Hospital Entrance by 7 am.

Eva Jormand

"That's it?" Laura's voice rose loud and irritated in the silence of the room. "No, welcome to DC, no enjoy your evening?"

She picked up her half empty wine glass and chugged it all down at once.

Charming behavior, Greenwald, snarked her inner voice.

Don't care, she thought back and poured herself more. Happy twirling circles belonged to another lifetime. This one contained elegant hotel rooms, pre-paid doormen and commandments that had to be followed.

Forget it. Time for dinner. She picked up the nightstand phone to order room service.

"Ah, Madam," said the disembodied voice, "A special dinner service has just been prepared for you. We can bring it right away."

"Oh," she said, and dropped the phone in its cradle like a hot potato. *Special service? Ready as soon as I pick up the phone?* Unconsciously, she scanned the room to look for cameras spying on her. Warning bells echoed back and forth in her mind. She could not silence them even with the buzz of wine in her head.

***

5:30 a.m. the next morning dragged into Laura's consciousness far too early. She punished herself for overindulging the night before by dowsing in a cold shower.

"I hate this; I hate this," she yelled in the shower stall, which got her through two minutes of wet wake up therapy.

An hour later Laura was out the door headed for the hospital. She wore a tailored suit and wedge heels, with hair in a French twist. A small shoulder bag was stuffed with her work shoes, scrubs to be provided by her employer.

The hospital, located between trendy Georgetown and a busy White House, was the go-to emergency hospital for the President of the United States. But the busy ER also served city residents, who inundated its facility with over 73,000 patients a year and that was just for emergencies.

Laura waited in the foyer as people flowed through the doors towards elevators, stairs and hallways, the reception guard checking every ID. She saw Eva Jormand heading towards her against the crowd.

The *person-who-decides if you get this job*, remembered Laura from the first interview.

Eva smiled and held out her hand. "Come. We'll get you prepped for the day."

They passed the guard, rode the elevator, and exited at neurology. They wound through corridors of the 'new building'—10 years old, 300,000 square feet and $150,000,000 to build and equip. Somewhere in this maze was Dr. Russell, his team and the start of her First Training Day.

Is a romp in the hay included? she wondered. *At least I'd get it over with. This waiting and wondering is for the bir...*

"You'll be shadowing Dr. Russell." Eva interrupted Laura's sex musings. "Surgery's at 8:00. He's excising a tumor pressing against the Brocas's speech area in the patient's brain. She's the wife of a mucky-muck politician. When she started slurring words, rumors spread about alcoholism. The wife cried foul. Next thing you know—here she is.

"I see," said Laura.

"She's a pretty typical patient—high profile with a life-threatening problem. Absolutely secret and confidential—for us. Someone else will leak the surgery to the media. It's a big sympathy factor—whatever the outcome." Eva watched her carefully. "We're throwing you in. Sink or swim."

Laura smiled, "I've got my life jacket on." *This I can do no sweat.*

At least, that's what she thought in the morning.

***

Dr. Russell finished three surgeries before noon, consulted two colleagues on radiological results, and had a mandatory catered staff lunch break. Laura stood within ten feet of him wherever he was, including lunch, excluding toilet breaks, which he didn't seem to need but she did.

At lunch, Eva joined them and sat next to Laura.

"How does he do it?" asked a bedraggled Laura.

Eva laughed. "He suggests you take a shower right after lunch. Perks you up."

"You're joking, right?"

"No joke. More like a tip. Then you can hit the meditation room next to the lockers for ten minutes."

Laura stared at Eva. She was serious.

Training Day One. Tips included.

Three more surgical events began at 1:30 with the last patient rolling to recovery by 7:00. Laura's back ached and she limped. Her stomach growled so loudly she started apologizing.

How could I have possibly thought today would include sex? I can't even stand up.

"Day's over!" whooped Eva to the staff milling around Dr. Russell's conference room. "Don't forget your copy of next week's surgical schedule."

"Whoo—hoo! Day's over. We're outta here!" The crowd of fifteen surged down the hallway, pulling a weary Laura with them—jostling, laughing and calling, "Eva, where'd you hide the limos? Com'on, fess up!"

Laura, still in scrubs, clutched her purse. Her copy of the day's schedule had gotten trampled underfoot. *Limos? I need a bed. What are they talking about?*

Confused, exhausted, too tired to think, she let herself be herded along, figuring they'd be outside soon enough. Then she'd call her own cab. *Don't need a limo—just a bed with no one else in it.*

They squeezed into the elevators, disgorged through the lobby, and headed towards two limousines idling at the curb. Before Laura could escape, she felt her hand grabbed, pulled towards the cars, and pushed down to squeeze into the warmth of the long back seat.

I surrender, thought Laura, head nodding from sleep deprivation, purse still clutched to her midriff. They drove through Friday evening traffic down 23rd Street towards Dupont Circle. The chatter subsided. When the limousines stopped and doors opened, Laura found herself standing in a narrow alleyway where a red neon sign blinked on and off like Christmas lights. Laura squinted. What she read was *Silver Touch Massage Studio.*

"Massage Friday," said Eva.

Laura stared at her. *Massage Friday?* She didn't have the energy to say it out loud.

"I grabbed you when we were leaving," Eva admitted, shrugging. "I thought you might like our twice a month 'relax your bones' night out."

A whisper of a smile formed on Laura's lips. *This surrender may not be so bad after all.*

***

By 9:30 pm, she was showered, steam-bathed, massaged, and starving. A deep relaxation oozed to her core.

The day's events turned over in her head as the group marched towards the Mai Thai Restaurant several blocks away. *A schizo-*

phrenic day. The whole kaboodle feels like John Russell—torture and pleasure strung hand to hand. The idea made her smile.

"Crispy duck salad, Thai bubble tea and black sticky rice with custard," she'd said to the waiter so hungry she could have eaten the pictures on the menu. Eva sat next to her.

"Mee Sue created this Friday night routine." confided Eva. "Mee Sue—I think you know her, right? She heads the team's Wellness Department."

Laura, sipping bubble tea, nodded. "John's idea was to have a masseuse attached to the team and follow everyone around. Mee Sue nixed that with a click of her fingers—up in the air. Like that." Eva imitated the gesture and laughed out loud.

"I'll never forget the look on John's face. Little, mild-mannered Mee Sue shaking her head, stomping her feet and hair flying across her face. She put her hands on her hips and pronounced, 'Oh, no, Mister Doctor John, Sir. That is very bad idea! Boring, old idea. You leave good ideas to be my job."

Eva was still laughing when the food came.

Chapter 18

The open limousine window framed Eva's face in the lamplight as she called out. Already half way up the hotel steps, Laura turned to listen.

"Orientation tomorrow, 8:00 am sharp—hotel lobby," she yelled as the car drifted into traffic.

"Got it!" Laura called back as the bellhop held open the door.

The hands of the lobby clock pointed to midnight.

God! Am I tired! Laura rode the elevator, walked down the corridor to her room, slid the key card into the lock and clicked open the door. She kicked off her shoes, sighed heavily and ran fingers through her now loose, untwisted hair. She turned around as she closed the door.

A wild, gut wrenching scream left her lips.

She heard it again, knew it rose out of her own throat. Terrorized and primal.

Backlit on the sofa, sat a man with glittering eyes, legs crossed, staring at her body and face.

She dropped her bag. "Oh, my God! Who...?"

The sofa lamp clicked on.

"I've been waiting for you," he said.

The man on the sofa cushions wore a tailored black suit, held a wine glass in his left hand, and an apology in his eyes. "I'm sorry to have startled you," said Dr. Russell.

He stood up.

"Waiting for me?" sputtered Laura. "What are you talking about? You're inside *my* room! It's midnight.! What are you doing in here?"

"Oh, yes... that."

He bent towards the end table, refilling his wine glass. "Care for some?" he asked, raising the cup. Laura, heart still pounding, kicked her bag towards the bedroom door, pushed her shoes out of the way and muttered, "That might help—if I can hold it." Her hands were still shaking from adrenaline shock.

A rueful smile spread across his face, "What just happened is an awkward blip for which I am sorry." His hand gestured around the room.

Laura threw back a gulp of wine, the last shreds of sophisticated behavior gone. *Did he expect to sleep with me? Tonight? Now?* Her head muddled itself up as she sat. "A blip...?" she asked.

"Well...if I hadn't fallen asleep, I'd have met you in the lobby."

"But you are *inside my* room."

"Not really."

"What do you mean, 'not really'?"

"Well, it's actually *our* room."

Laura shot off the couch. "Our room? Our room. What happened to mutual consent? Or transitions, or overload? Do you know how much..."

"Laura—stop.

She stopped.

"Calm down."

She tried.

"And breathe."

He looked at her and said, "Long day. Too much."

She nodded.

Moments passed.

"The 'not really' is that my office reserves an executive suite for both of us—separate bedrooms with shared central space. You are standing in our central space right now. That is your bedroom over there." He pointed to her door. "This is mine, over here." He pointed to the other wall.

Laura stared. A floor to ceiling drape now pushed aside revealed a connecting doorway.

"I had an emergency consult after work. Then a political meeting disguised as a social visit got squeezed in, too. No time for explanations. I'd have told you all this except I wasn't here—and then I fell asleep. That's my 'blip' speech."

Laura chugged more wine, coughed and shook her head.

"You're right—long day," she said, but kept staring at him.

"Something still on your mind?" he asked.

Of course, something's still on my mind, she thought but couldn't get the words out.

He waited. "Yes?"

She cleared her throat. "So, are we supposed to…"

"Not tonight," he said leaning over to refill her glass. "We're both exhausted." Dr. Russell raised his glass to her, stood, walked to his room, and shut the door.

"And good night to you, too," sputtered Laura. He had closed the door before she finished.

So much for jumping in and getting it over with. How long will it take to figure out what the hell's going on? She stomped to her room and slammed the door. It was stupid and childish. But it made her feel better.

Chapter 19

Ocean storm; waves pounding rocks, birds calling.

Dreams shattered.

The clock radio wakeup voice blared over its background sea sounds. "6:30 am wakeup... 6:30 am wakeup... Press red button to turn ..." She swatted the red dot on the machine, sat up, and poured a glass of cold orange juice from the decanter on the nightstand. Well, it worked. She was up.

And where was that damn catalog? She couldn't get dressed without it.

They'd sent the catalog to Somerville two weeks ago. Laura was to go shopping—all expenses paid by Dr. Manhattan Enterprises. That should have been fun. Except for the *Catalog*. She had to buy according to the guidelines.

And the prices. Oh, my goodness. The prices.

On her own, she tried buying two $500 blouses. It had been near impossible to match the blouses in the catalog with what was on the Neiman Markus hangers. Her eyes hurt so much from squinting at the pictures and then at the hanging blouses that she ended up with a headache.

By the third shopping trip she had a revelation. Who did she think dressed Lady Gaga and Angelina Jolie? They didn't shop till they dropped. No, ma'am. Personal shopper and wardrobe consultants, that's who. Those expensive looking sales ladies might actually have a purpose.

So, catalog in one hand, Dr. Manhattan Enterprises charge account in the other, Laura bought. Five stores, seven trips and six outfits later she completed her assignment. The sales women, proud of their selections, remarked how the outfits spotlighted Laura's natural beauty, her auburn hair, her slender body.

The same comments from so many different sales ladies made Laura wonder if John Russell had his consulting team put the catalog together just so his assistant would look sexy.

Today she had to show her outfits and pass the team's dress code. She wondered how much the sexy versus business part would strike the eye. Hospital uniforms were easy. It was the other clothing—the 'street uniforms' as John called them—that would create the important impressions. *And what impressions did he want her to leave,* she wondered *when the bill came to $12,576.00 and still counting?*

"We all need fashion advice at first" Eva had said. "It takes practice to buy right and that comes with a price tag. John helps out till you get the idea."

Laura stood in front of the closet. One hour to dress and get downstairs. Where was that damn catalog when she needed it?

***

Today's team consisted of seven people clustered around the lobby's coffee bar. George Penunos, her lawyer, and Eva Jormand were the only people Laura knew. Eva stood out amidst the group, her long black hair richly cut, grey-tailored suit, black heels and neck beads refined and elegant.

Has she been one of Dr. Russell's women? Laura shook her head. *Why can't I get this stuff out of my mind today?* As she wrestled with that question, the next one pushed into her brain. *How much does everyone know about what the whole contract says?*

There was no time to consider. Eva approached. "We've been waiting for you. Grab a coffee and we'll get started." She walked towards the mezzanine stairs and into a meeting room, the group following behind. She motioned Laura to the center seat at an oval table where a large stack of documents lay. Then everyone else sat, each person facing smaller stacks than Laura.

"We have twelve hours plus of lots to do. Introductions first." She smiled. "Meet Laura Greenwald. Just hired, terrific qualifications, and, maybe, just maybe, nearly as personable as I am."

Laughter, hand shakings and "Welcome... glad to meet you... congratulations..." echoing. The morning had begun.

A schedule of the day, hour by hour, sat on the top of the document piles. Confidentiality, ethics, privacy, dress codes, competence, hospital regulations, clinic requirements, health requirements, contact information, emergency procedures, foreign travel, payments, expenses, confidentiality (*Again?* Laura thought), licensing and on and on. Until it stopped.

Eva locked eyes with Laura. "We had a thousand applicants," Eva said.

Laura gaped. *A thousand applicants? How did I ever get...* began her thought.

But Eva was talking much faster than Laura could process that information. So, she gave up and focused on listening.

"What you do, Laura, you do very well. Your skills passed scrutiny with flying colors." She stopped, took a deep breath. You will receive training in the other skills required for this position. You'll find no diplomas or certificates for what we *really* teach here."

Laura blanched. *Eva couldn't... wouldn't bring up the Sex part in front of everyone... would she?*

Everyone waited, breathing audible.

"You'll practice it over and over. John will insist on it. And he's a good trainer—annoying, but good."

Oh, shit, thought Laura, *here it comes.*

"When you're done here, you'll be big time, honey, worth every single penny they'll try to pay you, and more."

Laura eyes widened and she stared at Eva. "*I can't believe she's going to talk about me and sex in front of everyone.* Her panicked thought sent an itchy, hot blush to her neck.

"The *It* we are talking about..." Eva paused and looked around. Every eye around the table was glued to her. "The *It* we teach here is *Endurance*—Endurance with a capital E."

Laughter erupted. Jolted, Laura forced herself back to attention. People smiled, gestured, talked over one another. Mini chaos had flooded the table.

Laura almost vomited in relief. The acidic anxiety dispersed so slowly she thought the lining of her stomach might puncture.

"All right, everybody! Let's come to order!" called Eva. "We've all been there. You know what John's like. We've all lived through his Olympic Endurance demands. If you don't give every ounce of body, mind, and soul, you won't last around here."

Eva now looked at Laura. "We're starting endurance practice right now." She held up the schedule so everyone could see it.

"It's 9:30 am. We've got a lot to do. Today ends in 12 hours—maybe."

***

Laura couldn't remember where the hours had gone or what they'd done.

"Don't worry." Eva had assured her. "It's a lot. We go over it all again and again."

The *It* she was talking about had started with team review of Laura's outfit.

They decided she needed a scarf, a larger purse to carry documents (hers was too small), lower heels for long days, wrinkle free jacket; return the one she bought (wouldn't travel well).

Up to her room, back down again—twice—before she passed.

Then the social engagements. Four afternoon lunches—invitations from prominent patients. The team now consisted only of Eva, George Penunos and Laura.

"Four lunches?" she exclaimed. "How can you possibly do that?"

"Watch and learn," smiled Eva. "Endurance," she said, "and skill."

Skill was right—Eva finessed her way through four lunches, consuming but somehow not consuming—and no one noticed. She looked as fresh at the 5:00 lunch as she had at the 1:00 snacks. *Really? Lobster, soup, salad and pecan pie for a snack?* thought Laura.

"I'm so sorry," Eva was saying to the 5:00 o'clock people, "but we have a meeting with Dr. Russell. Could you possibly excuse us?"

Good-byes were said, compliments given, and then they stood in the cold winter evening.

"Another hour or so and we'll be done," Eva said as the limousine drove up. As they got in, Laura did her best not to stumble, she was so exhausted.

"You see why we recommend comfortable shoes," remarked George Penunos. Laura barely managed a smile, closed her eyes, leaned back. They drove to the historic W Hotel, (*Really? Just an initial?*) where Dr. Russell waited. He opened the limo doors looking just as fresh as Eva.

"Welcome, ladies and..." he bent his head into the car, "...gentleman. We're meeting a few folks at the POV Bar, up top. Elevator's this way." He sounded as perky as if he'd just had a three-hour nap.

Endurance? thought Laura. *This is downright magic.*

The POV Roof Top Bar boasted floor to ceiling windows overlooking the White House and Tidal Basin monuments—all lit with street lamps and snowy reflections. The view was lost on Laura, whose delusional brain only looked for a bed as John Russell led them through the busy dining room. They ended at a corner table where several people were seated.

John Russell turned to Laura. "I'd like to introduce you to Senator Hiram Jenks of South Dakota, his wife, Dorothy, and their daughter, Marina. I think everyone else has already met."

Laura produced a smile on her face. "A pleasure to meet you."

They sat.

The waiter appeared.

Laura ordered a double espresso. Her eyes needed propping open.

When the waiter left, Dr. Russell said, "I'm going to head straight into business. It's late and I have a feeling some people might be tired."

He winked at Laura.

She blushed. Was she the only tired one here?

"…are too many eyes around my clinic building. Not a big deal most of the time, but in this case, I want to make absolutely sure."

Laura commanded her wandering mind to pay attention.

The story came out. Senator Jenks was facing an election year. His wife had developed unusual neurological symptoms and the family wanted health concerns kept private.

Dr. Russell offered to investigate the problem in another country.

Laura's eyelids popped open. *Another country?*

The plan was for the senator's wife and her daughter to 'take a winter vacation' while the Senator stayed home. The vacation had been scheduled at Dr. Russell's medical resort in Ciudad Cariari, Costa Rica, near the capitol. Dr. Russell held surgical privileges at the hospital close by and would conduct an evaluation of her condition and possible surgery during their stay.

Laura, wide awake, no longer needed espresso—except it was being delivered. Cup and saucer tinkled as they shifted into place in front of her. Marina smiled tentatively at Laura. *Now why was Marina doing that?* she wondered.

"…and Laura…" continued John Russell, "you'll accompany Mrs. Jenks and Marina. You'll leave Tuesday morning—I'll follow on a later flight."

Costa Rica? This Tuesday? Really? This is her orientation? Thoughts crashed together in her head. She didn't need that espresso anymore.

***

It was after 11:00 pm when Laura kicked her shoes off in the middle of the hotel suite and turned on the light. Tonight, the sofa was empty. John would be another 45-minutes finalizing instructions with the family.

That's what he'd told her.

What she'd told him was her passion for a long hot shower in the large bathroom of her comfortable hotel room.

She loosened her clothes, dropped them in front of the shower door and turned on the water. It poured down, hot and strong and she lost herself in the rhythmic drumming of water on her head and shoulders.

Ten soapy, hot minutes later, washed clean, Laura emerged, hair and body towel-wrapped and patted dry. The idea of thirty more minutes by herself was delicious. She tiptoed into the common area, bent down, and picked a mini-scotch from the under-counter refrigerator.

It was then that the hand grabbed her by the elbow.

Chapter 20

It was her scream. From her body. She knew it. It ripped through her vocal cords and shattered her ear drums. She felt herself pulled to her feet. *I won't be raped again! I won't!*

She heard the scream again, felt herself start to struggle.

"Laura! It's me."

"Oh... oh, my God... sorry!" She clamped her hands to her mouth, towel suddenly dropping.

"I thought... it's only... I mean..."

He stood there smiling.

She stood there naked.

"We finished early," John said.

"I...see that," she stuttered.

"I guess you do," he said, looking.

"Oh, my God..." she squeaked, grabbed the towel from the floor, and fumbled with it.

John stood watching, observing, not moving.

"You are very beautiful," he said.

"Thank you," she mumbled, twisting to get the towel around herself. "There," she said with a tuck. Wet hair flopped across face and cheeks.

"So, ah... everything finished up well?" she said, figuring she'd try sophisticated nonchalance instead of freak out. Except her mind deserted her. She stood stone statue frozen.

John smiled, shrugged out of his coat, held it between them. "Care to use this for the moment?"

"Uh, thank you, no. I think I'll be fine—I mean—I'm just going to bed and…"

Disregarding every word, John came over and settled the coat on her bare shoulders. Then he gave her a gentle, encompassing hug. Without conscious thought, Laura found herself leaning into his warm chest. She closed her eyes and nestled there.

Such a long day, she mumbled inwardly, confused about what she was doing but too tired to care. It just felt good to stand there together, laying the day's stresses aside one by one.

BBRRINGGG! BBRING! screeched a phone. Laura's head jerked up. It collided with John's chin. Jaw and teeth crunched together on a piece of his tongue.

"Oouuch!" he yelped and stumbled back, blood dripping from his mouth.

"Oh, my God!" she cried. She struggled free and ran to find ice. "I'm sorry. I'm sorry."

BBRRINGGG! BBRING!

She grabbed the phone, yelled into it, "It's the middle of the night. Unless you're dying, call in the morning!" and then hung up. No one called back.

Oh, jeez," thought Laura, *find me my bed.*

By midnight, she'd patched him up, tucked him in bed, and included a goodnight kiss on the forehead. Still bent over the bed, she giggled. He chortled. She laughed. He joined in. They ended up clutching their stomachs and gasping for breath. She finally pulled herself together, made it to her own bed and fell into an immediate and exhausted sleep.

***

That had been last night.

This morning, when Laura opened her door, she was fully dressed.

John sat in the breakfast nook with a tray of croissants, bagels, smoked salmon and cream cheese with strawberries and melon slices on the side.

She pointed an index finger at the coffee cup. "Hand me over one of those, Sir Galahad, or die!"

Oh, my God, did I really just say that?

John Russell snorted, poured the cup and patted the table in front of him. "Sit," he said.

She sat.

"Eat."

She ate.

The aroma of coffee floated throughout the suite. Companionable and easy. She was drawn to the Sunday-morning-ness of him. *This whole work-sex-two-year-contract thing might just work out— like friends with benefits... or something—including a big fuckin' salary. And the coffee tastes soooo good. I could get used to this.*

His voice broke her thoughts apart. "Eva left today's schedule on your iPad."

Laura stared at him. "I don't have an iPad."

"You do now." He bent down and pulled out the tablet from a briefcase at his feet. "Company property—yours for the duration." He took a sip of coffee.

"Eva will prep you for Tuesday." He looked at her. "The Costa Rica trip is one of those last-minute things we run into. Not a bit deal. It's good training." He looked at his watch. "I'm gone all day but we're scheduled for dinner tonight. 7:00 reservation."

He pushed back his chair and got up.

"But..."

"She's waiting downstairs. See you tonight."

And he was gone. Just like that.

***

Travel orientation for Costa Rica consumed all of Sunday— addresses, documents, e-tickets, protocols, and all the rest. She also received a lecture on Costa Rica's health care system. Eva stuffed the official guide to *Successful Medical Travel in Costa Rica* into Laura's purse.

"Read that on the plane," Eva said. "Make sure no one sees the title—wrap it in brown paper or something. You're supposed to be on a vacation trip, not a funeral tour."

By the end of another grueling afternoon, Laura laughed at her own naïveté. She'd thought orientation would involve John Russell and sex. She was drained, but certainly not by that part of the contract.

"It's the details," Eva commiserated. "You'll get used to it. Monday's a day off. You need to be rested and ready for airport action on Tuesday."

"Action?" she asked. "Where am I going—the Wild West?"

"Nothing to worry about. I'll be at the airport to handle whatever comes up." Eva stood. "I'm going home. Don't forget. Dinner at 7 p.m. tonight. John will get you in the lobby."

"I was wondering…," began Laura.

But Eva had gone.

Her watch read 6:00 p.m. "Oh, jeez," she said and ran for the elevator.

***

She waited in the lobby dressed and ready. John Russell never appeared.

Laura finally retreated to her hotel room after thirty confused, angry minutes. Stripping off her clothes she uncoiled her hair, removed makeup and hoped a hot, soapy shower would wash away her irritation. It didn't.

Her thoughts yelled and twisted in her mind.

Thought you were beginning to get the routine?

Thought he might actually care? Thought you'd get some resp…

Oh, SHUT UP.

In desperation she pulled on tights and top and began her mind-body routine—kick front, kick back, side, side, side. Kick front, kick back, side…she stopped.

What's under the table?

Dropping to her knees she found a half-folded sheet of paper hidden from view by the fruit basket. It lay between couch and table leg. She picked it up.

"*Laura,*" it read, scribbled in hard to read cursive, "*Evening meeting cancelled. Had another call to attend to. Very sorry. Please order yourself dinner. Eva will meet you Tuesday at airport with tickets. See you then—John.*

He must have left the note on the table. Maybe it slid to the floor as she raced in to get dressed.

I should be relieved, she thought, *happy to have an explanation and privacy.*

But all she felt was tired, homesick, scared, and wildly out of place. All weekend she had been pulled this way, tugged that way. Come here. Go there. Stand down. Show up. Look smart. Talk right.

What have I done? she wondered. *Has $700,000 bought my life?*

Chapter 21

On Tuesday morning, Laura arrived at Dulles Airport with Mrs. Jenks and Marina in tow. They were timid travelers, and she felt like a nanny leading two children.

Eva met them dressed in a tailored black suit, high heels, and white pillbox hat holding a tray of steaming coffees. She smiled, chatted, and never offered Laura or her charges a drop.

"What are you doing dressed like a stewardess cartoon?" she asked.

"Hopefully, nothing," Eva replied in an enigmatic tone. "Let's get you to your gate and get your two puppies to sit down and relax."

When three reporters showed up, Eva stopped smiling. How they'd found out about the trip and gotten through security was anybody's guess.

They zeroed in like an invasion force on Marina, Mrs. Jenks' daughter. Blood drained from the young woman's face and she bent over in her seat to grab her purse and clutch it to her middle.

"Are you and your moth…" began the nearest reporter.

Eva's black suit, pill box hat and coffee tray bulldozed into the middle of the sentence.

"Oh, how wonderful to have such handsome gentlemen in our little airport!" fluted Eva.

What was she doing with that southern accent? wondered Laura. eyes glued to the drama unfolding just feet away.

"May I offer you handsome gentlemen some of our complimentary Brazilian coffee. We are so…" Eva bent slightly to offer a cup.

"Not right now, ma'am," said a second reporter, irritably trying to elbow Eva out of the way.

What is she doing...?

Without warning, the coffee tray tipped. Ten cups crashed to the ground, brown liquid splashing cream and sugar crystals over trousers, phones, and faces. Eva, collapsing to the ground, had grabbed the arm of the reporter next to her. He was on the floor next to her. The high heel of a shoe, cracked and broken lay inches away.

"Oh, I am sorry!" wailed Eva, now on her knees, grabbing napkins, wiping everything in arm's distance. "I don't know how that happened. Please let me..."

"Boarding for Flight 729 to San Jose, Costa Rica. First class passengers..."

Laura grabbed her two charges and fled to the line of people boarding the plane. Her heartrate jackhammered until all three of them finally strapped into their seats.

A text from Eva rang out on Laura's phone. She still had time before takeoff to answer it.

"What do you think of my crowd dispersion techniques?" it asked.

"You should try out for Hollywood," she texted, remembering back to Sunday's never-ending orientation for the trip. *Crowd dispersion techniques?* she'd thought while Eva lectured. She'd even rolled her inner eyeballs, trying to keep the outer ones on Eva. *When am I ever going to need that?* she'd thought at the time, *I'm lucky I can still pretend to be listening.*

Laura switched her phone to airplane mode. It was only 10:00 a.m. She leaned back and closed her eyes. *What else am I not going to expect on this job?* she wondered.

***

Four and a half hours in flight, one hour in the San Jose airport customs and ten minutes guiding her two charges and luggage through the exit line, Laura scanned for someone holding a big sign with their name on it—someone to take over—to pick them up, put their luggage in the car, and drive them to safety.

The pamphlet Eva had stuffed in Laura's purse said every year two and a half million tourists walk through the gates of Costa Rica's airport, fifty thousand of them arriving for medical procedures. *With Mrs. Jenks it's now 50,001,* thought Laura.

"There!" yelled Marina, pointing towards a block of letters spelling "Jenks" with a smiley face attached. Laura maneuvered them through the bustling, noisy crowd, raised her arm, and waved at a short man with a round face.

"Perfecto, señoras y señoritas. I am Manuelo. I take very good care from here for you. Come, come, see, this is the best way. We go." He grabbed two suitcases, tucked one under his arm and pushed his bulky way forward to a tattooed Ford Escort. "Just a small way more and you be at your casa. Manuelo is at your service."

The "small way more" turned into an hour of traffic, heat, and smoggy exhaust. "It is las fabricas, senoras, I ask you many regrets. It is the end of work. But... en realidad... the cars not so less in the middle of working time, either. San Jose—she is busy, busy."

***

By evening, the Jenks' were settled in their villa and Laura lay fast asleep in hers on the living room's bamboo sofa.

John Russell walked in, tie removed, collar unbuttoned, perspiration beading on his forehead. He dropped his briefcase on the coffee table, opened the slider panels to the pool, and pulled off his shoes. Two morning surgeries and a postponed flight from DC had kept him in work mode for over 15 hours.

He sat on the edge of the sofa where Laura lay and rested a hand on her shoulder. She stirred.

"Long day?" he asked.

"That seems to be an ongoing problem," she mumbled, struggling to sit up.

He smiled.

Humid evening breezes stirred the hanging vines on the patio and rippled the pool water. Unseen jungle frogs croaked songs and bats silhouetted a darkening sky. Bamboo walls, bamboo ceiling, and bamboo furniture in the common area separated their two bed-rooms. No mistaking it. They were in the tropics.

"Drink?" he asked.

I was supposed to be in Washington, DC. What am I doing here? her groggy brain kept asking. *Do I want a drink?* It was a no brainer to say, "Yes. Thanks."

At the liquor cabinet he retrieved a tall blue bottle with a large black label. Transfixed, point-down in the wooden floor next to the cabinet, was a machete. Next to the machete stood a basket of green coconuts. He pulled one from the basket, placed it on a wooden block, hoisted the machete, and in one swift motion lopped off the end of the coconut. Then he poured the coconut water into glasses followed by liquid from the blue bottle.

"Cacique Guaro Superior with coconut milk, senorita. National drink of your host country, straight from the cane sugar fields and the palm trees." He handed her a glass.

"Thank you." She looked at the machete on the floor next to his feet. "That was quite a show."

"Men used to light women's cigarettes with a flourish. Instead, we can now lop off coconut heads with machetes. Same kind of show, don't you think?" he said as he sat on the couch.

No, she thought, *I don't. A machete has way more to say about itself than a match.*

And for a while they sat in quiet silence with their national drinks until Amparo, Manuelo's wife, served dinner.

***

It was past midnight when they finished.

Rest day tomorrow.

Work the next.

Laura relaxed against the sofa cushions, watching the fireflies on the patio. Good food and tropical night noises created a background lullaby. *I've almost forgotten why I'm here,* she thought.

The sofa scrunched as John moved.

"Are you awake?" he asked.

"Kinda… maybe… a little bit."

"Will you sleep next to me tonight?"

End of cozy. Her eyes flew open, her throat needed clearing, her breathing got ragged. She choked.

"Just sleep. Nothing else. I promise."

Silence.

Which extended.

John Russell swished the remains of his drink in its glass. "Look, it's been a 10-day haul for me. I'm dead tired, overextended, wound up, and I'm constipated."

"I'm supposed to fix that, too?" snapped Laura before she could stop herself. She giggled, clamped a hand over her mouth which made it worse.

"You failed to mention those special skills in your resume," he chided.

"A girl can't reveal all her secrets." Laura waggled a finger at him. It felt silly. What she needed was time to think, to decide what to do—only there wasn't any.

A few moments passed. *What the hell,* she finally thought. *This part of the job has to start sometime. Might as well be now.*

"Okay, Senor Juan, I'll sleep in your bed, but you get me in my night gown—and that's got pink elephants all over it." *Did I really say that?*

"Really?"

"No, I lie. It's a see-through negligee—but you have to keep your eyes closed."

"I can't do that."

"You can't?"

"No."

"How do you sleep?"

"I don't."

She swatted him on the shoulder. It loosened her up. *A little flirt always helps.* "You lie," she continued.

"Of course, I'm lying—about that, but not about the no-funny business."

Laura shook her head. "This conversation is nuts. I'm going to shower, wrap myself in a robe and find enough courage get into bed next to Mr. No-Funny-Business."

"Great. Only…" he hesitated.

She waited.

"It might get hot in the robe."

***

Laura showered off the day's dust and grime. She brushed her hair, lotioned her skin, and put on a negligee. It gave her time to de-stress. Except her brain was on a free-for-all. *You're just lying down next to the guy-nothing else—no big deal.*

Only it felt like a big deal all the way through the living room and into John's bedroom. In the dimness of the moonlight, her heart beat faster. *Maybe I'll quit right now.*

Moving toward the bed, she bent and pressed a palm to the mattress. John Russell's profile formed dark ridges against the light—wide-browed forehead, straight nose, strong chin. Cheek bones high and defined—skin stretched taut across them, small hollows created underneath. Lips, neither thin nor full, lay together in a soft, straight line as he slept, his breathing deep and easy. From its rhythm, she could tell it might be a while before he woke.

He slept with a light sheet tossed across his groin.

Ok. No clothes… well, she hadn't asked what he would wear. Her own nightclothes sported no pink elephants. It was a knit gown in a shade called "eggplant." It clung gently to her breasts and hips, and then dropped to her ankles. An all-around good solution to an unclear situation.

He stirred.

She stopped breathing.

His eyes opened. "Hi," he said.

"I thought you were sleeping."

"Good surgeons come full alert in an instant. Part of our training." He slid his left arm along the mattress to shoulder height, palm down, and patted the mattress.

"Come, lie down. I don't bite."

"You still scare me."

"Even when I'm asleep?"

"You're not asleep."

"I would be if you'd lie down."

He patted the bed again. "No bed bugs. I promise. They check at least once a year."

She hesitantly stretched out one half of her body on the bed. The rest of her hung on the side.

"Hang gliding doesn't count," he said.

"It does for me."

"You won't sleep."

"I already did."

"No, you napped. That doesn't count."

Without warning, he rolled out of bed. The sheets dropped from his waist. Moonlight spotlighted every naked genital he had. He padded to her side, placed both arms under her knees, lifted them several inches off the bed, replacing them at mattress center. Then he went for her upper back.

"Ok, okay, okay. No need to be pushy," and scooted the rest of herself towards the middle.

"Comfy?"

"It's okay," she grumbled.

He returned to his side of the bed, pulled the night light out of the wall socket, scrunched up his pillow and pretended to fall asleep. A few moments passed.

"You're not sleeping," she said.

"No, but I would if you'd rest you head on my shoulder," Moments passed.

"No funny business?"

"None."

So, she decided. He rolled over, opened his left arm toward her, and she lay in its crook.

They were soon both asleep.

***

Morning sunlight trickled through the window.

Laura lay in an empty bed. A tangle of feelings filled her head like knotted knitting yarn. She capped them all, got up and opened the bedroom door. John sat at a table, coffee in one hand, Wall Street Journal in the other, bath towel fastened at his waist.

"Good morning, Ms. Greenwald. Pool's available if you'd like to dunk before breakfast." He raised the coffee cup, "Or just have some brew." He went on reading; she went on contemplating. Several minutes passed before John spoke again.

"It's a rest day. I'm staying at the villa. But Manuelo can take you out if you want."

"Thanks." She hesitated. "I don't know what I want. I'm pretty wiped-out."

"Welcome to the job," he said, then smiled and put down his paper. "Endurance. Remember Eva's orientation speech on that?"

I don't think I'll ever forget it, she thought.

"Have a seat while you decide."

She sat.

John reached into his briefcase and handed her a glossy, tri-fold brochure with a map on the back. "This describes us—Villa Nueva Esperanza. We're a medical retreat and resort. Research shows people who are relaxed and have had mental preparation for surgery heal faster than if they're tense or frightened. I designed this place with that in mind. Take a look."

Laura reached for the brochure.

"Mrs. Jenks and Melina are already cued up for the masseuse and the theater." He paused a moment, then said, "I come here three or four times a year—just myself—no work. It heals me. I love this place."

His self-revelation, brief as it was, comforted Laura. They'd spent last night sleeping in the same bed and she was ready to talk more. *At least about something other than Endurance lectures and work. Maybe this job will turn out okay.*

Laura looked up to ask a question. Coffee cup at his lips and eyes locked on the newspaper, a self-contained silence had inserted itself between them walling him off from conversation. *Or maybe not.*

The trifold brochure lay open on the table. She read, "Pool, jacuzzi, masseuse, meditation rooms, private cinema, and on-site tour services in a relaxed, tropical setting."

***

In the end Laura stayed at the villa. Her day turned into a long swim, longer massage and lunch, prepared by Manuelo's wife who was a certified chef.

In halting English, Amparo explained Costa Rican custom served the main meal at midday. She prepared a sampler of platos tipicos for them and explained the dishes —sopa negra (black bean soup) surrounded by salted patacones (fried mashed plantains), arroz con gambas grandes (fried rice with large shrimp), fresh vegetable salad and, for dessert, a salad containing the Marnon fruit whose seed is the cashew. To quench thirst, she provided machete chopped pipas (green coconuts) with a straw inserted to sip the juice.

Just as typical as the meal, Laura fell asleep after lunch on the patio in a state of what she would later call simply "blissed out." When she woke, she ordered a massage, floated back to her rooms and opened the bamboo door. John lay reading on the sofa where Laura had sprawled the night before.

"Feel better?" he inquired.

"Intimately better." Her cheeks flushed. "I mean, ultimately better…" She gave up. "Yes, I feel good."

He put his book down and smiled. "Angelica's massages are notorious," he said. "It's hard not to melt into bed when you're done."

131

Laura nodded in slow motion. *He's back to normal talk mode. In and out he goes,* she thought.

John stood. "Would you join me for a quiet siesta together?" He got up.

Laura's brain assessed his bedroom request in slow motion. Her eyes drooped from good food, even better massage and a nap. Her heart beat slow rhythms and blood did not turn her face brilliant red. *Hmmm. No freak out for me. How interesting.*

She felt drunk on the relaxation. For the moment, his request roused not an ounce of anxiety. The unembarrassed part of her wanted to nap again—and this guy had been pretty comfortable the night before. When she said, "Lead the way," it didn't surprise her.

They lay next to each other on the bed, Laura snuggled into his arm and fell asleep.

How odd is this? was her last thought before melting into the lazy afternoon.

Chapter 22

She awoke suddenly, blinking away dream fragments, her body in motion.

His left arm rolled Laura onto her side tight to his chest. Her cheek rested on his pectoral muscle with her stomach flat to his. Auburn hair tangled around his bicep.

"What..."

"Shhh." He gently pulled her head back to his chest, wrapped arms around her, and began to knead the knotted muscles on her neck. First one hand, then another. Squeeze, stop and release. Squeeze, stop and release. Shivers of tingling energy released down her spine.

Like a curling cat, she arched into his fingers.

He tightened. She arched. He released and she let go. She arched, he released, she let go and he tightened. It pulsed. It rang in her ears. Wet and moist and drunk with the tropics.

Both hands slid down her back, pressing places that flashed sparks down her spine. Her back rippled into his stomach and he drew her even closer. A pulsing erection pressed tightly upwards to her belly against her panties, sticky and oozing wetness at her vulva. His hand slipped under her panty band and cupped the fullness of the soft, rounded flesh beneath. Her buttocks moved back to press into his hands. In a movement of unutterable skill, he rose to his knees, snaked both thumbs around the band of the panties and pulled them down past her knees as she arched towards him. When he resettled on his knees and elbows, his penis rested between the moistness of her legs and vulva.

In a sudden movement, he slid a hand under one of her buttocks and squeezed—rough, hard, punishing. She gasped. Her head arched back and pelvis thrust forward from the hurt, plunging into his hardened penis. At the same time his teeth found the flesh under her neck and bit—she cried out. But he calmed her with-tongue strokes ending at her ear and then encircling the lobe.

His breathing turned shorter, faster now both keeping time with the other. He thrust into her, deep and hard—claiming his possession, staking control. She surrendered to the pure sensuality, mind disengaged, pleasure chills running down her back, sliding to her pubis, tugging at vaginal walls, filling them with moisture.

Then he pulled out.

And pulled away.

So unexpected was it, she cried out.

On all fours he bent over her. With hands and forearms, he caressed her hair, her face, her lips. "Shhh," he whispered. "I'm not leaving."

He leaned back, bent at the knees, then pulled her legs over his shoulders. The fullness of her womanhood lay open to his mouth. He spread her legs wider, bent his head and found her nub. Sucking and licking and tongue thrusting into the wetness of her, over and over, and sucking more until her orgasm burst forth in yelps and groans. As she finished, he flipped her over, pulled her buttocks onto his rigid cock and entered her from behind. His fullness was insistent, demanding, constant as he drew her further onto himself. Sweating and panting and breathing—and on, and deeper—and on.

He pulled out, flipped her to her back and thrust into her from above, acutely aware of the empty seconds his cock had been outside her warmth. Her arms enfolded his torso, legs encircled his pelvis. Breathing increased, sweat slipped between their bellies while the hypnotic rhythm of heartbeat took over.

The orgasm burst through both of them together.

And burst again.

Silence.

Then laughter.

Peals of laughter from both of them.

He flopped onto his side next to her. "Sorry, I can't keep myself up."

More laughter.

Where did that come from? she wondered in a foggy blur of muddled thoughts. *I don't think I really want to know.*

They breathed. They lay still. They drifted along with the evening breezes.

Some while later, Laura leaned up on an elbow, head propped in her hand and asked, "What was *that*?"

"You don't know?" he replied.

"Of course, I *know*, but… actually—I don't. It was—intense."

"Agreed." He was lying down with hands under his head on the pillow.

"You set this up," she said.

"I did not."

"You plied me with massage and special food."

"No comment," he responded.

"That's it?" she asked. *I was so afraid of the sex. Now I'm multi-orgasmic? What's going on?*

"It happens," he said, and slipped out of bed.

It happens? That's all he has to say? She could feel herself getting annoyed again.

But John returned with two pina coladas in coconut shells. "Let's sit on the verandah and sip coconut. It's going to be quite a while before we'll be this relaxed again."

They slept together side by side that night, enfolded in Costa Rica's lazy humidity. John had guaranteed the next day would be horrendously busy.

***

"I'm not hungry," she protested at 5:30 a.m.

"Eat," he commanded. "I don't need a nurse who drops in the afternoon because there's no time for lunch." He was all business—No hint of yesterday's orgasms ever having taken place.

Back to work, she thought. John's abrupt, demanding attitude was like burning up in the local volcano. She did not know that it would be thirteen hours later, every single one of them laden with exhaustion, before the work day would end.

Hospital Hotel la Catolica, a top-notch facility, cranked out tests results, procedures, machines, lab reports, diagnoses, reviews, doctors, nurses, carts, gurneys, charts, monitoring devices and needles with such efficiency she thought the responses were fake. There was no time to stop for food. Snacks grabbed between consults proved inadequate.

Mrs. Jenks had stopped polite smiles by 3:00 p.m. and Laura was not far behind. It was John Russell's Olympian endurance that did not flag. At 6:00 p.m. he concluded their day, marched everyone into the white limousine and returned all of them to Nueva Esperanza. No word was spoken on the return trip. He sat face forward, absented into thought, personhood withdrawn until they arrived at the villa.

"We'll all meet here tomorrow morning at 8:00," he announced. Enjoy your evening." He opened his door and walked away. Manuelo helped Mrs. Jenks. Out of the car. Laura was left seated on her own.

What the hell, she thought.

John looked back, called, "Laura, walk with me." She trudged after him towards the cottage, annoyance and exhaustion close companions. He closed the door, turned and said, "Strip off your clothes."

She froze.

"Laura, this is part of the job."

She gaped at him. The pounding in her temples increased to thunder. "I thought…"

"Consensual? It is. I'm asking you to drop your clothes right now." He waited. "You ready to walk out? Or are you going to consent?"

A numb awareness trickled from her ears to her brain. *Walk out? Stay?* She was so tired it was hard to think. There'd been times she had sex when her partner wanted it but she wasn't so interested. *We all do that sometimes if we care about a relationship,* she thought.

Or a job, sniped her inner voice.

"Right here in the foyer," John instructed.

She untied scrub pants in slow motion. The pants fell in two wrinkled stacks at her ankles.

"Step out of them." He waited.

She did so.

"Now the underpants."

These too landed in a bunch at her ankles. He stepped close, put the index and middle fingers of his right hand into his mouth, then pushed them down through her pubic hair and into her vagina and began slow rotations. His left hand tight on her buttock, John bent to encompass her mouth.

She whipped her head to one side in wild refusal, rebuffing the kiss. *He won't have my face. That I won't let him touch.* Instead he bit at her neck, his breathing harder, faster. She closed her eyes and refused to release into him, even as his strokes sparked desire and response in her body.

I'm deciding this—I can walk away. I said okay. We already had sex. I'm just doing it again.

He withdrew his hand from her vagina, pulled at his own pants, lifted her onto his penis and backed them to the wall. He fucked her over and over again—hard driving thrusts that demanded strength from legs and arms and crotch—and again. Until his orgasm burst into her like a wild wind.

When he was done, he put her down, walked away to his bedroom and closed the door behind.

Laura stood there, confused, half naked, her body tingling all over from John Russell's handling. *If you'd let yourself go,* she said to herself, *you'd have had an orgasm, too.*

She couldn't get a handle on things. *Was I raped—or did I just have pushy sex?*

She pulled up her pants and walked to her room. *What the hell is going on around here?*

Chapter 23

Manuelo maneuvered them through Costa Rica's morning traffic—an hour and fifteen minutes to the airport. The last three days blurred into one for Laura. Hospital corridors, surgery rooms, radiation machinery, plastic gloves, sexual encounters, consults, pituitary tumors, smiles, frowns, tears, and exhaustion.

Mrs. Jenks' brain lesion had been found and excised with gamma knife radiosurgery. When Laura had asked questions, his curt responses were always, "Look it up. It's medical tourism worth millions here. We're part of it."

Meals turned tasteless as the unrelenting work schedule continued with bodies too tired to care. Each day had held the unpredictable, each action the possibility of failure.

She bent her head and drew in the silence of the car. Mrs. Jenks and daughter were staying eight more days. Dr. Russell would return in two; Laura received a bonus, her airline ticket and three days to recoup at home.

"Not your easy introduction to work," John admitted. "Take a break."

So, she'd decided to go to what felt most like home—back to Somerville.

***

Sam met her at the Davis Square subway stop with flowers and a big hug. He held her at arm's length in the gloom of the underground lights, assessed her tired eyes and said. "Whoa, babes. Looks like you could use a drink. Let's get you home."

And they'd gone together into the comfortable familiarity of her previous life.

That night Laura awoke in a cold sweat. Drops of perspiration plugged her ear canal. She lay naked next to Sam, his breathing a steady rhythm of untroubled conscience. The sheets, crispy before their lovemaking, now lay rumpled between them.

Twenty-four hours ago, I was packing my bags in Costa Rica. The rumbling thoughts banishing sleep.

"We need to review your performance before you go home," John Russell had said. He hadn't pushed or asked for sex. Her relief was palpable. He didn't seem to notice. An early dinner was set on the patio.

"You've done a good job, Laura." He sat in the padded bamboo chair, sounds from the night jungle in the background.

She smiled, a thin and tired line.

"With both parts of the job."

A thinner, tighter line appeared on her face.

"You'll find your balance. When you get there, you'll know. It will be, 'Not tonight, John,' or even, 'John, I need a fuck right now.'"

She glared at him.

"Sex and success get all tangled up. It makes people stupid. You and I completed a hard surgery really well. You got exhausted—but I got pumped up."

"What on earth are you talking about?" Irritable and uncomprehending, Laura started to get up.

"Sit down!" he ordered. "I'm not finished yet."

She sat down. Both dinners remained untouched.

"People pumped with adrenaline get stupid. Been there, done that, don't want it anymore. I can guarantee when you finally get pumped up, you'll be climbing all over me."

She gaped at him

"I don't see…"

"You haven't experienced it yet," he interrupted. "So, no, you don't see." He leaned back in his chair. "You're getting paid to protect me," he finished.

"To *protect* you? *You?*" She stared at him. Shock and outrage flashed across her face. "I don't believe this." She shook her head.

John produced a tired smile. "I know. Not yet, anyway."

She stood and pushed back her chair. "I've got to finish packing. I'm not hungry." He didn't protest. When she rose the next morning for her flight, Dr. Russell was nowhere to be seen.

***

Three days of Sam and dinners, picnics, Duck Tours, Boston Harbor Tours and lovemaking dug a deep hole for Laura to hide in and forget.

She laughed hard and played harder, hoping her fears and confusion would be ground into dust and buried. She was having sex with two men at once and one of them was her boss. She had a crazy job and a contract that bound her forever. *What is happening to me?*

She clung to Sam at night with a ferocious desire to experience only him. He laughed, saying if this were the result of her new job he totally approved.

And then, like all things in life, the three days came to an end.

***

Monday morning. Laura waited in the DC airport for her luggage to offload from the Boston flight. She planned to stop at her apartment before work even if it meant arriving late.

"Nobody's gonna care except me," she said and dialed Eva Jormand to let her know.

"Hi, Ev…"

"Boy, am I glad you called in. Emergency surgery—10:30 am—at the hospital. Get your butt over there. It'll be touch and go. Read the email."

She shook her head. *This whole adrenaline endurance thing is for the birds. What I need is sleep.*

141

The emails laid it out in black and white. A Supreme Court Justice's granddaughter rode her boyfriend's motorcycle without helmet or license. Along with several gin and tonics under her belt and a humungous machine, she drove around the supermarket parking lot, crashed into a line of shopping carts, upended the bike, struck her head on the railing, deflated an eyeball, concussed her brain, and broke both arms. Although stabilized, Dr. Russell's diagnosis spoke of intracranial pressure release, ocular inflation and orthopedic surgery. Keeping this out of the political spotlight was going to be a nightmare for someone.

The Town Car arrived ten minutes later to retrieve her from the DC airport.

"Good morning, Ms. Laura." Daniel smiled his words into the rearview mirror. "Going to be a busy morning for you?" inquired the chauffeur as he handed her a brown paper bag.

"I think so, Daniel. What's this?"

The bag crinkled open. Two fresh baguettes smothered with brie and sundried tomatoes stared back at her. Laura stuffed one in her purse and began on the other. So far, her on-the-job food experience was 'not much of it and way too late.' The command 'Eat!' rang in her ears. This time she did not quibble.

***

She paid the Uber driver, pulled out her housekeys and trudged up the front steps dragging her luggage behind. It was 9 p.m. The emergency surgery had spread across an entire day, surgeons from multiple specialties each taking a turn. Laura's only focus now was to eat and go to sleep.

Stumbling into her apartment, she thrust her suitcase in a corner, dropped her purse on the counter and plugged in her phone. Only then did she notice the numbers on her cell. Four messages from Sam. She hadn't checked her phone once during the day.

Oh, God. Had it been just last night? Sam lived in a universe nowhere near the planet she walked on.

She couldn't talk. She could barely walk. "Sorry," she texted, "just home now. Will call tomorrow. Promise," then punched 'send.'

She grabbed a beer from the fridge, ordered Thai takeout, then flopped on the couch, combing fingers through her hair.

I'm back in the country 12 hours and can barely stand up. How am I ever going to manage two years of this?

Chapter 24

The phone jolted Laura awake. Groggy from sleep, her hand groped towards the noise.

"Laura, Eva here. This is a heads-up. You're scheduled for a physical today. We need to catch you up on our regular routines. Meet me at the hospital 7:00 am sharp."

"Oh." she said. *Is there anything called' private time' in this contract?* The phone clicked. Laura moaned and got up.

***

Eva waited near the security guard in the hospital foyer.

"Don't you ever sleep?" she asked Eva.

"We all have our jobs."

That was totally unhelpful.

They ended up at an office with large windows and a central conference table. An appointment book lay on the table.

"This room is our office on hospital days," she said. "There's an exam room there." She pointed to a door. "That's where you'll have your physical today—which," she paused, "will include a gyneco-logical exam."

"I just had one," Laura protested. "I sent you the report."

"John likes to re-check things—especially when you've been outside the US and sexually active—even if it's with John."

Laura felt her neck flush with embarrassment. "How did you know that?"

"He told me."

Laura looked down. Her blush now included earlobes and fore-head.

"No need for embarrassment, Laura," she said, her tone tinged with empathy. "It's part of the contract."

Where have I heard that before?

Eva leaned forward. "Only a few of us know the full details of your contract. We've all signed confidentiality clauses. We check for sexuality transmitted diseases, make sure your birth control is in place, and do a pregnancy test. Better to have redundancy than slipups."

"I don't..."

Eva interrupted—not her typical behavior. "I'm sorry. Not really an option. John is financially generous. It helps to remember that in circumstances like this."

Humiliated and angry, Laura didn't feel like remembering, but stepped toward the examination room too overloaded to resist.

Thoughts of the huge salary floated through her mind. *Damn the $700,000. Has it bought this part of my life, too?* She opened the door and stepped into the exam room. *I'll have to figure that out—only not right now.*

With the way things were going, Laura wondered how long it might take before she figured anything out.

***

The work day finished as it began—in the hospital office with Eva. Laura had been informed of an afterwork cocktail networking party hosted by the American Neurological Association. John required attendance for at least half an hour. Everyone's homework was to bring him names of three of the neurosurgeons and what their current projects were.

Laura cocked her head to one side. "What in heaven's name for?"

"It's typical John," said Eva. "Keeps him up to date on who's doing what. Then, if he needs help with any projects, he's got a ready-made list."

I'll be home by 7:30, calculated Laura. *Not too bad.*

"Last minute gatherings are part of the deal," Eva explained. She opened an eighteen-inch closet door in the corner. "One of these dresses should fit you well enough."

Several outfits hung with matching accessories. "You'll need to keep some of your own dresses here, but, for now..." Eva looked down. "Your shoes..." A pause. "Oh, well, no one'll be looking at your feet. Rooftop view's too nice."

The dress fit and when Eva unpinned Laura's auburn hair, the aqua and red-sand patterns of the fabric danced in the lamplight.

"Okay, madam, you're good to go."

***

The DNV Building thrust its head ten stories into the night air. Rays of the setting sun hit the DC skyline and melted into the gold ribbon of the Potomac River. High top tables replaced pool chairs in a space where it was possible to rub shoulders but still find privacy. Gas-fired heat towers kept the crisp air pleasant.

Laura stood and watched the crowd relaxing to stand and stare, from the day's intensity.

Drink first; then the name game. She wandered to the bar and ordered a Chivas Regal. The smooth scotch blend always won her vote over single malts. She had just taken it from the bartender, when a voice spoke over her shoulder.

"I see we have something in common."

She swiveled. A tall, dark-haired man stood behind her. His suit jacket fresh, white shirt rumpled, tie loosened. She raised her eyebrows in response. He held out his hand.

"Dr. Stephanopoulos. And you?"

"Nurse Greenwald."

He laughed. "Point taken. Stephanopoulos, Apollo Stephanopoulos."

Laura burst out laughing. "Apollo—hard act to follow. No wonder you don't lead with that name." Still laughing she added her own.

"Well, most people call me Arlo."

So, Arlo it was for the first half hour. Until Laura glanced at her watch. "Oh shit," she blurted.

"And the matter is…?" he inquired, brows raised.

"I've got to bring three names to work tomorrow orI might as well not show up."

"Really?"

Arlo bowed and gestured with an arm. "As your Greek knight in shining armor, I inform you that my job is 'fixer-of-problems.' Come, distressed princess, and I'll introduce you to my fellow knights. Do you get extra credit collecting five names instead of three?"

"I'll let you know."

He brought her to a high-top table with five chairs, each one occupied by a neurologist. Arlo brought two more chairs; names were taken, more drinks ordered, Laura lost herself in the bantering conversations.

It was 10:30 when drinks and dinner-style hors d'oeuvres closed down, 11:00 when she stepped out of the cab at her apartment. She'd lost track of time, accidently left her phone in the cab, and by the time she retrieved it, she realized she'd forgotten to call Sam.

"Shit," she said, "shit, shit, shit."

***

Sam's dead silence said it all. Hurt. Angry.

"Sam, I'm sorry. The day—it just kept walloping me—I had to…" but he wasn't listening. Her new job loomed like a glacier in the background.

She'd make a mistake. She knew it. He knew it.

"Hey, don't stress. We'll talk tonight. No big deal."

That had been at 7:00 the next morning. Then came five hours of watching Dr. Russell provide cutting edge diagnoses in his Virginia offices with ten patients, thirty minutes per patient, before lunch. The depth and detail of the dialogue allowed patient and healer to alternately lead, negotiate, question and resolve. No session ran over; no session ran under, and no tension rose between participants.

When noon break came, Laura could barely keep her eyes open.

"Okay, how does he do it?" Laura demanded when she saw Eva at noon break.

"Do what?" asked Eva.

"Ten patients in five hours and everybody leaves happy." Laura stopped. "Well, maybe not happy, but—satisfied."

"I'm sorry," smiled Eva, "It's my fault.

Laura gaped at her. "What?"

"It's your orientation—or the lack thereof. Let's have lunch. I'll explain."

***

Linen draped tables overlooked the winter gardens. They filled plates and looked for a table where they have privacy. Eva spread a napkin on her lap and took a sip of water before she began.

"John's expertise is the medical field. His patients' expertise is their own bodies. That's his philosophy. So, first he has his patients attend sessions with nurse educators. Depending on how complicated things are, they can have up to three visits before meeting with the Big Doc. No one goes in cold turkey."

"They don't get annoyed at all that?"

Eva sat back and thought. "Well, let's see. During that time, tests get run and questions get answered. So, most of them feel they're prepping for the Big Visit. That's how his schedule can run without a hitch. Plus, if they choose, they can get wined and dined."

"Wined and dined?"

Eva nodded towards the French doors behind them. "There's a lunch option when you book appointments. Client dining area right next door."

Laura turned around and saw a second dining area she'd not even noticed.

"Patients can choose to plan a day on the town with friends or family—around their appointment, of course. We contract with tour guides who charge reduced rates. Fancy dining room, great food, personal tours of DC. What's not to like?"

In Costa Rica, John practically chanted his pitch about relaxing patients before surgery. *They feel better and heal faster.* She'd heard it over and over again.

And now, his philosophy of life was in every bite of lunch she ate.

***

Later in the afternoon, Laura noticed the text from Apollo Stephanopoulos. "Come for a drink after work."

She replied, "Can't. Exhausted."

He texted back, "Tomorrow?"

A long pause…a long thought…then, "Ok."

"Great."

A third man in my life? she thought. *What am I doing?*

***

That night, Laura called Sam as soon as her apartment door closed.

No response.

Good, she thought, *I really didn't want to talk tonight.* She felt guilty. Her unanswered call said, "I didn't forget you." It was her way of 'proving' she had remembered. Tests like that were never a good sign.

Laura dropped her purse on the counter, poured a half glass of wine, sat on the sofa, deposited her feet on the coffee table, sipped wine and closed her eyes to savor its taste.

This was her evening routine. Some people ran, swam, walked; some went bar hopping. She went to couch and wine—always fine wine—subtle flavors, soft aromas and fluid dynamics drawing her in.

Wine tasting was a body-mind sport.

Four ounces in a crystal glass.

Several nights to enjoy a bottle.

Those same nights to identify the markers of this wine.

How pleasant her body-mind was beginning to feel.

The phone rang at 7:10 p.m.

"Hi, Laura. How are you?" Sam's voice scattered the goodness of body-mind and wine.

A glass of wine will get me through this, she thought. "Meditating—so I'm..."

"Well, let me join you," he interrupted. She heard him pull a beer from the fridge.

"It's not quite like that..."

"Yeah, yeah," he interrupted. "Explain all you want. A drink is a drink." And she laughed, because, in fact, it was true.

They skirted the difficult issues, made nice with the rest. A conversation to soothe, not agitate. When it was over. Sam asked, "Talk to you tomorrow?"

Tomorrow was Friday. Tomorrow? It was drink-after-work-day with someone who was not Sam. She paused.

"Uh, Sam, I just, it's—well, I worry I don't know what they'll ask me to do at the last minute—like yesterday. I don't quite have a handle on it yet..."

A pause. Silence. Awkward was back again.

"Uh, Okay."

"What about Saturday morning? That's good." She said it in bright, sparkle tones so maybe he wouldn't focus on her flat-out 'no' of her Friday response.

"Sure... ok. Give me a buzz when you get up."

"Will do."

Click.

***

It didn't work out at all according to plan.

Friday morning, she labeled as being Mostly Manageable. Three clients observed, two hours of case review, one hour-long term planning with Eva and Dr. Russell. Five neurologist names handed over with no reward for extra diligence. She was ready for lunch.

Quail eggs stuffed in grilled red peppers over rice served with cold tomato bisque—if desired.

Unlike most other days she'd dined at the clinic, all fifteen staff members crowded the buffet. She looked for Eva, trying to keep her irritation in check. Eva stood in line at the soup tureen.

"Okay, what did you forget to tell me?" she asked.

Eva looked stricken. "Oh, your orientation…"

"Right, Eva, I know. Just tell me what's happening I don't know about."

"It's massage Friday. You went to one already—only today we quit at 2:00. I forgot to tell you."

"I see," she said, annoyance dissipating. She decided for understated enjoyment. "Tough to take, but—I'll manage."

***

By the time 5:00 o'clock rolled around, Laura had been stretched, patted, massaged, scraped, bathed, scented, rubbed, and manicured. At six o'clock she was meeting Arlo. The taxi deposited her at Fiola di Fabio, thoroughly mellowed and ready to wait. She took a seat at the back, ordered lemonade and watched the Friday night Washington, DC crowd.

When Arlo walked in the door, every head in his path turned to watch, even the men—tall, poised, dark hair, dark eyes and a big chest of muscle that stretched the second-to-the-top button of a white shirt. His collar was open and jacket slung over his left shoulder.

A model's stance, she thought to herself.

"I was," he said.

"You were what?"

"A model."

151

She stared at him. "How did you know what I was thinking?"

"I've seen the look before."

"What look?"

"The look on your face just a minute ago."

She blushed. "I didn't know I was that obvious."

"You're not, but the look is." He smiled and sat next to her on the bar stool. "It paid my way through medical school. A few risqué pictures here and there, but mostly straight forward—got to Esquire front cover one time. Once you're trained, it never quite goes away." He smiled again. "Let's sit down."

He took her hand and shouldered his way to a table by the window.

"What luck," Laura exclaimed, "A prime time table with a view."

"No luck about it—reserved by my very own hand."

A waiter appeared bubbling with pleasantries. "Signore, Dr. Appolino, a great pleasure for us that you have come again. Please, please, signorina," he said, and pulled out her chair.

She sat.

And smiled.

"May I suggest..." said the waiter, who proceeded to arrange the meal choices, bring the perfect bottle of wine, and somehow create a bubble of privacy for them in the middle of the Friday night crowd.

Arlo told her about himself. "Dad's electrical company in Greece got demolished during political rioting. His cousin sponsored him for emigration to the States a few years later, so we all came over. The only job he could get that would pay enough to support seven kids was in the Boston dockyards. I was the sixth son and nobody else even thought beyond high school."

"So, how did you get from the dockyards to fancy Friday night dinners?"

"Ah." He looked down, his voice carrying pain.

"I'm sorry. I didn't mean…" Laura began.

"No, it's okay." He shook his head. "It happened a long time ago."

Laura noticed his next sip of wine was more like a gulping swallow.

"I was six when it happened. My oldest brother smashed his back on the docks. It put him in a wheelchair. When I was ten, he shot himself in the head. I was the only one at home when it happened. Made me want to fix the world."

"I'm so sorry," she said.

He raised his glass and drank again. "Not a problem any more. It got me here—fixing the world."

They both laughed just as the waiter appeared with appetizers.

Her heart sank. "I'll probably have to doggie bag half my meal," Laura told Arlo. "Big lunch at work today."

"One of John's Friday specials?"

She stared. "How did you know?"

"I trained with him."

Her eyebrows went up. "Oh…I didn't realize." Her heart skipped several panicky beats. *Does he know about John's special assistants—about what I do? Has that leaked out?*

"Anything wrong with that?" he asked.

"Uh…no. Of course not." Laura unfolded her napkin and put it on her lap. It gave her time to consider a calm response. "I suppose I shouldn't be surprised—but, well… it feels like in DC everybody knows everybody."

Arlo thought for a moment. "That may say more about neurology as a profession and less about the number of people living in DC." He paused. "How many neurologists do you think practice in the U.S.?"

"Not a clue."

"In total we're a group of about 16,000." He took out his cell phone and pulled up the calculator. "Now divide that by 50 states and DC—that'll be 51 into 16,000." He did the calculations. "So, you've got about 353 per state, but of course, they're not evenly divided…"

Laura put up her hand. "Ok. Ok. You win," she laughed. "It's the profession."

Over the course of the evening, different dishes appeared one at a time—seared foie gras, white asparagus baked with Parmigiano, Chesapeake soft shelled crab tempura, cheese and fruits, gelato, and coffee. Two bottles of wine accompanied—one white, one red.

Somewhere, halfway through the courses, Laura asked, "You never married? No kids?" *I can't believe I'm asking.*

He smiled, looked pensive, then shook his head. "Almost. We…" He stopped. "There was a woman. I thought I loved her. We got pregnant. She had an abortion without telling me. It ended our relationship." Arlo shrugged. "It made me realized how much I wanted a family—how sacred life is—especially if you've created it."

"I'm so sorry—I didn't mean to intru…"

"It's a perfectly normal question," he said. "So, what about you?"

"Me?" *What about me?* "Oh, I've been in pursuit of career…" she deflected, avoiding painful stories and moving on to others.

At midnight, unrequested, the waiter came with the check. "Many apologies, signore," he said with a small bow. "It is that we close just at midnight."

Laura glanced around. She and Arlo were alone in the dining room. *Six hours over dinner? No wonder I ate the whole meal.*

Fiolo closed its doors behind them with polite smiles and "please-come-backs." When the doors locked, Arlo stopped on the sidewalk. He put his hands on Laura's shoulders and turned her to face him. "I'm at the Newseum Residences just around the corner. Would you come for a nightcap?"

Her thoughts began to race. *Do evenings with guys always have to end with sex? Why can't we just have…*

"Stop," interrupted Arlo. "What you're thinking is all over your face." He tipped her chin up and looked directly at her. "It's just hard to end a lovely evening in the street. I hoped you felt the same way."

She scanned his face, his eyes, his mouth. *This is what it's all about—why I changed jobs—to be where it's happening—to take some risks. Arlo's been wonderful.*

She decided for the nightcap. They talked for hours in his living room and fell asleep on the couch until noon. Their goodbye consisted of a midday coffee at nearby Union Station. He hailed a taxi to take her home. It was 2:30 p.m. by the time she arrived.

When she called, Sam didn't want to hear her excuses. When they hung up, the conversation with Laura had with herself was even worse.

I'm having sex with my boss. I'm having sex with Sam. I've met a new guy I really like. What am I doing?

She locked her front door, changed clothes and with a vengeance began to kick front, kick back, side, side, side.

Chapter 26

Monday morning, Eva stood by the Keurig machine in the hospital office making herself coffee. A platter of breakfast breads was on the credenza. It stretched next to the fruit bowl resting near the yogurt cups that bumped up against the napkins, spoons, and forks.

"Grab some breakfast, Laura. We get special catering from Whole Foods the days we're here."

"I didn't know that." *What else am I not prepared for?* she wondered. The enigmatic morning text on Laura's cell phone had been: *7:00 a.m. meeting, hospital conference room."*

Eva picked up an overstuffed leather satchel, hauled it to table, pulled out files, forms, pens and sat bent over sifting and picking.

"Sit," she said.

Laura sat.

Eva placed a stack of forms in front of Laura.

"So—we're going to backtrack." Eva smiled.

"Backtrack?"

"Yes, ma'am. That 'deer-in-the-headlights' look you keep having reminds me at the wrong times we haven't finished your orientation. The contract says, 'Orient during first three days.' I confessed to John we hadn't. He bit my head off." She bent over towards Laura. "See, I'm missing a part of my ear." Eva smiled, but it only made Laura nervous.

"You're excused from morning hospital rounds. Let's get started."

***

Two hours later Laura had been lectured to, re-lectured to, signed papers, double signed them, scratched out old dates, put in new ones, read out loud a page labeled 'airport codes' or maybe 'emergency evacuation procedures' or possibly 'carrying passports' or…she couldn't remember what at the moment. The stack of papers eventually shifted from Laura back to Eva.

"Any questions?"

Laura shook her head. The session had been brain torture.

"Good," said Eva, pulling out a new file with *Gynecology* stamped in big, black letters on the cover. "Here's how it goes—we review your birth control and vaginal health and most likely take it over."

"Eva, I just had an exam and I don't…

Eva's hand rose like a road block. "Let's see what you've got first. I'm sure it's fine—but, we double check everything." She pushed more papers towards Laura. "And you sign off here. We missed a beat because of the Costa Rica deal. Ani was too busy so John decided you could fill in. Thought it would be good training."

A pause.

"Was it?" asked Eva.

"Was it what?" asked Laura, cocking her head, totally confused.

"Good training," said Eva.

Laura forced her face to blank stare mode. *Is there no privacy here? Whether or not I 'get it on' with John is none of her damn business.* That was how she felt, but she was beginning to realize in this organization her idea of private vs business was way off. *And what the hell does* vaginal health *mean?*

Seconds passed before her response broke the silence. "Yes, I have to say it was…effective."

An enigmatic smile crossed Eva's face. "Good." She started to rise. "We've got fifteen minutes to get you checked in for the gyneco…"

"Not just yet." Laura's words sliced through the air.

Startled, Eva froze.

"I don't understand what is considered personal information around here and what isn't," said Laura. "What I do with John is private. And personal. Only it seems he reports everything back to the whole world. I feel like a dissected rat."

Eva took a moment to sit. She steepled her hands together on the table. "In our work, anything you do with John is considered business. Surgeries, dinners, meetings, travel, bedroom, anything. *He* is the business. He reports to me anything he considers necessary. What you do when you are not together, we consider personal—mostly."

"*Mostly?*"

Eva's enigmatic smile appeared again. "Well, we do have to check for vaginal health iss…"

"What the hell do you mean by *vaginal health* issues?" interrupted Laura midsentence.

"Sexually transmitted diseases pretty much. We hope you use condoms outside, but we can't be there to supervise. I'm sure you…"

Laura stood. She'd had enough of Eva for the moment. *I've had enough of this job, too.*

You can quit. The words flashed through her mind.

Not ready for that option yet, she thought and realized she was having an argument with herself. Part of her could see Eva's point. Another part felt offended and invaded. She couldn't make up her mind one way or the other in the fifteen minutes before the appointment.

Oh, what the hell. Confused decisions make for confused outcomes. Her father always harped on that. She decided, at the moment, to follow the 'program.'

Two weeks and four days—that's how long she'd been at work and she didn't see an end to confusion anywhere on the horizon. John Russell told her the learning curve would be steep. She never thought it would be straight up.

***

Dr. Rashmi Sanjana had been thorough, direct, warm, and funny. But there was no mistaking who was in charge. He took blood work and swabs, replaced Laura's IUD, and inserted an intrauterine device of his preference.

"My patients tell me this one is most comfortable. Plus, it has a 99% efficacy rate and lasts for a number of years—according to research," said Dr. Sanjana. "However, I'll replace this one next year," he added.

"Why would you do that?"

He shrugged and said, "Dr. Russell wants it that way. He said your job affects the amount of work he can do, especially when he's traveling. A pregnancy would affect everything, so, he goes for super-prevention."

"Oh…"

The doctor shifted position. "The IUD can get a little uncomfortable today. Should settle by tonight." A business card slipped across the table. "My contact numbers are here if you need me."

He stood up. "That's it for today, Ms. Greenwald. A pleasure to meet you." He closed the door behind him with a gentle click that barely disturbed the silence.

A big part of Laura felt nauseous and violated. Then there was the other part of her—the part that answered the ad, moved to DC, said yes to John, stayed overnight with Arlo. The part that had brought her here. *What's the big deal about getting a new IUD and blood tests? People do it all the time. And they get fucked by their bosses for way less.*

She held her hands over her ears as if she could shut out the battle inside herself.

***

Late Friday afternoon of the same week, Eva handed Laura a list—her life's schedule for the next month summed up in little bullet points. She'd given a lot already—body exams, blood tests, eye tests, urine tests, skin test, shots, photos, measurements, inoculations. Her whole overstressed life summed up with little dots was the last straw.

- 12 hospital days
- 12 clinic days
- 15 surgery assists
- 2 massage Fridays with Team
- 6 dinner evenings with high profile clients
- 1 weekend retreat—Shenandoah (*What the hell is that?*)

Her headache burst—swift and devastating. Through a nauseous haze, Laura heard Eva call for the Town Car and she was sent home.

***

The first week of her bullet list training Laura found pain in muscles she never knew she had. With each new ache her stamina grudgingly increased. Her personal life shriveled to the width of a grass blade—one night hanging up on Sam's phone call; another throwing her cell phone across the living room in frustration, a third falling into bed before 8:30.

On Day One of that week, she had entered what looked like an astronaut's command center. A black rectangular metal table at the center, wires, straps, knobs, lights, cameras, computer displays, overhanging metal arms. Her task was to stay glued behind the lead surgical nurse and help when directed. "You'll get a Completion Certificate from the Institute when you're done training," Eva explained.

Laura blinked. "Institute? What institute?"

Eva ignored the question. "Let's get you prepped for surgery," she said. Later she offered three sentences in explanation. "Too many neurologists wanted post doc training with John. To manage the demand, he started the Neuroscience Training Center six years ago. Ani's going to head it up once she finishes her studies."

"Listen up, everybody!" A strident voice interrupted further talk.

The surgical day had begun.

***

The patient with chart #1065 was a 37-year-old married architect, with children who had a tumor growing near his optic nerve. When he could no longer see numbers on the computer, he'd consulted a doctor.

Why did you leave it so long?

Well, the headache pills kept working; there were the kids; family, work, wife, house, car—who had time to breathe?

And here he was anesthetized, terrified, and dependent on strangers to give him back his life.

John Russell strode into the operating arena, already talking. "Let's do the run down. Patient name, birthdate and procedure."

He repeated the mandated pre-surgery call, now a national requirement after so many lawsuits from botched operations; then thrust his hands into gloves being held open for him and began.

The surgery lasted three hours. It left Laura exhausted while Dr. Impressive headed off to another operating room.

"Coming, Greenwald? You're on observation for this one," said the lead nurse.

"How does he do it?" asked Laura. "He's does four in a day and I'm ready for bed after one."

"You build up. By the end of a month you'll be a pro." The nurse smiled and headed to the next operating room.

Laura crossed her eyes.

***

Toward the end of Week One Laura stopped arguing with herself.

I need to know.

What in heaven's name for? You'll make a mess of it! Leave it alone.

I can't keep thinking about who's been...

You could if you... She never finished because the target of her mental argument walked right past heading to the cafeteria. Without thinking, Laura said, "Eva, may I ask a personal question?"

Eva stopped. "About...?"

The lunchtime crowd behind them began piling up. Laura maneuvered them to the wall determined resolve her conflict one way or another.

"Were you ever, well, I mean... did you ever have—my position?"

Eva laughed. "Me? No. I'm not a nurse. I don't qualify."

"Then how did you end up with John—doing all this?" She shrugged her shoulders. "I mean, your job is, well, unusual."

Eva smiled. "Let's walk and talk. I'm hungry." They started down the corridor.

"I met John at a how-to-build-your-business conference. I did high end marketing with a firm in San Francisco. He was at Mass General and married. I liked his approach and he needed mine. Couple of years later he called. We brainstormed and here we are, minus wife. I like it—mostly."

Laura took a deep breath. "Did you ever—uh—sleep with him or anything?"

Eva stopped and looked hard at Laura.

"Me? No. Not even 'anything.' John is very specific and very careful. One woman only. No other entanglements. 'My marriage debacle taught me lessons I'll never forget,' is his mantra. He doesn't stray, doesn't sleep around, and never gets into trouble."

Laura looked down. She wanted to stop but needed to calm her fears. "Who else knows about my position?"

Eva started to cross her arms but instead readjusted the shoulder strap of her purse. "Laura, I've said this before. Only a few people know the details of your contract. The lawyers and myself." A pause ensued. "Anything else?"

"No. That's it. Thanks." She began to turn away but Eva put out a restraining hand.

"You still interested in lunch?" she asked.

Laura had lost her appetite somewhere around question one, and her headache had started with question two. "Sure," she said brightly, "Just what I was thinking."

Liar said her inner voice.

Nope, she retorted, *learning to play the game.*

***

"What's this Shenandoah weekend retreat thing on my schedule?" That had been a Monday question to Eva. Now that it was Friday, the only thing she'd been told was "away weekend with John. He goes every so often."

Packing for the upcoming weekend should have been easy. It ended up being the worst disaster of Week One—which, for Laura, had not been a flaming success to begin with.

She needed to know 'is this a work weekend, or a play weekend?' and Eva was nowhere to be found. So, she stopped John in the hallway. "What's planned for the Shenandoah weekend? I need to pack and thought…"

He sliced through the middle of her sentence. "Laura, I don't have time to decide what to put in your suitcase. Figure it out. We pay you for your skills, and you're not showing any right now." He left and she stood in the hall, face flushing, hands clenching, blood pounding.

"Fuck you!" she yelled after him. And shocked herself. She'd never done anything like that before.

Damn him and damn me. If screaming obscenities down the hall is part of the fucking learning curve he's talking about, I quit."

She breathed deep breaths. For a while. Until she was able to move.

Chapter 27

The river wound its way through rocky gorges below Redoubt Peak in the western Shenandoah Valley. It tumbled, splashing and pushing southward through oak and pine. The house perched on a ledge of granite jutting into the river, just enough land for a field-stone patio, one container garden and two life preservers hung on the retaining wall. The sides of the house, made of ten-foot-tall glass panes, blurred the line between inside and outside.

"What do you think?" asked John.

"It's gorgeous." Laura didn't want to admit it. She was still carrying his arrogant comments like an irritating backpack.

He took her elbow and guided her along flagstone steps. "It's been a long week," he said, walking, talking, then unlocking the door.

Is that his idea of an apology? sniped one part of Laura's brain as they entered. Then, she jolted to a stop. "Oh, my goodness." She gaped. Every thought in her brain fled. She simply stopped breathing for seconds.

The expanse of beauty before her took every agitated thought, every feeling, every idea and replaced it with a panorama of harmony. Windows formed a border so transparent Laura could not tell where glass ended and forest began. Views from the living room extended over the patio cliff, to the roiling river below and onward to a waterfall shaded by hanging branches. On the table a dinner had been left by the caretaker; wine uncorked; placemats set.

John looked around, "Laura? You ok?"

"I'm—I got caught up in—well—this." Her arms spread to encompass the living space in front of her. "Wow."

He walked to the center of the room to drop his coat on the coffee table. When he didn't hear her footsteps, he turned, stood by the couch, but did not approach. In a gentle voice he said, "I wouldn't want you to feel any expectations this weekend. We both need a rest," he smiled, "and time to get to know each other."

Laura didn't move—her suitcase in hand and coat still on.

John waited.

He doesn't get it, she thought. *He treats me like a dead animal one minute—then drags me to a peace retreat the next.*

"Laura? Are you coming inside?" A puzzled look crossed his face.

"Are you going to treat me like shit again?"

The words bulldozed out of her mouth. Politeness had vanished like cockroaches when the lights switch on. *Did I say that out loud?* she wondered, but on she went anyway.

"I'm exhausted, hungry and working 15-hour days. That I can handle. What I can't handle is your screaming like a psychotic banshee when I ask you a simple question. And now you want me to relax?"

They faced each other as silence deafened the space between them.

Laura stood still, not knowing which way to move. She closed her eyes, too tired, too overloaded, not wanting to deal with what was facing her.

Moments passed.

The *ziiippp* of a zipper opening scratched the air. John tugged a package from his suitcase. When he straightened, he held a bottle of 2007 Gaja Barbaresco.

"I know you like red wine," he said. "I stowed this in my clothing so it wouldn't break."

"I see." *He gets to fly off the handle and then expects me to...*

"Laura..." His voice interrupted her brain chatter. "I'm sorry I offended you. It wasn't on purpose. I'm not even sure what I did." He shifted his weight from one leg to the other.

She stared at him.

"When I work, all I focus on is the problem and how to fix it." A crooked smile tugged at his lips. "I'm told I can be pretty dictatorial."

"That's an understatement, Dr. John. And what you did was scream bloody murder at me for asking what to pack."

"Would you accept my apologies—for screaming *and* not remembering it?"

He's turning human again—maybe. Her exhaustion seeped in. Her muscles released and she moved one step into the room. *It's Friday night. And that's a $200 bottle of wine.*

"I'll have a glass of that wine," she said pulling her suitcase behind her not accepting or rejecting his apology. *Can't deal with any more right now.*

Time to shut out the rest of the world.

***

The wine worked its magic. John displayed his charming side over cold Vietnamese salads and hot noodle soup. Somewhere between the salad and the soup, she decided to try relaxing into the weekend. It took two glasses of wine, but Laura finally accepted John's continuing attempt to apologize for something he couldn't remember doing.

So, when he asked, she said yes—with a condition.

"Just sleep. No sex. Agreed?" she said.

"Agreed," he said.

***

They slept in the same room and the same bed, holding exhaustion as company. Neither woke until late into the morning.

Laura lay on her side, skin illuminated by sunlight, her breathing regular and deep. John raised himself on an elbow and gazed at her body silhouetted beneath the sheets. His penis stiffened as he watched her. Moments passed before his hand rose to encircle her waist and pull her toward him. She stirred, her eyelids fluttering. Then they flew open and she screamed.

166

"No! Get off! Get off!" Hysteria edged her voice as she struggled wildly, thrashing, grabbing the mattress, pulling away.

John's arm whipped away, an abrupt release that sent her gasping and rolling to the other side of the mattress. Unmoving, he waited, watched for her eyes to focus. When they did, he spoke. "It's me, Laura. You're here. No one's going to hurt you."

Her raspy breathing pumped static into the silence between them. John waited. Laura breathed. We agreed to no sex last night." Her voice held accusation.

"None intended," he said. His tone rang of truth but she wasn't satisfied.

"Except you had a hard on."

He smiled. "If I had sex every time, I got a hard on, I'd be in bed all day. What I agreed to last night was no sex. I didn't realize it excluded holding you."

"Oh," she said, confusing thoughts rumbling in her head. *Every one of my buttons is being pushed—and then some. I don't know what's coming out of my mouth next.*

"You okay?" His face held a look of concern but he moved neither closer nor farther away. "Is there something I should know about?"

Laura teetered on the edge of the mattress. She didn't want to go over the whole stupid story of her rape—not now, not ever. "No, nothing in particular, John. I was…just startled. That's all."

Liar! roared her inner voice.

"I see," he said.

From his response, she figured he wouldn't push her lame excuse any further right now. *Truce declared—and lots more to learn about this guy called John Russell.*

"May I hold you now?"

And here it comes. Laura looked at him warily.

"Not every man is a sexual predator, Laura," he said.

A flush spread across her face. *I didn't hide my feelings very well.*

He smiled. "However, we all have our sexual needs." He slipped off his side of the bed, stark naked and comfortable. "The more powerful a man is, Laura, the bigger his sex drive—my opinion and experiences only." He paused. "Except there's truth to it." He padded toward the kitchen." I'll make coffee. You up for some?" he asked, but didn't wait for an answer.

***

John made breakfast and then invited her for a walk. Crisp mountain air invaded Laura's lungs and refreshed her thoughts. She followed him downriver and up the path towards Bear Peak Summit where the water fell and the gorge began. The mountains chased each other onward to the distant horizon, while the valleys held on tightly to cloud shadows. She watched the river splatter and sparkle. They returned three hours after starting, cold, exercised and no longer on edge.

He started the fire and they lay side by side on the sheepskin rug, heads propped on overstuffed pillows, mugs of hot toddy balanced on stomachs. Long sips of the hot Scottish whiskey and the toasty warmth nurtured a sense of companionship.

"Thank you for being with me this weekend," John said after a while.

"You're welcome—" responded Laura, slow and groggy "—I think."

He moved his mug to the floor and turned. "You think?"

"Yes, I *think*."

He cocked his head, waiting for her to go on.

He brought it up, so... "You can be an arrogant, rude, nose in the air, narcissistic jerk sometimes, Dr. Russell," she said.

He laughed out loud. "Ah," he said. "My bad manners. I've been told about them—just not in such vivid language. I'm sorry you were offended." He sipped at his drink. "But, and I hate to say this, I guarantee it will happen again. I juggle thousands of details every week—any one of which could turn deadly. It takes every atom of energy I have to do it well. So, when I work, all I can focus on is work—period."

"A little politeness can't be tha..."

"It's not in the cards—or I'd be doing it." He rolled back on to his pillow and looked up at the ceiling.

"You've got a big job, Laura. You're also extremely well paid. Whether I remember the incident or not, what I'm telling you now is this—what to pack is your problem—unless we tell you differently. Consider my inappropriate response part of your training."

Silence took over. Laura watched the fire, thoughts whirling.

Minutes passed before she spoke. "You said this job has a steep learning curve."

"True," he acknowledged.

"Straight up is more like it."

"At some points," he acknowledged.

She didn't respond.

"Do you understand my impolite bedside manners any better now?"

"I don't know." She sipped more of the hot toddy. "Drinks and fireplaces help—for now."

You aren't going to ask the other question? Laura closed her eyes in response to her own prodding. Minutes more passed. It took a while to decide.

"John?"

"Hmmm?"

"Does this job make me a prostitute?"

He shifted position.

"Do you feel like one?"

"I can't figure out how I feel. Consensual sex isn't part of any typical contract."

"You want to leave or quit?"

She shrugged. "What would you call me, considering what I'm doing?"

"I call you Laura. What else should I call you?"

"John, stop."

"No, Laura, you stop." He rolled off the rug, walked to the windows and stared out. "The act of sex is as natural as the act of eating. It's people who turn it into something bad. Sex in the wrong place with the wrong people at the wrong time for the wrong reasons is bad. Breaking laws, committing adultery, screwing around without thought to feelings or personal damage—that's wrong. But two adults having consensual sex that doesn't hurt anyone is not. Period."

He swiveled to face her. "Ouch!" he yelped. "Damned floor splinter." Bending down to extract the sliver she heard him say. "Stay where you are. I'm getting the champagne to celebrate."

What's he talking about? "Celebrate what?" she asked. *This man is...,* but he'd started talking again.

"That you're not quitting."

"I didn't say I was quitting."

"Didn't sound like that a minute ago."

"Well, the job takes some getting used to," she said.

"Laura, there's one part of your job contract that's not typical," he said."

"Only *one*?" retorted Laura. *What world is this guy living in?*

"The thing that's truly different is I wrote down *all* your duties in black and white. I didn't cover up the sex part."

"Get a life, John. The contract I signed is different—*really* different. You know that."

He brought the champagne over and sat on the rug.

"Look at it from my perspective. We're a sex-soaked society with people who work more hours and get less vacation than any other nation on earth. People spend huge amounts of time at work. They meet their future mistresses while they're working, sleep with their secretaries or bosses, have sex in the closets, affairs with the staff, impregnate the interns, pay for abortions, dole out coverup money—it goes on and on. Everybody's involved in cover ups. I may need good sex and good company to do my best work, but I sure as hell don't want that as a business model."

He stretched his neck and arms. "So, I designed my own model. That's the contract you signed. What's expected of you—sexual as well as clinical—is written down—spelled out—beforehand. That's the only difference." He paused and then added, "And maybe the really big salary."

"You think?" she said, stalling for time while the argument raged in her head.

He's got a point.

But he's just so fucking arrogant and dismissive.

You're being paid $700,000 a yea...

"The truly dumb part of it is," he said slicing into her thoughts, "when they finally put something in black and white, it's all about how to fix being stupid about sex—harassment complaints, lawsuits, trials, job terminations, ruined lives, media mongering. That way of operating is insane."

With one hand he reached for a scotch bottle on the coffee table, poured the single malt into his now empty glass and swigged it down. Champagne bottle in the other, he poured Laura a glass of fizzling liquid. "Here. Time to celebrate."

"Celebrate? Celebrate what?"

"Your decision to work with me." He looked at her as if she were an inattentive kindergartener. "That's what this conversation is all about—or hadn't you noticed?"

Laura gaped at him. *Maybe he's bipolar,* she thought. *That would explain how cuckoo he can get.* But she had a feeling Dr. Russell and his contract wouldn't be so simple to figure out. "I thought this was a toast, John—you just drank it by yourself."

He watched the flames flicker in the fireplace. "Sorry. Sometimes, even this cabin can't keep work from messing with my brain." He smiled. "Shall we try again?"

Laura sighed. She reached for the scotch bottle and poured it into his glass. Then she splashed some on top of her own leftover champagne and gulped it down.

Ick. Terrible, she thought and shivered as the fizzy mess slid down her throat. "You haven't answered my question," she persisted. "Would you call me a prostitute?"

Another shot of scotch fell into John Russell's glass.

"You're my surgical nurse and my sexual companion. We've just enjoyed a day getting to know each other. Does your contract say on Saturday, June 15 at 2 pm, Laura Greenwald must have sex? No, it doesn't, but if both of us wanted to, we would have. How does that make you a prostitute?"

With the scotch and the champagne, the fire and the exercise, she wasn't quite sure she had an answer his question.

But then, again, neither had he.

***

They slept together Saturday night. "Laura," he'd reassured her, "the contract says 'mutual consent.' If you are feeling chaste this weekend, then so be it."

She'd gone to sleep nestled in his arms, taking comfort from the warmth and the closeness without sexual demand attached.

I think I'm beginning to understand how… but she fell asleep before the thought was finished.

***

Fresh river trout, herb salad, and home-made blueberry pie served midday Sunday signaled the end of the weekend. Packing took five minutes. Laura's mental review took longer.

I told him he acts like a jerk. He said my telling him isn't going to change anything, but…you never know.

Sex is consensual—I think. Regardless of what the contract said she still wasn't so sure of that.

This whole job thing might work out. That was a better thought than what she'd felt two days ago.

He sure does own some great real estate.

She smiled and walked to the car, suitcase in tow.

***

Daniel began the drive back to the city.

John Russell turned on his computer and was engrossed in business details before they even left the driveway.

Laura took one glance at her cell messages and locked the phone in her suitcase. She refused to start city life on the drive home.

Sam wanted to come down.

Arlo wanted to come over.

John told her to be prepared for a trip.

She wanted to take a nap.

It was a no-brainer.

She took the nap.

***

Tough was an understatement for the second week of orientation.

Unrelenting practice at the hospital put Laura second in line as John's neurosurgical assistant. At the clinic, she now explained diagnoses and prognoses to patients, each case submitted first to John for approval and signature. Graphics professionals designed the PowerPoint presentations, but it was Laura who explained them to the patients, interviewing, educating, and discussing in preparation for their meeting with Dr. Russell.

On Wednesday she squeezed in dinner with Arlo.

On Friday she fled home to rest.

On Saturday Sam arrived.

She'd tried to stop him but realized it was time to 'have the discussion.'

So now they sat in her apartment, Sam's carry-on bag and visor leaning against the wall, coffee cups between them.

"Sam, I can't."

"Or you won't."

"It's hard to explain... really..."

"You're different, Laura. You took a new job; you moved; you work all hours; you're silent, you don't talk."

"I don't mean to be so… changed." she groaned. *This is no fun.*

"I don't know where I fit in," he said.

She bit her lip. "I'm sorry, Sam. I wish I could make everyone happy."

Silence. He wasn't filling in words or making it easy for her.

"But it doesn't work that way," she finished.

He raised his coffee cup. "No, it doesn't."

They sat for a while. The coffee aroma drifted through the tiny apartment. He leaned back, arms crossed behind his head, eyes closed, and feet on the coffee table. "So, here's my plan."

"I'm listening."

"Let's go have a delightful day. We include some lovely museums along with some exquisite sex. Tomorrow we continue being delightful with whatever we choose. Then I go home and you stay here."

Laura filled his cup and said, "That just leaves us where we already are."

He put his arm on the back of the couch and shifted to face her. "Nope. There's the silent difference."

"What's the silent difference?"

"It's all the hopes we don't say out loud but keep on thinking. Now I won't have any. I go home and don't have expectations. You stay here and do the same."

"Oh." She couldn't deny the burst of relief flooding through her, and the cloud of sadness that came with it.

"Look, Laura. Life moves on. We're in it. I don't see you floating the word commitment around. If I'm wrong, let me know."

She looked down. *"No, you're not wrong."*

"So, I go home, and we're friends—with benefits if you like— or friends without.

174

She started to speak but he interrupted her. "I was getting jealous. It's a yucky place to be. I won't go back there."

"I wouldn't want you to, Sam. You're a great guy."

They had a delightful weekend.

He went home to Somerville.

She stayed in DC.

And Monday morning came around way too quickly.

Chapter 28

"Saudi Arabia," he said blandly.

"What?" She crossed her arms. "That's where we're going? Saudi Arabia? In two days? I don't have a visa. You need one, right? They don't let just anybody in. It…"

He crossed his arms. "You've got one."

"How did that happen?"

"You sound like a petulant three-year-old."

"Answer my question." She stuck her chin forward.

"We applied for you."

"But don't I have to sign something?"

"We had some help with expediting."

"Oh." His range of influence kept annoying her.

"Readiness—part of the job. You have two days. That's generous. It'll be shorter in the future."

She opened her mouth with another question. "Ok, how long are we staying?"

"Undetermined."

"A day, a month, a week? You must have *some* idea."

"Depends on what happens."

"How am I supposed to pack for that?"

He shrugged. "I thought we discussed your packing issues. This is part of the learning curve. Call your predecessor if you like. I'm sure Ani's available for a few questions."

This is definitely annoying. "Never mind." She paused, then turned and said sourly, "No wonder this job pays so much."

"That it does." He turned and opened the door. "We'll provide you with an abaya to wear in Saudi."

"Abaya?"

"The robe women wear over everything in public. You'll be offered the hijab head covering also. That's optional. You'll get guidelines for visits to Saudi before we leave." And then he left, his instructions still reverberating in the air.

I'm well paid; she thought, more sourly than before. *I'm well paid; I'll get through this; yes, I will.*

***

The next two days left no room for breathing—clients, case histories, diagnoses, surgeries, meetings, people, faces, politics, eating when she could and the occasional emergency call. "We're building you up," was all he said. "Mind and body."

She talked to Sam once since he'd left, a bittersweet chat about this and that.

Arlo called twice. They'd squeezed in 6:00 appetizers at the Komi Grill. He'd offered his apartment when he saw her exhaustion but she still had work to do. She called an Uber, rode home and read the guidelines for females traveling in Saudi Arabia.

- Prohibition on unaccompanied female travel. Drivers available as needed.

- Conservative business dress required—Cover most of body.

- Use of head scarf suggested—avoid unwanted attention.

- Abaya worn over clothing in transit between meetings and in public.

- Contact between men and women severely regulated.

- Never offer handshake.

- No alcohol permitted.

- In the privacy of your own room these codes may be relaxed.

There was more, but those were the basics—confining and unpleasant. She looked at her closet with forlorn eyes and wondered how conservative she could get.

***

The overnight flight took twelve hours. First class on Saudi Air included bed seats, private cubicles, and showers. The wakeup call came with hot towels and robes.

"Wear your jammies for sleep," Eva told her. "Change to street clothes on the plane. Avoids wrinkles. Ceremonial greetings happen before you leave the tarmac."

Eva slid a photo in front of Laura and pointed. "Like that." Condoleezza Rice, the once Secretary of State, stared back at Laura, demeanor restrained and elegant as she descended from the plane in dark suit and modest heels. "The Saudis don't like dealing with women, but Condi is a hard act to follow."

So, Laura stripped and showered, disappeared her long auburn hair into a French twist and buttoned into a dark, tailored suit with long skirt and ankle boots.

John waited for her. "You look professional—and restrained. Well done. Walk slightly behind me on my left. Let's go." They descended the plane's gangway to the tarmac.

Out came the red carpet, white keffiyeh headdresses double wrapped with black agal cords and white thawb robes. They marched on the carpet into a terminal lined with ornate chairs and marble walls and listened for an hour to translated conversations while being served tea and elaborate trays of food.

A limousine was ordered specially for them. Two banks of leather seats faced each other, with a small pop-up table between. A Saudi man she did not know sat in a seat observing both of them. They faced a forty-five-minute ride to King Faisal Hospital.

As soon as the car started, John pulled out a file from his briefcase and placed it on her lap.

"Read this. I want to hear your first impressions." Arms crossed, he turned back to the window and did not bother talking again.

He's folded up into himself again. What's going on here?

She waited a few moments. When no one spoke further she opened the file and started to read

"Many apologies, Miss Greenwald, for the interruption." The man in the seat opposite was addressing her. "I will accompany you and Dr. Russell on all parts of this trip." He leaned over and placed a folded black fabric on the table. "You must wear this abaya when you leave the car. It protects you from unwanted attention." He raised up another fabric. "This hijab head cover will be even more approved by our people." A pause. "If you wish."

She wasn't sure what she wished. John Russell, beside her, gave no opinion.

She took the abaya. "I'll decide later about the head covering..." She paused. "Thank you."

The journey continued in silence. Laura continued reading.

Spinal muscular atrophy: a genetic condition of consanguineous marriages.

In Saudi Arabia, wedding customs tend to promote selection of partners from first- or second-degree relatives in arranged unions. This ancient practice has led to higher occurrence rates of genetic disorders. Spinal muscular atrophy is one of these disorders.

Symptoms occur in early middle age if patient lives to adulthood—progressive deterioration of back muscles; wheel chair use eventually required. The symptoms are often confused with cerebellar ataxia where balance, movement and body control are progressively lost.

Pages of pictures and detailed descriptions filled the folder, spilling onto her lap. Laura lapsed into a pressured speed reading.

"So?" Dr. Russell interrupted her concentration.

"What?" She was still reading.

"So—conclusions, please."

"I'm sorry... I haven't..."

"Doesn't matter... conclusions, please."

Okay, she thought, *if he wants uninformed, half-baked ideas he can have them.* She started. "Well, I think…"

"No, Laura. A conclusion—no 'I think.'"

"Fuck you!" she said—no, she thought. *It was a thought, right?* She hadn't said it out loud, had she?

"Ok, ok, take a minute," a half-smile twitching across his face as he waited.

Laura glanced at the Saudi sitting opposite. Dr. Russell shook his head.

"It's okay for him to hear what you have to say… go ahead. Tell me."

"I don't like doing this. But you want it, so you got it."

John Russell shrugged. "Go ahead."

"To me, it seems as if someone's trying to hide something. The data in this file reads more like a disorder of incest, not a brain disease from some tropical insect bite as is suggested." Laura took a deep breath. "Excuse my English but my question is, who's been screwing who and when did that somebody get screwed?"

A deafening silence thundered inside the cab.

Their Saudi host sat exquisitely still—except for a twitch he could not control below his left eye. Dr. Russell, unmoved and rigid, continued his crossed-arms stare out the window. Laura closed her eyes and counted heartbeats, now up to 110 and rising. She bit her lip, kept her hands clasped, eyes on the floor and said to herself, *I'm not taking back what I said. He wanted a fuckin' conclusion so I gave him one.*

The limousine dragged through three traffic-filled blocks. In the middle of the fourth their host spoke. "I apologize to you, Dr. John Russell."

John uncrossed his arms, turned toward the man sitting across the table and smiled. "I told you, Khalid. She's good at what she does. And she tells it like it is. She won't slant an opinion because it's nicer. We knew that before we hired her."

***

King Faisal Hospital was a sprawling complex of medical buildings, staff housing, health gyms, restaurants, marbled halls, and atriums. It was one of the very few settings where unrelated Saudi men and women freely inhabited the same air space.

Women of Saudi birth wore hijab scarves or full niqab head coverings above scrubs and white coats. Non-Saudi females walked bare headed. Laura had been too busy with incest versus bug bite brain damage to decide what she would do.

"But it is not the first cousin of anybody here, or even the fifth cousin," Khalid had protested in the conference room they'd gone to after arriving at the hospital.

"Aamir is engaged to Hada. She is not his relative—a connected family, yes, but not by blood. He was counseled to so marry. It is that his family... they suffer too many such... problems. What you say cannot be. There is some mistake."

Khalid's gaze speared through John Russell, demanding a different response.

Laura wished she could disappear. She kept her eyes down cast and hands folded. *A full head veil might actually have its advantages,* she thought. Khalid refused direct speech with a woman, so John inherited the role of go-between.

The face of a beautiful young girl—perhaps 18 or less—stared out from the files on Laura's lap. Tresses of dark hair tumbled around her shoulders. She and Dr. John were here to decide this woman-child's fate. A future honor killing hid its ugly tentacles between the words that had marched from Khalid's mouth.

"We will have to do some tests on the child..." began John.

"You may not look upon her or touch her, Dr. Russell. Haddiyah is not a child but a royal woman grown and betrothed. As royal blood of a Bedouin tribe her life—and your life—would be in danger."

A silence fell that swallowed all movement. John Russell waited. When time had passed, he said, in quiet monotone, "My colleague, Ms. Greenwald, will examine the patient. We are well aware of the cultural rules here—as well as their dangers."

Khalid bowed his head. "I beg to have my rudeness forgiven, Dr. Russell. My thought was for your safety." Moments passed. "It was the future mother-in-law whispering words of doubt into her husband's ear that made a cause of this situation."

He took a deep breath before beginning again. His voice held strident undertones. "The family of the groom now demands proof that the bride is clean of genetic defect. They, too, have been counseled. We know that dangerous secrets can hide behind such 'tests,' as you call them."

John Russell exhibited no facial changes, no leaked emotions. In a quiet voice he asked, "Shall I withdraw from this case?"

Khalid dropped his head. "No, Dr. Russell, your skill is much respected. I only remind you that we in Saudi live by a strict code and its violation might lead to death." A pause. "We shall proceed."

And proceed they did.

***

They brought Haddiyah under false name to the second floor of the north hospital tower into the private office of the hospital's Chief of Genetics.

Laura examined the young woman so fatally caught in a trap not of her making. Had Haddiyah acquired a brain infection on a family trip to Indonesia, as the family claimed, or had Haddiyah's mother been unfaithful nineteen years earlier with a close family member— thus transmitting a genetic disorder to her daughter through the unnamed father?

Similar symptoms, but sure as hell different consequences.

An exhausting, secretive day.

Laura had seen no rest since the tarmac that morning.

In the examination room, everything she said, touched and saw had to be documented.

Twice during the exam, Haddiyah dropped to her knees facing Mecca when the muezzin's call to prayer rang out, and remained so for the twenty minutes of worship that occurred five times each day.

By the time the exam was over, the voice recorder into which Laura dictated was stuck to her sweaty palm. She slapped it into Dr. Russell's waiting hands, fled to the room which had been given to her in the hospital residence and fell asleep before she reached the pillow.

It had been a very long day.

***

A cell phone thrummed its way into her sleep. The dimming seven o'clock evening light struggled through blinds in her west facing window.

"Okay, okay." Muttering and groping, Laura swiped her phone. "Hello," she rasped in a flat, tired voice.

"Laura, it's John. You up?"

"Well... I am now."

"Good, we need to talk. I'll be right over." He hung up.

She'd fallen asleep in her now wrinkled clothes. Eyeliner smeared both cheeks; lips were chapped, tongue dry and she was having trouble sitting up. Her room included a bath with broad sink and long mirror. When the doorbell rang, she was washing her face. Blobby soap ran from onto her white blouse.

"Hold your horses, I'm coming," she yelled.

John Russell stood at the door. He held a wide tray covered with woven cloth. He shouldered sideways into the room, laid the tray on a side table and swiveled to embrace her.

"You were magnificent."

His lips descended on hers, abrupt at first, then seeking, caressing, spreading her mouth open with his tongue. His hands massaged her neck and then pulled her closer. His erection was hot. The warmth of his chest seeped through his open shirt buttons.

Tired or not, her body responded to his touch. His fingers tugged at her twisted hair until it gave way and auburn locks tumbled down. Grasping scalp hair in both hands, he squeezed, pulling her head back, exposing throat. He kissed her there, then began unbuttoning, unzipping, undressing, caressing everywhere and elsewhere all the way down to her sex. There he found the nub of her clitoris. And stayed until she cried out in pleasure. And once again. Then he entered her, standing, pushing against the wall as she arched into him—and he kissed her mouth again and again before he emptied himself into her. And it was done.

"You are magnificent, may I state a second time?" He pulled her lips to his again.

"Are you supposed to be here?" was all she could manage to say.

"No, not at all. The Saudi's are pretty touchy when it comes to this boy-girl in the same room stuff."

"So, how'd you get in?" She couldn't believe she was in a women's dorm room with a man in Saudi Arabia, they'd just had orgasmic sex and this is what she was asking.

"I said you needed some medical help for exhaustion and I'm responsible for your health. They gave me a special escort for the 'crazy American doctor'—not happily, but, here I am." He smiled. "Anyway, we're moving to the Ritz-Carlton."

She stared at him. "Now?"

"You didn't think we're staying at the hospital residences, did you? This country's hard enough. Overnight at the Ritz with dinner. Pack up."

"What's that?" She pointed at the lumpy coverlet over the tray.

"Oh, that's some 1964 Seagram's Crown Royal Whiskey. Khalid had it stashed away, except his mother-in-law is moving in. He said she'd find it. He liked your work, so he's passing it along. Saudis can lose their hands for having liquor."

Laura gasped, then shook her head, trying to get… well… normalized was the word that floated through her brain. She went to wash her face.

"None of that, Laura. They gave me thirty minutes. Only five left. Throw on your abaya. I'll get the suitcase." He turned. "Oh, and be sure to look sick."

"Looking sick won't be a problem," she said, struggling to get hair pinned out of sight. Several long locks tumbled out of the two hair pins she'd found before John grabbed her hand.

They strode toward the waiting limousine with Laura struggling to keep up.

He winked at her. "You're magnificent," he said, "but let's get the hell out of here."

Four minutes later they were gone.

Chapter 29

It lay on fifty-two acres of prime land. Rows of palm trees lined the entry and a gleaming hotel of palatial proportions crowned the scene—the Ritz-Carlton at its most sumptuous. Included in the 492 guest rooms were the Royal suites—one of which Khalid's family had reserved for them—a cavernous extravaganza of more than 4500 square feet.

Khalid had been adamant. "Oh, no, you cannot sleep in an ordinary room. You come from very far with knowledge and personnel. Our country is difficult for the Westerner. May you find rest and peace within the walls of this magnificent hotel." The room was his gift for their remaining time in Saudi Arabia.

They stood in front of floor-to-ceiling windows at 9:00 p.m. of the same day they'd arrived and looked over manicured gardens to the city lights beyond.

"Welcome home," he said. "We're here for two nights, kind of."

"Kind of? What does that mean?" She was exhausted and she could feel the edge to her voice. Laura drifted toward a bowl filled with dates and apricots.

"'Our flight leaves in the wee hours of the morning a day from now. So, we 'kind of' have all day till midnight tomorrow when we leave for the airport… and tonight, of course."

He moved behind her, slipped his arms around her waist. "Thank you for your body this afternoon. It was delicious," he whispered, his arms tightening. She could feel his erection grow as he pressed against her buttocks.

Laura stiffened. "John—look at me. I've worked a 20-hour day in a very foreign country filled with white robes, turbans, women behind masks, 110-degree temperatures, desert sands, kings and princes, strange rules, deadly secrets, honor killings, and having sex in an all-female dormitory guarded by men with guns who could kill us. I don't know what's up with me, my body, my mind or my anything."

Her verbal litany ground to a halt while her blood pressure kept rising. "And you—all you can think about is sex." Laura walked to the balcony windows at the other end of the cavernous room and looked out. "I think I need that bottle of Khalid's whiskey."

***

The whiskey bottle sat between them on the coffee table. John topped his glass, but Laura shook her head.

"So," he said, "what's with the attitude I'm getting?" They sat kitty-corner on the couch watching the night sky brightened by the distant glow of city lights.

"This trip's weirded me out," she said. "All the male-female stuff, what you can and can't do, every woman behind a black robe—it's all about who gets to control what." She took a deep breath. "I can't sort it in my head. Then throw in what you and I are doing—a whole other set of weird rules. It's messing with my brain." She looked unhappy.

"I've done my research," he said. "We live in a rugged world. The contract I designed keeps everyone safe."

"Maybe…" She looked down.

Minutes passed. When John finally stood up, he moved behind the couch and put his palms on Laura's neck. A slow, rhythmic massage began. He moved it inch by inch from her shoulders to her scalp. A hum of relief escaped Laura's lips.

He bent next to her ear and whispered, "I want to have sex with you now, Laura."

She was too tired, too filled with alcohol, and too relaxed to search for reasons why it wasn't a good idea. *I'm a consenting adult* she thought a little petulantly. *Right now, I don't care one way or the other …so—what the hell.* She closed her eyes and let herself be persuaded. *No big deal.*

***

It was midnight when Laura felt John roll over and pick up the bedside phone. Groggy from sex and lack of sleep, she fell back to dozing, only to have him shake her awake moments later.

"Shower before dinner?" he asked, then burst into laughter at the look on her face. "I ordered dinner. Twenty minutes. Royal suite requests are rush-rush."

In response, Laura dragged the blankets over her head and groaned.

"That sounds like a no-shower to me," he said. He tossed something onto the bed calling "There's your robe," and disappeared into the shower room.

Twenty minutes later a white shirted waiter, with tablecloth, wheeled in dinner, set the table by the dark expanse of windows and left. Flat bread with hummus, spiced chicken, rice, yogurt drink, coffee and candied stuffed dates for dessert. The meal was filling and they ate in silence. Both tired. Both willing to forgo conversation.

"May I offer you my bed tonight?" he asked pushing back his chair.

Do these guys ever give up? she wondered, full of food, and beyond exhausted. *I need an isolation chamber right now.* "No, thanks," she said.

"If you change your mind, feel free to join me." He placed his napkin on the plate, crossed the fifty-feet of ebonized hardwood floor to the first of the master sleeping rooms and closed his door with a soft click.

***

Laura recalled her trip to Saudi as a whirlwind Disney night sweat—sheiks, robed virgins, head dresses, unimaginable wealth, sand cities, sandier deserts, and the ever-present echoes of the muezzin's call. She wondered how much her memory was already distorting what she could remember—all of it seemed like smoke from a genie's lantern.

Her last memory was that of a desert warrior who had burst the door open into their suite—bearded, broad-shouldered, white robed and turbaned, followed by two body guards. A chastened Khalid came last, carrying a titanium briefcase with combination lock.

The man in the robes stood tall in the middle of the room and crossed his arms.

"The woman must remove herself," had been the first booming demand from the bearded mouth.

Laura, her own mouth open to receive food from a breakfast fork, froze, gaping at the Arabs invading the enormous room. John nodded to her. She put down her fork, gagging on the last mouthful, and removed herself, shaking and coughing, to the nearest bedroom.

Dr. Russell turned to face the man whose behavior was so shocking. In a culture where guests in one's home were inviolate, this man's rudeness signified he had to be a major player in the family who owned this royal apartment.

"Speak!"

The order had been directed to Khalid whose brow dripped beads of sweat into the climate-controlled elegance of the room. He came forward.

"Many pardons, Dr. Russell." Dressed in western style suit and without head covering, Khalid lowered his head in apology. His grip on the titanium case did not loosen and John Russell saw the trembling of his hand. "I would present my father, Sheik Abdullah Fareed…"

"Enough!"

Khalid stopped mid-sentence and moved to his original place behind the sheik.

"You will do your testing here. These vials of blood and other information of our family must stay in the homeland."

Don't do it, John, prayed Laura. She had kept the door ajar, ear pressed to the opening. *If we stay, we might be involved in an honor killing.* Blood pounded in her ears.

"Do you understand what I am telling you?" demanded the sheik.

"I do. The vials of blood and information may stay here as you desire." A steady, slow rhythm from John's breath washed through his words and into the room.

"I did not think you might be so easily persuaded, Dr..."

"However," interrupted John, "my colleague and I will be leaving tonight as planned."

"You can finish your report so quickly?" the sheik asked in surprise.

"No. We cannot. Everything will stay here as it is. I never compromise my work or my staff—especially not under pressure. You know that, Sheik Fareed. And that is why your family requested me—not someone else."

John stood.

Abdullah faced him.

Five full minutes passed.

Suddenly, as abruptly as he had come, the sheik swirled and strode from the room. "Khalid," he ordered, "Leave the case with Dr. Russell."

Then they were gone, the door left wide open, with the roar of tension flooding out behind them.

Khalid, now alone, unlocked the handcuffs chaining him to the titanium case, and placed it on the floor between them. He grasped John's hand. "Many apologies, my friend, for this unexpected intrusion. I could not stop it." And then he, too, disappeared, closing the door behind him.

Results, diagnosis, and recommendations were to be completed in one week. Khalid would fly to the U.S., be briefed, and then return home, the bearer of family news.

When John had explained all that to her, Laura asked, "What happens then? To Haddiyah? Or her mother?"

He looked at her. "I don't know. They never tell me."

***

The flight back arrived mid-afternoon. Laura fled home with an Uber driver who could not stop talking. She fumbled for her keys and raced up the stairs. When the apartment door closed on the world behind her, she burst into tears.

"Stop it," she yelled, slapping herself twice on the cheek. "You're okay. It's all okay." But panic began to rise.

Luggage pushed to the wall, shoes, jacket, clothes stripped away, she plunged into the shower. She stayed for twenty-five steamy minutes, letting the water wash away fear and exhaustion. When she finished, she dragged on a plush robe and selected a special wine. From the cabinet. On the sofa. she sat and swirled wine while tension slipped away little red drop by little red drop.

The trip to Saudi Arabia had brought home a different Laura than the one who left just a few days earlier.

And I have no idea what this new Laura is going to do.

Chapter 30

"I'm getting up!" she yelled at the alarm.

Today was White House Day.

She needed to "White House" her dress, "White House" her shoes, "White House" her hair-do and her purse.

The work in Saudi Arabia work had promoted Laura to 'no-longer-in-training.' "But you'll be learning every day," John reminded her, "starting tomorrow with the White House."

His preparation for her big day had been succinct. "We arrive together. We stay together. We smile. We stay in sync." We disagree only in private.

They went in the Town Car, she and Dr. Russell. Daniel drove to the Northwest gate—far from the usual entryway. Navy guards walked them through interior checkpoints, escorted them past the West Wing, down the red-carpeted press corridor, and into the center hall of the "House of the President."

"Nice to see you again, Dr. Russell," said the medical secretary addressing him from her desk situated in a small space not meant to keep people waiting.

"Dr. Commander Jordman is briefing the President. He'll be back in a minute." She smiled. "Coffee?"

"No, thank you," they both said at the same time.

"We're 'in sync,' Dr. John," she quipped as they sat.

"We are," he said, closing his eyes and lapsing into silence.

A framed photo of the President shaking hands with Commander Jordman, MD, hung on the wall, dated three years earlier.

Laura had done her research. A designated physician with black bag and implements of emergency care always accompanied the President. Always dressed in street clothes, never standing out, always close by. When not dealing with travel needs of the most powerful person in the world, that same physician, selected from the armed services, headed up the twenty-three-member White House medical team.

As she waited, Laura watched John Russell's closed eyes, tensionless posture, even breathing. *How does he do that?*

Without warning, he opened and focused his eyes, stood and stretched out his hand.

"Roddy, great to see you!"

Laura had not even heard the door open.

Roddy Jordman, medium height, solid build, and decked out in dress whites, ushered them inside his office. "Sit. Sit. Coffee? Donuts? They're gluten free. Very good." Jordman waved them towards chairs angled in front of his desk.

"No, thanks, Roddy. We're fine."

John's pre-meeting instructions to Laura had also included—No coffee. No food. No distraction from eyes, movements or words of the teller of the story.

So, she sat, listened, watched.

"Well, then, let's get to it." Dr. Jordman shuffled papers on his desk. He looked down, then up.

"The Vice President's daughter is three months pregnant for the first time. She's having headaches—morning and afternoon, pretty bad. Family history shows brain tumors here and there. In addition, she and her husband went to Rio for a week at the Olympics. 'Zika territory unlimited,' may I quote from her. As you know, Zika has been identified as a significant cause of congenital damage to fetuses. This was announced after they were in Rio or they would have canceled the trip."

He sat forward. "She's terrified. All our testing comes up negative—on every count. Scans, blood work, sonograms, ultrasounds.

All negative. We'll retest in a month or so just to be sure. And that's the good news."

"And the bad?" asked John.

"She's talking about not keeping the pregnancy."

"What reasons?"

"She says it's 'too risky if we didn't catch everything.' I'm quoting again."

Silence.

"You know how terminating a pregnancy will spin politically—right?"

"I do, indeed," nodded John Russell. "And you want us to…?" His sentence trailed off as he waited for Jordman to finish.

"When we told her our results yesterday, she got distraught, said we missed something. Her headaches were coming from somewhere. POTUS and the Vice President would like to offer her a full second opinion—unbiased, discrete. We thought you could offer that."

John said, "I see."

Laura wondered why they had even invited her. What they needed were extra lab tests and a good bedside manner. John had more than enough of that—when he wanted.

Jordman sat back in his leather chair and spread his hands. "Psychology isn't my job. I've got no clue what she'll decide. But, whatever she decides, it'll impact a lot of people and a lot of issues."

"Where is she now?" John asked.

"At home—waiting for a call."

"Your thoughts, Laura?" Dr. Russell had turned to her.

I'm on the spot again, came her first thought, *like with Khalid.* Except she'd learned from the wild drama of her Saudi training: keep a steady face; focus attention; speak your mind with confidence.

"How much time do we have?" Laura demanded.

Then she felt like curling into a ball and rolling under the table. *Your first words as White House consultant and not one single, tiny allusion to medicine?* The mental yell echoed back and forth as a blush crept up from her neckline.

"An excellent question," began Jordman.

The blush fled, replaced by a tachycardic heart rate over what he might say.

"I think the time frame depends on what is suggested and what she accepts," he finished.

"Laura can handle that," said John without hesitation.

I can what? This is craz...

"Ok," Jordman said, shattering Laura's silent refusal. "Let's set it up. She's promised one appointment. Maybe two. Depends on how good Ms. Greenwald is."

***

The walk from the White House to Greenberry's Café took twenty minutes.

"No talk, just breathing," John commanded.

So, they sat and ordered. Eggs Florentine, four rashers of bacon, and steaming 'Morning Challenge' lattes served in soup cups.

He broke silence first. "You've been quite the surprise, Ms. Medical Consultant Greenwald. Well done."

Laura blushed, then blushed about blushing. "What are you talking about?" she asked. "I said six words. That's it. None of them had anything to do with medicine. So, you're a crock of..."

She didn't finish but instead bent her head to sip latte and ended up with a whipped cream nose.

He laughed.

She blushed.

"You have no idea how good you are." He paused to let his words sink in. "The only pertinent thing we needed to know was time frame. Roddy put all the medical details in a dossier. Asking questions would have been a waste of time." He paused. "Oh, yes, one more thing."

"What's that?"

"You don't come across as an arrogant know-it-all."

She smiled. "Great review, John. Good quote for my resume."

"You don't need a resume," he said. You've got a job."

Laura blushed, and then blushed about blushing.

***

They walked to the hospital after breakfast.

John disappeared into afternoon surgeries.

Laura took a taxi across the Potomac to the Virginia clinic and reviewed the White House file in the privacy of an office there. By 6:30 p.m., she was rubbing one very stiff neck. "Time to go home."

She stood, bent at the waist, closed her eyes and stretched fingers to floor... five seconds... ten... fifteen. The silence soothed her achy brain and body.

"This is how you spend my hard-earned dollars?" said a voice behind her.

Laura popped up. John stood framed in the doorway, his pin striped White House suit still crisp and elegant. "Daniel said you were still here. He expects a call from you at midnight if you keep on researching like this."

She brushed away loose hair from her neck, "I wanted to get this right." An arched eyebrow from John kept Laura explaining. "There's a lot of reading between the lines in this report. Dr. Jordman is pretty adept at that... uh... style. I like him."

"He likes you."

"I didn't want to leave till I understood it all."

"That might take forever." He loosened his tie. "How about not leaving?" A pause. "Have dinner with me. Stay over."

"Oh." She stood still.

He walked behind her.

"Stiff neck?" he inquired. He put both hands on her shoulders. A strong, steady muscle rub began. It moved up her scalp, his fingers rubbing the skin, then grasping and releasing her long hair at the roots. Energizing, soothing, sensual. She hadn't planned to stay. A quiet evening at home was what she'd wanted. Except her plans crackled apart as John's hands massaged tired muscles and achy neck.

He pulled over a chair and eased Laura into it. His fingers moved to upper arm, kneading tensions from the muscles, and on to her fingers. She forgot dinner, home, patients, work. The world narrowed to the fingers on her body—touching, moving, releasing the day from her mind. Calf muscles, ankle, feet and toes. Delicious.

Then his mouth was on hers. And dinner was forgotten, as was going home.

***

A growling stomach awoke her at 3 a.m. She'd been asleep on the couch next to John, without dinner or drink. Now she was ravenous. She rolled off and went to the office fridge. Yogurt, fruit, juice, gouda and goat cheeses.

"Up so early?"

"Yup." She said in an abrupt manner bent bare naked looking in at the food.

"Uncomfortable?"

"Nope, hungry." Her words were clipped.

"You okay?" he asked.

"Not really." A pause.

"Ah," he said, "The job."

He crossed his arms at chest level, genitals curled and lazy between his legs. A runner's lean body, built for endurance. And she, buck naked with goat cheese falling out of her mouth, sharing her distress with an equally undressed employer.

It was ludicrous. So, she laughed.

It was bewildering. So, she cried.

From somewhere he pulled out a blanket and wrapped her in it. A quiet knock on the door left behind soup mugs, cucumber-dill sandwiches and tissues. A towel now wrapped his waist and his slowly awakening genitals.

"Sit," he said. She sat.

"Eat," he continued.

"Good leadership skills, doctor," she retorted.

He smiled.

"Talk," she said.

He talked.

"There are different stages in getting adjusted to this job."

"Like what?" Laura sipped at the hot soup, and grabbed a napkin as it started to dribble.

"Well, let's see. The most evident one is just Getting Adjusted—the interview, the big salary, the 'do-I-want-this-job, the 'why-me'—all that kind of stuff."

"That's pretty unforgettable."

"It is, "he said, picking up a sandwich. The conversation broke as they both ate. When he began again, he said, "Right now I see you in the midst of Stage Two—I call it 'Easy Learning.' That's all the medical stuff. There's a lot to learn, but it's pretty straightforward."

He paused.

She breathed.

"Then comes 'Hard Learning'—all the relationship 'stuff'. It's the you-and-me, sex-and-work, and what-about-the-rest-of-the-world stuff. That's complicated—and a bitch to navigate." Another pause. "I guarantee there ain't no employee handbook on caring for a CEO's sexual health."

"Haven't seen any." She almost smiled, except her nose was dripping. "Sorry. Tissues?"

He handed her the box. She tossed the soiled ones towards the trash can. They fell on the floor neatly circling the container. "I never get those in.

Mini sandwich stuffed in mouth, she continued, "Except yours."

"Except my what?"

"Your contract."

"Why don't you just get married—like to some nurse—or something?"

He sipped at his brandy. "I did get married. It fell apart. I'm too involved in work to be a family man. I told you that already. And, to be honest, I'm not really interested."

Without thinking her hand tugged at the top of his towel. "You seem to be…"

"That's a whole different slice of pie."

He took the soup mug out of her hands and when they finally awoke to the clanging of his wake-up alarm, it was hours later.

***

Laura showered and dressed in John's apartment. They ate breakfast together. Bacon, eggs and fruit topped off by a latte supremo with enough caffeine to last Laura the entire day.

She felt good—maybe the sex last night, maybe their discussion, maybe just getting used to things. Didn't much matter. It felt just fine to sit and eat. She'd figure the rest out later.

Poor John, she thought with a bit of a gloat. *He's got to go to the hospital today, and all I have to do is get to the other side of the mansion for a quiet day of resear…*

"See you at noon." John's brusque interruption shattered any gloating.

"But I still…"

"Finish it up and get to DC for noon. Getting results faster than you think you can is part of the job." Then he opened the door and left.

"Crap. Just ask John how to mess up feeling good."

She strode to the first-floor clinic offices through the connecting door of the house. "If he wants quick, he'll get quick. No good-bye, no what-a-nice-evening—no 'nuthin,'" she muttered on the march to her office.

"Good morni…" attempted the clinic receptionist.

But Laura strode by, not hearing the words through the jumble of her own thoughts—until she was too far down the corridor. *Now, I'm even acting like him,* she thought. She gritted her teeth. *I'm gonna have to train that man—I don't give a damn what he says.* This job took some getting used to—whatever stage she was in. She reached her office door.

On to the next stop—one Vice President's daughter with an atomic bomb of a problem.

***

"You finish?" he asked when she arrived.

She nodded. It was noon and the hospital corridors rumbled with lunch carts.

"You make the appointment?"

"Yes."

"Good. When?" His speech was Morse code. She'd get used to that, too—eventually.

"Friday… Friday morning." She could be word-efficient, too.

"Good. I'll be there."

"No, you won't. Just me."

His raised eyebrows spoke the question. "Ooooh—kay," he said, dragging out the word. "Give."

"Well, Mrs.-Vice-President's-Daughter said, 'No guys and no one who knows my dad.'" Laura's smiled a crooked smile. "Sorry, but you fall into both holes."

They were walking towards the operating room.

"Good work," he said and disappeared behind scrub room doors.

The same doors popped open two seconds later. "Laura, snap out of it. You're attending this surgery—and you are clearly not attending. Go."

Four surgeries, two toilet breaks, one lemonade, and no food later, the clock hands showed 6:30 p.m. Exhausted was too mild a word for how she felt. She saw John shrugging into a sport coat. He smiled.

"Drink before you go home?" he offered.

"You mean before I collapse?"

"You're tired?" He'd crossed his arms on his chest.

"Exhausted is a better description."

"Good."

She snarked back, "How compassionate of you."

"Whoa!" Both his palms went up. "Hold your horses! I meant good for endurance—you need the build-up training."

Laura grabbed her purse and started for the door. "Not tonight I don't."

She had no idea how wrong she was going to be.

Chapter 31

A twenty-minute Uber ride on Rock Creek Parkway, a twenty-five-minute traffic jam and an overheated radiator finally made Laura open the Uber's door and walk the last mile home. She struggled up the steps with achy feet to find a package squashed behind the storm door. Her name was on it, so up it came with her, into the apartment, through the door and onto the floor with everything else.

Home. *This feels sooo good.* In seconds, she was cross legged on the couch, eyes closed, wine glass in hand. The phone rang ren minutes later.

"Hello?" Her voice blurred with relaxation.

"Did you get the package?"

"Who's this?" Wide awake now, damn it all.

"It's Arlo. I've been leaving messages, but..."

"I know. I know. I haven't been answering. Sorry."

A pause.

"Did you get it?"

"A few minutes ago—so, yes and no."

"I want you to open it now."

"Pushy, pushy, Signor Appolino," was her response.

"No, really, Laura, open it now."

"Ok. Hold on." She got up, padded across the room, used scissors to slice the tape. and pulled to open the box.

Inside lay an envelope.

Inside the envelope lay an invitation.

She opened the invitation.

"Oh, my God! Is this real?" She could almost hear his smile.

"I thought you'd enjoy the diversion."

"Well, yes, but—is it real?"

"It is. So, is that a yes or a no?"

"No. I mean, of course, it's a yes. I mean yes, not 'no'."

He laughed. "I think you said yes. Did you see the gift card?"

"There's a gift card?"

"In the envelope at the bottom."

She opened the envelope wider. Enclosed lay a brochure from the Anna Sui Fashion Line entitling the holder to five of the outfits shown.

"Arlo, what's this all about?"

"I want you to come with me—Friday to Sunday—transportation and fancy dinner—all included. And you get to keep all the outfits—unlike Cinderella."

"We barely know each... I mean..."

"My dad said I must have an escort—if I don't that would be 13 at the table—a British no-no. He's being honored for his service."

"What service?"

"Dad? Oh, he's a self-trained computer geek, along with being a dockside worker—dock work was the only job he could get when he came here. He did geek stuff enough in his spare time to prevent a major UK hack. They couldn't announce it—too dangerous. Instead, he's being honored with a small dinner and a big check."

"Well, then..." She took a breath. *I can't believe this is happening.* "I guess I'm in."

"Then get to work, honeybuns—you only have two days. Gotta choose them dresses!"

It was 1:30 in the morning when Laura retreated from the Anna Sui Fashion website with a ransom's worth of wardrobe and 24-hour guaranteed delivery.

After all, she was going to meet the Queen of England.

***

"You knew?" she asked, incredulous.

John smiled. "I did."

"That was mean," she said back.

"No, it was training. Can't assume you know what the next hour holds—ever." He was still smiling.

"Oooo—kay..." she dragged out.

"So, tell me again when you got to sleep last night?"

Her smile went crooked. "All right—I concede—you win." She didn't move from his office. He looked up again. "Give," she said.

"You want to know how I knew." He leaned back in his chair.

She nodded.

"I'm sorry. It's my policy to never reveal my sources." He steepled his fingers and looked at her.

She knew the look. She turned and closed the door behind her.

***

The next day Laura saw ten Thursday patients and spent two hours in prep time for her Friday interview with the Vice President's daughter. She arrived home, stumbled over her 24-hour delivery package and fell into bed without dinner.

"Fuck this endurance training," was the last thing she could remember.

Chapter 32

Her name was Anika. She opened the front door herself.

Tall and slender except for a popped-out belly over a navy-blue maternity dress, the Vice President's daughter smiled at Laura and invited her in. They sat in the wood paneled library of the Georgetown home with tea and biscuits in front of them.

"Sure," she said. "I'll work with you. Whatever you tell me will clarify what the first tests showed."

"That's a yes? You agree to a full second workup on your condition?" *This had been way too easy*, thought Laura.

"Of course. If I'd been polite with no hysterics, everyone would have kind-of-on-purpose dragged their feet—you know, to get me past the three-month pregnancy mark. At the three-month mark, you don't have the same choices." Anika sat back. "It's DC politics," she said. "You learn the game after a while. But it still makes me crazy."

Laura nodded. She reached over and took a biscuit, sipped her tea, crossed her legs. *I hope she thinks I know what she's talking about.* The learning curve on this job just kept getting steeper.

Forty-five minutes after arriving, Laura left with a packet of signed papers, a date for Anika's next appointment and two extra hours before her next client. *I deserve a medal for this one.* She looked at her watch and decided to take herself out to lunch.

***

That afternoon a self-satisfied Laura reviewed her schedule. *Three more patients to go, then home early to pack up for London. Let's see—Buckingham Palace, Westminster Abbey, London Brid...*

A loud knock shattered her daydreams. Eva stood in the doorway. "Emergency patient. Coming in at 4:00. John wants you to see her."

"What?" Laura straightened. "What patient?"

"But I'm going to England tonight. He knows that. I'm booked with patients till..."

Eva looked at her watch. "You'll have time. John wanted you specifically."

He's doing this on purpose, raged Laura.

The afternoon ground on.

By the time her last patient left, an angry Laura knew what exactly what John Russell had done. *I'm ready for a jet set weekend and he's stretching me out—screw his endurance training. Now I'm beyond late.*

She ran out of the building at rush hour and reached home at 6:00—hours later than she wanted. Arlo rang her doorbell at 7:00.

Bedraggled, sweaty, with hair falling into her eyes, Laura pulled her suitcase to the door and opened it. "I have to take a shower..." she started, wishing John Russell would shoot himself.

"No time. Gotta get going." Arlo grabbed her suitcase. "Great shower on the plane." Then he grabbed her hand, and they raced down the stairwell to the waiting taxi.

***

The engines of the Gulfstream 550 thrummed around her as they flew. The private jet boasted showers, private rooms, four-inch memory foam sleep-beds, lounges and dining service. The menu proclaimed caviar and lobster for dinner with bacon and cheese omelets at breakfast. What was not to like?

A steamy shower, refined dinner, and Arlo's company polished the edges from Laura's exhaustion. But now she lay prone, exhausted, and alone in one of the jet's sleep beds, muscles twitching and achy. Her mind bounced through the day's events but came to rest on her morning visit.

Her time with Anika, the vice president's daughter, had opened up an unprompted and sincere connection.

"I love my father," Anika had said. "I love the President. I respect the medical staff. But everything at the White House' is salted with the *Big P*."

"The big P?"

Anika laughed. "Welcome to my world. P stands for Politics with a capital P. You never know when someone's pulling strings. So, you gotta assume they're doing it all the time."

Laura watched Anika's face, her every of concern written in the tension of her lips and furrows on her brow.

"I'm not an ostrich with my head in the sand. Abortion is a political atomic bomb. I know that. But I couldn't just use Dr. Jordman. He works for the White House and he's a guy. He'll never understand what it's like to make a baby from your own body. I didn't until I got pregnant. How could he?" Anika looked down and sighed. "And, I wanted a woman doctor, not a man."

"I'm not a doctor."

"I know. All the better—you won't have the 'attitude.'

Right about that, she'd concurred.

Laura's eyelids drifted downward and she fell asleep.

***

Nine hours and 3700 miles later, Laura found herself standing one third of a mile from Buckingham Palace. From Heathrow, they'd driven to London's Taj Mahal Hotel, walked between antique Rolls Royce sedans that bookended the hotel's portico, and into a Victorian lobby filled with leather couches, overstuffed pillows, mirrors, porcelain lamps, chessboards, plants, oriental carpets, and a bar graced with outsized Renaissance portraits.

In contrast, their third-floor suite boasted Danish modern design. Minimalized lines and engineered comfort soothed away the sensory overload of Victorian decor. The two bedrooms, living room, and breakfast alcove all overlooked a garden patio bursting with flowers and umbrella covered tables.

"Nice, huh?" said Arlo.

"An extra bathroom for the live-in help would be nice," quipped Laura.

"Smart ass." He put his hands on her shoulders and turned her towards him.

"Laura…"

He paused. She tightened.

Not so soon, she thought. *Please not so soon.*

She couldn't relax. He massaged her neck. "You're tired…and tense," he said. "I feel it here," his hand moved, "…and here."

She nodded, mute, feeling a panic spot coming into bloom as her temples began to throb. *He's not a grabby kind of guy. He'll…* But the old memories kept pushing their way in.

His hands slid over her neck, kneading, pressing, deft and sure. Part of her wanted to retch—the other part wanted to arch her back and purr like a cat because it felt so fine. In the midst of the tug-of-war turmoil, she closed her eyes.

"Laura…?"

"Hmmm…?" was all she could get out.

"I'm sorry to tell you, but—we have a meeting at the Palace in an hour."

"What?" she chirped, coughed, swallowed the wrong way. The world snapped back into shape back. "Oh, my God. I have to take a shower, do my hair, get dressed. I'll never make it! Where are the bags?"

"I wanted to tell you before, but—well—you seemed so ex-hausted."

"That was thoughtful," she said, and felt guilt about what she'd been thinking.

The question hit her in the shower.

Coughing and sputtering, she grabbed at the handrail to steady herself and turned off the water. *How come I get terrorized about*

Arlo—but only get pissed off with John's shit? What's wrong with me?

***

Laura made it to the waiting Rolls Royce with one-minute to spare. She forced her unsettling questions into a mental lock box. *I'm sure they'll find their way out sometime—only Not Now.*

"Hi." She beamed at Arlo. The excitement of the day was taking her over. "I made it."

"I see." Arlo, casually elegant in dark suit and vest, turned her in a circle with an admiring look.

"Great dress."

She slid onto the limousine seat and he followed. He didn't stop staring at her.

"Thank you, sir. You bought it." She smiled.

"But I'm not wearing it," he replied.

The drive consumed less than five-minutes. Gates opened; gates closed; identifications displayed; limousine halted at main portico; they descended.

Laura and Arlo had arrived at Buckingham Palace.

***

Later, she recalled hazes of color, protocol, Victorian furniture, food, conversation, waiters, flowers, and sunlight streaming through shining windows. But the warm friendliness of the people she met at this very British event stood out most in her memory.

A briefing took place first—the do's and don'ts of basic royal etiquette. They received a booklet, five-minutes of introduction to the aide who would accompany them, sixteen-minutes of practice tea with cucumber sandwiches and olives.

Then, they walked red-carpeted hallways to a silk withdrawing room and came face to face with Dr. Alexandros Stephanopoulos and wife.

"My mom died eight years ago," came Arlo's whispered explanation.

"Oh."

"In the Congo."

"Oh." *A dock worker father and a Congo dying mother?* But there was no time to inquire.

The door opened. A black-suited butler conducted them further down carpeted hallways, stopping at the dining hall directly opposite the throne room. The marble mantles, ten-foot-tall porcelain vases, velvet draperies and fourteen places set at a long table prodded Laura to stand in more regal posture. She entered, her nervousness giving way as the gold utensils, crystal goblets, antique dishware and sparkling chandeliers designed an afternoon of memories for a lifetime.

The three-hour luncheon with the Queen and Prince created a mini-history of British food with cultish names: Bubble and Squeak cakes, crumpets, Scottish lobster tail, black truffles, candied beet root, herbed Yorkshire pudding, pork pies, piccalilli, and desserts of Eton Mess pudding and berry trifle.

Table conversations filled the room with secrets not again to be revealed. The Queen honored Alexandros Stephanopoulos for his service to the United Kingdom. His gifts included a three-week European river cruise, 100,000 British pounds and an invitation to return for a week at Holyrood Palace in Scotland whenever the Queen would be in residence.

"He stopped a takeover of the British electrical grid," whispered Arlo about his father, "just by fiddling around on his time off."

"Oh," said Laura, nibbling on blueberry trifle.

"Even better, Dad's invitation to visit the Queen in Scotland includes guests."

"Oh." She sat up straighter. Sudden visions of wild moors, Scottish Highlands, and British royalty flooded her mind. Vivid images brushed aside a creeping tiredness from the night's plane ride.

Arlo leaned closer. "Would you like to go?"

"Wouldn't miss it." She smiled and squeezed his hand. *I like this guy.* As soon as she thought it, her heart pounded into double time. She started to cough, pulled her napkin to dab her mouth, and hoped it hid her distress.

One night with John, she thought, *the next with Arlo? How's he going to...*

Neither her mind nor her heart would slow down.

"You okay?" Concern flooded Arlo's voice. "Can I get you a drink?"

"Nap," she answered.

"Righto," he said.

"Very British," she quipped, trying anything to keep up the distraction.

"It's been a long day." He glanced around. "We're almost done. I spy some closing formalities. Got another half hour in you?"

Laura nodded although she knew it would take hours longer. *Arlo's father is gonna want time with his son.* She raised a hand to stop one of the roving waiters. "Another cup of coffee, please."

The waiter inclined his head. "Yes, Madam, right away."

***

The royal limousine drove them all back to the hotel. Alexander Stephanopoulos, arm intertwined with Arlo's, led the family group into the lounge. They nestled around a table, ordered drinks, and their private celebration lasted another hour. Laura smiled here and there, but behind her eyes floated daydreams of sleep fairies and feather beds.

She remembered Arlo's insistence on separate bedrooms for the trip.

"I don't want a trip deciding whether you will sleep with me or not." It wasn't up for discussion and he didn't talk about it again. She remembered feeling a palpable relief when he'd insisted. *Lord help me if I fall in love with Arlo while I'm working for John,* she thought.

By the time they reached their hotel suite and said good night, her mind had turned off. She wanted to swear she felt her head hit the pillow, but...

***

Bang. Knock. Rattle, rattle.

Laura rolled over, startled and alert. Her doorknob twisted first one way, then the other. She couldn't move. *Who's breaking into my room?*

"Laura?"

"Arlo?" *Why is he whispering?*

"Are you up?"

"How could I not be up by now?" She struggled out of bed. "Hold on…"

She wrapped herself in one of her new acquisitions—an $800 hand-dyed silk robe. Cynical thoughts of having to perform as payment for the weekend skittered through her mind. *Except he sounds more like a kid with chocolate candy in hand.*

She peeked out the door. "Arlo—it's 3:00 in the morning." His tall, handsome figure, in Ralph Lauren satin lounger, stared back at her, a grin split his face almost ear to ear.

"We've got twelve hours left in London. Get up. Get dressed. We're going exploring." He thrust a cup of hot coffee through the door and strode off to shower.

"*Oh*," thought Laura.

She shook her head. This boy-girl stuff was very confusing.

***

They started at Balan's Soho in Old Compton Street, washed down two 4:00 a.m. kedgeree breakfasts with hot toddies, explored markets at Camden, strolled through Hyde Park and gawked their way through Westminster Abbey. They bought street vendor Indian curry for lunch and ate on a bench squeezed between a tired dog walker and avid pigeon feeder.

Laura, in-between a bite of curry and wiping her mouth, noticed Arlo's watch. "Oh, my God. It's 1:30. Don't we have to pack our bags, get ready, get out, or something?"

"Bags packed and ready to fly. Valet service, my dear. They provide everything." She noticed his self-satisfied grin.

"Well, Mr. Self-Satisfied, make sure they get to the plane. I need my fancy clothes in the operating room. Keeps up my image."

"Providing is my pleasure." He bowed; she giggled, and they both ran for a taxi. Even private jets had to comply with schedules.

This is one nice guy. And I have a real problem on my hands.

Chapter 33

On the return flight, Laura fought with jet-lagged images—Saudi Arabia, an Esquire model turned brain doctor, a brain doctor turned employer, Costa Rica, sex, New York rape, the Queen of England, the Shenandoah Valley. The visions crashed together in her head with a clang and a clunk.

On her first days back at work, she'd shake her head hoping something would settle out. But the question returned—again and again. Like an imprinted duckling, Laura veered off path whenever it appeared.

You gonna sleep with both of them? Same week? Alternating days?

"Laura!" Fingers snapped in front of her face.

Now that was really annoying.

"Focus or remove yourself from surgery."

More than once that week she refocused and drifted, refocused and drifted.

John Russell's Olympian pace prevailed the entire week. Friday was Massage day. By Wednesday her attention fixated on that one event. Arlo called to say hi. Sam called to check in. Her mother called to ask for a visit. Her two-minute semi-disjointed responses all ended with "I'll call you later." She really had to snap out of this.

***

"Okay, that's it. Dr. Allen finishes up on this surgery. Laura, scrub out and come to my office in ten." John Russell exited surgery. Other nurses closed in as Laura backed out, gloved hands held high, elbows bent. She pushed through double doors and headed to the locker room. *What just happened? Is this my performance shakedown?* She wouldn't know until she got to his office.

She knocked and walked in. He looked up from the work on his desk.

"Sit." She sat.

"Water?"

She shook her head.

"I want you to come to the Shenandoah this weekend."

Oh, God, not now. She looked down. She wished he'd screamed at her for distractedness.

"Something the matter?' he asked.

"I…" She couldn't look at him. "I don't I think…"

"Laura, look at me."

She looked up.

"Are you all right?"

She shook her head.

"What's the matter?"

She burst into tears.

He waited, quiet, attentive.

Damn. His charming side is showing up and I need him to act like a jerk right now.

"Dr. Russell…"

"This is a 'John' type conversation, Laura."

"I think…I'd do best this weekend…" *Why can't I finish the damn sentence?* She trailed off.

"Staying home?" he finished for her.

She nodded, tissue under nose, and blew.

He sat back. "There are no 'have-to's,' Laura. You don't seem to get that."

I am nowhere near ready to have this conversation. "I guess." The two words came out in a mumble.

John Russell burst into laughter. "That was such a not-Laura-Greenwald answer." He chuckled for a while.

She glared and watched him bite his lip to keep from smiling. "It's not funny."

"But you are." He struggled not to chuckle. "You've been with me four months, right?"

She nodded, crossed her arms.

"Your contract says you can leave whenever you decide, yes?"

"I never signed up for mandatory birth control exams."

"Mandatory? I think not. You're welcome to refuse such services. You are even welcome to formally grieve the issue. It's your privilege. Those exams have never been 'mandatory.'"

"Well, Eva damn well makes them sound like it."

"You have an issue with Eva?" He leaned back in his chair.

"I don't know who I have a goddamned issue with. It sounded like you. Are you passing everything off onto Eva?" She no longer slumped in the chair. The angry edge of her voice rippled down her spine.

"If you have an issue with how Eva does her job, then there is a process set up to deal with that. And that process is not coming to my office and complaining about it." Laura sat rigid in her chair. "I told you," he continued, "the learning curve here is steep. It's $700,000 a year steep. And it doesn't include just clinical skills—it includes everything."

"Did you sign a contract that required you to attend to my every single demand?"

She shook her head.

"If you choose to linger in the city this fine weekend, it is your privilege to do so." He sat back, eyes still searching her face. Laura unfurled, one limb at a time.

"I see." She let her built up anger push the next question out. *Time to test the waters.* "And what if I decide never to go with you?"

"Then we negotiate. After all, you did sign a contract."

Laura gaped at him.

"That's all for now. Close the door after you, please." He went back to work, head bent over papers, oblivious to the woman standing and breathing in front of him.

***

"Wake, wake, I know you remain. Come to the door." Knock. Bang. "Helloooo." Pause, then all over again.

"What the hell is that?" Laura sat on the couch with her morning coffee. She gazed out the second story window from which only tree branches could be seen. Her mind had meandered far from home.

"Lori. You are there, sitting. I know. Open." Knock. Bang. "Now, please." Bang.

Shit. It's Saturday. The damn security door downstairs isn't worth...

"Open, please."

Oh, what the heck. Her peace had been shattered anyway.

"Okay, okay. I'm coming."

Two locks, and one hard-to-turn door knob later, she stared at her visitor.

"Mee Sue?"

"Yes, yes, who else? Now, let me please...," and in she came.

"What are you...?"

"Yes, yes, thank you. Dr. John, he send me. He say you stress too much. Not good."

She flopped a duffel on the floor. Out appeared a self-inflating massage mat, essential oils, candles and one lavender-filled eye pad.

"Towel, please." She held her hand out. Laura hesitated. Mee Sue glared. Laura fled and returned with the commanded item. "Dr. John say you not to stress."

Laura gaped at Mee Sue.

"Lie down." Mee Sue's index finger pointed to the mat on the floor. "No good you wait. Now please."

217

Laura lay. Then she was prodded, kneaded, oiled and rolled over. The phone rang. Mee Sue banished it under the couch cushion. More prods and trigger points and neck releases and hair pulls. Two hours later she was done. Laura, eyes closed and mind drifting toward sleep, remained motionless on the mat.

"You bring it later. Now is rest." Mee Sue gathered her things, opened the apartment door and left. Silence descended.

The last image to cross Laura's mind threw her into a boxing ring. A two-headed John Russell danced forward, one hand encased in an enormous glove, the other naked and palm up. Magnificent jerk or empathic soul. *Punch him or hug him?* She stood undecided and frozen as he approached.

***

The cushion vibrated. Bzzzzpt... muummm... Bzzzzpt... mmmuuum.

One eye stretched open. One mind unhooked from its dream ladder. Bzzzpt... mmmuuum. Then...silence.

Face down on the couch, a stretch, a yawn, a roll over. Then she fell off as the couch vibrated again. Bzzzzpt....mmmuum.

Turn off the damn phone, Greenwald. She shoved one hand under the cushion, pat, pat, pat some more—*there, got it.*

She punched the phone's white center button.

"Hello?"

"Hi, sweetheart..."

She heard the familiar voice of Apollo Stephanopoulos. '*Sweetheart?*' thought Laura. '*When did that happen?*'

"I called five times. Got worried. You okay?"

"Sorry. I'm pretty out of it this morning."

"Morning? It's five in the afternoon. Laura."

She put her feet on the floor, head still groggy. "It's really fi...?"

"You don't sound okay."

His interruption jangled her brain, slowed her responses.

218

"Laura, I want to see you, only now I'm worried."

Silence. "I'm okay. I took a nap." More silence. "It's fine. Come over."

"Good. I'll bring dinner." He sounded relieved. "You sure it's okay?"

"Arlo, it's fine—Thai food's just around the corner, if that helps."

"Uh—I already kind of ordered dinner this morning."

"How could you do that? What if you couldn't come or I was sick or..." She stopped. "Sorry I'm being such a jerk."

"Accepted." She heard him jangle keys and shuffle papers for a moment. "I called you all morning. This food takes hours to prepare. If I didn't order early, it wouldn't be ready for dinner. Yes or no, I'd have a great dinner. Win-win either way."

Laura laughed. "Okay, I'm hooked. What are you bringing?"

"Well—I'm bringing the chef."

"The chef?"

"And we're ten minutes from your house."

***

The chef came with a big white hat and sharp knife.

He brought his own dining table, linens, cutting tools and a square black box.

He banished them to the hall and then called them back in.

The apartment had been transformed to banquet hall.

Out of his black box onto the table came the symbol of Chinese national food.

Lush meat, encased in crisped skin, sliced and served as they watched—Peking Duck.

Next came crunchy, glassy, sesame toasted jellyfish and pine cone shaped sea cucumbers.

Winter melon, shiitake mushrooms and Chinese cabbage lay in separate bowls.

Into glass flutes was poured the dry Riesling wine.

Bowing and backing out, the chef wished them a pleasant evening.

Laura looked at the handsome, semi-stranger sitting across from her, at the food transformed to artwork, and felt peace for the first time in months. "Arlo?"

He looked up and smiled as he finished putting the napkin on his lap. "Yes?"

"You haven't applied for the head butler's job at Buckingham Palace, have you?"

He winked. "Not unless you come with me."

***

It was midnight when he rose to leave.

Laura put her hand on his arm. She made a simple request. "Come to bed with me."

Their love making was gentle. Passion, tamped down by full bellies and the late hour, twinkled around the edges but did not materialize. Contentment did. When they were done, she lay in the curve of Arlo's arm and drifted into sleep.

***

Laura jumped. The phone rang, started, stopped, then began again. 7:00 a.m. Sunday. *Emergency*, yelled Laura's thoughts.

"Everything okay?" Arlo had turned towards her.

"I don't know." She had the phone in hand, heart pounding. "Hello?"

"Hello, Laura."

John? Why is he calling? Eva does emergency calls, not John.

"John, what's wrong? Do I need to get to the hospital?"

He chuckled. "No. I've been up for a while. Wanted to make sure you were okay. Did you enjoy Mee Sue's visit?"

What the fuck? It's 7:00 in the morning. Laura almost spit into the telephone, but knew Arlo was watching every movement. She bit her lip. "Yes, I did. Thank you."

220

"I hope I haven't intruded."

She hung up on him.

"You have to get going?" asked Arlo, his head propped on his hand.

"No." She smiled. "John needed to ask me something." *Not a total lie.*

"Odd time to do it" laughed Arlo.

"You know John," she deflected.

And I need to strangle him.

Chapter 34

Huddled over her phone in the clinic lunchroom, Laura typed S-E-X. *Too broad a search, but what the hell.*

Oversized boobs and butt cracks grabbed first place. That was on Instagram.

Love advice for women snatched second brought to you by *Your Tango* horoscope website for any kind of female relationship you could imagine.

Information based articles minus breasts and booty cracks came in third. Those appeared on-line in *Psychology Today* and *Women's' Health* magazines.

Not helpful.

When she typed C-O-N-T-R-A-C-T-U-A-L S-E-X, Fifty Shades of Grey popped to the screen. Not what she wanted either. She stuffed her mouth with salad and kept scrolling.

Contrasexual, promosexual, intersexual, retrosexual. Then philosophy of sex, politics of sex, education of sex, medical procedures for sex, sex therapy and sex scandals.

Sex contracts were available for marriage, dating, casual sex, gay sex, lesbian sex, no sex and—well, you name it. Except for legalized prostitution, the internet scuttlebutt showed sexual contracts as unenforceable. If one of the partners said, "I quit," the problems start. Forget the contract. You can't sign away constitutional rights.

Nothing she read described her contract. Her job wasn't "sex work." She was consenting to it even when pushiness and seduction happened. Arlo's Saturday night dinner had been seduction. That had worked and she hadn't minded at all.

What was making her so—so—weirded out?

Sex with her boss? Not usually a great idea, but it happened all the time.

Sex without possibility of marriage or children?

That was even sillier. She'd had lots of sex without marriage, no kids in sight, none wanted, and no guilt. So did a zillion other people.

Two partners in a week?

Lots of people did that. Lots of people did two, three and four partners all at once. She didn't cotton to that approach, but—whatever.

Exclusivity?

She tossed that over for a while but got nowhere. John was exclusive with her. She was the one not exclusive with him. He didn't care—unless she got pregnant. Otherwise, she had a very clear contract to be with him for a long while.

No love involved?

She respected John. She even liked him when he wasn't being stupid. Her frustration soared around his dismissive, imperious work behavior. But during personal time, he was charming, funny, thoughtful, and very good in bed—but—fall in love with him? Not a chance. Enjoy personal time with him? She already had.

And Arlo? What about him?

Oh, jeez, I'm getting a headache.

She had fifteen minutes left on lunch break when her phone rang.

"Laura—Eva Jormand here. Emergency surgery in Costa Rica. Flight leaves at 6 p.m. Get home and pack. Daniel will pick you up 3:00."

And that was that. Just another day at the ranch.

***

Their plane landed in Costa Rica early Friday morning. They drove to the Villa, rested a few hours, and arrived at the hospital by 9:00 a.m. Hours later Dr. Russell removed and biopsied a cerebral tumor from a well-known multi-millionaire, whose real name was nowhere to be found in the hospital records.

A sunny afternoon and food filled evening at Villa Nueva Esperanza helped Laura and John recuperate from the surgery and sleep loss. They ordered massages, sat in Jacuzzis, ate Amparo's cooking and had lazy afternoon sex. Laura, overtired and far from home, refused to think about anything and focused on the brilliance of the tropical setting.

Sunday afternoon provided a smooth return flight. Home by early evening, Laura dropped her flight bag on the floor. She checked the kitchen drawer for her mobile phone, another company regulation learned when Daniel confiscated hers before the first Costa Rica trip.

"Miss Laura," he'd smiled in apology, "what goes outside the country stays outside the country." He gave her an international phone with all US numbers blocked.

Staring back at her from her private phone, she saw five calls from Arlo, one from her mother, and three from Sam.

I'm getting another headache. She meditated on wine for an hour before dialing. When he answered, dissatisfaction and hurt radiated in Arlo's voice. She wondered if his male instincts felt the lurking sexuality she had not mentioned.

"Arlo, it's the job. I disappear sometimes and I can't tell anyone anything." Even this small revelation made her worry about contract boundaries. They arranged to meet after work for tapas.

Then came the call to her mother.

"No, mom, I can't visit now."

Mumbling.

"Yes. It's the job. You and Pop could come here—take a vacation. I'll arrange for accommodations."

More mumbling.

"I know you're the after-school sitter for Atticus…"

Thirty minutes to reassure her mother everything was fine.

Sam was next. *Why had he called?*

"Keira's in Boston?" she squeaked after he explained.

She and Keira, Laura's "best friend for life," had met in Ireland during Laura's nursing semester abroad. Kiera had showed up in in Somerville asking around the local pubs for Laura who had forgotten to tell her best friend about the move to DC. Keira stumbled onto Sam. Along with stumbling onto him, she stayed with him. They were an item now for as long as Kiera's stateside job lasted—or maybe longer. Sam wanted to tell Laura.

No, she could not visit Somerville right now, but could they visit in DC, etc., etc.?

When she hung up, Laura looked for a headache pill. It didn't help. She tried a second one and went to bed.

***

Exhaustion oozed from her pores by the end of the week. Five surgeries, fifteen clinic patients, an evening with Arlo, another two in Dr. Russell's discrete, high level, closed-door neurological consultations.

John Russell assessed her condition at a glance. "More endurance training. Getting control of your emotions would help, too."

"God damn it, Russell," she spit back at him, "Don't you ever say thank you?"

"Thank you for illustrating my point."

She got so pissed off at him the adrenaline rush stayed with her all day. Last night's conversation with Arlo skimmed along with the flood.

"Stay with me this weekend, Laura," he'd asked. "Hotel-like accommodations in my ridiculously fancy building, right downtown, at your service." He paused. "And me, too."

Caring, concerned, and an ex-model? She liked him.

"You've got me all weekend, Apollo Stephanopoulos."

***

The call came just as she and Arlo were dressing for dinner reservations Saturday evening at the Plume Restaurant.

"Eva Jormand here."

Laura hated hearing those words.

"Emergency surgery at the hospital. Four hours or more—can't determine. Meet John in an hour. Scrub in by 7:30."

And that was that.

Arlo's face went blank.

Laura's posture fizzled. Her stomach clenched.

"I'm sorry Arlo."

"It's your job, right?" he interrupted. "You said that last week."

He turned and began to unbutton his suit jacket.

"Arlo?"

"Just get it done. I'll cancel the reservation. Someone will be thrilled and it won't be me."

He turned to her. "The job is not your fault," he said, "but from my point of view it's damned intrusive."

Her shoulders slumped as she shrugged on her coat. "I'm beginning to see that," she mumbled.

He looked up as the front door clicked open, his erect model's posture lost, coat dragging in his hand. "You'll come back when you're done?"

"I'd like that—if you don't mind."

"I'm being a bad sport. I miss you already."

His face held a rueful smile. She kissed him and disappeared down the hallway.

***

Bedraggled and fizzled out, Laura tiptoed into the apartment at 2:00 a.m. She took a shower, a drink of water, dropped her clothes in a pile by the bedside, and pulled herself over to Arlo's bare back. He did not turn. She fell into restless dreams that plagued her until dawn.

In the morning, she could feel the hairline fracture between them begin to waggle its finger. He made fried eggs and she cut up fruit. The coffee brewed while the day clouded over. After breakfast

Arlo picked up the dishes, walked to the sink and stood with his back to her.

"Do you want me to get out of your life?" he asked.'

"Oh, my God, no, Arlo. Not at all."

"I like you, Laura—a lot." He turned around, faced her while leaning against the sink. "There's something more than your rushing off to surgeries—except I can't put my finger on it."

"Arlo, you kn…"

"No explanations, Laura."

She heard the firmness in his abrupt interruption. Her stomach clenched.

"Whenever I ask what's going on, you deflect my questions." He raised his palm to stop her protest. "I'm sorry. That's what it feels like."

Silence. Then Laura went to where he stood and gave him a hug. "I'm sorry, too."

He put his arms around her. "So, you admit I'm not crazy?"

Laura nodded into his shoulder. "I admit you're not crazy. But I still can't talk about it." She pushed away from his chest and pulled his face toward her lips. The kiss left them panting.

"Let's get some fresh air," he said.

They walked across the National Mall to the Botanic Gardens, raced to avoid the downpour, took a cab to the Eastern Market for lunch bought from crowded market stalls and counters lining long aisles. They held hands, chatted, laughed, and avoided words of conflict.

By mid-afternoon Laura had run out of steam.

He asked to drive her home; she preferred a taxi. He gave her a hug; she kissed him on the lips. Neither of them knew what would happen next.

She sat for an hour on her couch thinking the same thought—*this fucking job is stealing my life and I've got a zillion months left to go.*

***

"How'd the rest of the weekend go?" John rocked back in the conference room chair, fingers steepled, eyes scrutinizing her. It was Monday morning.

She glared at him. Sunlight streamed in the window. "You're my employer. It's unprofessional to get personal and professional all mixed up.

He ignored the comment. "You're six months into this job by my reckoning."

Laura nodded. *So?*

"Six month marks the completion of Full Training Phase."

"And that is…?"

"Graduation from the Institute training program. You'll get a certificate in a week or so—same as the docs studying with me—except I trained you double, maybe triple time."

"What's the difference if I'm post-Full-Phase-whatever-you-call-it?"

"Post-Full-Phase-whatever-you-call-it," he said, "means I won't deflect celebrity surgeries to other nurses—which I was doing. I started not deflecting on Saturday night."

"And you were going to tell me this when?"

"I'm telling you now.

I can't believe this guy. Posture rigid, face blank, Laura's mind counted. *Is Arlo my first casualty? What about Kiera and Sam? Or two years of my life? What's this job costing me?*

She bit her lip.

"More coffee?" he invited. She shook her head.

"Not fun stuff." He drained his cup and added, "Plus, secrets complicate life—the biggest one—for you, anyway—is going to be having sex with me."

Abrupt, intense, without warning, she blurted, "How many girls have been here?" *Where the fuck did that come from?*

John stared at her. "What are you talking about? I haven't had any girls here."

"I mean—how many women have had my job?" Laura's stood rigid with tension.

"Three," he said. "The job is different with each person, but there are commonalities."

"Like what?"

"Like what you're facing now."

"And what's that?"

"Balancing work with personal life."

"What happened?"

"People made choices."

"Such as...?"

"Sorry. That's confidential." He rose, walked to the window, and looked out.

"You're screwing up my life," she said.

"No, I'm not. Making decisions you don't like is doing that."

"That's not helpful."

"Happens to be the truth." He stood. "Surgery in thirty-minutes."

She stared, thoughts still roiling. *You're gonna throw a million-and-a-half-dollar job away for a little nooky with Arlo?*

"I'll scrub in," was all she could think to say.

***

Arlo called on Wednesday afternoon with tickets to a concert at Constitution Hall.

"Think it's safe?" he asked.

"I do until I don't."

He laughed. "That's fair. Wanna give it a try?"

"Yes."

They met for dinner after work that night. He drove her home and stayed.

Maybe this will all work out, she thought, *or maybe I'll just run out of luck.*

Chapter 35

Mid-week in late August a phone call sent Laura to work at the hospital instead of the clinic. An agitated staff greeted her. Eva waited at the office door, John Russell nowhere to be seen. "You're on."

"What do you mean, 'I'm on?'" demanded Laura. A wave of panic rose in her stomach.

"The Vice President's daughter reported severe headaches and nausea this morning—thinks she's miscarrying. John said you should assess and recommend."

"Where's John?"

"Not here. He said you could handle it."

Laura pulled off coat and boots. "She's here?"

"Ten minutes, tops," said Eva.

***

Hands washed, medical file on the screen, Laura observed Anika as she sat, dignified in anxiety—high boots, calf length maternity skirt, hands crossed.

"I haven't been feeling well. I thought it was just pregnancy tired. You know. Everyone gets it. But the headaches got worse. My husband insisted I come."

Laura smiled. "I'm glad you did. Checking things out makes everyone rest easier. Let's get to it."

She began exam basics—temperature: normal gestation weight, blood pressure: whoa! —way too high. Not good. She took it again, then entered the data on the medical tablet. *Oh, jeez,* she thought. *Really not good.*

More questions, emergency blood work, a call to the obstetrics chief one floor above.

"Everything okay?" Anika asked.

Laura hoped she wouldn't ask—of course, that was ridiculous. If it had been her, she'd have asked ten times by now. She was already ticking off fifty possible complications and she wasn't the pregnant person here. *Keep your head on straight, Greenwald—matter-of-fact pleasant.*

"Your pressure's a little above what we like, but that could be anything. Let's not worry unless we have to. We'll do some…"

A knock interrupted Laura mid-sentence and the door swung open; Outside stood a large, motherly, grey-haired, African American woman in a white coat. Her empathic eyes, ample breasts and large hips radiated a 'mama's here now' presence, comforting and all-encompassing.

Oh, my God. She's the answer to every prayer I ever had for today. Laura stood to address her. "We're so glad you could come. Anika, this is Dr. Joycelin Mirembe, head of hospital obstetrics."

Anika started to rise. Dr. Mirembe bustled into the room and put gentle hands on Anika's shoulder. "Please sit. It's my pleasure to help. Now, let's see how we can do that." She sat at the computer and began to type her quiet, insistent way toward answers.

The clock said just past 9:00 a.m. *All this testing could take till 5:00.* Laura's job was to sit with Anika until everything cleared. She tried not to slump at the idea. *Long day ahead.*

Except it wasn't. Two hours later exam results were completed and returned—blood tests, urine tests, ultrasound and physical. Laura threw her hands in the air. "A modern-day miracle."

Anika shook her head and laughed. "More likely, just modern-day political pull."

"Politics influencing health care?" Laura quipped. "Never."

Dr. Mirembe swept into the exam room and conversation ended.

"We have the test results. Do not be nervous." She sat at the computer. "All the information and resources of the world are here at our fingertips."

Silence descended as she tapped on the keyboard.

"Miss Anika. We have found your baby is fine. That is the true blessing."

Laura watched Anika struggle to restrain tears.

"But we do find numbers on blood pressure higher than we like. We want to keep an eye on that."

A pause, then, "Also, there is some protein in the urine—not much—it may be a partial cause of some of the increase in headaches. We want to avoid a condition called pre-eclampsia. But our monitoring will take good care of that."

She lowered the computer top. "And finally, we found you are dehydrated. That happens a lot. People forget to drink enough water. So, we see there is nothing to worry us at this moment, Miss Anika. We'll keep a good eye on everything. You should be a proud mother very soon."

Dr. Mirembe winked at Anika, leaned forward and said, "Drink more water. Dehydration creates lovely headaches. We'll see you in a week."

Anika smiled, then began to cry. "Sorry," she said and burst into tears. "Thank you."

Chapter 36

Traffic on Rock Creek Parkway was bumper to bumper—going the other way. Friday nights everyone wanted out of the city. She wanted in. Destination—Georgetown.

Laura hadn't wanted the invitation to the family's annual late summer party, but Anika insisted on it the same morning of Dr. Mirembe's "all's well" pronouncement.

"You have to come. It's a late invite. I know—really bad protocol. Only two days away. But I'm hosting at my house—won't be so formal. Mom and Dad are coming. They keep pestering about meeting you. You'll have to come by yourself—is that okay? No time for security checks for anyone else. Please?"

It had been impossible to refuse.

John gave Laura two full bear hugs when she told him.

"Well done, Consultant Greenwald! You're making a name in White House circles—and being quick about it, I might add." He punched in his secretary's number. "Darlene, get me a lunch reservation for two at East Moon."

He looked up. Laura was staring at him.

"What?" he asked. "You think I'm going to let you walk into the lion's den without basic training? No way."

He insisted on a long lunch in elegant surrounding.

Then he lectured her over a two-hour meal about the workings of political dinners.

Even when it's not political, it is.

People remember more than ever happened.

Don't trust anyone.

It's all about image, stupid.

Mouth full of food and finally exasperated, Laura demanded, "What am I doing? Going into a war zone?"

"No," he said, "more like walking through an abandoned mine-field after the truce is over."

"That bad?" She grimaced.

"Can be."

Mee Sue showed up in Laura's office on Thursday morning.

"Mr. John, he has sent me for advising," she'd said.

"Advising on what?"

"On fashion, of course," said Mee Sue, confused about the confusion. "He did not say this to you? No matter. No problem. This will be definitely a no-problem."

She walked around Laura's desk and looked her up and down. "Must be 'upscale family relax' to make you dressed up and down all at a time." She pulled out a catalog, pointed at one page, then another, marking pictures of sandals, a flowing mid-calf skirt, loose knit top and lace camisole under garment. "It is order in this minute," pronounced Mee Sue happily, disappearing as abruptly as she had come.

The fashion package arrived at work Friday morning. Laura, as semi-volunteer party-goer entering her first political mine field, was released from afternoon duties. She returned home, washed, dressed, and finally found herself in the chauffeured limousine sent by the Vice President's daughter.

Six o'clock traffic made it a tricky maneuver to stop in front of the O Street, Georgetown home. Her chauffeur opened the limousine door at a three-story rectangular brick box of a home worth several millions of dollars. Filigreed iron steps led to a recessed entryway. He rang the bell and waited. Moments later the door opened and Laura found herself pulled into a world of warmth, smells, laughter and curiosity.

"I'm so glad you're here!" bear-hugged Anika. "Come in. I want you to meet everyone."

And everyone she met, from the Vice President and his wife, to brothers, sisters, three Senators (dad's friends), two football stars (husband's college buddies), accompanying friends and spouses, two stockbrokers (Anika's college buddies) and one Harvard Business School professor. The fireplace in the great room held a bouquet of summer flowers. Shawls and sweaters were removed and iced martinis held for cooling. Appetizers served in several rounds presented the flavors of Japan, Thailand, Brazil, and Italy.

After two martinis, she loosened up. Several of the unaccompanied men vied for her attention. Laura responded with her own flirtations. She was flushed and excited by the time the accident happened.

The cry burst over the chattering, noisy group.

A catering tray wobbled as its waiter tripped, tried to regain balance. His oval plate held high and piled higher with tortellini's, bruschetta's and spicy oil dip, tipped from his white gloved hands, tilted precariously, slid onto Laura's neck, down her shoulders and clattered to the floor.

Shocked silence deadened the room. The oily goo dribbled down her hair, greased her sweater, poured pasta and olives all over skirt and sandals.

Laura froze. It had been a long week full of way too-much. She stood there, allowing the goo and the smells and the olives to slide earthwards. She shook her head. Several tortellini fell to the floor. When she threw her hands in the air, capers and mushrooms popped away. She brushed an olive from her shoulder and burst into laughter as a pimento dripped onto her foot. "I give up," she cried.

The paralyzed silence suddenly crackled with hoorahs, applause, "way-to-go's," and supportive chatter. Someone helped the waiter to his feet while Laura gave him an "I'm fine" hug. She stood still dripping in oil and tomatoes as Anika rushed over.

"Oh, my God; oh my God—I'm sooo sorry... Don't worry; we'll fix you up in a jiffy." Waiters converged like a hive of bees to remove the mess; guests murmured regrets. Concern reverberated through the room.

"A few minutes delay, ladies and gentlemen," bellowed Anika. She pulled a toweled-down Laura towards the hallway. Anika's mother and father moved to oversee guests with Anika's husband close behind.

A well-oiled family, noted Laura's brain, filing away the observation.

Anika guided Laura down a polished oakwood hallway to the lower floor stairwell. They descended into a spacious suite opening onto patio gardens hidden from street level. At the other end of the room was a large bath room and shower, white robes, towels, shampoo and recessed heat lamps.

"Make yourself at home," laughed Anika as she waved Laura into the shower. "I'll bring you some outfits—I can't wear them anymore." She patted her stomach. "We're about the same size. At least—when I'm not pregnant. Choose whatever you want. What a blooper!"

They laughed. Anika turned to go. "I have to get everyone seated. We'll serve the soup course. That should take half an hour. Will that be enough time to clean up?"

"I'll be fine. You have half of Washington to attend to."

"Thanks! You're a peach! Outfits'll be here on the bench." Seconds later she retreated up the stairs.

Laura shampooed three times before the spiced oil and bruschetta garlic gave up on her hair. She towel-wrapped it, enfolded herself in a plush robe and turned on the heat lamps Ten-minutes down, twenty to go. She closed her eyes and took a deep breath.

Three loud knocks on the door made her eyes fly open.

"Anika?"

The pocket door slid open. Carlyle Janett, a senator from Wyoming and protege of the Vice President, stood in front of her. She'd been talking to him right before the accident. Several dresses hung draped over his arm.

"What are you…?"

"I brought these down for Anika. Thought it would save her some time." Without pause, Janett dropped them on the toilet seat, pulled the towel loose from her hair, the cord loose from her robe and lifted her face towards his lips.

"What...?"

His left arm circled her back, pelvis arching forward, hard lips covered her mouth. She struggled but he was rock hard with weight-trained muscle, phallus stiff and bulging against her thigh.

Panic deluged her. "No, Stop it. Get off of me!"

Her frantic body wiggled, tensed, struggled. Pictures of the first rape flooded her and she collapsed back in time—screaming, ineffectual. Janett's right arm clamped her shoulder in place while his mouth and tongue closed on her nostrils, seeking a way in and up. She gagged.

For an instant he stopped and rasped words into her ear.

"You wanted this. I could see it. I could feel it."

His words shoved Laura through an inner explosion to a vortex of white-hot rage. Her panic stopped. Her vision sharpened and her mind turned a razor edge to the problem at hand. Carlyle Janett's ridiculous, arrogant, self-serving excuse for a rape got her so pissed to shit that a raging fire exploded in every cell of her body.

She dropped like a rock, throwing him off balance, his two arms holding her dead weight between his legs. He bent for a better grip. Laura stood and slammed her bare knee into his turgid cock. His testicles, held in perfect target shot by jockey shorts, were rammed by her powerful knee stroke.

The scream was piercing. He doubled over. She broke his nose with a well-placed elbow. He collapsed onto the tiled floor, bright. red blood dripping onto his blue Van Heusen shirt. She stepped over him, picked up the dresses, grabbed comb and brush and closed the door behind her.

Laura saw a vague outline of herself reflected in the sliding doors to the patio. Wild, wet hair, open robe, two garments clutched in one hand. She pulled the wrap closed, brushed her hair, then stepped panty-less into a teal blue dress with belted waist.

Sounds filtered from inside herself and from upstairs—her rapid heartbeat, the clink of glasses, her shortened breath, congenial laughter, the throb of her temples, the scraping of chairs. She wiped her saliva covered nose with the belt of the robe, then dry-heaved just before preventing a full vomit.

She found her sandals by the couch, wiped off as much oil as she could, then slipped them on. She looked at the clock. Thirty minutes from when she first came downstairs. Laura moved to ascend the stairwell, but stopped. Eyes closed, she breathed deeply for two full minutes.

She recalled how fuckin' expensive those self-defense lessons had been—private classes. They'd been worth every damn penny.

***

The limousine drove her home along deserted city streets.

She'd floated through a four-course dinner of specialty cuisine, two rounds of after dinner drinks and numerous compliments on her ability to "weather the storm" like a pro. The senator from Wyoming had disappeared. He'd called to say an "urgent matter had become a crisis and please to excuse," and so on.

Clock hands finally pointed to 10:00 pm. She could hear John saying, "Ten o'clock is the earliest you can escape political family dinners. Anything before that says you didn't really 'bond.'"

"Bond? What is this—a wedding?"

"Of sorts," he said. An enigmatic smile had passed over his face. He'd leaned forward. "You've moved to the higher circles pretty quickly—be cautious—follow the etiquette."

"Okay, okay," she remembered retorting, dumbly ignorant of whatever prompted him to say any of it.

Frazzled and fragile, Laura felt adrenaline surge and fall away. Arrhythmic heartbeats made her jangled and irritable. She barely noticed when the chauffeur walked her to the front door, or when she keyed herself into her apartment. She paced counterclockwise for five minutes, and then changed directions for another five.

"I'm a mess—a total, miserable, fucking mess," she said to no one in particular, then sat on the couch with fingers yanking her hair and scratching her scalp. A vague thought that she might need help passed through her mind. She laughed outright. "Can't you just see the headlines—White House medical consultant admits to nervous breakdown. Just great."

"Shut up." she yelled at herself. At some point which she couldn't remember, she saw the phone in her open purse. She reached for it and dialed a number.

"Hello?" said the voice.

Laura didn't respond.

"Hello, are you there?"

Silence.

"Laura, answer me. I know it's you from my caller ID. Are you all right?"

"No."

Silence.

"Are you at home?"

"Yes."

"Stay there. I'm coming to get you."

***

In what seemed three days but was only thirty-minutes, John Russell plunged into her apartment. No knock, no bell, no call.

From the couch, she peered at him, squinting, shading her eyes.

"How'd you get in?" Slurred, hard to hear words.

"Nothing was locked. Laura. What the hell happened?"

Her hair was wild, red gashes ran down both cheeks, eyeliner smeared towards her mouth and she was shivering in full body tremble.

He knelt, and put his hands on her shoulders. Then he slipped them down to her waist to loosen her arms which she had clasped tightly around her waist. He ended with a hug as big and undemanding as he could make it. And waited.

In a while, he couldn't tell how long, shivering stopped and shoulders relaxed. A flask of brandy appeared from his back pocket.

"Chug this."

"I don't..."

"Drink!" he commanded.

"Okay, okay," she retorted, a grump in her voice.

"That's a familiar tone. Get rid of it and drink up."

She did. Twice.

"Jeeeez—uhzz!" she coughed.

"I'm taking you home with me."

"I'll be fine."

"Home. With. Me." His man of steel face stared at her.

Easier not to argue, she thought. She glared instead, crossed her arms, stuck out her tongue, stalked to the door. She stopped, looked over her shoulder and said, "You coming, Dr. Russell, or am I supposed to go by myself?"

"Is that a snide Laura Greenwald remark?" A grin tugged at his mouth.

"You'd better wipe that smile off, Russell, or I stay put." She watched him with a belligerent stare.

"Yes, ma'am." His face clicked into semi-neutral. She marched through the door, down the steps, and swaggered to the car—face smeared, hair rumpled, stupid and trembling. John, right behind, tried throwing a wrap over her shoulders. It fell off. "Damn!" filtered up from the sidewalk as he bent to retrieve it. She was already in the car.

Laura huddled in the back seat, the air conditioning blasting, John next to her. Daniel drove down empty streets toward Virginia. It had been just two hours since she'd left the party going the other way home.

"Brandy." A small tumbler appeared in front to her.

"No," she mumbled.

"Not a question."

"Don't want it."

"I don't care. Drink it."

He glared.

She glared back, then took the drink. He poured her another.

She downed three more brandies before they arrived at John's mansion. Hot soup, buttered baguettes, and chamomile tea awaited. Wing chairs faced the bay window and held in the beauty of the summer gardens in moonlight. Her shivering retreated, heart rate slowed, breathing relaxed.

She spoke. "Thank you."

"You're welcome."

Time passed.

"It was awful," she said.

"I imagined it was," he said.

She talked.

He listened. "I see," he said when she finished.

"Will anyone find out?" she asked.

"I doubt it."

"Should I tell anyone?"

"That's up to you." A few minutes passed before he spoke again. "Legally, it's a he-said-she-said deal. Evidence shows you attacked him."

"You gotta be joking." She flushed.

John didn't respond to her comment. After a while he continued. "But—and, this is a biggy for a politician—he's got a broken nose to explain."

"Oh, right. How…? She stared at him.

"By faking a police report."

She continued to stare.

"He'll call, say he got mugged. Police will come, no witnesses, broken nose. What's not to believe?"

She shook her head. "I've got a lot to learn about this town."

"You'll get there."

"You know—I couldn't believe his fuckin' arrogance. How fuckin' dare he say *I wanted it?*" She gritted her teeth. "I hope he needs a new nose and can't ever breathe right again. Along with a new suit. Fuck him." She took several deep breaths and stretched her neck by bending her head side to side. "Chen Li, my martial arts instructor, taught me to elbow up and in—shove the nose up towards the back of the skull—more complicated than a straight on smash."

Now it was John's turn to stare.

She pursed her lips. "Not so bad for a little lady, huh?" He was still staring at her. "You're right," she continued. "I'll get used to all this. If it doesn't drive me nuts first." She stood up. "Let's go to bed." He didn't move. "Come on, Russell. Adrenaline's gone. I'm wiped out."

"You're a laugh a minute," he said and got up.

Chapter 37

When she woke in John's spacious apartment, she found herself alone, a handwritten note on the table. She stretched, unkinked her neck and read.

"Sorry. Emergency consult. You were sleeping like a baby. Thought you'd be okay. Have Daniel drive you home."

She had to admit—*Good job last night, Greenwald.* The previous night's terrors seemed to be evaporating with the sunlight. *Chen Li would be proud.* She decided not to eat, dressed, called Daniel and waited for him to bring the car.

It happened on the way home—the Question. It burst into her mind like a child's stray baseball breaking a kitchen window—*Why did I call John for help? Why not Arlo? What made me call the one jerk who pisses me off all the time?*

Calling a girlfriend was out of the question. The job cut them out of her life months ago. *I wouldn't have called a girl, anyway. I needed a man.* That man would have to witness her mewling, messy, gasping collapse and tell her she was still okay—still alive—still clean—still beautiful.

John was that man. *Or, maybe the contract made him that man.* She screwed up her face and tilted her head as the thought bounced around. She and John didn't have a marriage contract—but still— the contract bound them—gave them obligations—one to the other. The contract made it okay for her to call and for him to come— expectations already spelled out. It made John *safe* and Arlo not.

Not for that night. Not when I felt so dirty, so unclean. I couldn't have faced Arlo. Not when...

She was still thinking about it when Daniel dropped her off.

***

Laura's last-minute decision to attend her family's Labor Day festivities in Cleveland happened on Friday of the next week. She wanted to feel surrounded by *home*—mother, father, brothers, children—that kind of home.

Flight reservations showed one seat available that afternoon. She grabbed it, threw clothes and toiletries into a carry-on and shoved the suitcase towards the door.

"I'm going *home*," she said out loud. Too late to call anyone. What would she say, anyhow? *I was almost raped and now I need to reconnect?* No—better just to show up.

***

Wet and drippy—Cleveland in a thunder and hail storm. Sheets of water and pellets of ice washed over the rental car windshield; the air conditioner churned out a windy cold that dried her eyeballs. Marco and Laura Greenwald lived on Lake Erie's Edgewater Drive, twenty-five minutes from the airport. Today it took a battering sixty of them before she parked in the driveway, elbowed open the dripping car door and sprinted to the portico.

She waited a moment to let her brain catch up with her body, then reached for the knocker.

It descended three times. She waited. Footsteps. Door opened just a crack.

"Yessss….? A hesitant voice.

"Mom?"

"Laura? Oh, my God!" She heard the chain lifting. Pulled into her mother's arms. Pulled into the smells and sounds and memories of home with all its ups and downs and "stuff."

"I can't believe you're here. Come in. Come in. It's not safe driving out there. Oh, my goodness." Hugs, kisses, more hugs and, "Marco! It's Laura!" poured out her mother. "Let me get that coat. Why didn't you call? I've got to tell your brothers. How long are you staying? You shouldn't be out in this weather!"

"Good to see you, too, Mom." Laura smiled and hugged her mother. For the time being, the rest of her life could take a hike.

***

A pre-Labor Day dinner with a very thrilled-to-see-her-family happened the next day in honor of Laura's unexpected visit.

Parents, brothers, spouses and children all visiting, all talking, all eating—a whirl of activity, with no time to think. Just what she needed.

And then came the Call.

It happened in the middle of dinner.

She excused herself and walked upstairs to her bedroom.

Eva. Costa Rica Emergency.

Surgery should be done today; could wait till tomorrow—maybe. Get there now. John on the way.

Laura closed her eyes.

She booked a last-minute flight first class flight via Miami at an outrageous price with no idea of what was happening in San Jose, Costa Rica.

Flight time—11:45 pm tonight.

***

"Leaving? Now?" Her father's sparerib hovered halfway between the table and his mouth. "What are you talking about?" Confusion and irritation echoed in his voice. He put down the rib. A retired naval commander, Marco Titus Greenwald did not like losing control.

"Laura," interrupted her mother, "I'm sure you can finish your dinner and explain to us all about your new job. I don't think your doctor would want to disrupt your family like this. Isn't that right, darling?"

"I can take you to the airport, Sis," interjected Simon. He wiped his hands and folded his napkin.

Simon's wife put a restraining hand on his arm. "Don't you think…" she started.

"Laura. What's going on?" Her older brother Atticus boomed the question out over the table and stood up. "Everyone. Be. Quiet. Now."

Laura did not move. She stood in the dining room doorway, hands by her side, numb inside and out. *Every time I take a breath, John Russell squashes it out of me.*

"I'm on emergency call. I have to be at a surgery in the morning," That is what she said.

I can't do this anymore, she thought. She whirled toward the door, tears streaming down her face. "Just leave me alone. Everybody, just leave me alone." She dragged out her suitcase and threw in clothes. "Who cares if everything looks like shit tomorrow?" She squashed the top closed, called a taxi from upstairs and tried to sneak out the front door.

"No, you don't, Sis." Simon waited for her at the bottom of the stairs. "You say goodbye to everyone. Then I drive you to the airport."

"I called a cab."

"Un-call it." He gave her a hug and dragged her back to the dining room.

Laura wondered if she'd be dead and buried before she ever got to Costa Rica.

***

Her flight went on and on. The Miami layover massacred Laura's sleep cycles and the bags under her eyes grew larger than her carry-on.

When she landed in Costa Rica, Manuelo waited for her at the airport. A change of clothes swung in the bag hanging from his shoulder.

"Senorita Lorita, you look so beautiful—even after such a heavy trip." His smile and nickname for her spoke of slower paces and tropical climes. She put on fresh clothes in the car as they drove towards the hospital through ever-present traffic jams. Cleveland's sugar maples and cloudy skies had converted to palm trees and sunshine. Laura shook her head to make sure it was all real.

John waited for them dressed in street clothes and apologies; a picnic basket dangled in his left hand. She stopped in her tracks, her face flushing.

"A picnic? Now? Is this whole thing a joke, John Russ…"

John raised his hand with traffic cop impact. "No picnic, Laura. This…" he held up the basket, "holds our lifeline to sanity." He waved it in the air and pointed to a table in the shade overhung by bougainvillea. "My guess is you haven't eaten. We have a long day ahead."

Laura realized she hadn't eaten since the night before. Her stomach growled. Her eyes drooped and her temper hovered near exploding. "A long day? I've already had a long day, John. Russell. You called in the middle of family dinner, remember?"

"No, I don't remember. It's not my job. Eva called you."

"Oh, for Christ's sake, John. "Stop…"

"No, Laura," interrupted John. "You keep wanting things to be easy. Only they're not. You have a job with extraordinary responsibilities—as do I. You also earn an extraordinary amount for doing it. I was inconvenienced, too, if you haven't noticed. Who's apologizing to me?"

Laura looked down. *Take a breath. He's got a point. Lots of jobs interrupt dinner—and life.*

"Breathe, Laura."

Her head jerked up. *He's reading my mind.*

They reached the shaded coolness by the table.

He pulled two rickety stools from underneath the table. "I want you trained for the big time. Real life is how I do it." He wiped his finger along the edge of the dusty table. "The Costa Ricans don't picnic much at work." He turned the stool upside down. "But I don't see any roaches here." John gestured to the now upright seat. "Sit. Eat. Recuperate."

She looked at him as if he were crazy. "I think I'll stand for a bit."

"As you wish." He shrugged and sat down on the second stool.

Laura watched Manuelo create their eating space. He cleaned the table top, laid place mats, bordered them with forks, knives and spoons. Then he laid two red-brown crockery plates in the center along with blue plastic glasses. Containers of food, homemade by Manuelo's wife, were removed from the basket and placed within reach. The smells from the hot meal anchored Laura into Costa Rica and left Cleveland far behind.

As a final gesture, Manuelo dusted her chair top and bottom, then set it with care on the ground. Laura sat. She had no strength left to think, talk, or resist.

She ate.

***

John stood next to Laura as Manuelo cleared the meal and dishes from the table. "Has your brain caught up with your body yet?"

She looked at him. "How did you know?"

"I've done emergency travel more than I care to remember—one minute you're here, next minute you're not. You learn to manage the trip effects. Part of the job. When we get back, Eva can give you the 'Tips.'"

"The 'Tips?'"

"All about how to handle the shitty parts of travel." He smiled. "It takes practice. You'll get there."

The hot meal had revived her.

"If I'm still alive," Laura retorted.

"Ah." He smiled. "I see you've reached the 'I-wonder-if-I-can-manage-this-job-and-fuck-the-money' point."

Laura flushed, shocked at how right he was.

"Seems I hit the nail on the head." He crossed his arms.

She hated being so transparent. "How did you know?"

"I've watched your predecessors face the same decisions—about seven months in—where you are now. This job is hard. The $700,000 salary seemed to be the tipping point in favor of staying. A lot of money for a lot of work."

She nodded.

"When they left after two years, each woman told me she'd earned every penny of the $1,400,000." He paused. "I like you, Laura. I want you to stay."

Laura pushed back her stool and stood. "When do we start the surgery?" At the moment, she had no idea what else to say.

Chapter 38

Eight hours for a critically difficult surgery to eliminate a squamous cell carcinoma on a cerebral blood vessel about to burst. Even saying it was exhausting.

High tech endoscopic, endonasal surgery.

On a critically important human being.

In secret.

A patient unknown to the surgical team.

Except for John Russell.

Who kept the secret.

Until it was over.

The patient almost died when a stretched blood vessel burst.

John Russell stopped the bleed.

Laura helped.

The surgical removal continued.

At 9:00 p.m. they admitted the patient, carcinoma removed, to intensive care for recovery.

Laura and John showered at the hospital. A snack basket awaited them—meaty hot soup in covered mugs.

Manuelo drove them home. "I see tiredness in the eyes," he said, and remained silent the rest of the trip.

John offered a single sentence. "I'll explain at the Villa."

Laura had no words and no sentences.

***

The moonlit patio at Villa Nueva Esperanza held two drinks, two chairs, two people and a light meal.

"Explain," she said.

He took a deep breath, tipped his chair back onto two legs. "Raul Castro," he said.

"Raul Castro, what?" she said.

"We operated on Raul Castro."

"What?!" It came out as a squawk. "Castro? Raul Castro? Is that what you said?"

"Do you need hearing aids, Laura?"

"Oh, my God." She was out of her chair. "Do you reali…"

"I do," he cut in.

"He almost died," she squeaked.

"I know."

She stood, paced one way, turned and paced the other.

"Laura."

"What?"

"Sit," he commanded. "Now."

She sat.

"You're overtired."

"Not any more, I'm not," she said. "I'm never, ever going to sleep again."

"Don't exaggerate."

"Fuck you."

"I know the feeling," he said.

"Why didn't you tell me before?"

"Protocol." He paused. "And this."

"What's the 'this'?"

"Your reaction."

"My reaction? *My* reaction? I think my reaction is pretty normal, don't you? I mean, if Raul Castro died on the operating table, we'd be on the global hit list. War could break out. You're way too 'Mr. Casual' for what we…"

"Your reaction is normal for a first timer," he interrupted.

Silence.

"After today, you will no longer be a first timer."

Crickets and frogs twittered. Laura stared. John untipped his chair and filled her glass.

"Drink," he ordered.

She blinked instead.

"Drink."

She drank.

The patio meal lingered in semi-sultry heat under a half moon. Laura could not relax. Exhaustion transformed to wired anxiety. Raul Castro, lying strapped on a surgery table for eight hours in front of her, played over and over again in her mind. She picked at her food and gulped glasses of cacique.

"Laura." John's voice came across the table in gentle tones. "He's alive. You're okay. This is life with the Big Boys. It takes training."

"Hmmm."

John gave up. He finished his dinner, went to Laura, took her hand and led her to the couch. "Here, lean up against me." She did. His hands began a firm, tension releasing massage on the tightened muscles in her neck.

"Ouch."

"You're tense."

"Brilliant diagnosis." But she let him continue.

It started as a twinge and whisper in her groin—a hot spot—a red poppy flower. It snaked through her spine and took up residence in her mouth. It became a sinuous, hungry, desirous tongue. It wanted. Now. No delay. She curled her body around and pressed to his chest. Her teeth nipped at his neck, his throat, his chin. Her hands reached around his back. She drew her legs up to kneel over him, crotch to crotch.

Her tongue licked his neck and slid to earlobe, inch by slow inch. A bite, hard, then a soft dry lick to his ear and then into it—deep, silky, breathy. His phallus stiffened, once, and then harder. Her body wound in close, molding, melting into angles. Her lips searching, parting, probing.

She licked the inside of his teeth and cheeks, withdrawing, inserting, touching inside. Her hands rifled through his hair, her pantied vulva pressed on his erection. He pulled her knit shirt high on her back, caressing, kneading, sparking tingles down her spine. Tonight, no brassiere strapped her flesh.

He pulled open his shirt, wrapped arms round her back and pressed loosened breasts against his chest, bodies held close and still, one to another. His hands moved underneath the sheer panties and held firm to her buttocks. His erection hardened against her. She moaned. He ripped the panties open and exposed her moistness. She crouched over his rigid manhood, wet, hungry, paralyzed with sexual need.

"Take me," she whispered, "take me."

Sudden pain ripped through her as he dug and scraped fingernails into the fleshy cheeks of her backside. She screamed with the pain, and thrust forward, loosening her legs. He thrust into her while pulling down. She cried with pain, desire and loss of control. Over and over he thrust—deeper, longer, heavier. One hand moved to her nipple, pinched hard, then kissed, then licked, and over again. Until finally, somewhere the red poppy in her groin exploded into a million pieces.

From somewhere she heard his cry follow hers. Then the night sounds closed over them and all became a silent, gentle sleep.

***

Laura woke on the couch just before dawn, tangled in legs and arms. Her body pressed against John's chest and groin. Breathing in the sultry air, she closed her eyes, feeling the warmth of his body, remembering their coupling the night before. Tiredness still tugged at her limbs and her brain.

Maybe I'll just drift back to sleep. Her mind started to slide back into darkness only to be shattered into pieces. A sexual desire rose from her gut so powerful it lit lightbulbs, drowned out yesterday's orgasm, crowded over reason, commandeered action. Her 'what-the-fuck-is-going-on-with-me' thought got lost in the avalanche.

She slid to John's phallus, took it to her mouth, inched moist lips towards its base, curled her tongue around the flesh, withdrew, licked the turgidity, blew throaty, windy breaths over it and licked again. Over and over and over and over until she was so wet, she dripped moisture to his legs from her passage.

Awake, alert, releasing a groan, John pulled her to him and thrust inside—gazing, watching, absorbing the soft, glowing morning light on her breasts. They copulated and fornicated and fucked and satisfied desire for a long, long time. Slow and fast and easy and hard. Wet, intense, wild, complete.

Hours later, in morning sunlight, Laura made love to John again. Her need seemed insatiable and John followed her into it with erection after erection.

When desire withdrew, step by step from loins and bones, they lay together and laughed. Wild, funny laughs, full of surprise and satiation. They breathed and listened and felt the gentle movement of the air.

Nowhere could Laura find an anxious bone in her body.

***

Later, leaning her head on her hand, she asked, "What happened?"

"What'd you mean, 'what happened?'"

"You know, like what happened to me?"

"I have no idea what you're going on about." He looked at her with curiosity.

"What got me so—sexed up. What happened to me? That's what I mean."

"Oh, that," he said.

"What's 'oh, that' mean?" she demanded, glaring.

"You get used to it."

"Get used to *that*? That was way beyond over the top, John Russell. What do you mean 'get used to it'?"

"Coffee first." He swung feet onto floor, stood naked in the sun and stretched.

Laura scooted out of bed, wrapped a robe around and said, "You better."

"I will. Coffee first." He wrapped a towel around his waist.

The aroma of Costa Rican coffee preceded Manuelo as he carried in a breakfast tray, placed cups and carafe on the table and withdrew. John gestured for her to sit.

"Okay—wild sex. Talk" she pulled out a chair.

John balanced his cup without spilling while he rocked back on the legs of his chair.

How does he do that?

"Last night's sex—it's the fallout from Risky Big Business. It doesn't show up with little things. I created your job because of last night."

She glared.

"Well, all right—not last night, but—like last night."

She glared more.

"Okay. Okay. I'll spell it out." He crossed arms behind his neck. "In DC, I got a reputation for handling risky cases—successful operations on big-time patients with big-time diseases. Money flooded in. Big Money with Big Risks—stuff most docs didn't want to handle. But I could and I did—like Raul Castro."

Laura stopped glaring. She hadn't heard this before.

John stood, went to the liquor cabinet and brought a bottle of bourbon to the table. He dashed an amount into his coffee cup before he continued.

"With the money, came the connections. The more successful I got, the more people wanted to hang around me. The Washington Post inducted me into DC's "Big Time' with a huge misquote under my photo. '*I can cure anything,* says Dr. Miracle.' What I'd said was, 'I don't take a patient I can't cure.' With a few drinks under my belt, I didn't think about what I'd said. But the morning paper set me straight. That's when I started watching every word I said and who I talked to."

He reached for a banana on the breakfast tray, peeled it, and cut slices into a dish along with strawberries. He poured heavy cream on the fruit and sprinkled it with ginger sugar.

"Every word?" she prodded getting him back on track. "That's a bit much."

"Easy with clients. Harder with the press. Fucking impossible with the women. My whole life style kept me pumped on adrenaline—taking the risks I took, getting the money I got, doing the social scenes I had to go to. It was one constant, testosterone-spiked, adrenaline high."

He stood, stretched and bent over the table. "Want me to top you off with some bourbon?" he asked. Laura shook her head.

"Dangerous surgeries would get me adrenaline pumped for hours after. I didn't have time to re-coup. I had too many surgeries. But sex—good, hard, heavy sex—always brought me down—on time and ready for the next day's operations. Anyway..." Sip of coffee. Deep breath.

"Anyway...?" pushed Laura.

"Well, that was you—last night."

Laura's cheeks throbbed with the blood of a furious blush.

"It's a bulldozer of a feeling," he continued, sitting down again. "You've got to have Sex with a capital S and No is not an option. Have I described last night, Ms. Greenwald?"

She nodded, face averted. *He's spot on.*

"When I was married, I wild-sexed with my wife. As newlyweds, we loved it. When I got divorced, somebody was always around for a good fuck—even several somebodies."

He steepled his fingers and rested his chin on them. "The trouble was, those somebodies were also around when I didn't want them—like—the next day. 'Thanks for the fuck and close the door on your way out.'"

Laura swirled her coffee. "I can imagine how well that went over."

He stood again, crossed his arms and turned toward the patio. "The dates I'd go on, we'd have dinner, go to bed, go home. Simple. Until 'involvement talk' started. 'Not interested—too involved with work,' I'd say. Some retaliated—paternity suits, theft of personal information, hiring a thug to rough me up. Any one of which is more than enough. I had way more than one."

He stopped talking. Laura waited. An important part of the story crouched at the edge of his silence. She could feel it.

"I was too work committed to deal with that shit." He kept looking at her until she began to grow uncomfortable.

She poured herself more coffee and brought it to the patio. "What happened?"

"The usual," he said. "I didn't deal with it--let things slide. Surgeries, research, money, parties, travel. No slow down time. I knew I'd lose my balance sometime—I just didn't know when." He stopped.

"Give," she prodded.

"It's not a fun thing to talk about."

"It was fun last night. Give."

"Nutshell version."

"Fine—give."

"Okay. Okay." He walked to the pool and gazed at the blue-white ripples stirred by the breeze. "Kendra was the last straw. She was French. Thin as a willow and just as beautiful. She'd dress in black with spiked heels, short skirts and…"

He stopped. "If you roll your eyes one more time, I'll quit and never talk about this again. That's a promise."

"Sorry…" she mumbled and bit her lip to keep it straight.

"No more disapproval of my maleness." He glared at her.

"Okay. Sorry," she repeated and looked down.

"Kendra—well, actually, Dr. Kendra—came from Paris to study robotic surgery. Every trainee had a supervisor. I was hers. She'd show up at the hospital in high heels—took them off for surgery. Said her calf muscles shortened up from years of wearing them." He laughed. "Hard image to forget."

I bet, thought Laura.

"She had an aura—like wisps of perfume. Every part of my body reacted to it. I spent hours in that halo of hers, just breathing it in." He pulled out a patio chair and sat, resting the bourbon flavored coffee on the garden ledge.

"She lived in the student dorms, went to the gym after work, studied at night and talked to her fiancée during lunch. 'There eese no time to waste,' she'd say. 'I must be a married woman to thees man I love.' When she said that, I'd get a hard on. I knew I was being stupid, but, Jesus Christ, I couldn't stop it."

"I can imagine," Laura said.

He stopped.

"Sorry. My bad."

John eagle-eyed her face until she forced it into neutral.

"I asked her to help me with a complex procedure—the last option for a guy with brain cancer who was all VIP—political, financial, social. We spent hours together, researching, practicing, sharpening skills. I got high from being with her so much." He drifted off again.

Oh, no you don't. I'm getting the rest of this story. Laura sat on the garden ledge and said, "John. Focus. Finish the story."

"Oh, right—well—the surgery went longer than expected—fourteen hours. Patient almost coded twice, bled internally, and blood pressures plummeted or skyrocketed. We were exhausted, wanted the damn thing over, and the patient in recovery. When that finally happened—I just—well, I kissed her. And it wasn't a chaste kiss. Then I said, 'Let's get a bunch of fuckin' drinks at the best bar in town.'"

Laura leaned forward. "Did she agree?"

"She didn't refuse. We got so drunk our waiter booked a room in the hotel, dragged us up elevators, down hallways and dumped us on the bed—clothes and all. We didn't notice—at first.

"And then?"

"When we woke up, sexual wildness decided to pay a visit. It had us both by the throat—and wouldn't let go 'til we'd had our fill. Then sleep and wake and all over again. Like last night. Only bigger. And more. I knew there'd be hell to pay but I didn't fuckin' care."

He let a long swallow of coffee slide down his throat. A pause, a breath, another cough.

"That was it?" Laura squirmed. Pebbles in the ledge wall pressed into her behind. *I'm not moving till he finishes this.*

"No. Hell had to be paid. The next day Kendra wouldn't look at me. I'd way overstepped. She knew it and I knew it. On top of that, I worried about harassment claims and emotional tangles clogging up our work. Stupid me, I still wanted her. I never thought she'd pull anything as stupid as she did." He leaned back in the chair.

An empathetic cringe for Kendra crept into Laura's gut as she waited for John to finish.

"Kendra showed up in my office a few weeks later with legal papers and attitude. She stood in the doorway and demanded payment for pain and suffering plus an all-expenses paid abortion and recuperation period."

John sat upright, crossed his arms. Laura watched his neck muscles tighten.

"She blindsided me. A sexual harassment suit—okay. But not this. I hadn't forced her; she was willing, able and un-drunk when we had sex. I still can't wrap my head around how my mind exploded when those papers dropped on my desk. I just stared at her."

Laura shifted position. "What did you do?" she asked.

"I asked her the question."

"What question?"

"The 'did you know I have a vasectomy' question. John stopped talking. Silence slammed onto the patio space. Minutes ticked by before he said anything.

"She stood there, didn't say a word. 'I'll do a DNA test,' I said. But she ripped the papers out of my hand and screamed, 'Theese eese what you men all say to we women. You say, 'It is not mine,' And I say, 'I hate you.' Then she ran out the door. I ran after her. She'd flung the papers all over the corridor. When I couldn't find her, I picked them up and cancelled the rest of my surgeries that day. I'd never done that before—or since."

Laura could no longer sit on the pebbly retaining wall. "What happened to her?" she asked, standing and rubbing her backside.

"Don't know. She quit the next day. Left for France. Administration investigated on our end but wouldn't share details. I kept my mouth shut, my head down, my record clean—and called my lawyers."

"I'm sorry," said Laura. "It sounds…"

"It was," he interrupted. "But it made me stop doing it."

Laura's eyes squinted into the question. "Doing what?"

"The 'Big Boys' stupid act."

"John, cut the double speak." She stood in front of him, feeling as if she were pulling teeth.

"The Big Boys—the untouchables—the men with power, money, influence, connections. It's like there's a semi-secret 'Club.' No women allowed of course. You know you've been given a membership card when you do some 'horrible-whatever-the-fuck-it-is-you-just-did-thing' and nobody does a thing. Nothing. Worst case scenario—you get hassled a little bit.

"Look what happened with me and Kendra. Administration knew I'd done something big and bad, but no one pushed. They didn't want to know. And they won't push—at least, until you shoot yourself in the foot too many times. If you're that stupid, they toss you as bloody bait to the media crocodiles." He drained his coffee cup.

I've met members of that shit club, she thought.

"Would you mind, Laura?" he asked.

She startled. "Mind what?"

"Getting me the bottle of Glenlivet scotch in the cabinet."

"Not the bourbon?" she asked and pointed to the bottle already on the table.

"Need the scotch to finish this fuckin' story off."

She padded to the cabinet, shuffled around till she found the twenty-five-year-old single malt, pulled it out, and brought it over.

"So, you're in this so-called Club?" she prodded.

"Nobody handed me a membership card. But people started acting differently. I'd say 'jump' and people jumped. I'd tell them to fuckin' get out of my life and they'd leave—no questions. I'd slap money down—threaten legal action. 'Poof'— problem, gone. It's addictive. I haven't met anyone who doesn't want more of it—at first."

He coughed, poured coffee and followed it with scotch, swallowed, and cleared his throat.

John never talks like this. Last night must have been some personal milestone—sure as shit was for me. Laura sat motionless, afraid even her thoughts might distract him.

"Some guys never have a clue about what they're doing, don't care, and don't stop till something castrates them. Narcissists believe in their own brilliance and everyone else's stupidity. DC is infested with that types."

John Russell took another swig of coffee. "Then there are the guys who've been there, done that, and want out." He suspended his cup in both hands, elbows on the arms of his chair.

"John, you sure you want to pour $450 scotch into your coffee?"

"Never surer—top me off again."

She did. *How much more can he drink?*

"A bit more," he said.

"John, it's a half cup of..."

"Just pour it, Laura.

She did.

Then she waited.

It took a few minutes. He sipped the scotch and coffee—shoulders relaxed; spine settling into the chair.

"I was lucky—I got out before disaster hit. Lots of men would rather go down in flaming disaster than give up Big Boy privileges. I knew I smashed Kendra's life. Part of me said 'Fuck her." He uncrossed his legs and stared into the scotch-filled coffee mug. "In the end, my moral decency hadn't quite expired."

"What did you do?"

"I called my lawyers." He shrugged. A rueful smile appeared. "What else do you do in DC except call the lawyers?"

Laura laughed. "In Boston, you call the doctors."

"I was one of the smart ones my lawyers told me. Most of their work was digging people out of their own shit. 'Lucrative business,' they said, 'but 'repetitive.' What I wanted was unique—creative. It might take up to a year to do, but noth…"

"Stop." Laura sliced through his sentence leaving John's mouth hanging half open. "Take a year? Unique? What are you talking about?"

He scanned her face. "Are you not with me, Laura? I'm talking about how your contract got written."

Hold your tongue, Greenwald. She took a deep breath.

Don't know if I can. "Your story meandered through some history, Dr. Russell. Excuse me if I got lost."

John raised his coffee and scotch mug in apology. "Truce," he acknowledged. Without waiting for a response, he continued. "It took them a year to develop. They'd tell me, 'So sorry. Nothing's been done like this—all new—has to be air-tight.' I decided to stay away from sex till I could be protected by a contract." He stopped.

She held out her coffee mug. "Throw a bit of that scotch into mine."

He laughed, poured the gold liquid into her cup, spilling it on the table as she tugged it back. "Whoa," she cried, "way too much." Scotch and coffee sloshed over her wrist. "So—tell—how did The Year of No Sex work out?"

"I substituted. Started getting massages. That's how Massage Friday at work. Share the wealth and get a happy staff. It was a good year. No hassles, no complications."

"You're expecting me to believe *that* after the I-Need-Wild-Sex stories you just told?"

A knock on the door stopped conversation. Amparo's voice called out. "It is time for prepare almuerzo. Will Senor John stay for the lunch plate?"

John caught Laura's eye. She nodded. "Yes, Amparo, we'll be here," he called out.

"Si, senor." Her footsteps receded.

Laura looked up. "We've been talking a long time."

"Too long." He put his cup down, stood, paced toward the patio, then back. "I'm telling you this because you need to know how important your contract is. Your contract keeps the whole organization safe because it keeps me scandal proof."

"Righ…" she began, but stopped when John locked eyes with her.

"I said the year was good. I never said it was easy. Temptation threw itself at me over and over—sexy and hard to turn down. For example: did you know the French have an etiquette for cocktail party seduction?"

Laura shook her head.

"Well, there is. I got an invitation to a charity ball at the French Ambassador's house. European décor, of course—painted ceilings, marble floors, French windows, manicured gardens—the works. Quite lovely."

***

John, dressed in black tuxedo and bow tie for the ambassador's ball, scanned the crowd as he held a martini glass to his lips.

"Dr. Russell, the miracle doctor," said a woman's voice behind him. "I have seen the pictures. They do you no justice."

An older woman, in a long, amber gown, hooked her arm into his. "Come, I will introduce you to the ladies who so desire to greet you." She laughed at his startled look. "I am Marianne, the ambassador's wife—it is my duty to make comfortable each person who enters our home."

Six women surrounded him before they'd moved more than a few feet. "I give you now to French comfort," smiled Marianne as she left. Excitement laced through the women's chatter as they probed for information about his 'astonishing cures.'

"I am so sorry. Patient privacy, mademoiselles," John repeated six times before he could shift the conversation to innocuous topics.

During the same time, a new and urgent problem arose. He needed to use his hands. They currently held his martini glass. He glanced around for help. "Would you ladies care for another drink?" He raised one arm to summon a waiter without waiting for responses.

"Yes, Monsieur?"

"These ladies would like a second drink." He placed his empty glass on the tray and smiled.

"Certainly, Monsieur. Right away." The waiter bowed and retreated, leaving John with empty hands. He spread his legs a few inches in military style and placed crossed hands in front of his crotch. The bulge in his pants had come and gone throughout the entire conversation, each time bigger and harder. This time it refused to go away.

John waited for the drinks to come, then said, "Excuse me, ladies. I must take a few moments to myself." He extricated himself and headed to the restrooms located off the opposite side of the ballroom. When he reached the empty hallway, he whispered a frustrated, "Shit. This is totally adolescent. For several moments he stood in front of the restroom door, eyes closed, breathing deeply.

"Jesus Christ!"

A hand caressed his neck. It slid down his back and pulled at his waist, turning him around. Inches from his face stood a woman from the group. Long, black hair pulled behind her ears, dropping straight to her waist. A white, long-sleeved dress V-necked to her cleavage. The long front slit in the skirt sliced upwards the top of her legs. John gave up trying to hide the rock-hard bulge in his pants.

'Thank you," she said. "I'd be honored."

"Honored? About what?" Her confusing words triggered the startled, blunt response.

"Why, to have a drink with me later…and perhaps something more? Did you not ask me again and again with your eyes in our conversations? Everyone could see it. After all, of what use are all those silly words except to make such a decision? Do you not practice so in this country?" She smiled. "I can see you are a little interested, no?"

***

John stopped his story. He put the coffee cup on the table, paced toward the patio pool, then came back. "Once I got to that certain point of power and money," he explained, "things like that woman kept falling at my feet. She was beautiful and willing. I was drunk and horny." He took a long swig from the cup and gazed out at the garden.

"What did you do?" prodded Laura. *If he stops again, I'll pull my hair out.*

"I wanted to take that French lady from nowhere for drinks and fucks. But Kendra had just happened. Five lawyers were being paid a shitload of money for a year to write the contract you signed. If I couldn't control myself for a few months, I was doomed for the long run."

Laura watched John drain the liquid out of his coffee cup.

"So, I voted for sanity. I stood there, my penis hard as a rock, and said, 'I'm engaged.'

"'Engaged?' She laughed in my face. 'I send condolences to your fiancée.' Her finger stroked my cheek. 'Liar,' she whispered. Then she left me standing in the hallway."

He sat at the table and leaned forward. "Not an easy year, Laura. But that's the long and the short of it."

His abrupt ending caught Laura off guard. "The long and the short of what?"

John scowled at her. "Didn't you ask me a question? Did I spend all this time pouring my guts out and you missed the answer?"

Oh, shit, here we go again. Retreat time. "No, I got it. Sorry." She looked down at her coffee. It was cold and she was tired.

John stood. "I'm going for a swim."

He stripped naked, walked across the patio and dove into the pool.

Chapter 39

The night before, Laura lost the argument although she tried her best. "DC is humid and overpopulated, John," she'd argued. "Costa Rica is sunny, dry, and beautiful. Staying a few extra days is a no-brainer.

He'd just stared at her. And now he waited in Manuelo's car with his arms crossed.

***

Wasted was the word Laura used when the trip was over. "I'm wasted, dish-rag-rung-out wasted."

She dropped her suitcase, unlocked her apartment, and stripped off coat and gloves. Five days only since she'd impulsively headed to Cleveland. Her window plant lay wilted on the sill.

"Some holiday trip," she mumbled. "I can't keep anything alive except at work."

Phone calls had piled up on her personal cell phone. Why did she keep that damn thing, anyway? Bloody waste of money. She was never home. Caller ID showed Arlo's name. She punched at the machine irritably.

She sat down, got up, stalked to the window and looked out. A dreary, grey afternoon stared back at her. "I'm just plain, annoyingly, humongously irritable."

She massaged her neck, turned from the window, selected a wine glass, poured it quarter-full, sat down, swirled the cup and began to sip. She sat in the dark, her legs tucked under for two-hours until she sorted out what she needed to do.

She didn't want to do it.

But the way things were going, what difference was that going to make?

***

The afternoon crowd at Church Key Restaurant was light. Laura took the cold twenty-seven-minute walk from the hospital to the bar as an antidote. She slipped onto the red leather bar seat, shrugged off her coat, silently mouthed 'waiting for a friend' to the bartender, and glanced along the plank of the bar top searching for the face. Not here, not yet. A few minutes' reprieve—not a long time—but she'd take anything she could get. She really didn't...

"Laura!"

Arlo pushed through the front door, hand and woolen scarf held high, waving at her across the tables. She waved back, waiting as he wound towards her. She reached to give him a hug but he avoided it, cupped her face in his hands and kissed her full on the mouth. Then he kissed her cheeks, her nose, her forehead and whispered, "I missed you, Laura. Can you tell?" He enveloped her in a bear hug. Her peripheral vision caught the bartender with full-on grin.

Arlo sat, then got up and pulled her toward a booth in the far back of the eatery.

"Give. How is Cleveland? Humid and hot like DC? Or sunny breezes across the Great Lakes with picnic baskets and red wine? God, it's good to see you! Am I being a jerk or what?" and he gave her another hug.

His enthusiasm opened her heart, pushed her decision away, made her forget it, squash it, mangle it, remove it. He ordered drinks. They talked. They laughed and they ate—double cheese and cilantro bruschetta, gnocchi with broccoli rabe, pine nut pesto, candied hazelnuts with ginger and lattes.

"Let's walk," he said.

"Now? Where? I can't move."

"It'll do you good."

"I bet. To which location in DC are you planning this after dinner walk, senor?"

"To my house."

Her stomach clenched and she stumbled.

I'm not ready, she thought.

"You ok?" Arlo asked looking at her face tighten. "The walk is great—city lights at night, fresh air, a warm hand to hold yours…"

I'll do it later, just not now.

So, she did not, not then and not there.

The walk home was delightful.

The hand that held hers was warm.

The city night lights were beautiful.

The air was fresh.

The welcome home lovemaking was best of all.

When it was over, she hugged him tightly.

He didn't see that she began to cry.

They fell asleep, warm, entwined, familiar.

And that was the last time in her life she felt she would ever make love to Arlo Stephanopoulos.

***

"What do you mean it's over?" he said the next morning, incredulous.

"I can't explain it to you." She looked down.

"After last night? What happened? What do you mean 'you can't explain'?"

"It's, well, I just can't. Something's come up. I…"

"Another man?" he interrupted. "Is that it? You met someone else?"

"I wouldn't really explain it that way."

"What does that mean? Are you sleeping with someone else?"

"Well—not really," she mumbled.

"What the fuck does 'not really' mean? Either you are or you aren't."

"That's not quite true." And around they went.

He never did understand and she never could explain.

It was 8:00 a.m. when she left his apartment.

He'd offered to drive her. She needed the two-mile walk to the hospital and work to settle her brain. 'No, thanks' were the last words she spoke to him.

She obsessed on the walk to work. Arlo was the kind of guy she could fall in love with. How could she ever explain a job contract with millions of dollars in salary plus mind-blowing 'protection' sex with her boss?

She couldn't.

And if she broke confidentiality? The consequences marched through her head like a grim parade.

Even without the 'sex part,' her job was a relationship killer— the secret keeping, the emergency disappearances, regular hours which were never 'regular,' life-and-death-on-a-string decisions. She could go on. It was too much for any relationship. The Job fucked up a stupid visit to her family—never mind a full-blown guy thing.

It isn't a job. It's a goddamned marriage.

Laura jerked to a stop, a dream-like vision clutching her by the throat.

She watched herself sign John's contract with a golden pen. When she'd finished, he slipped an enormous, diamond studded wedding ring onto her left hand. "You may say your vows later," said his ghostly voice as he faded from view. She turned. Arlo stood in a doorway, arms extended. "Arlo—I'm married," she cried.

"Miss? Miss?"

Laura, startled from her daydream, lost balance. The strong arm of a hospital security guard held her steady. "Are you well?" he asked, brow wrinkling.

"Yes. Yes, I'm fine. Thank you."

"It's safety, you know—can't be stopping in the middle of a going crowd, Miss."

Laura fled into the hospital foyer, cheeks flaming with embarrassment. *Secrets fuck up everything, including a walk to work.*

***

John mentioned it at the end of the week. "You've grown into the job," he said in clipped communication mode. "And," he paused, "I see you've decided to stay."

"It looks that way," she said.

"Good."

I gave up Arlo; sacrificed my home, lost girlfriends, and have a fucked-up sex life. 'Yes, damn it—I'm staying. Money and glitter won the vote—this time.

"Laura?" John stood in his office doorway. "What are doing? Your client's here—they're paging you."

"Oh. Sorry." Laura turned to go. Her left foot twisted. Pain shot through the leg. *Shit, shit, shit.*

"By the way," his voice called after her, "I squeezed you in for a 5:00 p.m. urgent care patient. You'll have to stay late." He shut his door. The words hung in the air, taunting and commanding.

I'm not gonna quit—not yet, she repeated over and over limping down the corridor. *'Power and money,' John said, 'I haven't met anyone who doesn't want more of it—at first.'*

A disembodied voice sliced through her thoughts. "Laura Greenwald—your client has arrived. Please contact the front desk."

She opened her office door, ankle still throbbing. *Back to work.*

Chapter 40

The late March sunshine burst open Washington's pink and white cherry blossoms. Wind scattered days of petals over the ripples. The air carried no trace of a hot, damp summer in the making.

Daniel dropped her at the Tidal Basin amidst spring sun and scents. She planned to meander the rest of the way to the hospital. A little over a year had passed since her appointment to The Job. One more to go.

She'd decided to stay in her Mt. Pleasant apartment with its woodland view and neighborhood feeling. It was unpretentious and practical. Her travel schedule over the one-year-left-to-go on her contract would never give the tiny space a chance to agitate or irritate. She didn't keep up with friends, did not entertain, did not date, and spoke to her parents less than once a month. Her mental mantra—*Million-Dollars-and-Growing*—had carried her through numerous irritations.

Arlo had called on and off for a month. After each call, she went for an hour run, order Thai food, and binge-watch *Game of Thrones*. As Laura walked to work, her mind replayed the night she blocked Arlo's phone number. It had depressed her for weeks.

"Arlo, how sweet, but, no, I can't," Her face scrunched up. She sat rigid on her couch that Sunday evening holding the cell phone to her ear. *I'm a fucking liar—I'd love to go.* She had just spent the weekend with her boss at his Shenandoah cabin. The mistake of mixing Arlo with John again made her cringe.

"Listen, Laura. I promise—just pick you up and drop you off. It's front row theater tickets to *Hamilton*. One of my…"

"No. Arlo. No." And she hung up.

Tears welled up and spilled over. Her irritating nose dripped onto her tee shirt. Even the *got a million-dollars-and-just-a-year-to-go* chant didn't impact the pain. Laura rooted around for a sleeping pill in the medicine cabinet and washed it down with a steaming hot cup of Sleepytime Tea. Somewhere in the middle of watching *Die Hard* for the fifteenth time she fell asleep.

***

That was months ago. Wonder what's bringing it up now. Her thoughts floated on the rhythm of her footsteps *All work and no play got me good at what I do. Work together—travel— recoup together. The 'Big Boys' might appreciate John's contract.* Laura smiled. *That would be a game changer.*

But she couldn't deny the days when black depression clouded every thought—when what was buried struggled for life. Laura dreaded those times. She'd flee to the cinema to watch movies back to back until every cell in her body wanted only sleep.

"Watch the hell where you're goin', lady," screamed the driver as he slammed on his brakes. Horns blared; brakes squealed.

Laura jerked to a stop. Her body stood two feet from the sidewalk in busy morning traffic. *How did that happen?* She scooted backwards onto the curb, brain jangled and adrenaline pumped. The inner fight to keep her one-sided, Contract-is-King life balanced was getting dangerous.

***

Adrenaline still pumping, Laura went to scrub in for the morning surgeries, but found a note from Eva on her locker instead.

"Schedule change. Come to my office."

"Everything okay?" asked Laura when she arrived.

Eva, making notations in a large folder answered without looking up. "Yup," she said, "John's on emergency consult. Wants you to observe first surgery with Dr. Lewis, then assist him for the rest of the day."

Eva closed the file, picked out several papers from a stack on her desk, and handed them to Laura. "Here's your schedule and billing forms for Dr. Lewis. We charge him for your hours."

Laura turned to go. "Eva?"

"Hmmmm?" She had already slipped back into work.

"Why don't you digitalize all this?" Laura gestured to the large manila file on Eva's desk. "It looks ancient when you pull out reams of paper instead of the computer."

Eva looked up in surprise. "Oh—this? It's your contract. John wants it separate from the digital records—too easy to hack—or copy. The full file's locked in a safe at the mansion. I'll call Daniel to drive it back to Virginia as soon as I'm done updating. You didn't know all that?"

"No," said Laura, "I'm still learning."

She closed the door, wondering if she'd hallucinated about being able to manage another year working with John.

***

The summer came. It included the birth of the Vice President's healthy granddaughter, three trips to Costa Rica, one more to Saudi Arabia, two separate emergency consults on site in South Africa and a Fourth of July trip to her family in Cleveland.

Laura picked the trip home to Cleveland as her first battle campaign.

She went into John's office the afternoon before her flight.

He'd leaned back in his swivel chair and crossed his arms behind his neck. "I hear you've taken a hefty four days off," he commented. "Good for you. Enjoy the rest."

"Thank you," she said but didn't leave.

"Something else?" he asked after a moment.

"Yes." She took a deep breath. The words she'd rehearsed until her voice rang firm and clear rolled from her lips. "Under no circumstances, John, including World War III, am I going to interrupt this trip. It's three nights away from work. Whatever problem the world concocts in that time will have to wait."

"Agreed," he said. "Everything's quiet on the western front. So, go. I promise not to call. Cross my heart and hope to die."

"Boy scout?" she asked.

"No. It just sounds good."

She laughed and left, relieved at how easy standing up for herself had been.

Two days later, in the kitchen of her parents' home, Laura's mother handed her the phone. "There's a lovely lady calling for you dear."

"For me? Okay...Hello? Eva? Emergency? South Africa...I see." She paused a moment, took a deep breath and let the blood rage through her veins. "Yes. Tell him it will wait—or—he can go by himself." And she hung up.

"Moms," Laura called out.

"Yes, dear?"

"Don't give me any more phone calls."

"Yes, dear."

***

She flew to South Africa with John on July 7th instead of July Fourth. The patient survived the operation, and John Russell negotiated another year of health consultation with the Johannesburg hospital.

When they returned home, Laura stood taller as she walked down the hospital and clinic corridors.

John glowered behind a dark cloud and avoided walking in the same hallway with her for over a week.

The iceberg between them froze the ground they walked on.

The day it melted was a late July afternoon. Supreme Court Justice Ruth Bader Ginsberg, keynote speaker at hospital auditorium, invited medical staff to meet her just before the speech.

"Eva," said John, tones brusque and sharp, "tell Laura to meet at my office 3:30 sharp. We'll do a quick in-and-out for the Bader meeting."

"She's coming in just a minute—you could..."

"No. You tell her." He thwacked the door shut on his way out.

Laura appeared in his office at 3:30, opened the door, and saluted. "Here as commanded, Doctor." She stalked to the auditorium several paces behind him, her pumps clip-clapping on the pavement. Without warning, he jerked to a stop, spun on his heel, and she "thunked" into him.

"Stop this!" he demanded.

Still looking straight at his chest, she said, "You owe me an apology."

Moments passed, neither moving.

Pedestrians began to give them a wide berth.

He shifted his weight, first to one leg, then the other.

"Okay, I admit. I promised not to call." he said.

"I know," she retorted, still staring at his chest. Silence. She didn't move. "So, I want the apology."

"I just said it."

"No, you didn't. You said I was right. That's a fact, not an apology."

Silence.

"Ok, I'm sorry," he mumbled.

"For what?"

"For God's sake, Laura! For what we've just been talking about." He almost stamped his foot in frustration.

"We haven't been talking, if you've noticed."

Silence.

"Oh, for Heaven's sake—all right—for calling you when I said I'd leave you alone."

"And for acting like a complete ass since we got back?"

"Yes, that, too."

"What 'too'?"

"For acting like a jerk afterwards."

She looked up, smiled and said, "That was like pulling teeth."

"No shit, Sherlock," he retorted.

277

But the glacier had cracked. They were back "on track"—*whatever that means,* thought Laura.

He looked at her. "You've grown up, Laura."

"*Gettin' there,*" she thought, *if it doesn't kill me first.*

Chapter 41

It happened late in October. 6:30 a.m. precisely.

On a Monday.

The Uber driver had opened the door to his Toyota Camry. She'd gotten out of the cream-colored car with its ivory interior. Her brown faux fur coat hugged warmth to her body.

She stepped out, gasped, bent over, and, clasping her midriff with one arm, vomited. Acidified coffee and cream splattered on the pavement. She tried wiping her mouth with a tissue from a coat pocket. Uncooperative fingers brushed at invisible coffee spots on the hem.

Damn that scallop dinner last night, was all she could think.

"Ma'am, you all right?" Can I help?" The young face bent low towards hers. "Jeez—this is my first pick-up… I'm sorry. You okay?"

She stood up, his steady arm on her elbow, a wobbly smile on her face. "I'm fine—I think. Scallops last night."

"Oh, yeah, that'll do it. My aunt has this scallop allergy thing real bad. At least you're at the hospital. We got you here in a jiffy— get well, okay?" he said, scurrying off.

Nice kid. Laura took a deep breath and felt the acid burn of stomach contents in her throat. She pushed open the hospital doors and willed her stomach to settle down.

***

By Wednesday, she wasn't feeling much better.

"Eva, I need time off—how does that work?"

Eva didn't look up from her work. "Hmm…, surprised you haven't asked before. Hold on; be with you in a second."

Eva's office at the Virginia mansion combined cozy home and efficient work space. Overstuffed pillows in the custom-made burl wood couch invited Laura to sink in.

"You look a bit peaked," commented Eva, when she looked up. "Go home for the day. I just did the arranging."

"No, really. I need to sleep in for about two days straight."

"Good luck with that." Eva bent over her computer. "Let's look at the calendar. We might manage one day unless you're sick—you know, like diseased? You're not sick, are you?" She looked at Laura, worry striping her forehead.

"No, nothing like that." Laura leaned back in the couch. "Just worn out. On-the-go hazard, I suppose."

Eva squinted at the digital calendar. "If you can hold off a day, I'll re-arrange your Friday clients—that'll give you three days in a row, counting the weekend. How's that?" Eva asked.

Laura never answered. She nestled deep in sofa cushions, fast asleep, one hand still holding her head in place. That was how she got an early ride home, two days' work release and four days off in a row.

***

The next morning Laura woke, took a shower, went into the kitchen, threw up, cleaned up, sat down and said, "I can't be pregnant. So, what the hell is going on?"

Her groggy brain demanded coffee. She managed to grind the beans, heat the water, place the filter, press the grind, and distill the black liquid into a mug. She added sugar and topped it all with frothed cream.

Beautiful. Perfect. Smells wonderful. Laura sat on the couch, pressed the mug to her lips, and took a long, deep sip. The frothing cream clung to her upper lip. She always loved to lick it off.

Seconds later it all came back out in an explosive cough. The sip had tasted like bitter lemons and, in shock, she'd swallowed the wrong way. Two full minutes of hacking cough left her in cramped pain. Exhausted and frightened she wiped up the mess, sat on the couch, and fell asleep.

***

Sunlight, an after-drizzle, grey afternoon color, poked around Laura's eyelids. It woke her.

She pulled on boots and jeans, tucked in the pajama tee shirt she still had on from the night before, and grabbed her coat.

Destination—pharmacy. Fifteen-minute walk—she damn well better stay awake for that.

The overstuffed shelves in the tiny neighborhood drugstore held more feminine products than she'd ever imagined existed. Searching for one label amidst the riot of packages taxed her ability to focus.

"You are finding what you need, Miss?" called a voice from the front of the store, which was, she estimated, only about ten feet away.

"Uh, yes, thanks." Laura refused to announce she was looking for a pregnancy test kit. She rummaged around on her own through overstocked shelves until she saw it. The three-pack of Early Response Fast Result test sticks lay next to the lubrication jellies.

No coincidence there, she thought. She pushed twenty-five dollars toward the clerk and left, collar pulled high to keep the wind from snaking down her neck on the way home.

There's no way I'm pregnant. Laura's brain trolled through a list of horrible diseases she could have—chronic fatigue syndrome, liver failure, cancer, fibromyalgia. Hunched over, she mentally stacked up her defense--*the newest, super best IUD ever made—and a guy with a vasectomy. That's a strong line-up.*

She sighed. *Except for the shit-load of sex they'd been having. No one's gonna 100% guarantee a vasectomy. Read it on the internet.* The mental joke didn't crack Laura's grim feeling.

John was her only sex partner. The work kept them under constant pressure. They coupled often, the fucking quick, intense, releasing.

Sometimes, they'd do it in the operating room after a hard surgery. One of the patients had come near to death. After Laura clamped the burst artery, it gave way a second time. Swabbing blood from the living brain tissue had extended and hampered work. When it was over, hours later, he'd asked for fifteen-minutes alone in the room to clear his head. She stayed with him.

His phallus had been hard, dense, dry.

"I'm going to take you now, Laura."

He stripped her scrub pants along with panties, grabbed her buttocks and hips and thrust inside—deep, deep inside. Her lubrication started the instant he spoke. His hard phallus met a wet, smooth welcome. They fucked hard as she bent over the uncleared operating table—panting, thrusting, lifting and coming—first she, then he.

Without a word she collected her pants and he his, and were re-settled when the orderly called from the other side of the door.

It had been like that many times. In the Virginia clinic, he would slot himself in for a half-hour of her clinic time. Then he would just fuck her. And she him. The harder they worked, the harder they fucked. Their teamwork showed in the clinic and in the bedroom.

On one Shenandoah weekend, he'd rolled over towards her. "You're keeping me on the straight and narrow," he said.

She laughed. "This is not so straight and it's not so narrow." She climbed on top of him, held her vulva over the tip of his penis and rubbed her moistness onto the sensitive tip. He gasped.

"Not so narrow," she whispered, and slowly lowered herself onto him.

When they finished, he re-phrased. "What I meant was…"

"Shhh," she'd said and put a finger to his lips.

But she knew what he meant. She'd watched him magnetize woman after woman, in situation after situation—they were captured by his charm and power; he by theirs—or just by their beauty.

She watched the weaving of webs time and time again. Power, money, greed, self-interest, ambition, fame, sex, ego, high stakes thrills. She wove some of her own. But never did John Russell or Laura Greenwald occupy the bed of any other but their own. Their antidote lay signed, sealed, and delivered in Laura's contract, stored under lock and key.

Laura slipped on the drizzly sidewalk in front of her house and nearly went down. "Shit! Pay attention, girl," she yelled at herself.

She took the steps two by two, ran down the hall, fumbled for keys, and fell over her own threshold opening the lock. She shed coat and boots where she stood, headed for the bathroom, grabbed a cup in one hand, and held the pregnancy kit in the other.

"I gotta get rid of this pregnancy idea and get on to whatever stupid disease I've got," she announced to the empty bathroom.

Laura placed the pink cardboard package on the sink top. Inside lay three, plastic-wrapped test sticks with instructions. She read, then talked herself through the steps.

"Okay—so I do the pee-in-a-cup crouch." She did that. "Then collect my pee." She did that. "And put a stick in the cup. No sweat."

It started when she pulled the cap from the pink plastic tube. First her index finger cramped; then both her hands began to shake. "Don't be a jerk," she scolded herself. Which didn't help. She sat on her hands and took three large, deep breaths. *Ready?*

Dip.

Remove.

Wait three minutes.

Read result—two pink lines, probably pregnant. One pink line, probably not.

Laura glared at the oval window on the stick, shut her eyes, felt her heart thunk an annoying, unsteady rhythm.

Her eyes couldn't wait three minutes. They blinked open all on their own. She was left watching her future creep its slow way across the stripes on the little pink screen.

And then it was over.

Chapter 42

Eva Jormand looked over her computer screen as the door opened. Rope lights twinkled in the arched window bays of the office. They turned the grey Monday morning almost cheery with their glow.

"You feeling better? Not so tired?"

Laura stood stiff and well-dressed inside the closed doors. Seconds passed before she spoke.

She said, "Eva, I'm pregnant."

Not for one instant did her supervisor's face change.

"Ahh, I see." Eva rested elbows on the desk, steepled fingers, unflustered, competent.

"Well, we've had that situation in the past." A sigh. "It makes for complicated decisions. An empathetic smile emerged. "I'm sorry you have to face them."

Silence—for a long time.

Eva interrupted it.

"Laura, you're not alone. We'll help you through whatever you decide."

More silence. Laura stiffened further. Her rigidity kept her upright. Her mind whirled.

"Laura?"

Laura struggled to focus. "Yes?"

"You know who the father is, I assume?"

"Yes."

"Is it someone who you want involved in the decision-making?"

"Yes."

A long pause.

"Well then…have you mentioned it to him yet?"

"No."

"Do you plan to?"

"Yes."

"Who is it?"

"It's John."

Eva's laugh tinkled in the air. "No, that's not possible. You know it. We all know it. His vasectomy, your IUD—it's 120% effective."

"No, it's not."

Eva stared at Laura.

Laura stood unmoving and stubborn-straight. "It's not impossible Eva. John is this child's father."

"How can you know that?"

"Because I haven't slept with anyone else in six months."

"What about that neurosur…"

"I broke it off six months ago. How do you think…" Laura spread her arms wide, "this whole 'job arrangement' affects 'the other guy'? Or me?"

Eva watched—waited for Laura to continue.

Laura folded her arms and let the sarcasm drain away.

"It was screwing with my head, So, I made a decision. I decided I could finish the contract by leaving whatever life I had behind—friends, boyfriends, home life, night life—everything. That's what you can't tell your recruits, right? That you're in this lock, stock, and barrel—head, feet and toes—no room left over." She took a deep breath.

"John and I had a shitload of a lot of sex after I made that decision. And I mean whole, big, fuckin' truck loads."

"Laura, pleas…" Eva began to rise.

"Sit. I will finish this and you will listen."

Eva sat.

"I don't love him—not my type—except he can be totally charismatic sometimes, and really good in bed..."

"Laur..."

"Listen. To. Me."

Eva did not speak.

"The money, the power, the glamour, the people. Totally hypnotizing, irresistible. I didn't have enough chocolate cake on my metaphorical plate, I suppose." A deep breath.

"So, I broke off with Arlo—and any-future-one-else. With John—there's only room for John and John's shit. Nuthin' else. It pays a lot. But, you know, I finally agree—the salary matches the job. I stopped feeling sorry for myself and grew some balls."

Moments passed before she continued.

"Only now I'm carrying his child. And that's a fuckin' complication."

"Laura, it can't be John's."

She stared at Eva. "You think I'm lying?"

"No. I don't know what I think. False positive on the test, possibly? That happens."

Laura just stood.

Eva took a breath. "Let's have hospital obstetrics check you out."

"Dr. Mirimbe is out of the country." Laura's words resounded in wooden monotone.

"Not a problem. I assume you did a home pregnancy test. We'll re-check it with the hospital lab. We don't need Dr. Mirimbe for that." Eva stood, rounded the desk, placed hands on Laura's shoulders. "It's fine. We'll work it through."

***

They sat next to each other in two chairs across from the nurse practitioner who scrolled down her computer screen.

"We like to be as certain as we can when we talk about results. Ms. Jormand put in a rush order for your blood draw this morning, Ms. Greenwald. Let me find the results… Ahhh, here they are." She squinted at the laptop, smiled at Eva and Laura.

"Let me give you a little background information first."

They nodded.

"Okay. So, pregnancy tests have false positives. I'm sure you already know that. When an egg is fertilized, it creates a sac with several layers to protect the fetus. What we're looking for is human chorionic gonadotropin, or HCG for short. It's produced by the outermost sac around the baby. That's what urine and blood tests react to.

"Home kits measure if there's HCG in the urine. Blood draw can detect much lower levels of the hormone. They also detect how much is present—not just yes or no. If you are below five milli-international units per milliliter, it's considered negative." She wrote 'mIU/ml' on a pad. "If you're above twenty-five, you're pregnant."

The nurse tapped on the keyboard, eyes scanning the screen.

"Testing too early with home kits can give more false positives." She continued scrolling. "So, let's see…your last period was…"

"About five weeks ago," responded Laura.

"Ok…so…we've got a reading of 20." The nurse practitioner looked up. "That's in the 'not-quite-sure' zone. It may be a little too early to tell what's going on."

"I'm too tired and nauseated for it to be unclear," said Laura.

"Those are certainly symptoms of early pregnancy," responded the nurse. "But results vary substantially with each person. Tiredness and nausea are also symptoms of, well, many other things." She smiled. "Perhaps we could retest you in a week or so?"

"Thank you. I'll schedule the appointment." Laura stood and walked out. She left Eva to find her way back alone.

***

The operating room with its well-known routines kept her frayed nerves under control. Mask, scrubs, ticking machinery—all kept her swirling thoughts bound to a central hitching post called 'focus.' But yesterday's discussions with Eva intruded, playing over and over.

"Yes, Eva," she'd said, "I'll go back to work and forget everything till next week's retest."

"No, Eva, thank you. I don't want more diagnostics to rule out what I don't have—not yet." *Is he going to ditch me like that New York jerk of a doctor? 'Sorry, you're not convenient anymore and have a nice life?'* She thought that over the first cup of coffee—which made her slightly sick.

"No, Eva, I won't say anything to John till testing is finalized." *Wouldn't want to interrupt his work just because he got me pregnant.* That was over the second cup of coffee, which she didn't drink.

"Yes, Eva, I'm fine." *Like hell you are—this is gonna be New York all over again. Only this time my whole life is gonna get shafted.* That was over her third cup of coffee.

Laura didn't know if the smell of the coffee or what she was feeling made her nauseous. She'd excused herself and gone to throw up.

"Ok, we're done here!" John's call rattled Laura back to the operating room. He turned.

"Good job, Laura. Thanks," he said removing his gloves. "You're quiet today. Recuperated?"

She nodded.

"Glad to hear it. Up for a drink after work?"

She almost vomited at the thought, shook her head and walked to the operating room doors while stripping off gloves. Seconds later she was retching into the locker room toilet bowl.

She looked at the clock.

It was going to be a long day.

***

5:00 p.m. found a bedraggled Laura at John Russell's office door.

"Got a minute?" she asked.

He nodded, distracted, glanced up from paperwork and said, "You looked wiped."

"I am." She hesitated. Not long. But it allowed his eyes to start drifting back to the desk top.

"I have a diagnosis," she said, hurling the words into his moment of attention.

"And that is…?" he asked

"Overworked. Dehydrated. Sleep deprived."

He gave a slight nod, said, "Glad it's not complicated."

She rushed in to tell the antidote. Rest and no extracurricular invitations for a week or more, thank-you-very-much. *That lie will keep him off my back for a while,* she thought.

"I see," he said, resuming his work. "Shut the door behind, please."

And that was that.

She stalked down the corridor lost in a mental rage, teeth clenched, fists balled.

Not complicated? I got raped and blackmailed in my New York apartment; I'm John's call-when-you-want-me sex toy, and my baby's the current pain-in-the-butt everyone wants disappeared.

Her next thought exploded with such intensity she jerked to a halt. *You can't have it all, John Russell. I'm gonna fight this one.*

Did she need a baby to protect herself? Was she the kind of woman who let men beat her, but don't-you-dare-touch-my-kids? How many insults would she take before standing her ground?

Laura's yell echoed down the hallway. "Fuck you, John Russell."

She didn't give a damn who heard it.

***

"Your score is 1,036," the nurse practitioner said. "A definite pregnancy," and smiled charmingly at Laura and Eva. "Congratulations. I know you've been eager for the results."

Laura rolled her eyes.

In the privacy of Eva's office, they began the conversation.

"You can't," said Eva.

"I can," replied Laura.

"It can't be his."

"It is."

"You'll be terminated, Laura. I know him."

"We'll do a paternity test."

"He won't believe it and he won't believe you. He's been through this before."

"Not with me."

"Even so."

And, on it went.

Laura left work early. She pulled the best vintage wine from her wine cabinet and savored its aroma before taking a long, slow sip.

"Shit," she cried and vomited everything onto the floor.

***

That next week, Laura hunkered down in the evenings with her computer. Together they deep-researched paternity testing.

She learned how to extract her own DNA by spitting into salt water in a cup, then dowsing it with dish soap and isopropyl alcohol. Interesting, but not helpful.

She ran through terms like restriction fragment length polymorphism and short tandem repeat analysis, mitochondrial DNA, nucleotide replacements, and acronyms like AABB, CODIS and mtDNA.

She read about dark-colored bands on the DNA chart being equal to fingerprint identification; about cheek swabs versus blood tests; that analyzing DNA from hair required a separate type of processing because hair cells have no nucleus; and how Y marker analysis, based on chromosomes passed from father to son, could identify DNA from different men.

She learned the difference between "peace of mind" testing versus "chain-of-custody-for-court" documents; costs between $70 to $500 with a five-day wait or pay $300 extra for same day results.

"But," Laura asked herself out loud, "the main question is—can Mr. 'I-Have-a-Vasectomy' get me pregnant?"

Bleary-eyed hours on the computer proved no one, *not ever*, said vasectomies were 100% guaranteed.

Failure rate very rare—yes.

99.7% success rate—yes.

100% success rate—no—never.

Laura descended into a cloud of depression.

John would never volunteer for a DNA check. He'd run around saying she'd been with someone else; should be more careful; remember the contract; blah, blah, blah.

Plus, she'd need the baby's DNA—before it was born.

Born? Did I say born?

Her head went into her hands. *What a fucking mess.*

Chapter 43

The baby's hand and its wailing cry speared through Laura's consciousness. It woke her in the middle of the night with a vicious terror. Sweat leaked into her eyes. Heart pounding, breathing rapid, she sat straight up, tossing bedcovers from her overheated body. Pregnancy had never been on her radar—and neither had abortion. Birth control was—well—like the air she breathed—a constant, reliable truth.

"What a mess." The words regurgitated over and over again. *Like throwing up, only in my head.* She knew an IUD pregnancy was risky, even if she got the IUD removed. High miscarriage rates, premature birth rates even higher, and always the chance of uterine infection or placental abruption. The image of her placenta tearing away from the uterus wall left Laura shuddering.

Even if I just 'got rid of it,' the whole thing could happen all over again—same players, same conditions, same consequences. Life had gotten jaggedly shattered by something so—ordinary.

She stalked to the medicine cabinet, tossed down a capful of Nyquil, and retreated to bed. For an hour she slammed one angry thought against another, only making her depression bigger and lumpier. The clock hands changed position in slow motion. Light from the street lamps elbowed its way through the windows. At some unknown point, her eyes closed and she fell into the dark hole of sleep.

***

'Thwack!' The door shut behind Laura's last patient. Done for the day. She closed her medical records laptop, rested her elbows on the desk, and rubbed her scalp until it tingled. Twelve patients on three hours' sleep. *I need more relief than a scalp rub.*

Laura stood up and bent from her waist to the floor. She curled upwards to standing position. Vertebrae crackled into place.

"Turning this place into a yoga studio?" John stood in the doorway, watching.

What is he doing in my office? His last patient was scheduled for 5:00 o'clock I checked. Laura planned on being long gone by then. "No." she grunted in response. "Stretching,"

John came in and sat down. His long, lanky frame took over the wing chair in effortless ease. "Haven't seen you in a bit. You ok?" he asked.

"Right as rain."

Silence.

She stretched through another several poses, looked up, stopped. He was still there.

"What do you want?" she asked?

"You," he replied.

"I thought you had patients till 5:00."

"Ever heard of cancellations?"

"I guess. I finish extra work when someone cancels. You were pretty clear about using time 'efficiently,' if I remember."

"I'm working."

"You are?"

"Yes."

"Now?"

"Yes."

"On what?"

"On sorting out what's going on with you."

"I'm fine."

He rolled his eyes. "You want documentation?" he said. "Here goes—you're avoiding me like the plague; you're hiding at the office, at home, and you're not talking to anyone—totally not the person I know."

"I'm not hiding…"

"Don't quibble over semantics. Something's changed. I want to know what."

She wasn't ready—too tired—too frazzled. "How about if we talk in the morning

"Surgery all day tomorrow." His tone turned icier by the second. "What about over dinner tonight?"

She took a breath. *Ready or not*, she thought. *On his invite? It might work'*. She glanced at the clock. 4:00 p.m.

"I was going to leave early—catch some rest…"

He side-swiped her objections. "Take a few hours off. Use the jacuzzi. I'll call Mee Sue. Have her do some reflexology. See you at 7:00—my side of the house."

Then he left.

She had been commanded.

Probably better this way.

Maybe.

Only no jacuzzi. Too hot for the baby.

***

John sat by the fireplace in a grey cashmere sweater and button-down shirt. Two wine glasses stood on the table. She entered; he motioned to the empty chair.

"You look lovely," he said. A smile touched the corner of his lips.

It was true. Mee Sue had worked Laura until tangled worries unwound. And, she had brought the "Hair Kit."

"No woman deep relax with bad hair. Dr. John say you are very not relax. So, I do hair relax and foot relax. You will be, oh, so very… ahh, how to say…" and here she put her finger to her lip in contemplation, "…so very… 'go with flow.'" Mee Sue beamed. "Good idea, you think not?"

She poked and chatted and massaged and cracked and combed and pulled and pushed and oiled and then did it all again. When she was done, Mee Sue pulled out what she called a "lounge dress," wiggled it over Laura's head and stepped back.

"Very relax, I see, Miss Laura. Do you not think this?" She twirled Laura around to look in the wall mirror. Laura had to admit—yes—she did look—well—radiant.

That had been a half hour ago. Now she stared at John—at fingers that had touched her in so many places; at arms which had performed so many surgeries and had held her in so many embraces. She looked at his hair speckling with grey, at his long legs, at eyes behind which lay an infinitely complex brain. Those eyes now caught hold of hers—and smiled.

"Sit," he said.

She sat.

"Drink," he said. He pushed a glass towards her.

She shook her head.

He raised his eyebrows.

"I, uh, started some medication," she lied. "It doesn't mix with alcohol."

"I see. So, I shouldn't decant the Penfolds Shiraz?"

She shook her head, smile wistful. "Not for me."

"Ah. Glass of Perrier, instead?"

She nodded. He pushed a buzzer, gave instructions, and waited for the Perrier to be delivered. Laura felt the rhythm of her heart, her breath as it moved in and out, smelled John's scotch as the ice cubes clinked in his glass. It soothed her. More muscles unknotted.

Better this way, she thought.

She studied his face again—cheek bones high enough to make his face gaunt when he lost weight; lips molded—not too thin, not too big. Hair floppy, part sexy, part elegant; neck too skinny; ears close bound to skull; strong chin just a bit too sharp.

And then she considered his eyes—eyes that opened, closed, and could shutter him away from the world. He would not like this news. He would close his ears, bind his eyes, and turn her out. No, he was not going to like this news.

"Shall we eat first?" His voice speared through her bubble of inner whispers. He stood.

"Oh, ahh, well, I thought…" she half rose, half sat.

"Laura, what the hell is wrong with you?" The clanging crash of his words lifted her like an explosive. She gasped, sneezed, swallowed the wrong way, and coughed in violent convulsions.

"Shit," he said, grasped her under the chest and thwacked her back. "Open your throat."

John's alcohol-polished demeanor morphed into sharp, irritated instruction. Dizzy nausea settled in as her cough subsided in fits and starts.

"I'm pregnant."

"Oh, Jesus Christ. What a fuck-up!"

His response was absurdly instantaneous. Not a whisper of hesitation; not an atom of concern; no measure of thought—nothing dampened the rejection.

Nothing.

Not the months of working together.

Not the hours of sexual pleasures.

Not the weeks of traveling or mutual respect for each other's skills.

Nothing stopped the wall of refusal that shone on his face.

"It's yours," she said.

"Can't be. Not possible."

"It is."

"No, you fucked up," he said, "Clean it up."

"It could happen again," she said.

"It may if you continue sleeping around." His tone held the face slap, the smear, the disdain.

"I haven't been with anyone else in over six months." She glared at him. "I'm seven weeks along, and, if you remember, Dr. Sex-on-the-Table, we've had a shitload of sex in the last six months.

Twice, sometimes three times a day, on occasion, if you remember. You worked me hard, Mr. Not-My-Fault."

Face flushed, straight-standing, Laura shot each word out with pistol force.

A condescending twitch tugged his lower lip.

"Vasectomy…"

"99.96% effective," she interrupted.

A raised eyebrow.

"Internet, I see," he drawled.

Silence. Her eyes raked his face and then fell steady.

"And your IUD?" he cooed, "Miss Internet?"

"98-99% effective," she said, straighter, taller.

"Well, there you go. They're all covering their asses." His cold smile broadened.

"No one, John—not one source—not one person—not one reference—not one mention—no one said 100%. Not anyone, not anywhere."

"Laura…" The ice in his tone announced decision. "There's not a chance in hell this thing is mine. You have any idea how many women have tried this on me? Letters in the mail from women I don't even know, naming me as father of their babies. I'm fucking immune to this crap—just surprised you'd try it."

He turned to leave. She grabbed his arm.

"DNA tests would show…" she began.

"Like hell! Go read your contract. Take care of it or get the hell out."

He turned, pushed open the door and vanished down the hall.

Chapter 44

Morning sunlight filtered through the hospital office windows.

"What are you going to do?" asked Eva. Laura sat facing her, oddly calm. Last night she'd Ubered home, tried to sleep, tossed, fidgeted, and in desperation re-watched early episodes of *Game of Thrones*—a perfect distraction.

John's response had been awful. Both of them tired, not ready, caught by surprise—still—no preparation would have landed a different result. Brutal, shut down, unbending, vicious.

"Didn't go well, right?" Eva inquired.

Laura shook her head.

"He's been through this before."

Silence.

"He was probably over-reactive to you in particular," continued Eva.

Laura cocked her head. "How come?"

"I don't know, really. Some comments he made. How he acted. I mean—John is John—he's not going to change. But he respected and liked you a lot. Comfortable together, I think. That wasn't always the case with, ah, well, some predecessors." A slight shrug. "Not much help, but there you have it."

Laura's smiled a tight smile.

"He's never been through this before, Eva."

"He's been through his wife plus six other attem…"

"Not. Through. This." Laura's interruption hammer-cracked through the room. "This is his child. No lies, no deception, no fancy foot work. His. Child."

Silence.

"What will you do?" asked Eva.

"Go to work for now." More silence. "Things won't go back to normal, Eva. If it happened once, even if the baby were, uh—removed—it could happen all over again. He thinks I betrayed him, and I think he's a fucking, self-centered jerk who won't even try to investigate."

"The contract does say…"

"I know what the fucking contract says. I just haven't figured out what to do about it yet. Give the girl a break!"

"Sorry…" said Eva, looking down at her hands.

"Gotta go. John and I are scheduled for surgery. That should be a barrel of fun." Laura pushed her chair back and got up. "I'll let you know what I decide."

***

"Going somewhere?" John's voice catapulted over Laura's shoulder. He looked at her, a bemused smile in his eyes. "You sailed past the locker room—we have surgery in fifteen-minutes. You going anywhere else?"

"Of course not. I—was distracted."

"Undistract then. See you in surgery." He disappeared into the men's locker room.

She blinked. Just like that. Like last night never happened.

She shook her head. She needed her brain unencumbered in surgery to avoid killing anyone—either John or the Senator from Arizona who awaited them on the operating table.

***

An emergency craniotomy for blood clot associated with malignant primary glioblastoma. Fast growing, possibly speech impairing, certain to recur again. A successful outcome, a short surgery, shorter time and an adrenaline punch at the end. Days like this usually ended up with John, sex and dinner, in that order. *What a mess.*

"Going somewhere?"

Startled, she twirled backwards, lost balance and found John's arm gripping hers.

"Whoa, girl," he said, laughing.

She struggled to get her balance, breathe, collect her thoughts. *He's crazy if he thinks I'll have sex with him.*

"Question too hard?" he prompted.

She straightened and shook his arm from hers.

"Do you have amnesia, John?"

"Ah. That might be nice—but no."

She waited.

"I thought you might need to talk a bit more." His face was guileless—unhaunted.

"You think?"

***

They ended up in the Bedouin Tent Room at The Compass Rose on T Street. Private, quiet, folded in fabric—a decent place for a difficult talk.

"Eat first," John pronounced. "Long day."

They sat without speech in the in slowly melting silence as food was ordered, prepared, and served.

They ate.

Smorrebord from Denmark.

Sambal Udang from Malaysia.

Chicken Torta from Mexico.

Then they discussed.

Brief, to the point.

"It's yours," she said.

"No."

"Then take a paternity test."

"No. There will be no testing, no further discussion. My offer is to forget we encountered this breach in your contract. That is, if you return to work unencumbered in the next few days."

"Unencumbered?"

"You know my meaning."

"And paternity?"

He sipped his scotch.

"You know that's impossible with our protections."

Another sip, then violent coughing as he swallowed the wrong way, grabbed a napkin and covered his mouth.

She ought to be concerned but thinking, *Good, choke on that,* made her feel better.

"Sorry," John said, and put the cloth down. "I'm not sure why you're doing this." He rose, still talking, "but, let's move on. I've paid the bill and your fare home. The Maître d' will call a cab."

He walked out.

And their 'talk' was over, just like that.

Or was it?

She looked at the cloth napkin, bubbles of spittle still shiny on the printed design. Laura rummaged in her purse, found the small plastic bags she always stowed for unexpected leftovers. She bagged the top of the napkin that had the spittle, tied it off with an abandoned rubber band from the bottom of her purse.

As she left, the maître' d' held a $20 bill in his hand.

"The gentleman…"

"Keep it," she said. "It will pay for the napkin."

Chapter 45

Laura went straight home, logged on to her bank accounts, made one call, one online appointment and waited. The phone rang fifteen minutes later.

"Laura, hi, what can I…"

"Can you get here tonight?" Forceful, hard, clear—her tone slaughtered objection.

"Where is here?"

"My apartment."

"Okay. See you in 30."

She waited.

***

When she heard the bzzzzzpt, bzzzzzpt of the front door buzzer, Laura pressed the release button. Moments later she ushered George Penunos into the apartment. She gestured to the couch, handed him a glass of water, and said, "You're my lawyer for job related issues."

"I'm sure I'm not here so you can remind me of that."

"No, you're not."

Silence.

He waited, shifted position, then asked, "Have you decided to mention why I'm here?"

She began; told the of the history of her pregnancy and finished with, "I want to know if I can legally test paternity with the napkin."

He sat back, steepled his fingers, said, "I see."

"Can I?'

"Sure. You took something from the public domain that was unwanted, except perhaps for the restaurant napkin which you paid for. However, none of this follows chain of custody. That makes any results useless in court."

"Court doesn't matter. John's insufferable ego—well, that's another matter."

Silence.

"What do you plan to do?" he asked.

"Go to work, get the IUD removed, do the paternity test, quit."

He raised his eyebrows. "In that order?

"I can do most of it tomorrow."

"And the baby?"

"It may not survive the IUD removal—so I don't have to decide yet."

"You sure you want to quit?"

She looked down, intertwined fingers squeezing and releasing. "Yes. No." Pause. "It's so damn sudden. It's not just a 'quit.' It's my life—except I can't be around John anymore—especially after this."

She stopped.

He waited, then spoke. "He's a brilliant man, Laura. You've learned a lot, earned a lot, and you'll be giving up a lot. Think about it. You're not the same woman who started here months ago."

"I'd be prostituting myself."

George sat back; eyebrows knit together.

"How is consensual sex between consenting, single adults prostitution?"

"Cause this time around, I'd detest the jerk and hate being with him. I'd only be doing it for the money."

More silence.

"A mess, right?" she said, a half-smile trembling on her face.

"You have choices," he said.

"I've got lots of choices, only they aren't the ones people in male bodies have to make. They're not even choices females in unpregnant bodies make."

He shook his head. "What do you mean?"

She shook her head. "I'm not sure I can figure it out yet."

After George left, Laura went to bed. She pulled up the covers, opened her book and began reading *A Child's Garden of Verses*.

***

At 6:30 a.m. she called the Virginia clinic and left the receptionist scurrying to reassign her patients. A 6:45 call to Eva Jormand secured a 9:00 a.m. IUD removal. Then she called Identi-Test Genetics. They told her same-day test results were available if the sample arrived at the lab by 11:00. Laura stored the napkin in the fridge. She hoped the saliva would be testable.

When she arrived at the hospital, her vision telescoped into a single hole pulling her forward through noisy corridors. The receptionist looked up as she pushed open the door and signed in.

"Ms. Greenwald?"

Laura nodded.

"We'll be right with you."

She nodded and sat.

She went with them when they opened the door, measured her weight, took her blood pressure, temperature and gave her a gown to wrap around her waist.

She undressed and waited and shivered.

Click—the door opened.

Click—the door shut.

In front of her stood an ample woman whose eye smiles could be seen even through thick glasses and long bangs.

"Good morning, Ms. Greenwald. I am Dr. Ayana Chepi. A pleasure to meet you." She held out her hand. Laura took it. Confidence prickled through the grasp and Laura stopped shivering. She looked up.

"As you know, Dr. Mirembe…"

"Yes, I know."

"I am seeing her patients until she…"

"That's fine."

"Good. Then I shall explain one or two things before…"

"Okay."

Dr. Aiyana Chepi smiled. "I'll make it brief then."

"Good," said Laura. She liked this woman.

"Your baby is two months grown. You state you are uncertain when you became pregnant."

Laura nodded.

"And you have a hormonal IUD."

Another nod.

"IUD removal before four months gestation is recommended. This reduces some of the higher rates of miscarriage, premature delivery and infections. But we do not know the effects hormonal IUD's have on further fetal development."

"I know," said Laura.

"Good," said Dr. Chepi. "Most IUD removals are quick procedures. There may be some complic…"

"Tell me those later."

A brief smile, a glance at her notes, then Dr. Chepi continued.

"Along with IUD removal we conduct a vaginal ultrasound to confirm fetal development is in the uterus, not the fallopian tube.

"Fine."

"Would you…" began the doctor.

"No. Could we please just do this?"

The doctor handed Laura papers on a clipboard.

"We need your signature."

Laura signed in eight places without reading. "Done," she said.

They began.

The IUD collapsed out of her uterus with a tug. She winced in pain; the ultrasound showed a normal pregnancy; the doctor smiled one last time as Laura interrupted final explanations. The clock read 11:30 when Laura fled the building and headed to the genetics labs, parcel in hand.

She arrived too late for same day results, but delivered the napkin sample, had blood drawn, put $300 more on her credit card, signed papers, and ignored the vibrations of her cell phone. She'd have to return tomorrow for the results.

Then she called Daniel. Yes, he and the limousine were available. She waited on the corner of 13th and Corcoran until the black limousine pulled up and took her across the River to the place where everything had started.

***

Eva looked up. "Oh, hi," she smiled. "I thought you'd cancelled for today.

"I did. I have."

Raised eyebrows.

"Soooo…you are here because…"

"I'm quitting."

Eva shut her laptop.

"I see." She stood up, moved from behind the desk and gestured to a chair.

"Will you sit?"

Laura shook her head. "I don't think so."

"May I?" inquired Eva.

"Please."

Eva sat. "How can I be helpful?" Her words bore no hidden agenda—just a simple statement that left the door to swing any way Laura wanted.

"Could you draw up the papers?"

"For you to leave? Should I take a few days so you can consider…"

"I want to sign them by tomorrow."

"That's a little…"

Laura's head shake interrupted Eva Jormand mid-sentence. "No, it's not… not for this organization—more like 'business as usual.'"

Laura stood motionless in mid-calf skirt, and thigh length jacket. Her hands stayed by her side, posture impeccable, auburn hair windblown. Purpose powered by appearance.

"Will you come in to sign the…"

"George Penunos will pick up everything. I'll sign in his office."

Eva nodded. "10 o'clock tomorrow, then?"

"That's good." Laura turned to leave.

"Laura—I…"

For the umpteenth time that day Laura interrupted

"I know, Eva. I'm sorry, too." A shadow smile drifted over Laura's mouth. "You told me what to expect, only I didn't expect it."

Then she left closing the door with a soft 'thunk.'"

***

The next morning, she went to see George Penunos.

The lawyer sat back in his chair. "Just tell me where to sign."

"No, Laura, you are going to stay put and listen to me."

She looked at him.

He looked at her.

She crossed her arms and legs as she sat. "Fine. Do it your way."

"Good." Papers shuffled. "I've looked at your financials. All benefits from Dr. Manhattan Enterprises stop as soon as you sign this. Eva created a special extension of health benefits in your case. The usual cut off is one month after resignation. Yours is ten."

"That was nice of her."

"I agree," he responded. "This document reviews confidentiality agreements. I am required to have you read them out loud."

"You're joking, right?"

"Nope."

"That's ridiculous."

George Penunos shrugged. "The sooner you start, the sooner we're done."

So, she read—about the cover story they suggested she use, about how she could never speak of her job or salary or clients or private time with John Russell—not to husband, sister, brother, mother, father, therapist, doctor, priest—no one.

About no severance pay and no bonus. About returning all computer and phone devices, wiping all digital accounts and about the suspension of any licenses she might have if she stepped over the line "above here indicated."

When done, she looked up.

"Satisfied?"

George stopped the recording and put his hand over the signature line. "You're sure?"

She nodded. Last night she had not been sure. She'd sat up until 2 a.m. and thought. And gone over. And thought again. She and the baby—thinking and breathing for two.

"I'm sure." Her voice didn't echo in this carpeted, curtained room with leather chairs and cushioned seats. The only sound heard was the scraping of pen on paper as she initialed each page, each paragraph.

Then it was done—cut loose, swinging free.

She looked up. "What now?" she asked.

"Well," George rocked back in his chair, hands behind his neck. "You're pretty well positioned money wise. Looks like $850,000 in the bank for 18 months. Not bad with taxes paid up."

"The job ate my life—no time to spend anything," Laura mumbled.

George smiled, leaned forward.

"You'll be fine, Laura."

"Maybe."

"Assuredly. After working with John, you're not going to have any trouble finding a job—I mean—a really good job."

"I guess." A pause. "You do remember I'm pregnant?"

He sat back again.

"Yes, there is always that." A pause.

Laura felt a chill run through her. She stood. "Thank you for your help, George" Then she walked out of his office, closing another door behind her.

She still had to get the lab results.

***

At the genetics office, the receptionist smiled, had Laura sit, brought a cup of coffee, and said, "Our client consultant will…"

"Fine. Where is he?"

Eventually, Laura was conducted to a conference room where Ms. Anurva Ananda introduced herself. She began speaking right away.

"You see we have a nice match with the parts of the DNA profile that you gave us." And she pointed. "But since we do not have…"

"Yes, I know…"

"In your case we would be glad offering you a no-charge re-try if you can get…"

"Not possible."

"Ah… I see…"

"Tell me what the report says."

"I will be liking very much to do that." Paper shuffling, silent reading, then Ms. Anurva Ananda looked up with a smile. "It is reported we can be saying the subject who spit on the napkin could be included as paternal contributor to the fetus. This we may be saying

309

very strongly if we were to be having the other 25% of the degraded spittle sample. The markers we have do suggest such a match."

"That's the only thing you can say?"

"Oh, Madam, this is a strong something. We are not saying anything such as 'exclusion,' Just—not enough evidence—not the 99.5%."

Laura stood. "Thank you. May I have the report?"

Anurva Ananda blinked. She shuffled papers back to order. "Oh, yes, Madam, right away. I will find for you a proper envelope."

Five minutes later Laura left with a proper envelope and improper results. It would have to do. She stuffed the DNA report into her purse and then headed—or rather drifted—down one street and off another. *Too much going on. Just need to think.*

She wandered from Georgetown over to Rock Creek—brisk, sunny, windy, rudderless and finally so cold she needed to be inside. A busy doorway caught her eye—people in and out, talking, hurrying, laughing, carrying. She slipped inside, searched out a corner, and hid. The menu and the bulging bookshelves claimed she was at 'Kramer Books.' *DC has such variety*, she thought.

A mug of hot cider clinked onto the tiny ceramic table spilling drops onto the envelope she'd drawn from her purse. Laura, daydreaming, had forgotten she'd ordered.

"Thanks." A smile to the waitress.

"Anything else?"

"Not now."

"Enjoy."

Crumpled inside the now-stained envelope lay the report.

"DNA partially degraded due to compromised collection procedures. Results suggest 75% accuracy rating versus 99.5% for well-preserved buccal swabs. Repeat analysis recommended."

More words explaining, then a graph of lines and streaks with numbers.

The best she could do.

Her cider grew cold. When the waitress came again, Laura shook her head. She was left alone—just her and the report. Sitting at the table for she couldn't remember how long. Thinking, drifting, wondering. Until the twinge.

"Ouch!"

"You ok?" mouthed a nearby couple through the hubbub of conversation and music.

"Yes, fine." Her nod, her smile, her lie.

"Shit." She bent over in pain. The couple was still staring.

"Gas, I think," said with a crooked smile for her crooked story.

"Ahh," they breathed out like a mantra and left her in privacy.

She gasped in pain again—silently. Laura rose, left a large tip and stumbled through tables toward the exit. The cold walloped her face.

"Oh, jeez, forget calling an Uber," she panted, leaping into the street, grabbing at a cab, wrenching open the door.

"Lady, I almost ran..."

"Sorry, sorry. Really. It's just—it's been—a really, bad hair day."

"Okay. Okay, just don't want no one hurt. Where to?"

"Home," she said, scrunched in the back seat.

But she never made it.

***

Fuzzy, hazy faces swam into view. "Where...?" she began but didn't have the energy to finish.

"Emergency room— Washington Memorial Hospital. You're fine," said the face way too close to her nose. Laura sneezed. A quick backing up by the unknown person, now smiling.

"How...?" *It's so hard to focus.*

"A cab driver claimed he had a dead person with bad hair in the back seat. It was a weird report, so security went to check. And here you are." The nurse stepped back. "Actually, your hair's not too bad." A pause as she read on her tablet. "Let's see how you're doing now."

She read for a few moments. "Oh, I see."

"See what?" Laura reacted to the words with a stomach clenching worry.

The nurse smiled. "The doctor will explain everything. Now that you're awake we can get you registered." She reached down and brought up Laura's purse.

"Cab driver left his contact info inside your purse if you need it... so... let's see...," she said, producing a sheaf of documents and pen for insurance signatures. She poked and prodded and, once done, said the doctor would be 'right in.'

The doctor appeared two hours later. The "zil-link" of emergency room curtains sliding along their rods startled Laura awake.

"Ms. Greenwald?"

"Yes?"

"It's good to see you again."

Again? What's he talking about?

"Don't remember me?"

Laura shook her head, struggling to sit up. Her purse began to slide off the narrow bed. The doctor caught it and put it on the floor.

"I'm Dr. Carmona. Dr. Luis Carmona. I'm happy to tell you my team averted your miscarriage. That's what made you faint in the cab—and why we took you in right away."

Took me in? Where? What is he talking about? "But I wasn't bleeding or anything—," she protested.

He placed a hand on her shoulder. "I understand. I looked at your hospital file. You had an IUD removed yesterday."

Laura nodded. "That's right."

He sighed. "We can't explain the high percentage of miscarriages that occur with IUD pregnancies. We just know it happens. In your case, we administered medication to calm the uterus. If we hadn't, you would have lost the baby."

Silence. Laura stared straight ahead.

"You need bedrest. That'll give everything a chance to settle. The plan is you sleep here overnight and we discharge you tomorrow afternoon." He smiled. "You're a lucky woman." Dr. Carmona hung the chart at the end of the bed. "Any questions?"

Laura closed her eyes and took a breath. "No," she said, and closed her eyes wanting the world to disappear.

The curtains made no noise as Dr. Carmona left.

How did he do that? asked one part of her mind. The other part of her curled into a ball on the bed and began to cry.

Chapter 46

Don't do it.

I want to go home.

They said wait till the afternoon.

I'll be fine.

No, you won't.

Laura threw off the hospital covers and slipped her feet onto the floor. The room's dingy light outlined her clothing hanging on the door. Her purse sat on the rolling table with the water pitcher. Dizziness swirled her head and she gripped the mattress to steady herself.

One step at a time. She started a slow walk towards her clothes. The action required every available brain cell. Getting dressed demanded even more.

Laura pulled clothes off the hanger, removed her hospital gown, pulled on underpants, buttoned her blouse and zipped up slacks. Each painful effort grew smoother than the one before. At the end, she closed her eyes and sat in exhausted silence. She needed time to take command of her plan.

Are you kidding me? You ain't got no plan except 'get outta here.'

Well, that's my plan—stand up and get the fuck out of here. Except I don't know where I am.

Last night the hospital had been bombarded with patients. Rooms were scarce. She remembered someone saying, "She's a clean patient—no infections. We can probably put her…" But the rest of the conversation turned too faint to hear.

Laura stood, slung her purse over her shoulder, and opened the door. Her room was at the end of a hallway. The nurse's station guarded the entrance where two corridors intersected. She looked at the wall clock. *3:15 in the morning. Home in an hour.* She started her march down the hall.

"Ouww," she cried.

Her cry rocketed down the hallway. The door to the patient room next to her had slammed into her arm. It pushed Laura backwards, but she caught herself before she fell.

"Oh, my God. I'm so sorry," responded a far too familiar voice. A body emerged from behind the door.

"Arlo?"

He stood in motionless shock. And stared. "Laura? What are you doing here?"

Shocked, exhausted, every defense cracked to smithereens, Laura said, "I'm pregnant."

"Pregnant? Is something wrong with the baby?"

She watched awareness trickle muscle by muscle through Arlo's face. Her cheeks flared with embarrassment. *I can't believe I told him. Congratulations, Greenwald, on making an awful day worse. Great work.*

"What are you doing in the neurology unit?" he persisted."

"Oh—that. No room at the inn. I got put where they found an empty room." She shrugged. "Some coincidence, huh? I suppose you were checking a patient."

A nod. Then a wry smile. He asked again, "You okay?"

"No." She looked away. "I quit my job and avoided a miscarriage. Not a great day."

His eyes widened. "Quit your..." Arlo stood stone-rigid, his face white, breathing doubled. He stared at her for a long while, then said, "John—it was John, wasn't it?" She could hear his teeth grinding.

"I told you it was complicated," she said, her eyes averted.

"You damn well did."

They stood in awkward, unbalanced silence. She wanted to explain; she wanted to disappear; she wanted to hug him; and wished she'd never met him. In the end she did nothing.

"Can I give you a ride home?" Arlo asked finally. "I'm finished here."

"I think it's best if you don't," she replied. "But thank you."

***

Against medical advice Laura signed the hospital release papers at 4:00 a.m. By 4:30 she was home on her couch. By 5:00 she had struggled into a shower where hot water beat on her face, thighs, and buttocks. At 6:00 a.m. she was in bed, folded into a dead sleep for twelve-hours.

When she woke, she wanted to dowse the pulsing anxiety in her stomach with alcohol, but chose sparkling lemonade instead. She kept pushing DVD's into the player and lost herself in the fake dramas until 3 a.m. Somewhere in-between she ordered a pizza. And somewhere in between she'd thrown it all up, crawled back to bed and slept another twelve-hours.

***

The scale showed she lost five pounds in two days. *Not good for the baby.*

The mirror reflected a haggard face. *No big deal—I'm not going anywhere.*

Her phone listed 26 unanswered calls. She didn't respond. *Who cares? I need a new life. It's hard to think.* So, she didn't bother.

This is bad for the baby.

Can't think about it.

***

Three days passed before Laura emerged, thinner and paler. She'd tried to eat, ordered food, but most of it sat untouched, wrapped in the refrigerator for a 'second try.'

Over and over she thought of her collision with Arlo. She kept feeling stupid, embarrassed, and finally panicked. *Would he confront*

John? Or call and scream at her? Or, never, ever talk to her? She binge-watched TV and made lists.

Today, she held one of those painfully crafted to-do lists in her left hand; a purse hung over her right shoulder, and she'd stiffened her spine with two cups of—*herbal tea? I can't get used to this 'being pregnant' stuff.*

First on her list was to have breakfast at a café (*need to eat),* then to call everybody who might think she was dead by this time ("No, mom, I'm fine;), and finally reorganize her neglected life (Yes, I'll be there for my eye appointment; My package hasn't been delivered...).

She accomplished it all before noon—except it felt like midnight. Her body sagged with the pull of gravity. She wanted home and bed.

You gotta eat for the baby, roared her conscience. *Now.*

She stopped at a restaurant. A glass of lemonade sat on the bar next to her as she waited for the take out order of chicken soup and cornbread. Her pale face, auburn hair and tenuous boundaries stirred nearby male attention.

A man from one of the tables came over and sat down. "Hi."

She looked at him. *I wish he were Arlo.* She said, "You. Go away. Now." When he didn't, she went to the end of the bar, crossed her arms, and waited for her package. Laura walked a mile towards home, called an Uber for the rest of the way and crawled into bed. The chicken soup sat by itself on the counter getting colder than it already was.

The next day she wandered through the National Zoo and the day after through five museums whose displays of mammoths, airplanes, and artwork merged into puddles of mud in her mind.

She took showers in the morning, meandered on walks during the day, drank lemonade at night and found she'd lost more weight. Not good, but she couldn't help herself.

It went on like that for seven days until the phone call came. She'd had lots of phone calls but this one she answered. Just like that—no rhyme or reason.

"Hello?"

Then she wanted to hang up, maybe throw up. But it was too late.

"Laura?"

She knew the voice. "Yes?" came her dulled response.

"Hi, this is Anika, the Vice Pres…"

"Yes, I know."

She was interrupting again. An unstoppable rudeness it seemed.

"I called the office…" A pause. "They said you weren't there anymore."

"That is correct." Another flattened response.

"Are you all right?"

"I'm trying to be."

Silence.

Anika cleared her throat. "Is it ok for me to talk to you?"

"Yes, of course." Laura grabbed a tissue. "I'm sorry. I've been…" She searched for—what? That damned contract cut through every word—tied up every story.

"I've been home, Anika. Kind of recuperating." It was a mistake the instant the words left her mouth.

"Recuperating? What happened?"

Big mouth," Laura sniped at herself. "I'm ok, Anika, really." Another pause.

"That sounds lame even to me." Her gentle tone made Laura smile.

"Yeah. It's lame." Three deep breaths. "You know, Anika, the deal is, I can't talk about it."

"Ahhhh…" breathed Anika. "Politics—welcome to the club."

They both laughed.

Laura asked why Anika called.

Anika called to arrange a consult about her next baby. Could Laura do that?

No, Laura couldn't do that on her own.

What about seeing Anika if Laura worked through the White House Medical Staff? The Vice President could pull some strings.

Laura hadn't thought about it and could she have some time to think?

Yes, she could and would Laura come over for lunch today?

Laura wasn't sure.

"Please."

"Well…"

"I'll add roast beef sandwiches from Stachowski's Market. Bet you haven't been eating."

"Well… I don't…"

"And Alka-Seltzer if you indulge too much."

"Ok, ok," laughed Laura the second time in three minutes. "Deal."

"Now?"

"Gimme a break, Anika—I need at least an hour."

She'd been in hiding for days. Time to emerge.

***

That same night Arlo called.

I'm on a roll today, she thought.

"Hi," he said.

"Hi," she said back.

"I thought we might have a few things to talk about."

"Probably."

"Can I come over?"

"Not to my house--not a good idea," she said.

"I don't want to talk on the phone."

"There's a café a few blocks away. We could meet there."

"When?"

"Now."

***

Arlo walked to her table at the Side Street Café.

Still handsome and sexy, she thought, *but there's too much water over the dam.*

He sat. "Mind if I order a drink?" She shook her head. "You want anything?"

"No."

He ordered, then looked around. Discomfort stalked behind him.

"Arlo. I'm sorry." She refused to look away. *This is my shitstorm to clean up.*

He had no room for niceties. "What happened, Laura? I thought we were good. Then you crash into me in the middle of the night, tell me you're pregnant, and it was John all along. It felt like you split my head open with an ax."

"I said it was complicated. Part of it is that I can't say anything." She took a deep breath. The waiter brought Arlo's drink, which he gulped and called for another.

"If you won't talk, Laura, why did you let me come?" He was angry.

Now she looked down. "I was hoping you'd figure it out on your own."

They didn't speak. His second drink came. Arlo stared at her for a long time.

"You're under contract," he said.

Laura did not respond. Instead, she watched him think—brows knit, eyes far-away. In a while he added, "There's something about sex in it."

She did not confirm or deny. Tears formed and overflowed.

"I see." A deep breath. More of the far-away look in his eyes. "So, that's how he does it."

"Does what? What are you talking about?" She reached for a napkin, dried her cheeks dry, and focused on his face.

"Keeps out of trouble—scandal free, so to speak. Avoids woman trouble."

"But he's around women all the time. He's flooded at social events. I've seen it."

"Laura," Arlo leaned forward, elbows on the table, "John's on *Washington Magazine's* most eligible bachelor list. He's probably on some national list, too. But you never see him written up in a gossip column. There's no girlfriend in sight. The scuttlebutt is he never takes anyone home. So—either he's gay or..." Arlo paused mid-sentence; his eyes locked onto Laura.

Her cheeks flushed. She looked away.

"Or—you are the secret ingredient."

Laura's mouth felt duct-taped shut. She said nothing, waiting for Arlo to complete the one-sided conversation.

He tip-toed into the next sentence like walking through a mine field. "But something happened--turned the whole thing into a wild card." It took a while before he said, "Must have been the birth control."

Laura sat in rigid silence with a weird, warm glow blooming in her stomach. *He nailed it.*

"Jeez-uz," muttered Arlo. "John must have gone crazy."

Laura tweaked out a small smile. Her nose dripped at the same time.

"I'm sorry," he said. "Are you and the baby okay?"

Laura shrugged. "For now."

"What do you plan to do?"

"May get a job offer on the White House Medical Team."

His eyebrows rose. "Is that good news?"

"For now."

He laughed and rocked back in his chair. "Talk about non-committal."

"Thanks for coming, Arlo." She reached her hand part way across the table.

He moved his chair closer and took it. "Could we get together once in a while?"

She wanted to say yes, how much she'd like to spend time together. What she said was, "I'm not ready, Arlo." She withdrew her hand.

"I see." After a moment he pushed back his chair, placed money on the table, and turned to leave. "Thank you for seeing me. It helps to know." When she looked up, he had gone.

Chapter 47

Laura composed the letter the next morning

John.

This is the napkin you spit into.

These are the results.

I never lied.

It was your baby.

You're a bastard with blinders on."

It had come easily, this parting letter of truth. She didn't want money; didn't care about revenge, didn't want the job back, could never do that job again.

But the pain in her gut kept on going.

Not physical pain. Not life broken-to-pieces pain.

It was the pain of being corrupted data—wiped out, erased, disappeared—here one minute, gone the next. The work, the travel, the sex, everything about her—just "x"-d out.

"Enough!" She erupted out of the chair, grabbed coffee, strode to bedroom, threw open her closet and put together a power suit of elegant understatement.

***

"You know he won't see you."

"How do I know that?"

"Because you know him."

"Did you ask?"

"No."

"Then ask."

Silence. Breathing.

"Okay. I'll be right back."

The "right back" turned into a half-hour. When Eva returned, she said with a blank face, "He won't see you. I'm sorry."

"Then give him this."

"I…"

"Give him this." Laura stood, held out a bulging envelope, addressed and stamped.

"He won't…"

"Put it in with his mail." She paused. "And he will—if you don't rub his face in it." Her arm remained stretched out.

A hesitation. Eva took the envelope.

"I planned to send it by mail—thought I'd try this first." She turned to open the door.

"Laura…"

"Yes?" A partial twist to regard the woman who had taught her so much.

"We miss you here."

A wispy smile touched Laura's face.

"Me, too." Then she closed the door, disappeared through hallways and onto the street.

***

"The job's unusual—but 'do-able.' You're certainly qualified," George Penunos said.

Laura sat, ankles crossed, hands in lap. "I know that."

"You really want to stay in DC?"

She stared at him without responding. He shook his head. "Sorry, none of my business. How can your ex-lawyer be of help today?"

"I need a recommendation," she said.

"That's standard practice."

"Nothing's standard about what happened with me."

The muscle creasing his forehead tensed, then relaxed. A pause. "Laura, I'm on your side."

"Nobody was on the side of my being pregnant, not even me."

"I'm sorry about..."

"Doesn't matter. It's irrelevant. I quit the job and I'll have the baby. Can we talk about the job recommendation?"

"I can set that in motion."

"What does that mean?"

"A memo to Eva. She gets it written up and then sends it to you."

"John doesn't write it?"

"He signs it—adds something if needed."

"How long does that take?"

"Two—three days—plus mailing."

"I'll pick it up."

"It's usually..."

"Nothing usual here. I just said that. Call me when you have it." Laura stood and left. She liked George. She just couldn't stand him right now.

***

"They had to pull some strings," Anika said.

"I figured," said Laura.

"Dad convinced the President you could stop medical emergencies before they got political." Anika smiled.

"You're kidding, right?"

"Not really," said Anika.

"I can't do that."

"You did with me."

"That was different," protested Laura.

"No, it was spot on." Anika continued. "It's a non-career appointment."

325

"Non-career?"

"It means, when the President goes, Dad goes, and you do, too." Anika looked concerned. "Is that ok?"

"Piece of cake," smiled Laura, "after what I've..." She almost blurted out the rest.

"After you've... what?"

"Oh, just... after what I've seen in DC."

"Tell me about it," responded Anika, smiling and rolling her eyes.

And so, life began again for Laura Greenwald.

***

Laura was hired under special appointment to the White House. Some flap had occurred about Laura not being a military nurse. Along the way somewhere, that complaint silenced itself. The FBI welcomed her with background checks.

She started four weeks from the day Anika first called. That made her almost four months pregnant. She requested her medical privacy be maintained. Except for her boss and Human Resources, they assured her the pregnancy would not be a topic of conversation.

Arlo didn't call again. She hadn't expected he would.

Or, had she?

Her disappointment told a different story.

***

When she walked into the White House medical offices, Dr. Roddy Jordman's first words to her were "Damn girl! Way to go. Good to see you. Excuse my English. I told them you were good— better than good. I'm still in awe of how you worked with Anika. Use it as an example all the time. No names, of course. Here, sit down."

"I didn't know I'd made such an impression."

"Well, you did. I followed your work—when I could—as much as John would let me. Friends or not, he's a master of privacy."

He'd better be, she thought.

"He did keep me abreast of your accomplishments—after I kept pestering him, of course."

"Why did you do that?"

"Because when I see talent, I like to know where it goes—and how it grows." He smiled. "It's never wise to be short on resources—medical or human."

He started to get up, but stopped, and sat back. "One last thing—congratulations on your pregnancy. Didn't know you had a special someone. Shouldn't be a problem—at least in the beginning. We'll adjust as you go forward. HR said you wanted privacy." He smiled. "At least for now."

"Thank you. I appreciate that."

"So, let's get you started."

Orientation took two weeks. It included special trainings with the medical staff, briefings with Dr. Jordman as well as accompanying him everywhere—office visits, presidential flights, state dinners, lunches, coffees, speeches, hospital reviews, and staff meetings.

In a moment of collegial exhaustion, after two 18-hour days and one flight to Illinois, he'd said, "They call my wife the 'White House widow.' This job is tough on family life." A pause. "On me, too." He smiled. "Puts a strain on things, you know?"

"Yes." *How well I know.* Laura closed her eyes against the images of how she and John dealt with the exhaustion/exhilaration cycle

"I wanted to get in as much training as we could before you tell me to slow it down." Concern edged his voice. "How're you holding up?"

The question dragged Laura back from daydreams. Roddy's schedule was a killer—doing it while pregnant meant she had to eat well, eat often, and 'fast sleep.' John had demanded she master the art. "Fast-sleep," he said. "Learn it or die."

Every trip she'd practiced cat-naps under his unrelenting tutelage. One day, he poured champagne on her head. Confused, startled, unsure if she were asleep or awake, she shouted, "Quit it, John. Now."

Instead, he kept pouring, only this time into two glasses. "Congratulations, Laura. I just woke you up. A toast to the new master fast-sleeper."

From that day on she used cat-nap fast-sleep. Her endurance levels soared. She knew it was one of the best things he'd ever taught her.

"Thanks for asking, Roddy. I'm okay," she lied.

***

Laura's official job duties started with a home visit to the Vice President's daughter.

Anika beamed smiles across the dining room table.

"Tell me, how is it?" asked Anika.

"How is what?"

"Your new job, silly. How do you like it?"

"I like it. And, thank you."

"That's it? No more details?"

Laura smiled. She was getting used to this—her responses more sincere, more heartfelt, less uptight. "Sorry, I can't say any more. You know the drill."

Anika rolled her eyes and laughed. "Boy, do I know the drill."

"Well, then, let's get started," said Laura. "First, let me congratulate you on your new pregnancy."

Chapter 48

Laura never knew what her job title really was, not in the beginning and not at the end. She tended White House patients, met lawmakers and law manipulators, consulted on diagnoses, and didn't ask questions. She'd known too much before. Better to be a cog in a machine, turning only where required. She moved day to day, collected her paycheck, and watched her stomach swell.

In the evenings, she'd sit on the couch, the same thoughts running an endless loop in her head. *A month into a new job; almost five months pregnant; no friends left; haven't told my family, and angry as shit.* When she'd had enough, she turned on the TV and watched standup comedy.

One Thursday night, she picked up the phone and dialed Arlo.

"Hello?"

Oh, my God, what did I do? I can't talk to him. I can't believe I...

"Laura? Are you all right?"

"Arlo. Sorry. I think this was just a butt dial."

"This was just a butt dial?" he repeated.

It sounded stupid even to her.

"I don't know."

"I'm coming over. Let me in when I get there."

"Okay."

When he came, she began to cry. He held her until the tears stopped. They watched TV together until midnight. Then he got up to go home.

"Can I see you again?" he asked.

"Maybe I'll make another butt dial," she answered.

"Maybe I'll be home," he replied.

"I hope so," she said, and felt a twinge in her stomach.

***

She saw him at 6:45 p.m. on the rooftop terrace of the hotel where she'd first been trained—he was hosting new post-docs for his 'Institute,' and she was the on-site medical staff for the First Lady's birthday party.

Laura froze. Her dress covered the gentle bulge of middle pregnancy, but she had filled out in other areas, breasts enlarging, cheeks full and rosy. *I knew this would happen sometime. Just wasn't expecting it tonight.*

John Russell nodded as he passed feet from where she stood. Trailing him in high heels and tailored suit was a tall, large-boned brunette with French twist. They moved well together, comfortable, unimpeded.

She knew he would not acknowledge her more than that once during the rest of their hours on the rooftop. "Conscious positioning," he'd called it and drilled her in the technique until it turned to habit. "Know where, with whom and with what you are dealing at all times—it keeps you in charge." She'd watched the power of it— in surgery, in the airport, at gatherings, everywhere.

"You really sure you want to stay in DC?" The question echoed in her head. She hadn't answered George Penunos then and still didn't know. But seeing John Russell shook loose an anger so profound she coughed from sudden heart arrhythmia and stumbled to find a chair.

***

"Laura, you can't dictate where you'll work. At the White House, it depends on where we need coverage and who has the skills for the job. I know you understand that." Dr. Jordman looked less than sympathetic.

"Yes, I know."

Jordman was not so sure. "I'll repeat for the record. You prefer not to work around Dr. Russell—is that your request?"

"Yes."

330

"You look tired," he said.

"Yes, sir."

Roddy Jordman steepled his fingers.

"I'm aware there were unresolved difficulties when you left Dr. Russell's employ." A pause. "Anything you'd like to share?"

She shook her head.

He sat back.

"I'll do my best, but I can't make any promises."

"Yes, sir. Thank you." She shrugged on her coat, closed the door and headed toward the street.

Last night had been her first encounter with John Russell since she quit her job.

She wanted it to be the last.

Only it wasn't.

***

She saw him a week later at the Guggenheim Museum's open house. Accompanied.

Then, several days later, at the National Science Foundation lecture series. Accompanied.

On Friday he was in the White House medical clinic. Accompanied.

She kept her mouth shut and lips sealed as her tension built.

He's stalking me, she kept thinking.

That's ridiculous, she'd argue. But John Russell's "showing up everywhere" behavior fertilized distasteful thoughts about him and his. *He never answered my DNA letter. How dare he pretend this isn't happening? What happens when I wear 'real' maternity clothing and talk about the father? Did he think I'd lie? What if I serve him with a fucking lawsuit for being the daddy?*

She would place her dishes on her coffee table, pull her feet from the floor, and stretch out on the sofa. *Too tired to think about it right now.*

***

331

On Monday afternoon, Dr. Jordman called Laura to his office.

"Sit down please, Ms. Greenwald." The formal tone was a warning.

"We've had a request."

She waited.

"For assistance on surgery."

She waited.

"Neurological complications."

Her head began to pound.

"A high-profile diplomat."

Her blood pressure rose.

"Wednesday—with briefings tomorrow."

"You accepted for me?"

"Of course. I'm your boss. You're a nurse and have the experience."

"And I'll be working with…?"

"Dr. John Russell."

She forced herself up from the chair.

"Roddy—I won't…"

"Sit down, Ms. Greenwald."

She sat.

"I cannot retract the request. As long as you are in our employ, this is part of your job."

The unstated alternative hung in the air.

"And if I don't…?"

Silence.

"I encourage you to attend the briefing," he said, and returned to the papers on his desk.

She didn't move. He looked up.

"That's all. Briefing's at 9:00 tomorrow morning in the conference room."

She still didn't move.

"Ms. Greenwald. I am a military doctor. In the military, when you are dismissed, you turn and exit. I suggest you follow the same guidelines."

Laura rose stiffly, exited, stalked to the White House chapel and sat cross legged in a chair for how long she did not know. When her brain loosened, she had a plan—take sick leave for the rest of the day (*this is making me sick, right?*), and show up for Tuesday's 'suggested' briefing. *Then we shall see what we shall see.*

Damned if she'd let John Russell take control of her life again.

***

The room held three people. They sat around a long, oval table—Dr. Jordman, Dr. Russell, Eva Jormand.

I should have worn my bullet-proof vest. Laura had not slept well. The irritated edges of her nerves scraped every thought that passed through her mind.

"Sit, please, Laura," said Dr. Jordman, motioning to the extra chair as she walked in.

She sat, back stiff, hands folded.

"Thank you for coming," he said.

She deemed no response necessary.

Jordman began. "Let's get started on…"

"Why do you need me?" Laura speared the question at John Russell before Jordman had finished.

"Your question is irrelevant to the…" attempted Roddy Jordman. But no one listened.

"You have the experience," John Russell lobbed back at Laura.

"Many people do," she said, "so, I beg to differ."

"Dr. Russell, Ms. Greenwald…" tried Dr. Jordman again.

"You always were direct, Laura," replied John Russell.

"You always were manipulative, John." *You're making a mess of this, Greenwald,* she thought. *Better shut up.* But she couldn't stop.

Roddy Jordman stood up. "Gentlemen, ladies, may we please…"

"You are needed on the case, Laura," John Russell insisted. He did not look at Jordman.

"You never responded to the envelope I left you."

"I never opened it."

WHAM! Laura's hand walloped the table. The smack rattled the water glasses on the table.

"You *never* opened it? Never looked inside? Didn't *read* it?" She leaned forward, her face red with incredulity.

"I did not."

"You're a bigger jerk than I imagined." The snarl rolled off her tongue.

John's face flushed. "You should have gotten an abortion and not brought it up—not flaunted the contract breach in my face." He glared at her. "We could have continued as we were."

Laura stood up so abruptly the chair toppled backward, and thudded to the carpet.

"This is your child." She took a huge breath. "How could you ever think we could 'continue as we were?'"

"Frankly, I didn't—but I wanted you either working with me or out of my town. It's too inconvenient for my…"

"Too inconvenient? Who fuckin' gave you the right to decide what's convenient for me?"

John smiled. Wispy sadness tugged at his mouth. "I've instructed you. Only you don't get it. The people with power make the decisions. The people with power decide what they'll do, get paid for it, and have big fan clubs cheering them on. That's who decides."

Roddy Jordman gaped at both of them. Eva Jormand stared at her water glass.

"Fuck you!" she said in a cold sweat, so angry she turned white. "You were going to wait till our baby is born—and then what? I sue you for child support? I can do that. It's not covered by your precious contract."

Laura stalked to the door. She stopped and turned. With ice packs under each word she said, "This. Baby. Is. Your. Son." She slammed the door and disappeared down the corridor while texting Roddy Jordman she had just "fucking quit."

In the silence, Eva turned to John. "You're sure the child isn't yours?" she asked.

"You know, I'm not so sure any more." John Russell stood. "Let's go, Eva. Can you find that envelope she's talking about?"

"I think so," she said, picking up her purse. They left, closing the door softly behind.

Jordman stood where he had first risen minutes earlier. He poured himself a glass of water and shook his head. "What a mess," he said to no one in particular.

***

Laura evacuated.

It took two days non-stop.

You're overdoing it, Greenwald.

Don't give a shit.

She packed bags, boxed clothes, sold furniture, gave things away, left a lot on the curb, and argued with the landlord about her rental contract. The air ticket to Cleveland was cheap; shipping the boxes was not. She didn't tell anyone she had quit her second job and was leaving DC. She didn't speak to Arlo. She never called her mother. She could barely breathe.

No talk. Just run. Now.

Chapter 49

John Russell sat alone in his office for over an hour, door locked, calls held. Eva retrieved the envelope Laura hand-delivered months earlier and walked across the hall. She knocked on his office door.

"Come in," he called, tone distracted and bent over the papers in front of him. She handed him the envelope. Slashed across the front were the words, *Don't Toss.*

"Sit," he said, "while I read this."

She sat. And waited. Minutes passed. "What does it say?" asked Eva.

He looked up. "It says this baby is mine."

***

Laura boarded the mid-morning flight. She'd only slept three hours. Exhaustion pervaded every cell of her body.

I feel like shit, she thought, so she'd upgraded to first class. *Only a ninety-minute flight.*

Doesn't help the nausea, whined an inner voice.

Oh, shut up. Laura squeezed her eyes closed and rested her head against the chair.

The stewardess stopped. "Are you all right, ma'am?"

"Yes. Thank you."

Liar.

She fell asleep before take-off.

An hour later she woke to her own screams as they echoed throughout the airliner cabin.

***

Arlo knocked on the apartment door. "Laura? Are you there?"

Silence.

"Laura, open up. It's me. I'm worried."

The downstairs neighbor had let him in the building and now stood several paces behind. Arlo kept knocking. Moments passed before he placed a palm on Arlo's back. "Hey, man, I'm sorry. She moved out a couple of days ago."

Arlo turned around. "No. I know her. She wouldn't just—drop out of sight. She's…"

"Sorry, buddy. She left me a bunch of her stuff." He shrugged. "'Things came up.' That's what she told me."

Arlo stared. The other man shuffled his feet and looked down. "Hey, I gotta get back downstairs. Let yourself out, okay?" Arlo heard footsteps retreat down the hallway and onto the first landing.

He took a deep breath, began his own retreat, then stopped. Struggling to loosen the cell phone from his jeans pocket, he speed-dialed a number. "Answer this time, damn it." Arlo had stopped leaving voice and text messages after fifteen calls. Now, at day four and call number thirty-one, he just dialed and waited. Three rings, four rings. He shoved the phone halfway into his hip pocket.

"Hello?" Weak, raspy, barely audible.

The phone dropped from half pocket to the floor. Then it disconnected.

"Shit. Shit. Shit." He fumbled for it and jabbed the screen back to life. "Pick up, Pick up. Pick up."

"Hello?" Weak. Sad.

"Laura—is that you? I called but…"

"I know," she interrupted. "I couldn't."

"I'm at your apartment. I…"

"I'm not okay."

Arlo stopped talking. Blood drained from his face. "What do you mean? What happen…"

"A big, messy, fucking miscarriage—on a plane."

Coughing, rasping and nose blowing from her end of the line squelched Arlo's barrage of questions.

He waited. She calmed.

"Where are you?"

"Cleveland Hospital."

"I'm coming out."

"No, Arlo…"

"Sorry, kiddo. On my way." He hung up, punched in Cleveland flight schedules and bought a ticket for that night's last flight to the Rock and Roll Capital of the World.

***

Eva canceled John's afternoon appointments and took him to a bar. They sat in a quiet corner. When the waiter came, she ordered John a double scotch on the rocks. The waiter turned back toward the bar to fill the order.

"Stop." The command in Eva's voice made him swivel like a soldier in training. "As soon my friend finishes his drink," she said, "I want to see another already on its way."

"Yes, ma'am."

She turned to John. "Talk," she said with the same command.

But John didn't talk. He sat and drank—one double scotch and then a second. Every so often he uttered, "Shit."

A while passed before he said, "Call my lawyers."

Eva looked at him. "Answer a question first."

"And what question is that?"

"Do you care?"

John Russell swigged the last of the scotch. "Doesn't make any damn difference if I care or not. I save lives. I teach others how to save lives. I won't have it fucked up."

"I see." Eva sighed. She shook her head.

Then she dialed his lawyers.

***

Arlo's flight to Cleveland arrived at 10:30 p.m. He used the plane time to cancel his next day's schedule, eat a meal and take a cat-nap. Laura had been taken to the hospital nearest the airport, ten-minutes away. With no luggage to slow him down, he was in a cab and on his way by 11:00.

"I'm sorry, sir," it's too late for visiting." The station nurse on duty was adamant. "After 10 in the evening we only allow family memb…"

"I'm her brother."

"I see." Her tone made it apparent she did not see. "We have no record of a brother…"

"Of course not. She's had a life-threatening event. There's no way she'd be cognizant of arranging those factors in an emergency. She can barely talk much less organize."

"Are you a doctor, sir?"

Arlo stared at her. "Yes. A neurosurgeon. Is it written on my forehead or something?"

"No, sir. It's written all over the way you talk. Go ahead. She's down that hallway—no roommate." She paused. He waited. "She does need her sleep, sir."

"I'm a doctor, remember?"

Arlo made his way down the hall, knocked on Laura's door, then slipped into the dimmed room. She was awake.

"Laura?"

"Arlo?" She turned her head and tried to smile. Tears spilled down her cheeks instead.

He bent to kiss her forehead, and whispered, "I'm so sorry." Then he sat, pulling a chair next to the bed. He took her hand until time and effort and strangeness melted into the background.

After a while he heard her whisper, "Thank you for being here."

He nodded keeping her hand firm in his. She turned toward him.

"I couldn't call, Arlo. My mind—it just exploded. *Get the fuck out* was all I could think. So, out I got." Laura struggled to sit up. She brushed Arlo's forehead, combing away the hair that had fallen onto his brow.

"Are you okay now?" he asked.

"The baby was twenty weeks. I hemorrhaged—a lot. A doctor was on board—that helped. They had an ambulance at the airport. The baby had already—come out—when I got to the hospital. The medic said the baby was stillborn. I got an emergency D&C. Now it's bedrest till the bleeding stops."

"How long?"

"Tomorrow afternoon, I think."

"Then what?" he asked.

"A glass of water, if you don't mind." They both laughed. He poured and passed her the cup.

"So, what's next for you?" he repeated.

"Hiding under my old blankets at mom and dad's house."

Arlo burst out laughing.

"What?" she demanded, tone peeved and impatient.

"That is the most Un-Laura-like comment I've ever heard you make." He bit his lip and tried to look serious. Then he poked her in the ribs. "Give it up, Greenwald." He kept at it till she laughed, cried foul, and begged for mercy. It took a few minutes before the nurse came in to demand order.

When she had gone and they stopped giggling, Arlo leaned back in his chair, arms behind his head and said, "So, Laura, what the fuck happened?"

***

"No, sir. Ms. Greenwald's contract does not prohibit speaking about the father of her child. She can sue for child support, talk to the media, show documentation. It's easy enough to do without breaking the contract. If she's got proof of fatherhood and doesn't divulge protected information, she'd win."

340

The five lawyers sat on one side of the oval table, John and Eva on the other.

"I see." John, elbows on the chair arms, rested his chin on steepled fingers. He stared at the table. Silence descended, broken only by the sound of seven people breathing. Minutes passed before he asked, "What do you suggest?"

Jennine Punati spoke for the group. "We suggest doing nothing for the moment, sir."

"Nothing?"

"Ms. Greenwald vacated her apartment. We don't know yet where she went or what she might do. We need more information to suggest..."

"Get it," John interrupted. "She probably went to Cleveland. Start there." He stood and left the room.

Eva smiled apologetically at the lawyers. "He's preoccupied," she said, then followed her employer out the door.

***

The cabin lights dimmed for an evening flight. Arlo refused dinner and rested his head against the seatback. He replayed in restless frustration his time with Laura.

"There's no DNA from the fetus?" asked Arlo, leaning back in the hospital armchair over a slices of takeout pizza he'd ordered at 2:00 am.

Laura's voice, thin and tired, spoke of bone deep exhaustion. She shook her head. "I was screaming in pain with blood pouring out of me. It didn't occur to ask for..."

He held up his hands. "I'm sorry—really. John's been such a fucking jerk over this. How could he think..."

"Arlo, just leave it alone. I told you what happened in Roddy's office." Laura looked down. "The machine I've been playing with is way bigger than I am. What did doing anything get me? Right into a hospital bed, if you haven't noticed."

He wiped his fingers of pizza grease and smiled gently. "The Laura Greenwald I know would think twice about what she could or couldn't do."

Arlo slept in the chair, freshened up in the morning, then took Laura for breakfast and a walk around the hospital grounds. Discharge was after lunch. They took a taxi to the airport. She retrieved her luggage and he bought a ticket back to DC.

"Promise me you'll think about it," he said.

"I promise I'll think about it."

He kissed her, then wouldn't let go. She started laughing.

"You're ruining a good kiss," he grumbled. "When can we talk again?"

"I don't know." She looked at the sidewalk. "When I'm better." She softened her noncommittal answer with a hug. Then she turned toward the line of taxis heading into Cleveland.

Arlo entered the airport and walked to the security line. If they'd screened his thoughts, they'd never have allowed him on the plane.

***

When she arrived on her parents' doorstep, Mrs. Greenwald exclaimed, "Laura, how wonderful! Come in. Why didn't you call?"

"Long story." She put her suitcase down and burst into tears.

No one asked any more questions that day and she was grateful.

Chapter 50

It took a while.

The healing, that is.

The first nights Laura dreamed. She awoke in deep sweats, ran to the toilet and vomited bile.

The second set of nights she moved to what used to be her big brother's bedroom.

"Why do you want to move into Atticus's room?" asked her mother.

"Just a hunch," replied Laura.

Her night sweats calmed and her nausea waited till morning. Atticus had always made her feel safe.

She slept. She lost weight. Afternoons found her cross-legged on the sun room chaise staring into the ripples of Lake Erie.

"Are you ok, dear?" asked her mother.

"I'm fine," she lied, wondering when she would ever feel okay again.

"I'm glad," said her mother. "You rest up as long as you need to."

***

One day she woke up and realized the world was still rumbling along and she'd missed weeks of it.

Time to stop hiding. She pulled out her phone, dialed the biggest hospital in the region and asked for the personnel office for nursing. Online applications might be the way to go, but personal contact never hurt. Laura gave her name to the receptionist and asked about positions in the neurology clinic.

"Just a moment, please. I'll transfer you."

A few clicks, and then a voice on the other end of the line said, "Good morning, Ms. Greenwald. We've been waiting for your call."

Her muscles froze. "What are you talking about?"

"I'm Dr. Hartwell, personnel director for nursing applications." A pause ensued. Papers rustled. "Let me see," she said. "Ah, here we are. I have permission to tell you that Dr. John Russell gave you a very strong recommendation. He said we should hire you on the spot for whatever you wanted to do—when you called, that is." More paper shuffling. "I must say it was quite unusual. And he's so well respected."

Laura's stomach clenched into a roiling, nauseous knot. *When the fuck is that man gonna get out of my life? How does he know what I'm going to do when even I don't?* Boiling anger kidnapped every thought she produced. *This is one more of his arrogant, underhanded, self-centered, miserable plans to shove me into a corner as far from DC as ...*

"Can you come for an interview tomorrow morning, say around 10:00?" asked the voice on the phone. A pause. "Are you still there?"

Answer the woman. "Oh, sorry," *I gotta sort out this shit.* "The day after would be a little better for me, if that's okay."

"Yes, that'll be fine. Thursday then. I'll send an email to confirm."

"Great. Let me give you my email..."

"Oh, not necessary, Ms. Greenwald. Dr. Russell already gave us that. He left your resume with us. You have an impressive skill set." A pause ensued. Laura did not respond. "It's been a pleasure to speak with you." The line went dead.

You're gonna figure out everything in 24 hours before the interview? jeered her inner voice. *You can't even stand up straight much less talk.*

A headache lurched its way forward. Laura dragged herself back to bed and crawled under the covers. She'd only been up for an hour.

Sleep. She waited, but her mind raced, one thought tripping over the next.

I signed a contract for $700,000 a year.

I signed non-disclosure clauses.

I went on duty anywhere and anytime my employer called.

I had consensual sex under contract with my boss.

I got pregnant.

I refused an abortion.

I lost my job.

I lost my friends.

I lost Arlo.

I lost my baby fathered by my ex-employer who refused to believe it.

I got harassed out of town.

I'm still being stalked by John Russell.

I'm hiding under the covers in my brother's old bedroom.

I can't stand it.

Sleep eluded her. She pulled on pants and top and sat in the back yard by the edge of the lake—still obsessing.

Sexual stupidity and powerful men, she thought. *The combination that kills. In the news. Every day.*

Will it never stop?

Arnold Schwarzenegger, Bill Clinton, Harvey Weinstein, Tiger Woods, Mark Sanford, Anthony Weiner, David Petraeus, Eliot Spitzer, Bill Cosby, the Catholic priests. The list went on and on and on. Very discouraging.

She shook her head and yelled to the clouds, "This country can't even discuss birth control without somebody getting shot." Laura got up and walked along the lakeshore edge, stopping in front of an oak tree. "No one's ready for a John Russell Contract—not even John Russell." she pronounced. The oak tree didn't respond.

I'd have finished out the contract. I've lived through worse.

An uninvited thought punched through her parade of logic. *Except for getting pregnant by a dismissive, narcissistic, controlling bastard who acted like you were...*

Gasping, she clutched at her stomach and bent over. Pain rocketed upward through uterus, intestines, chest. "Shit," she sobbed. Laura dropped to the grass and rocked back and forth. *What's happening?* The searing agony would not ease.

For an endless time, she lay there, panting and gagging. When the last pains sputtered out, she slid her hand down to check the jeans fabric between her legs. *How much have I bled out from the D&C? Do I need the hospital?*

What she found was nothing. Nothing but dry, clean fabric.

***

"Doctor?" A pause. "Did you want to attend?" persisted the intern.

Silence.

"Sir?"

Dr. Apollo Stephanopoulos, in soiled scrubs, stood facing his locker. The afternoon surgery had extended far longer than usual. "Sorry. Got a bit distracted." He laughed, but the feeling didn't reach his eyes. "Run that by me again?"

"Yes, sir. You wanted a reminder about the training—Dr. Russell's new procedure. Invitation only—you were on the list. It's in thirty minutes."

"That's today?" He paused. "Totally forgot." The paper memo from John Russell's office had arrived several weeks ago. Observation of a new method in the hospital's operating theater—with commentary. Arlo, just back from Cleveland, had been in no mood to respond to the man whose actions had shoved Laura straight into a miscarriage. He'd wadded the RSVP into a ball and slam-dunked it into the nearest wastebasket. Now he was facing the decision a second time.

"What should I tell Dr. Russell?"

"Tell him I'll be there."

***

Not one blemish, not one blood spot, not one bruise.

"Bloody hell," yelled Laura at the full-length mirror. Not one drop of blood. She looked at herself—pale, naked, and too thin by a number of pounds. "I made up that whole fucking, agonizing pain in my crazed little mind."

She snatched her clothes from the floor, pulled them on, then ran her hands through her hair, pulling at the roots. *Thousands of people show up in the ER*, she thought, *only to find they'd panicked themselves into the symptoms—heart fine—mental status a mess.*

"Damn you, John Russell!" she yelled. Every loss, every disappointment, every angry, hellish moment of the last months threw venom into her words. "I'm not living like this anymore."

"You all right, dear?" called Laura's mother from the first floor.

"Yes, mom, I'm fine," she called downstairs. She added, turning to the mirror, "And, I'm sick of lying to everybody."

Her purse lay on the chair by the window. Three strides took her within snatching distance. She flung open the bag and rooted around. "Where's my damn phone?" The inside looked like her life felt—a complete wreck. She dumped the bag upside down. Her cell clattered to the floor, along with everything else.

She retrieved it, speed dialed, and waited, pacing the bedroom as the phone rang. Voicemail. *Shit.* She hung up, punched in the same number; got the same non-response.

It could be hours before I hear back, she thought. Her fingers flew over the phone's screen. Ten-minutes passed before she stopped, wrenched her suitcase from the closet, threw in clothes, toothbrush, toiletries, and took a shower.

When Laura bumped down the steps with luggage, her mother stood blocking the front door.

"Young lady, you are not leaving without telling me what's happening and where you're going. I've been very worried about you. However," she put her hands on her hips for emphasis, "disappearing is not only ungrateful, it's unacceptable."

Laura pulled her mother into an embrace, still wet hair clinging to cheeks and neck.

"Mom, I love you, but it's a long story and not over yet." She let go, grabbed her suitcase and raced down the front walk to the waiting Uber. "I'm going to DC," she called. "My plane leaves in 90 minutes. Gotta go."

***

Dr. Russell stood in the operating arena next to the robotic machinery. His executive nurse and a patient who had undergone the procedure sat next to him.

"And so," he concluded, "as the video shows, this minimally invasive, prototype robotic tool can access deep level brain tumors, distinguish between cancerous and healthy tissue *as we operate,* and remove all of the invading cells at one time. No second guessing from MRI images or going back to 'clean up the borders.'"

The fifty neurologists in seats behind the observation window rose, almost as a unit, and gave their lecturer a standing ovation. Arlo Stephanopoulos stayed glued to his chair.

"Hey, man," said a friend next to him, "get your ass up. That was damn impressive." He dragged Arlo to standing position.

John Russell bowed to the crowd. "Thank you all for your time. Please consider training at my Institute. It has been my honor to bring such new technology to our community."

People jostled out of the room, everyone tired from a long day and the two-hour, blow-by-blow descriptions of videotaped surgery.

Arlo turned his cell phone back on. Laura's two text messages popped onto the screen. He stopped dead in the middle of the corridor and punched the message icon.

"Arlo, I need to talk to you." Text number-one.

Text number-two sent twenty minutes later. "I'll be in DC at…"

"Dr. Stephanopoulos—so glad you could come." A hand clapped Arlo on the back. "I hadn't gotten your RSVP. Wasn't sure you'd…"

John Russell's face swam into view amidst the crowd flowing from the lecture area. Next to him stood the woman from the surgical theater—tall, possibly five-foot-nine, dark hair pulled back, intelligent eyes, no smile. Laura always wore flowing clothing. This executive-nurse came dressed in a business suit.

"Russell." said Arlo woodenly. He stood, phone in both hands, trying to reply to Laura's text but unable to do so.

John shepherded them out of the jostling crowd to the side of the hallway.

"I can see you want something more than a hello, John," said Arlo. The nurse-in-a-business-suit widened her eyes at the drenching irritation in Arlo's response.

"I'd like you to meet Susan Blacking, my new nurse." John turned to his companion. "She's with me quite a lot. Thought it would be good to introduce the two of you."

"Point taken." Arlo, raised his phone and began to text. Susan Blacking's eyes widened even further.

John persisted. "I was wondering how Laura's doing. If anyone knew, I thought you…"

Arlo stepped back and crossed his arms. He spat out his next words, a loud, piercing voice above the noise of the crowd. "Your fucking everywhere information network hasn't told you yet—is that why you're asking?"

People shied away from the disturbance.

"You got her pregnant then put her in the hospital," he continued, even louder. "I thought you'd have figured out how she is by now—or don't you care?"

Passers-by slowed, turned to watch.

"Sir?" Susan Blacking interjected, the arteries in her neck throbbing. "I'll wait for you at the front door." She disappeared through the circle of people gathering around them.

"Arlo," commanded John Russell, posture rigid, almost trembling in anger. "Stop right there. Laura has been prohibited from divulging any informa…"

"She didn't say a word, John. I pieced it together on my own. You had a contract that involved her being your…"

"Stop!" roared Russell. The darting glance John gave the crowd showed how much he wanted this conversation shut down.

"I wonder if Susan Blacking is also your…'

"Stop! I can sue you to hell and bac…"

"Good try, Doctor," retorted Arlo as he shouldered out of the crowd, away from John and the emotional blast furnace they'd created. He noticed no one had pulled out any phone cameras.

"Too damn many people need John Russell. That's the fuckin' problem," Arlo mumbled as he headed for exit and the freedom of open space.

Chapter 51

Laura's plane landed at 7:00 that evening. She powered on her phone. At best, Arlo would know—at worst, he'd advise.

There it was. The text had come in at 6:00 p.m. while she was still in flight. *Glad I didn't wait to hear from him—I'd still be in Cleveland.*

"No hotel," it said. "Stay with me. Easier to talk. Separate bedrooms available if needed. Have something to tell you, too. Take an Uber."

What was he going to tell her? It couldn't be as insane as what she was planning. *Maybe he's gone crazy, too,* she thought. He'd have to be a little whacky at this point to hang out with her.

***

John called the emergency meeting two hours after Arlo shouted his obscenities into the hallway crowd. Four lawyers, John Russell and Eva Jormand.

"Yes, sir," said Jeannine Punati, "Just as you requested. Right after we found out about the miscarriage, we contacted all the Cleveland hospitals with your letter of recommendation—told them it might take a while for her to call. She made her first call today."

"Did she accept an interview?"

"Yes, sir. For tomorrow morning—at Cleveland Hospital."

"Good." He paused. "Can she sue for damages over the pregnancy or miscarriage?"

"Anyone can sue for anything," said George Penunos, "especially if a lawyer's willing to take the case. But, since you're still paying health, it's unlikely she'd get monetary damages."

"I don't give a damn about monetary damages," retorted John. "What I care about is the media circus if she goes to court."

Silence.

Jim Johnson broke it. "I suggest we wait. Her job interview could settle everything—or not." He leaned back, hands clasped behind head. "You don't want to play your hand before the cards are dealt."

John Russell scrutinized each face in the room. "Okay. Keep me informed." He stood. "Walk with me, Eva." They went to his office, leaving the lawyers to gather papers and turn out lights. "Your opinion?" he asked.

"About?"

"About Laura. You think she'll break her contract—talk to people?" John's lips set in a tight, thin line. He crossed his arms. "My verbal boxing match with Arlo this afternoon was thoroughly unpleasant."

Eva studied her employer. She saw the age and pressure lines forming along his brow, the tension in his posture. "Laura's gone through a lot—add in a late term miscarriage in the middle of a plane flight?" Eva shook her head. "Hide? Work? Fight? Something more creative? At this point, I couldn't even pretend to predict what she might do."

"I see."

They stood in silence broken only by the tick-tock of a wall clock.

"It's late. I'd like to go home if you don't need me for anything further."

"You want Daniel to drive you?" he asked.

"No, thanks," she said.

Eva left a distracted John Russell staring out the windows onto a darkened garden.

***

"You did *what*? cried Laura, laughing so hard wine sloshed over side of her glass and spattered the granite counter top.

"I couldn't help myself." Arlo smiled, elbows on the counter, drink in hand. "He was so...self-involved."

"*Self-involved*? That's the best you can come up with for Doctor John and his destructive, thoughtless behavior?" She leaned over the counter and grabbed the bottle of single malt scotch by Arlo's elbow. "Hand me your glass," she demanded. "I can see you haven't had enough to drink yet."

"Whoa," he yelled as she poured the liquid until it flooded over the top of his tumbler.

"Sorry. My bad." Laura looked around for a towel. She came back, wiped up, and added, "You're gonna need a whole lotta booze to hear what I've got planned."

His laughter died out.

"I see. Want something to eat first?"

Laura rubbed her neck. "I'm grungy; I'm so pissed off I can't sleep, and I'm hungry. I don't know which is worse."

Arlo walked over to Laura and lifted her chin with a gentle touch. "You take a shower; I'll get the food. Then we tackle the pissed off together."

"Deal."

***

It took an hour to shower and eat. When they were done, the hands of the wall clock pointed to 10:30.

"More wine," he asked, "before getting you un-pissed?"

"Don't you have work tomorrow?"

"You're more interesting than sleep. Sit." He pointed. "Over there."

Laura remembered it as "The Talk."

'The Talk' took two hours. She was more awake at the end than the beginning.

"There's a good chance it'll work," he said when she was done, feet resting on the coffee table, head propped on couch pillows.

"You're just being supportive." She'd gone to the sink for a glass. "I need an honest response."

I am being honest. I think you've got a damn good chance."

"Except?" she asked.

"Except what?" he countered.

"You're holding something back, Stephanopoulos. Out with it."

He faced her. "You sure you don't want more time to rest up? Or think? If you do it tomorrow—just hours after..."

She interrupted. "I can't wait. It's gotta be tomorrow. I'm so angry; I could vomit every five minutes—only the nausea makes me take the next step. If I stop, I'll eat myself alive from the inside out."

"Okay, okay," he relented and enfolded her in his arms. "I think it's time for some shut eye."

She nodded.

"Tonight, you get your own bed." He went to the guest room and opened the door.

"Apartment key's in the night stand. I'm outta here at 6:00 in the morning."

Exhaustion fogged her mind. "Thanks, Arlo," she said, a meager smile at her lips.

"You let me know—if I don't answer, you text—agreed?"

"Agreed."

***

Laura allowed herself to sleep in. She wanted to be fresh for what faced her. The witching hour was twelve noon.

She showered, styled her hair, and applied makeup with exquisite care. The night before they'd discussed what she should wear. Now, she critiqued the effect as she reviewed her reflection in the mirror. In the back of her mind she could hear Mee Sue saying, "business elegant with dash of sexy. Very good, Ms. Lori."

I miss her.

The uninvited thought slashed through Laura's concentration. Other memories she'd kept in lockdown pressed forward, clamoring for release. *I'm not letting them in. Not now.* She reached for her purse. Time to go.

I should call Daniel to chauffeur me over. That would take some balls. She laughed at the thought.

But Daniel had always been kind. She would never use him as a pawn in a showdown with John Russell.

Chapter 52

Laura ignored the receptionist, walked past the desk, and strode down the hallway.

"May I help you?" The woman's protest echoed down the corridor.

"No." Laura said without stopping.

"Ma'am," she called. "You need to check in. We'll call you for your appointment." The scraping of a chair and the receptionist's rapid footsteps followed her down the hall. She stopped abruptly, turned, and set a blazing gaze on the woman coming after her. The receptionist tripped as she backed away from Laura's fiery face"

"I'm here on business." She stood stone firm in grey suit and black boots. "I know exactly where I'm going."

Face flushed with indecision, the receptionist stood immobilized. The front door opened and the phone began to ring. The harried clerk turned and scampered back to familiar territory.

Laura checked her watch. *Almost noon.*

She knew John's schedule by heart—he always started and ended consults at exactly thirty minutes. Lunch always at noon. She headed to Dr. Russell's office and waited outside the door, opening the purse hanging over one arm. It took a few seconds to rearrange the contents.

"Thank you so much, Doctor," said the man exiting the office. He saw Laura in the hallway and held the door for her to enter.

"It's always a pleasure," said John's disembodied voice from inside the room.

"It may not be this time." Laura stood in the doorway.

"Laura." He rose from his chair, his hands just shutting the desktop drawer.

John never could tolerate being one down.

"What are you doing here?"

"I thought we could discuss that."

Laura felt nausea grapple upward as she spoke. *I will not throw up. I've got nothing to be afraid of.*

"There's nothing to discuss," he said. John relaxed and broadened his stance. "Or," he continued "we could discuss the consequences of breaching your contract."

In an instant, her anger exploded. It came from behind her eyes, cauterizing every nerve cell still spewing anxiety, incinerating every last shred of nausea. *I'm going to skewer him. How dare he try that 'you've been a bad girl tone' with me.*

She stalked to his desk. "You can rip up and throw out your precious contract—which I never broke," she replied in a measured, level voice, "and do the same with your goddamned consequences, Dr. Russell." "They're not worth the paper they're written on."

"You're going to lose your license to practice, Laura."

"Oh, I don't think so, John." Her tone turned buttery. *Time to show I'm staying till the finale.* She chose a chair and sat. "But I'd be happy to discuss that in court if you like.

He glared at her but did not move.

"See? We might have something to talk about after all," she said cheerily.

Laura watched the flush creep up John's face. It disappeared seconds later. *Struggling for emotional control,* she thought. *Good. And he pissed me off again—even better.*

She patted the chair kitty corner to her own. "Come. Sit down. We can have a nice chat."

The undertone in Laura's voice pulled a reluctant John Russell from behind his desk, but he did not sit.

"Don't be stubborn, John. I'm staying until we're finished—if we do it quickly you won't fuck up your afternoon schedule."

You've grown a pair of balls, she said to herself.

"Laura, I'm calling security." He reached for the phone.

"I'll leave on my own—if you insist," she said, but stayed seated. "Just to let you know, though, my next stop is the Washington Post, and then my lawyer. "She smiled.

A lawyer? said the voice in her head. *You don't have a lawyer. And you don't even know where the Washington Post is.*

Oh, shut up.

John pulled his hand back.

Gotcha, thought Laura. John Russell, sitting or standing, was now at the negotiating table.

"Besides your broken contract, Laura, what is there to talk about?"

"I never broke my contract. Whether or not somebody guessed what was in it is another matter." She let the statement sink in. *Don't get sidetracked, Greenwald.* "Let's start with—did you look at the test results? And don't be stupid enough to ask what test results. You should have done that months ago."

She watched his jaw clench.

"I kind of looked over the test results."

"*Kind of?* What the hell does that mean?" *Punch the pompous jerk into kingdom come,* exploded a voice from somewhere inside her head. Only a death grip on the armchair kept Laura seated. She forced herself back under control.

"It means I didn't quite believe..."

"No shit, Sherlock."

"Laura." His tone was steel hard.

Shit. Overplayed that one. "What?"

"It you want to have a discussion, stop interrupting." He looked down, shifted his stance. "I know you're angry."

"That's an understatement," she said slowly, each word dripping sarcasm.

Silence.

Shit, he's gonna stop talking. She held her breath—and her tongue.

But this time he continued. "I looked at the test results. I also hired a paternity professional to review them."

More silence.

"They were... ah... convincing."

Silence.

"And...?" she prompted.

"I'd put too many precautions in place to father any child. I thought it was a scam."

Laura fought an inner fury and incredulity grown so huge they blurred her vision. With excruciating care, she eased the next words out of her mouth.

"How could you ever think I'd stoop to such a stunt? After all our time together, all the crises we've gone through, *that* is what you thought?"

He shrugged—an elegant, offhand gesture. "All women have that capacity—especially when defending their young." Belief reverberated through each word.

"I'm not a coyote with a litter of pups, John." She felt ready to rip his pretentious testicles off.

"You're being dramatic, Laura. I didn't want to believe the DNA results. I admit that. I'd covered every contingency. There shouldn't have been a pregnancy with me involved."

Laura stared at him in stony, frigid silence.

"The DNA test suggested differently." He crossed his arms. "Regardless, I do not allow anything to interfere with my work. If I was, in part, responsible for the baby, I reasoned you should be compensated for your inconvenience."

Inconvenience?

She came to life. "You call my life being blown away and a miscarriage on an airplane 'an inconvenience'? I can't believe yo..."

"Stop."

Laura stopped—a knee jerk reaction to months of crisis training in surgery from the man in front of her. *Shit,* she thought, *when will I stop taking orders from him?*

"I'm not to blame for how women act around me." John, more relaxed, put his hands in his pockets.

Silence.

"My life has to stay scandal free. No dirty linen, no dangling threads. And especially no babies. That's how I keep moving when other people trip over their own stupidity."

"So now I'm dirty linen?"

"You could have been."

His casual disdain was spellbinding.

"And you needed me out of DC…?" The sentence dangled.

"You were unfinished business—with scandal potential." He stopped for a moment. "I'm sure you can appreciate that. Anyhow, I've already made up for the trouble you've had."

Breathing—now it came shallow—now hard. She could feel a vice-crunching headache in the making. "John, what on earth are you talking about?"

"Job interviews in Cleveland, of course. I had to use significant influence to make sure you'd get good results wherever you went. It should take care of any difficulties you've experienced."

Laura gaped at him. She couldn't believe this guy.

"No thank-you's?" he asked coyly.

Her head exploded. *Screw it,* she screamed at herself. *Get to the point with this asshole—forget the fancy chitchat.*

"I want an endowment," she said, face blank, and stone cold neutral.

Silence. He stood frozen in place.

"An endowment?" The confused look on his face made Laura want to clap.

"Yes. Two and a half million dollars, plus health benefits." *Keep him off balance.*

"WHAT?" he yelled. "Are you crazy?" His face flushed. "What the hell kind of blackmail is this?" "John leaned over the desk, palms gripping the sides, arms straightened. "*Endowment*? How delusional have you gotten?"

Laura leaned back. Her breathing calmed. *Bull's eye. Got his attention.*

"A business endeavor I think you'd love to support," she said. Smooth. Easy.

He glowered but didn't speak.

He's worried. She watched in grim satisfaction as John ground each flailing emotion from his face, banished every spark of fear from his eyes. He'd taught her that technique for surgeries—when unexpected crisis threatened a patient and fear pounded the physician's mind.

Smile. He'll hate it.

She sat, hands folded on her lap, and smiled. "Everything I do is above board, Dr. Russell. Your founding contribution would be just a little more than my original two-year salary—that is—if I hadn't become an 'inconvenience.'"

John Russell unfroze. His right hand reached for the telephone and he dialed. "Security to my office, please." He his eyes locked onto hers.

Asshole. He's still testing. "John—put the phone down."

"Security's coming any minute, Laura. I'm…"

"A pompous ass is what you are, John. You didn't dial security or anybody else. Every extension here has three digits. You dialed two."

She crossed her legs. Icicles dripped from each vowel of every next word. "You have one last chance to listen to me or I'm out the door and you won't need any security—except for the journalists."

A smile tugged his lips. "You always did notice the details." He turned and gazed out the windows.

"And you were always good at manipulating them, John."

"Okay, talk."

Laura's breathing turned ragged. *He's gonna go ballistic on this one. Make it fast.*

"A non-profit—Sexual and Legal Wellness in the Workplace. Two employees—me and a lawyer. Endowment to keep fees down. My license unthreatened."

John remained immobile for seconds, back rigid, arms crossed. When he turned, every facial muscle was positioned into a tight, professional mask.

"I see," he said. "And you want me to write a three-million-dollar check on my lunchtime?"

"Two and a half," she corrected.

"You don't want me to sign a contract?" he asked, pulling out the chair and sitting at his desk.

"We'd have to write that up. But the check first. It won't be used until the endowment is legal. Lawyers create special accounts for donations like this.

What invisible, non-existent lawyer are you talking about? screeched her inner voices all at once.

"Donations?" John raised his eyebrows.

I need to get this very clear—and loud. "Yes, John. My request is for you to endow a non-profit organization dealing with sexual wellness in the workplace."

"It's a significant amount of money."

"And you have 'significant influence'—I believe you mentioned using it to 'make sure I'd get good results wherever I went.' Well, here I am."

"I damn well didn't mean this." Anger boiled under the words.

"And I damn well do." Laura straightened in the chair. "I came to get the kind of help I can use. You used my body. You fathered my baby. You harassed me out of two jobs in this city. You will not threaten, interfere, ignore. or restructure any part of my life—ever again."

She stood up and put her purse under her arm. "Have you decided to write that check? Once I leave, I'm not sure I'm going to want to take it."

He leaned back. "Not take three million dollars if I offer it later?"

"Two and a half," she said. "This isn't a game, John. I have to decide if you're worth dealing with." Her headache came down full force. She winced and felt a tickle of nausea threaten. *I'm exhausted.*

"These things take time, Laura…" He spread his arms trying to imitate a helpless gesture.

"No, they don't, John, not around here." *He's pussyfooting. Get the hell out.* Laura stood.

"Here's my phone number." She left a card on his desk, closed her purse, and exited the office.

This 'thing' Arlo gave me better have recorded the whole conversation—every single, irritating word of it. The mini-recorder looked like a flash drive. It lay in a side pocket of her slim bag. She hoped her arm hadn't blocked the sound.

She called an Uber before she reached the front hallway.

John dialed Eva's office. "Get the damn lawyers over here—now."

Chapter 53

Laura opened the apartment door with Arlo's key. She stripped; each piece of clothing splayed on the floor where it fell as she ran. By the time she yanked open the shower door, the nausea exploded. Dry heaves rampaged through her until she sat on the tiles and turned on the water. It beat on her head in warm waves until her shivering stopped. *I'm fine. I'm perfect. No one got hurt.*

When the panic squeezed itself to a trickle, she towel-dried, pulled on jeans with a sweater and called Arlo. *Mid-day—he probably can't answer.*

"Stephanopoulos."

"Arlo, it's me." She yanked a brush through her wet hair. The pain kept her focused. "I'm going to the Washington Post. I can't stop, Arlo. I can't stop." She refused to cry, so, instead plowed forward. "I'm not going to let him. I won't."

"Laura, take a breath…"

"I took a shower."

"Good." He waited. She calmed. "You told him about the endowment," he said. It was a statement.

"Yes."

"What did he say?"

"He has to think about it."

"That's reasonable, Laura."

"He's so fucking arrogant, Arlo."

"Yes, he is." A pause ensued. "But he always has been."

Her breathing remained erratic.

He waited, then said, "Laura, I want you to listen with excruciating care to each word I say next."

Moments passed before she whispered, "Okay."

"If you can't deal with John, if you get sick every time you see him, or get so angry you can't breathe—then forget the endowment, forget your business, forget a life here; and get your damn ass back to a safe job in Cleveland."

Her audible intake of breath echoed over the connection.

She hung up.

***

"No, sir," Jim Johnson said, "it's unlikely she'd win much." The lawyers sat across the conference table from John Russell and Eva Jormand. Sixty minutes earlier Laura had left. The discussion had been going on for fifteen of them.

"There's no way to prove you harassed her or that she had out-of-pocket expenses. You still pay her health care—so, everything was covered."

"It's the media I'm worried about—or haven't you been listening?"

"You might consider suggesting an endowment contract with a non-disclosure clause," Johnson suggested.

John exploded. "You already put that fucking clause in the previous contract and what damn good did it do?" Even with Eva's restraining hand on his arm it took several moments before he calmed down.

"Sir," said Jim Johnson, "the original contract we created was always outside the 'standard of practice.' Nothing illegal by statute, but it always held potential for media interest. Considering the scope of Ms. Greenwald's duties, it might well be judged null and void in court."

"She'd ruin herself," snorted John.

"But you'd get dragged along with her, sir."

Jennine Punati intervened. "Can we listen to that recording again?"

John Russell shrugged, pulled out a small recording device and set it on the table. Fifteen-minutes later Jennine summed up the recording. "Glad you keep a recorder in your desk, John. It's helpful to hear what went on. The problem is, she denies breach of contract, said she'd go to newspaper and lawyer, but doesn't say about what. Nothing actionable here."

"Then we'll keep working on it," he persisted.

"Shall I transfer the rest of your patients to someone else today?" asked Eva.

John nodded. "I'll be with the lawyers for a while."

***

Arlo knocked on his own door before slipping the key into the lock. He stepped inside the darkening apartment and called out. "Laura?" he called.

No response.

He flicked on the lights, walked to the wine cupboard, and poured himself a glass. Laura's call had made a hard day worse. He stared through balcony windows at the city lights as the wine relaxed his tightened muscles. "She's gone," he whispered to the empty room.

Barefoot, groggy from afternoon sleep, Laura slipped behind him and encircled his waist. "No. I'm not. I didn't go."

He tried to turn.

"No, Arlo." She held him in place.

"I'm sorry I hung up. You were right. I wasn't thinking straight. If I can't manage how I feel, I should get my ass out of town. I took a run, a nap, and decided to stay."

He twisted to face her. "I thought I'd lost you again."

"Put down the damn glass and kiss me," she said.

***

He'd been irritable all afternoon. "Who'll make the call?"

"Marina Brown," said George Penunos.

"Why Marina?" retorted John. "Laura's doesn't know her."

"Exactly," said George, "She's less likely to refuse."

"Refuse two-and-a-half million dollars sweetened with health benefits?" John laughed. "Not likely."

"Sir," said George Penunos, "I advise you not to underestimate what she'll do."

John glowered, but didn't respond. Instead, he stood and walked to the door. 8:00 p.m. Long day.

"I'm going to eat dinner. Make the call. Let me know what happens."

***

The ringing phone lay in her purse on the other side of the room.

"Laura, don't answer. You're exhausted. Let's order dinner first."

Listening to the recording she'd made of her visit with John had taken away her appetite. *If I eat anything right now, I'll throw up.*

"Let me get this one, Arlo. It'll only take a second." She crossed the room and scrabbled inside her purse. "Hello?"

Arlo watched Laura rigidify muscle by muscle.

"I see. Yes." A pause. "No. Email is fine, but there's no sense sending it. I won't accept non-disclosure clauses or donor anonymity." Another pause. "If Dr. Russell wishes to withdraw his offer of endowment, that is his decision" Silence. "Yes, I understand." Laura began to tap her foot. "Thank you." Then the disconnect.

Arlo raised his eyebrows. "They offered, but you declined." He patted the space on the couch beside him. "Come. Sit."

"I didn't decline—I 'managed.'" She realized her appetite had returned in a blazing rush. "Let's order dinner."

***

Laura rolled out of bed the next morning. She felt safe, strong, and no headache in sight. *Haven't felt this good in a long time.*

She and Arlo had discussed plans the night before. They wrote strategies and counter strategies as the clock hands moved toward one in the morning. When they could no longer focus, he went to bed and she put the to-do list on her nightstand. She read it over before falling asleep—all the contact numbers for lawyers and newspapers.

"No final decisions and no confidential disclosures tomorrow," Arlo had said. "Only checking out who's good to work with." He repeated it ten times.

"Okay. Okay. I get it," she complained, but he'd made his point.

He concluded by saying, "Separate rooms. I need my sleep, and if you..." She'd kissed him in the middle of the sentence and left him standing alone in the hallway.

Laura took last night's list and placed it in the center of the kitchen counter. She showered, ate breakfast, and hung on to the feeling of safety in Arlo's apartment. Then she picked up her phone and began dialing.

Eleven phone calls later with mind-numbing repetitions of what she wanted, she heard herself say, "Yes, Wednesday is good. First twenty-minutes free—and after that? Yes, I understand." Then she grabbed the to-do list, took a big marker and placed a fat, red check next to the first item—lawyer specializing in workplace harassment issues.

Next on the list—journalist. She picked up her phone and began another round of calls.

The first time she heard it, Laura couldn't distinguish the knock on the door over the sound of the phone connection ringing. She pressed the disconnect button and listened. Definitely a knock. *Did Arlo come home for lunch?* She shrugged, slid off the counter stool and went to the door. Through the peep hole she saw a woman in a business suit holding an envelope.

With the chain lock on, she opened the door. The woman looked vaguely familiar. "Yes?"

"Laura, I'm Marina Brown, Dr. Russell's lawyer. We spoke last night."

"How did you know where I was?" she shot back, then wanted to kick herself. *Damn John and his fucking information network.* She pulled herself together. "What do you want?"

"Can we talk?"

Laura shook her head. "Not in the apartment. You can't come inside."

"In the hallway?"

What the hell. "Just a minute." Laura closed the door, slipped the apartment key from her purse to her pocket and stepped into the corridor.

"Okay." She started to cross her arms, then dropped them to her sides. *No defensive postures. Management Training 101.*

"Dr. Russell would like you to read over this endowment contract."

"Does it include gag rules or requests for anonymity?"

"I suggest you read it and decide for yourself."

Laura crossed her arms. "Yes or no?"

Marina Brown looked at the package. "There might be some conditions…" The sentence dangled in the silence.

Laura pulled the key out of her pocket. "I thought I made myself very clear last night. There's nothing further to say." She turned to unlock the door. "Except I might point out you are an unauthorized visitor on these premises."

She opened the door and stepped into the apartment. "If John has anything further to communicate, he should schedule an appointment. It appears I'm easy enough to find." Laura deadbolted the door and felt the blood pounding at her temples. Grabbing her phone, she punched in the numbers.

"Hello? Yes, this is Laura Greenwald. Wednesday is not fine. I need to see you today. I've got an emergency and, boy, am I willing to pay."

***

Laura left the apartment at 3:30 dressed in a power suit, high heels, and large document purse. She strode forward with such intensity the Friday commuter crowds gave way in front of her. When she raised her arm and stopped a taxi, no one argued who had signaled for it first.

"14th and K, please." The lawyer's office was located less than a block from the Washington Post building. *And that's not a coincidence,* she thought. It gave her inordinate satisfaction to know that.

She arrived early. The secretary's desk was empty, so Laura sat alone in the reception room, legs crossed, purse on her lap. *Focus.* She closed her eyes.

"Ms. Greenwald?" inquired a voice. A business-suited, African-American woman of middle age and professional demeanor stood in the doorway. "Come in. Let's see what we can do about your emergency."

***

"She didn't touch the envelope."

"Didn't even look at it?"

"No."

Silence.

"She said she was clear about what she wanted," continued Marina Brown.

Silence.

John Russell sat behind his desk, hands steepled, neck muscles tightened. "I won't be pushed around."

"No, sir."

He held out his hand for the envelope Marina had not been able to deliver. "Thank you." He opened the contents and did not bother to look at the lawyer again. The door clicked shut, leaving him alone in the room. He swiveled his chair and stared out the windows. "Shit," he said, "shit, shit, shit."

***

"Johneen Johnson—doing law for twenty-five years. Workplace codes and harassment. Just me and my paralegal. We keep things tight and efficient that way. She's on jury duty—which is why I get to answer my own phone today." Johneen folded her hands on the desk. "Now, what's your emergency?" She laughed. "I sound like a 911 operator."

Laura hadn't intended to tell the whole story. But, in the end, it all came out. The contract, the sex, the salary, duties, travel, people, surgeries. She described the pregnancy, the loss of her jobs and the airplane miscarriage. The last words made her tongue feel like dry cotton.

"That's quite a story," Johneen commented. "But no Friday afternoon emergency that I can see."

"I'm not done." Laura tightened the grip on her purse. Words should have been shooting out of her mouth but none came out.

In the silence, Johneen leaned forward. With gentle voice she focused the conversation. "Ms. Greenwald, you had an appointment for Wednesday. What changed? What made you need me today—right away?"

"She was outside my door."

"Who?"

"John's lawyer. I never gave them my address. It's not right. It scares me and annoys the shit out of me at the same time."

"What does?"

"John's damn spy network."

Her words came out in a rush—how Cleveland Hospital had Laura's recommendation from John even before she'd applied, her panic attack, the decision to stop running and fight back, the DC plane trip, discussing ideas with Arlo, requesting a two-and-a half million-dollar endowment, and finally, John's lawyer standing outside the apartment door with the envelope.

"I never told him where I was staying; Arlo's building is locked; it has a security doorman. Marina got inside anyway." Laura crossed her arms. "That's when I called."

"I see." The lawyer folded her hands on the desk. "Why ever would Dr. Russell want to give you so much money?"

Laura's gaze was direct and unflinching. "To put things right. He won't see it that way, but I do." She held up fingers on one hand

and began to count. "He fathered my baby, was a fucking, arrogant jerk about it, and wanted me disappeared. Oh, yes, the baby conveniently disappeared, too—on the plane ride outta here."

Four of her five fingers were down. Laura paused, then added, "My pregnancy ripped his precious 'Scandal Clause' to pieces."

"Scandal Clause?"

"Oh, sorry. John's name for the sex part of my contract. He said it would keep him safe from, and I quote, 'the sexual temptations thrown at the feet of powerful men.'"

Johneen's facial expression remained unreadable. "Okay." A pause. "What's your business pitch?"

"Two employees—myself and a lawyer. We'd research more effective methods of managing sexuality in the workplace. Healthy ones—a total break from deny, hide, prosecute, and get ruined."

The lawyer looked skeptical. "That business idea would have a two-and-a-half-million-dollar appeal to him?"

She shrugged. "John tried his own idea. It turned into a big, out -of-control mess with me. And I'm not going away."

Leather squeaked as the lawyer sat back in her chair, elbows on armrests, fingers steepled. "What do you want me to do?"

"Get me a $2,500,000 endowment with his name all over it, no gag rules, no nursing license threats, and no harassment. Exactly what I told him when I went to his office yesterday." She crossed her legs, resettled the purse in her lap. "The thing is," Laura continued, "if I don't jump on it today, John will set some god-awful plans in motion. And I'll lose—again."

"What would make him agree to any of what you're proposing?"

"You."

"Me?" The lawyer's eyebrows raised. "As much as I appreciate your business, Ms. Greenwald, I'm not that good a salesperson."

"As Officer of the Court you would be. He wants to keep his shoes clean and his name out of the media. Adding a lawyer to the mix promises to drag everything through the muck."

"And if he won't agree?"

"Plan B."

"Which is?"

"The media—with a capital M."

"I see." The lawyer smiled. She opened the computer on her desk. "Okay. I can make a call—follow it with email and letter—easy enough for a first step." She pulled a folder from her desk "It'll take me some time. Meanwhile," she said, handing over some forms, "sign these and make yourself an official client."

Hallelujah. I've got a lawyer.

"Shit," was the next word out of her mouth.

"Change your mind?" Laura tugged the phone from her purse as Johneen watched.

"No. But Arlo's expecting me at home."

"Shouldn't he join us?" asked Johneen.

"Yes," said Laura, "he should," and began texting. *This woman is my kind of lawyer.*

***

At 8:45 p.m., in front of Arlo and Laura, Johneen dialed John's private emergency number.

"Dr. John Russell's emergency line. How may I help you?" Eva Jormand's voice rang steady and clear over the office speaker phone.

"Attorney Johneen Johnson. May I speak to Dr. Russell, please?"

Silence. A rustling of clothing fabric as Eva moved. "This is a medical emergency line. May I ask how you got this number, Ms. Johnson?"

"Of course. Ms. Greenwald gave it to me. She's here in my office."

"Isn't this a bit late for…"

"I believe Dr. Russell will want to take this call, Ms. Jormand," interrupted Johneen.

373

"I see. I'll check with Dr. Russell."

The phone went silent. They waited.

"What if he won't..." began Laura.

"Ms. Johnson?" John Russell's voice boomed out over the speaker phone.

"Yes, Dr. Russell. I'm right here."

"What is this about?" Tense, rigid, clipped. Laura knew that hunched over tone, could see him grip the phone, control his breathing, cross his leg.

"I am Laura Greenwald's attorney. You are on speaker phone and her verbal proposal will be confirmed by email and letter."

"What proposal?"

"Immediate cessation of personal harassment by your lawyers."

Silence. Breathing. "I don't know what you're talking about."

Laura flushed. She half rose from the chair. Arlo grabbed her hand before she could get further. Johneen shook her head. Laura sat.

"She also states that any action on your part against her nursing license will be fully prosecuted."

"This is ridiculous." His disembodied voice flowed through the room.

"And Ms. Greenwald wants a meeting with you tomorrow morning at 10:00 o'clock to discuss an endowment."

"Ms. Johnson, it's time to terminate this call." They heard clothing fabric rustle as he took the phone from his ear.

Johneen raised her voice—quick, loud and directed. "I guarantee you won't want to deal with Plan B."

A long pause—line still connected.

The lawyer nodded at Arlo and Laura. "Plan B, Dr. Russell, is the plan that moves forward without you."

Silence.

Laura shifted position, lips and mouth dry with nervous agitation. She zipped open her purse, searching for a mint. Johneen responded to the noise by thrusting out her hand palm up and shook her head.

Laura froze.

Time dragged. An imaginary noose tightened around her neck. She labored to breathe in the rigid stillness of the office. Hand entwined with Arlo's, she leaned back into the couch and closed her eyes.

When John's voice sliced through the phone lines, it asked a question. "If such a meeting were to take place, where might it be?"

Laura's eyes flew open. She jumped out of the couch in an explosion of silent excitement, raised her arms, pirouetted around the couch, kissed Arlo, and hugged Johneen Johnson still sitting in her executive chair holding the phone.

Chapter 54

They met at 10:00 am the next morning in the breakfast lounge of the Hamiltonian—a hotel whose location matched the elegance of its décor—next to the Washington Post and across from Johneen's office.

John Russell came dressed in cashmere sweater, dark trousers and power. George Penunos strode behind in pinstripe suit, white shirt, briefcase and knowledge.

John had called the lawyer as soon as Johneen Johnson hung up. "Marina Brown made a mess of things. I want you at this god-damned meeting tomorrow. You know how Laura thinks."

"She's formidable, sir," George said, "much more than when you first hired her." He'd paused before speaking again. "You also need to know that having me involved in this meeting could be considered a conflict of interest."

"I don't give a shit about you conflict of interest. You work for my company. I'm the one paying the bills and I require your services tomorrow morning," John had said, and ended the call.

How well I know them both, Laura thought when she saw George Penunos accompanying her ex-boss.

"Good morning, gentlemen," said Johneen Johnson who stood at easeful attention next to Laura. "I thought we would sit over here." She moved forward, maneuvering the two men where she wanted them.

She's on the offensive. Laura smiled and followed behind her lawyer but in front of John Russell. They approached a square table with four chairs. "You here, please, Doctor, and you, sir, next to him."

Laura watched John's jaw muscles clench. He sat.

"Ms. Greenwald?" Johneen gestured to another seat, then pulled out her own chair. "I've already ordered coffee and croissants for us." She removed the envelope from her document purse and placed it on the table. "Shall we start?"

The lawyer gave no time for either man to speak. She placed several sheets of paper on the table.

Laura clamped back a jolt of laughter. She'd never seen John so well managed. *I've got a lot to learn.*

"Ms. Johnson..." George began.

"We need to read this first, Mr. Penunos. Then we can chat."

John's face reddened.

He's definitely pissed thought Laura and couldn't help smiling.

"So, let's move forward or we'll be here all morning." She looked at John. Curt, almost imperceptible, he nodded.

"All right, then.". She picked up the top sheet, read it aloud word for word, then pushed the paper towards John. "By signing this document, Dr. Russell, you're acknowledging Ms. Greenwald will prosecute to the full extent of the law, and also make public, to the full extent of her ability, any harassment, past or present, by your lawyers or employees of your firm—such as trespassing in private apartment hallways without permission."

"Ms. Greenwald had a contract..."

"No contract includes stalking, personal harassment, trespassing, or threats." She raised her eyebrows and looked at George. "Unless you have created an illegal document." Johneen pointed. "We are forewarning you with a statement of intent. Please sign at the bottom, sir."

"Why bother? This isn't a contract; it's a statement. You told me. I heard you. So, we've finished Issue Number One," retorted John.

"As you wish. I'll notate you preferred not to sign. There are signature lines for all of us. It's useful in court—or with the media—they love documentation." She turned to George Penunos. "And you, sir?"

"He won't sign," said John.

Johneen withdrew the paper, wrote her statements, then pushed it towards Laura. "Your turn."

A second sheet was produced. "This document states that you remove any threats made by your firm to her nursing license."

"I have done no such thing," stated John, with bland disinterest.

Laura exploded out of her chair. "You goddamned…"

Johneen's restraining hand snaked out and encircled Laura's forearm. "Sit," she commanded.

Laura sat.

John leaned forward. "Ms. Greenwald signed a non-disclosure contract which she has clearly broken," I'll prosecute her to the full extent of…"

"Dr. Russell," interrupted Johneen, "shut up." Her eyes dead-locked with John's. He stopped. Laura gaped. "Your coming here says you have something to lose, to hide, or both. So, I…"

A waitress appeared—four coffees and croissants balanced on a tray. Johneen pointed to the next table over. "Would you put every-thing there, just for a bit?" She pulled a credit card and twenty-dollar bill from her wallet. "Get me the check. And keep this for yourself."

The waitress beamed. "Thank you, ma'am. Right away."

The lawyer looked at the two men. "I don't care about the food. It's the receipt I want—proof of this meeting." Cell phone in hand she then snapped a picture of the them, catching Laura's face in the corner. "We're in public. That makes this photo legal. Thank you, gentlemen."

Dr. Russell's face remained immobile. The face of the lawyer sitting next to him drained to white. *George is getting castrated,* thought Laura, frozen in fascination as she watched the scenario play out.

"Now, this business about a contract." Johneen folded her hands on the table in front of her. "Legally, it is likely not worth the paper it's written on. Not if we pull it apart paragraph by paragraph. Which we would do in court. Also, the salary and benefits are astounding—which would lead anyone to think something unusual is involved. I haven't seen the document itself—yet. I'm sure it would make interesting reading."

John stood, his face so hard-set Laura imagined one muscle twitch would scrape skin bloody against its rigid surface "I want to speak with my lawyer." Without waiting, he turned, and strode to the foyer, leaving George to follow in his roiling wake.

Laura turned. "That was amaz…"

The lawyer stopped her. "Still negotiating. We wait—in silence." Johneen's hands remained folded on the table, her breathing even, eyes unfocused.

***

Fifteen-minutes passed.

John and his lawyer returned.

They sat at the table.

"Give me the document about the nursing license," said John.

Johneen pushed it across the table. He scribbled his name and pushed it back.

What did George say to him? wondered Laura.

"Excellent—Issue Number Two completed," said Johneen and handed the document to George. "Everyone needs to sign as witness." Her face remained pleasantly neutral as she gathered signatures.

Where has this woman been all my life? thought Laura.

"Now--Issue Number Three. Ms. Greenwald's request for a charitable endowment."

John's right eye twitched; his jaw muscle contracted.

He's worried, thought Laura. *That's what happened in their little hallway chat.*

"Ms. Greenwald informed me you are an advocate of sexual wellness in the workplace," said Johneen.

He looked at his lawyer who gave a slight nod. "You could put it that way, I suppose."

"And you are concerned about the consequences of inappropriate sexual conduct in such situations?"

"Yes. It should be a concern for everyone, don't you think?" retorted John.

George Penunos flushed. A miniscule shake of his head told Laura his lawyer thought John had just said too much.

"I absolutely agree, Dr. Russell," said Johneen. "It's a nationwide and global issue—I've been working with it for twenty-five years."

Laura watched John register surprise—a slight widening of the eyes, an intake of breath where it shouldn't have been.

Johneen's next comment slipped in with perfect timing. "I specialize in workplace codes and harassment—got in on the ground floor." She stretched and shifted position. "My, how things have changed since I..."

"Can we get on with this?" interrupted John.

He's nervous and doesn't want her grandstanding, observed Laura. *I've never seen him like this.*

"We surely can." Johneen thumbed through the documents. "Ms. Greenwald is asking for a charitable endowment. Her nonprofit company will address sexual conduct in the workplace—something you just stated should be everyone's concern." She leaned back in the chair. "It seems a worthy endeavor to underwrite—don't you think?"

"She doesn't have a company," he said, a semi-snarl sandwiched between each word.

Johneen's eyebrows went up. "And how would you know that, Dr. Russell?"

"There's no wa...," began John.

"Shall we remain on topic?" interrupted Penunos, pointedly looking at John. "We're not making commitments—just listening."

"Just so, Mr. Penunos." Johneen selected the top sheet from the pages on the table. "We'll move forward now, Ms. Greenwald, unless you have questions."

Laura shook her head.

"Sexual and Legal Wellness in the Workplace." Johneen let the words drop into the silence. And waited.

"What the fuck is tha…"

George interrupted again. "Could you explain what that is, Ms. Johnson?"

This woman is brilliant. She's playing John, and he's falling right into her trap., thought *if I could find a lawyer just like—*

Laura's sharp intake of breath stopped the conversation. Heads swiveled toward her. She flushed. "Sorry, just a cramp…" She bent to rub a non-existent pain and hide a smile. *Johneen Johnson—would she take a job with me?*

"That is the name of the nonprofit Ms. Greenwald is creating. Incorporation procedures are in process."

"Well," drawled John, "come back when you've got it all togeth…"

"No." Johneen's voice sliced through his sentence—unbending, cold, clear. "Ms. Greenwald is offering you an opportunity—one that will not wait." She looked at George. "Would you like a few moments to think about the gains, rather than the losses, that might come from this?" She began placing the papers into an envelope.

George turned to his employer before John could interrupt. "I suggest we at least look at the documents. We can decide to do whatever we want at any point."

"I won't be pushed around." John's face flushed.

"No one is pushing, Dr. Russell," stated Johneen with quiet certainty. "However, sometimes facing consequences of what you've done in the past may feel that way."

John stood—abrupt and sudden. George rose faster, grabbed John's arm and said, "Sit down. Now." Moments passed as they stared at each other. John finally sat.

"Continue," said George.

"Two employees—Ms. Greenwald and a lawyer; endowment of $2,500,000 to support reduced fees; Dr. Russell's endorsement and no gag rules." She looked up. "But you knew that already."

She handed the envelope to George. "This describes the proposal in more detail." "A special escrow account will be created until full incorporation occurs." Johneen nodded to Laura. "That concludes it." She looked at Laura. "We'll be leaving now," she said, and they both rose.

The lawyer shrugged on her coat. "I know it's the weekend. However, the deadline to hear back from Dr. Russell is Monday at noon. After that, Ms. Greenwald is no longer interested. It's all in the packet." She smiled at them.

"I have a question ab…" started George Penunos.

"I'm sure you'll have more questions after you've read the documents. Call me at that point. It's been a pleasure" Johneen extended her hand.

George ignored it.

Laura smiled.

The two women left.

John Russell looked at George Penunos. "God damn," he said. "Find out who the fuck that woman is."

***

Johneen sat at her desk, printed out something from her computer, and handed the information to her client. "Take Arlo with you."

Laura read the words on the paper. "Korea Spa? In Virginia? What's all this?"

The lawyer l. "How are looked at her. "How are you feeling?"

Laura quashed a wave of annoyance as it boiled up. "Exhausted. Too tired to be elated. Isn't it obvious?"

"It's very obvious," replied Johneen. "You have my marching orders. Call Arlo and get your asses over there. Relax at the Spa. You'll love it. It'll get you ready for Monday."

***

"I won't."

"That's your decision to make," said George Penunos.

"Where the fuck did Laura find that lawyer?"

George shook his head but remained silent, waiting for John Russell to bridle his temper. Lines around the lawyer's mouth tightened as he pushed several sheets of paper across the desk. "This is a list of different decisions you could make. Along with consequences."

John nodded.

The lawyer pointed to the first one. "We'll start here—what happens if you decide not to negotiate."

"Negotiate?" growled John. "Being bull-dozed is more like it."

"John." George's voice carried a steely, disciplinary tone.

"What?" Irritated. Unconciliatory.

"Stop whining and start thinking."

"How dare…"

George stood up. "Call me when your tantrum is over." He walked to the door, opened it, and was in the hallway before John called out.

"Okay. Okay." He raised his hands. "I'll listen."

The lawyer assessed the man behind the desk. Rigid, unbending, but not stupid. George returned.

"If you decide not to negotiate," George said, pointing again to the first sheet, "…to ignore this whole thing, I guarantee Laura will go straight to the media—Washington Post first, internet next. You'll be the new poster boy for sex scandals."

John glared at him. "You have a crystal ball somewhere?"

The lawyer did not speak. He stood and retrieved his briefcase. "It's late. Let me know when…"

"Sit down," said John, "please." He squeezed out the last word.

George did not sit.

John picked up the sheet under discussion. "How can you be so sure she'd do that?"

"Because she's pissed to shit and has nothing left to lose. She's quit her $700,000 a year job to save the baby you wouldn't acknowledge, and put up with your stalking until you went too far. Then she had a public miscarriage on an airplane trying to get away. You might owe her something in restitution, Dr. Russell."

The lawyer pointed to the paper. "But, if you ignore her—if that's your decision—you have a lot to lose, and she knows it. If I wanted to cut off your balls, I'd go straight to the media. That's how I know what she'll do."

The doctor rubbed his temples "I see." Sarcasm gone, he gestured to the chair. "Would you care to sit?"

George assented.

"What other options are on your list of horrors?"

"Fund the endowment but negotiate different terms—like include stipulations but increase the dollar amount. I explain that on the second sheet."

A laugh erupted from across the desk. "And I should send Marina Brown to try again?"

"I didn't say it would be successful—it's an option."

"Right. Next?"

"Agree to the endowment. You've got the money. It's good public relations. You did publicly agree with the principles of her company."

"Don't remind me."

George scrutinized his employer's face before adding, "She's going to make you work with her."

"What the hell are you talking about?" John's face reddened with angry disbelief.

"You wanted her out of sight—she's saying 'no fuckin' way, Jose.' She'll put you front and center as an advertisement for her business." The lawyer paused.

"How do you know that?" demanded the doctor.

George shrugged. "It's what I'd do. Your endorsement and no gag rules? It's a pot of gold." He uncurled from his position and leaned forward. "She's punching back hard—and doing something worthwhile. Smart cookie."

Chapter 55

Five minutes before noon on Monday, Laura asked "Would you?"

"Would I what?" asked Johneen Johnson, standing behind the desk in her office.

"Work with me. Be my lawyer. You'd be perfect."

Johneen laughed. "Hold your horses, Miss Laura. You're light years ahead of me. Right now, we're just waiting for a phone call.

Laura plowed ahead. "It wouldn't be full time—not at first. I could rent that room over there." She nodded towards a closed door on the other end of the office. "I scoped it out. It's totally empty. Not even a bookcase. You're wasting resources in..."

The phone rang. Conversation stopped.

Once. Twice. Three times.

Johneen Johnson, Attorney at Law."

"Ms. Johnson, George Penunos here."

"Good to hear from you, Mr. Penunos. You are on speaker phone."

Laura sat, hands curled in a fist, turning white.

"Dr. Russell has agreed to discuss the documentation."

Laura's arms shot up in a fierce victory 'V'—eyes sparkling, lips clamped onto the taste of success.

Johneen glared at her client and sliced a hand across her throat. Laura froze. The lawyer waited in silence while the phone connection echoed zips of static. Moments passed.

"Are you still there, Ms. Johnson?"

"Waiting for you to proceed," she said.

The words *kneel to the queen* shot through Laura's mind.

"Dr. Russell will meet with you in his Virginia clinic office Wednesday at 10:00."

"No."

"I'm sorry?"

"I said no. We meet in neutral territory. The Hamiltonian Hotel. Today. 5:30 p.m."

"The doctor is operating today. He won't…"

"He's done at 3:00," interrupted Johneen. "5:30 will be fine."

"I see you've done your homework."

"I see you're pussy-footing around." Johneen allowed a snap in her tone. "Don't." A pause. "A private table will be reserved in the lounge. 5:30 p.m." She hung up and turned to Laura.

The lawyer's countenance was so somber Laura felt her stomach lurch. "What's the matter?" she asked. "I mean, they're going to meet with us, right?"

"Closing the deal—it's the trickiest part, most likely place to fail. I never celebrate before closing a deal. I prepare. And you, Ms. Greenwald," she pointed at Laura's chest, "need to rest. Go home and be back by 5:00."

Rest? I'd need a marathon to calm me down right now.

Laura left the office, rented a bicycle and pedaled around the streets of the National Mall. She allowed memories of the Korea Spa weekend to wash through her—ten luxurious hours with a man she was falling in love with—massages, salt rooms, Jacuzzis. When she stopped for late lunch at a food truck, she texted Arlo. "Coming home late. Big meeting at 5:30. Have drinks ready."

***

Arlo rested on the couch facing the balcony windows. He'd had a tiring work day. A soft mechanical whir of blinds lifting filled the apartment. Late evening light from the street lamps bathed the living room in a soft glow. Ice clinked as he poured whiskey into a glass and waited for Laura to arrive home from her meeting.

387

***

Laura slouched against the back of the taxi seat, eyes closed, document purse folded in her lap. The meeting had drained every spark of energy her brain cells could produce. The details of the evening replayed in her mind like a Sunday night soap opera. *My brain is chopped hamburger. How does Johneen do it?*

She remembered George coming dressed in power suit and navy tie; John in casual cashmere, looking as if not a worry could touch him.

He's good, she'd thought, *"but I'm one up—nothing to lose, everything to gain, and John to thank for putting me here."*

"Good evening, gentlemen." Johneen Johnson stood tall and impressive—black suit, tailored slacks, gleaming white blouse with buttons starting at her cleavage and pearls to hold the neckline in place. "Shall we begin?" She gestured towards booth style seats at a corner table with a 'reserved' sign.

"We'd rather..." started George. But Johneen and Laura, strategizing for a half hour before the meeting, had seated themselves in the chairs opposite. John and George found themselves behind the table in the booth backed against the wall. When Johneen leaned forward to make the first statement, her weight slid the table a few centimeters closer to the men.

"I've spent the afternoon getting the documents ready for signature..." she began.

"Ms. Johnson," interrupted George Penunos. "We have a few items to discuss."

The look of surprise on Johneen's face fooled even Laura. "We do? Whatever are they? Ms. Greenwald was clear there would be no negotiating her terms for the endowment."

"Dr. Russell wishes to address the breach of previous contract..."

"In a courtroom," interrupted Johneen, "right about now, I would call out, 'irrelevant and unproven.' I would be sustained and you know it, Mr. Penunos."

Laura watched a very slight twitch snap across John's left cheek.

"Regardless," continued George, "we want it stated in writing that Ms. Greenwald continues to be liable for non-disclosure rules from her original contract. It's obvious she's told you about them...'

Thwack! Johneen's fist pounded the table. *Thwack!*

Laura's hand flew to her chest; conversation shattered; John's face flushed, and water glasses spilled.

"Act as if you have a license, Mr. Penunos." The ice coldness of her words froze George's response before he uttered it.

"If you devised a contract so full of holes it won't stand on its own, I suggest your employer find a new attorney."

Johneen sat back and crossed her arms. "Under no circumstances will Ms. Greenwald's attorney-client privilege be breached or besmirched—by you or anyone else. What my client has discussed with me is locked away—by law—from prying fingers. Feel free to sue her for breach of contract. That is an entirely separate matter not to be included in these discussions."

Spilled water from the table top glasses dripped onto John's lap. He blocked the stream with a napkin and stood up with a jerk, shaking the glasses and spilling more water.

"I'm done." He pushed the table back toward Johneen and Laura. "If you think you can blackmail me for two-and-a-half-million dollars, then think again." He threw the wet napkin on the table top, turned his back and strode toward the exit.

Johneen raised her eyebrows and looked at George. He shook his head.

"I see," said Johneen. She produced an understanding smile.

What does she see? wondered Laura. *I don't see anything.*

"Ms. Greenwald and I will eat dinner here, Mr. Penunos. Since Dr. Russell is no longer at table, what are your plans?"

Laura looked at Johneen as if she were crazy. "Din...?" she started to ask thinking, *get me the hell out of here.* But a head shake from Johneen cut her short.

George extracted himself from behind the table. He stood, stared at the two women, picked up his briefcase, and said, "Thank you, ladies."

Laura swiveled to watch as he left. She grabbed her purse and said, "I'm leaving. I'll call…"

Johneen's clamped a hand on Laura's forearm. "Stay seated, Ms. Greenwald. We are in the middle of negotiating. I just executed a move. Now we wait. We are in a restaurant at dinner time, so we order."

Laura gaped at her. "What negotiations? No one's here. They both left. End of story."

"No, not end of story by a long shot."

Laura, too exasperated to understand and too tired to say anything, glared.

Johneen folded hands in her lap. "George and I are in the middle of a game. It's been going on since they walked in the door. That's what lawyers do—play tug-of-war for results that favor our clients." She took a sip of water.

Laura kept glaring, so Johneen continued. "I assume," she said, "John is used to getting his way?"

"That's an understatement," retorted Laura.

"As you can see, things haven't gone his way; he's angry and keeps losing control. Dr. Russell just wiped out their game plan. That leaves George to pick up the pieces. He's not going to announce, 'Be right back—gotta fix this so you can get a million bucks.'"

Laura smiled despite her irritation. "With John it'll take days. Why stay?" She was desperate to get home.

"He'll be back tonight."

Laura stared at Johneen as if she'd sprouted two heads. "How can you be so sure?"

"Because tomorrow we go to the newspapers."

"How would he know that?"

"Because George knows you hold the power spot. You don't give a damn if everything goes public. John does. George is reminding him of that right now."

Laura sighed, dropped her purse on the floor and picked up the menu. She ordered, barely picked at her food when it came, and watched the clock. There was little conversation. Johneen ate and reviewed documents.

"...you keep that woman from making..."

"...get hold of...it doesn't help when..."

Johneen looked up. "They're coming. You can hear them a mile away."

***

Laura couldn't remember when it happened. Maybe twenty minutes after the men returned. Maybe sooner. The waitress had been paid and given orders to leave them alone. Johneen was discussing the two-and-a-half million-dollar escrow account. It was late. Laura was exhausted.

"...and I won't sign *any* document before we discuss the consequences of Laura breaching the original contract. I'm going to the men's room. Think about what I just said. "No signature without that." John put his palms on the table and started to get up.

She remembered George's tired face and Johneen's eye rolling.

And then The Voice spoke.

"Sit. The. Fuck. Down."

Shit. Who said that?

Laura found herself standing, finger pointed like a gun at John Russell's chest. "Sit." exploded the command so powerful her body rigidified in statuesque intensity. "Down. Right where you are. And. Shut. The. Fuck. Up." Her snarl so ferocious that John sat the instant her words hit his eardrums.

"Listen with care, Dr. John Russell. Never, ever threaten me again." She leaned over the table like a wolf paralyzing its prey. "Because if you do, you will never, ever call a part of your life private again. I will rip away pieces of your world you never knew you

391

owned and thrust them into the limelight so fast and so deep your testicles will shrivel from the sunburn."

She shook from fury bottled for so long it could shatter crystal. Heads began to turn in the sparsely occupied restaurant. Laura could care less.

"We made a damn good team, you and I. But you pissed it away with your arrogant stupidity. You just had to have it your way. Talk about people being stupid." She leaned closer. "You just made the worst fucking mistake of your life."

Laura felt Johneen's hand on her arm. She shook it off and kept going. "You trained me, fucked me, fathered my child, harassed me out of jobs, and then thought an interfering pat on the back would make it all go away according to plan."

She reached over and pulled at Johneen's documents. "See these?" She raised the pages and tapped them with her finger in front of John's face. "This is what *I* plan—with or without you." Laura dropped them back on the table and locked eyes. "I don't give a fuck if you sign them or not—I win either way."

She grabbed her purse, "And, if you're stupid enough to think there's only one copy of that goddamned contract, think again." She pulled on her coat. "Before I signed, you left me alone for a long time to read it—remember? 'Call the lawyers when you're done,' you said. Well, I did. But first I took a photo of every page—every single, fucking page." Laura straightened, turned her back on the room, and left.

John sat motionless, his face drained of color. George reached for the documents on the table. Johneen waited, hands folded in her lap. Polite murmurings heightened in the dining room. Laura had produced a show. It had been noticed.

John turned to his lawyer. "Thoughts?"

"My thoughts?" said George still reading documents "My thoughts are don't underestimate her."

"That's it?" Peeved tone.

"Yes." Stolid, bland tone. "At this point it's all you need to know."

***

Water and soap from the bathroom sink splashed over her face. It stung her eyes. She tried toweling it out. "Oouuch."

"You okay?" called Arlo, his tone worried.

"I'm fine. Pour me a scotch. I'll be right out." *Fine? You mean drained, exhausted, rung out—not 'fine,'* grumbled part of her, *you're such a Pollyanna.*

Arlo stood silhouetted by the living room windows, lights dimmed, drinks on the table. He opened his arms and she went to him, standing for minutes without speech, her head on his shoulder.

"How'd it go?" he asked.

"Not sure," Laura mumbled into his shoulder. "Left before it was over."

"I see." Genial, empathetic, warm.

"I blew up."

"About time."

She smiled. *I'm in love with this guy.* "Where's that drink?"

***

The buzzer from the street entryway sounded—loud, disruptive, startling. 11:15 p.m. Entwined with Arlo, drowsing on the couch, still in street clothes, Laura startled to alertness. Arlo raised inquiring eyebrows. She shrugged and shook her head.

"I'll check." He unwound his arms, went to the wall receptacle and pushed the call button. "Yes?" Short and firm.

"Arlo, it's Johneen Johnson."

Within three minutes, the lawyer's no-nonsense presence dominated the living room. She turned up the lights, spread documents on the coffee table, placed ink pens beside them. Then she sat in an upright chair and faced her startled client enveloped under Arlo's protective arm.

"Sign here…and here," said Johneen, tapping several points on the pages. She swiveled around to find her purse.

"Johneen?" ventured Laura trying to get her attention.

"Yes?" The lawyer frowned in concentration, glancing over the table as she rearranged several sheets. "I ran these off so quickly, I'm not sure they're in the right…"

"You're forgetting something," interrupted Laura.

Johneen looked up. "Forgetting something?"

"I left before the meeting was over—you noticed, right?" Laura said.

"Of course, I noticed. You announced it to the whole restaurant. A perfect exit. Couldn't have done it better myself."

"For God's sake, Johneen, just tell me if he signed the damn agreement."

Arlo's shit-eating grin was contagious. He leaned over, picked up the whiskey bottle, and poured himself another glass. Laura Greenwald was back on her feet.

The lawyer looked surprised. "I thought you knew, Laura. I thought you left so I could finish without distraction." The lawyer's grin outmatched Arlo's. "Excuse my English," she said, "but you were a mother of a powerhouse. People gave me the thumbs-up when I left. No way John wants you out there without having some say. Not the way you took over."

Laura gaped at her. Things still did not compute. "Johneen, just tell me what happened."

The lawyer folded her hands in her lap. "When you left, Dr. Russell insisted his lawyer go over every word of the agreement. George kept telling him the only real issue was, and I quote— 'She doesn't give a fuck any more—don't underestimate her.'"

Johneen winked. "It took a half an hour of reading every word out loud. Fifteen minutes along, I handed the waitress an extra fifty bucks."

A thin smile tugged at Laura's lips. "Add it to my bill."

"That'll be the least of my charges," said the lawyer, smiling. "So, here's the deal—Dr. Russell signed a contractual promise of $2,500,000 for an endowment, money to be escrowed this week—no strings attached, endorsement to follow, nine months to establish business and transfer monies from escrow to a functioning non-profit. If you're not up and running within nine months, all monies. including start-up advances, must be returned to Dr. Russell."

She stopped to catch her breath. "We argued about the number of months for non-profit set up—nine was the best I could do. It should be enough if we pull every string we've got. George was pushing. He's a decent lawyer—when he's not minding an angry bull."

Laura sat straighter on the couch, face covered in disbelief. "Damn," she said. "We did it."

"We did," said the lawyer. "Except—and this is big—it's a damned tight time line—and they know it." Johneen sat back. "But it's been fun so far, don't you think?"

"You're twisted," quipped Laura, "if you think that was…" but Arlo grabbed her arm, pulled her up, and smothered her in kisses— thorough, deep, long.

"Ladies and gentlemen, time to focus," called Johneen.

No response.

The lawyer got up. "Stop that!" she yelled in their ears. "We're on deadline tighter than a camel's ass."

Laura pushed away from Arlo. "We? Did I hear you say 'we'?"

Johneen paused, distracted by the question.

"Ms. Greenwald," redirected Johneen. "Right now, we focus on this paperwork—it needs to get done—and soon." She pointed. "Sit and sign."

Laura sat, signed and handed back the documents. "Work with me," she persisted.

Johneen placed the signed pages into folders. She looked at Laura seated opposite with Arlo beside her. "Ms. Greenwald," she said, "I've known you for three days. You charged into my office with your 'emergency.' Drama, suspense, sex, money, success—like a TV soap opera on speed."

She put down the papers down and sat back, hands folded in her lap.

Oh, boy, I know that gesture, thought Laura.

"I like to consider partnerships with care. Legal marriages are serious. Not something you just jump into."

Laura looked down. Her eyes sparkled with tears of exhaustion and disappointment. "I'm sorry. I just thought…"

"So, here's my offer," interrupted Johneen. She paused and waited for Laura to look up. "You rent the 'wasted resource' of a room in my office. You hire me, as needed, by the hour for nine months. At nine months, when the endowment is yours, we have a discussion about what's next."

Laura began to cry. "Yes," she said, "yes, yes, yes."

"I won't be cheap."

Laura wiped her nose with a cocktail napkin, smiled at Arlo, then said to Johneen, "Stand up, please."

"Stand up?"

"Yes. Stand up."

The lawyer stood. Laura covered the distance in two strides, opened her arms, and enfolded Johneen in a bear hug. "Yes, she whispered, "Yes, yes, yes."

***

"Think they'll be able to do it?" John sat behind his executive desk; curtains drawn across the window to shield the blackness of the hour.

"Maybe, maybe not," shrugged George Penunos. "It's tight. I gave them enough time to work it so Ms. Johnson didn't throw it back in my face. But nine months is short. What happens next is a crap shoot."

"Any wrenches you can throw in to slow things down?"

"Possibly," responded the lawyer.

John leaned forward, tiredness creeping across his features. "It's late. Get me your list of options in the morning." He started to rise.

"No."

John gaped. "No? What the fuck kind of answer is that?" he demanded, half sitting, half standing.

"It's an answer that says 'no.'" The lawyer didn't move.

John sat, tiredness wiped from his face by war paint. "Look, Penunos," he growled with a laser beam glare. "I'm done for today. Get those goddamned ideas to me tomorrow or don't bother to come back."

George extracted an envelope from his briefcase. "I thought we might run into a difference of opinion." He placed the letter on the desk. "My resignation's inside. Figure the rest out yourself. I'm done." He pulled on his coat, walked to the door, and closed it behind with a soft click.

John Russell stared at the empty room. His temples began to throb. The headache had been coming on since he signed the agreement two hours ago. He picked up the phone and speed dialed a number.

"Hello?" Susan Blacking, the nurse who replaced Laura, had a low, soothing voice.

"Susan, it's John."

"Are you all right?" Worry echoed over the phone. "Eva calls when there's an emerg..."

"I'm fine," he interrupted. "Just fine." He stopped. "I'd like you to come over tonight."

A sharp intake of breath, then a muting of sound. When the line opened again, she said, "Sir? I'm so sorry. If it's not a medical emergency, I can't really..."

He hung up. "Piss on it all."

John Russell left his office, pushing the door closed with a thudding slam. "Damn it." he yelled down the empty corridor. "Things are gonna be fine; just fucking fine."

He strode through the darkened clinic towards his apartment, punching numbers into his cell phone.

The phone rang five times before a sleep laden voice answered. "Hello?"

"Eva? John here. We've got a bit of a problem..."

---The End---

About the Author

The author, Sydney Stern, has been a psychologist, lecturer, supervisor, educator, and consultant for over 35-years. Family systems and multicultural therapies, sexual abuse treatment, and psychological assessment are her specialties. She has lived in different cultures, spoken different languages, and worked with people ages 5 to 85 from the inner cities to schools and universities. Her professional writing skills and experiences live on in the stories she tells.

The Scandal Clause

Ordering Information

The Scandal Clause
by Sydney Stern

ISBN: 978-1-7336435-9-7

Bridgeland Books
PO Box 4277
Winter Park, FL 32793
www.SydneySternBooks.com

Made in the USA
Middletown, DE
26 May 2020